A CERTAIN SLANT OF LIGHT

A CERTAIN SLANT OF LIGHT

C.P. DU TOIT

ISBN: 979-8-88785-042-9 (Paperback)
ISBN: 979-8-88785-043-6 (Hardcover)

Library of Congress Control Number: 2024942924

Any references to historical events, real people, or real places are used fictitiously. Names, characters, and places are products of the author's imagination.

Book design by Allison Chernutan.
Edited by Emily Kudeviz and Carol Kudeviz.

Printed in the United States of America.

First printing edition 2024.

emily@fracturedmirrorpublishing.com
Fractured Mirror Publishing
Knoxville, Tennessee

www.fracturedmirrorpublishing.com

To my father, whose love of fantasy
sparked my own imagination

And to my mother, who gave me the
gift of words

prologue

Sometimes I dreamed about screaming. They were not my own screams, but those of someone nearby, someone I knew, someone I cared about.

I could not say who exactly cried out. As is the way of dreams, the details hovered around the edges, shimmering like fireflies always an inch out of reach. Still, each scream echoed in my skull. A thud resounded in time with the cries. And suddenly there was the sound of metal on metal, then hushed voices and whispered words.

Through it all, I could see nothing but a wisp of white fabric and, behind it, the wooden beams of a ceiling far out of reach. The site was at odds with the noise: the horror of gurgling, pleading words, the cries of a woman.

But no matter how many times I had this dream, I could not control my dream-body. I could never see what was happening. All I could feel was a keen sense of wanting as I reached arms that felt too small, too pudgy, towards ones that had always wrapped me in comfort—arms that had always felt smooth like velvet and warm like thick blankets.

I wanted those arms, and the lack of them made me cry.

1
rite of passage

"SAHLE?" MY MOTHER ASKED, SOFTLY SNAPPING FINGERS in front of my unseeing eyes.

We were sitting in a coffee shop downtown, easing our weary feet after an afternoon of browsing boutiques in search of what my mother called my "birthday suit." I had promptly advised her that the black lace blouse we purchased should never again be referred to as such.

"Hmm?" I blinked at her as I tried to focus on the present. "Sorry, did you say something?"

She rolled her eyes, muttering under her breath about staring into space. "I asked whether or not you're excited for tomorrow."

I looked at her with a quirked brow.

Tomorrow was my twentieth birthday and, for the life of me, I could not muster an ounce of enthusiasm. I should be excited. It was not every day that my friends threw me a secret surprise party—albeit one that I found out about as soon as the planning began. But I despised parties. Any sort of bustling, crowded event was a strange mix of terrifying and tedious. I hated the heat and press of too many bodies, the background chatter that groaned, the nearly perceptible buzz of energy that floated in the air.

If I were being truly honest, I would admit that my hatred did not stem from the parties themselves but rather how they made me feel. I was a solitary sort of girl, someone who much preferred a quiet walk along a country lane or a comfy reading nook on a rainy afternoon. And, no matter how old I grew, how many birthdays came and went, I never failed to say something stupid and impulsive in front of a crowd of people.

My friends would not call me shy, even if there were a quietness to me. I had a tendency to speak my mind freely the moment something rubbed me the wrong way, and I had a sparking temper that flared whenever I was backed into a corner. For all of these reasons, it was healthier for everyone involved if I avoided the large events my friends insisted on throwing.

But my mother knew all of this. Despite the fact that we looked nothing alike, our personalities were fairly similar. I found a kinship with the knowledge that she, too, found large gatherings anxiety producing rather than joyous as normal people did.

I drained the rest of my coffee and a hairline crack along the mug's edge scratched the corner of my lip. "You know I'm not," I responded with a grimace.

But my mother just laughed, tipping back her blonde head as she chuckled. It was my turn to roll my eyes at her and, despite my derision, I smiled. I had always loved my mother's laughter, the way her blue eyes crinkled at the corners and shone with mirth as she let loose almost bell-like giggles.

My own laugh was nothing like hers, at least not to my ears. I guffawed and even snorted at times. And when my own head tipped back in fits of laughter, it was not gently waving blonde hair that glided down my back.

My own head of hair was dense and curled like tightly coiled springs that seemingly defied gravity. They had grown long enough in my late teens that they did now fall towards the earth rather than springing out at odd angles, and in the last years I had grown to not despise my hair. I would not say I loved it, but I no longer looked in the mirror with dread.

My skin was also darker than my mother's. While hers was the color of fresh cream, mine was a lustrous, warm beige. I tanned several shades darker in the summer and went a sickly shade of yellow when I spent too many hours indoors.

But what I did have of my mother were her eyes. Those gray-blue eyes that shone in laughter—that color was the same as mine. My eyes were set at a slight slant while hers were not, but the color was near-identical. And for that I was always thankful. It was something I could grasp onto, something that marked me as hers.

In truth, the eyes could have been as much from my father as my mother. My hair texture, my skin coloring, the shape of my features all looked like my father. They were not exact replicas, as if an errant great aunt had also lent the upturn of a nose or the arch of an eyebrow, but I saw myself more in my father's darker coloring and tightly coiled hair.

I brushed one of these coils back from my face as I kept the disbelieving look trained on my mother. "I don't do well with crowds."

"So you continue to tell me," she replied. "But Sahle, these are your friends. And they'll all be there to celebrate you."

"There to celebrate the existence of alcohol, you mean," I murmured under my breath. Several of my friends jumped at the idea of any event where they could slurp down straight vodka as fast as their throats would allow.

My mother's face suddenly changed, and it was as if a gauzy veil of emotion draped across her usually bright smile. "Yes, well, some parents aren't as relaxed as we've been with that sort of thing. Your friends will grow out of it in time and with more exposure. But promise me something?"

I nodded, transfixed by her shifting mood.

She took my hand where it sat on the round bistro table between us. "You're getting older, Sahl, and with that…some things are going to change. You'll lose some friends. You'll make new ones. And at the end of it, all you'll be left with are your memories of being young, being at your parties, being with the friends you had in that moment. Cherish them, OK?"

Both eyebrows raised at her now, but something in her earnestness kept me from laughing, from making light of her seriousness. "OK, Mom."

She nodded once, as if confirming something in her own mind. Then she drained her mug and stood. "Shall we head home? Someone has to decide what they'll wear with their new top!"

I laughed as I climbed to my feet and followed her out of the shop. Only my mother could make me excited about a birthday—almost.

I awoke the morning of my birthday with a splitting headache and an overwhelming sense of dread. I rolled out of bed and stared at myself in the mirror as I brushed my teeth. Welcome to twenty, I thought as I looked into my gray-blue eyes.

Between my own classes that I attended at the local college, lunch, and a barely suffered-through bite of birthday cake at home with my parents, time seemed to slow and race interchangeably. But before I knew it, it was time to head to the birthday party I had been dreading.

My dad offered to drive me, even though I said more than once that I could call a rideshare. Strangely, he insisted. That is how I ended up sliding into the smooth leather interior of his sedan as we headed out into the evening.

"You excited, Sahl?" my dad asked me.

I rolled my eyes. "You and Mom keep asking me this like I

suddenly changed my mind about birthdays."

My dad let loose a low chuckle, the sound warm and deep in his chest. He was a quiet man, one who listened more than he spoke—except to me. I felt he spoke to me more than anyone else in the world. "We know you, and how you feel about it. But turning twenty is a big deal. We want you to take in the experience. It's important."

"That also sounds like Mom," I responded, watching the lights of suburbia whisk by. They were the lights of slightly too large houses with slightly too large lawns, slightly too big department stores on slightly too wide avenues. "She said something similar yesterday while we were shopping. Something about savoring this because one day all I'd have are memories of my friends."

"She's right."

"You two are too sentimental. Next year, I'll be twenty-one and I'll be back at the same party with my same friends. I don't think much changes in a town like this."

Strangely, my dad did not say anything for a moment. I watched as his grip tightened on the steering wheel, and I wondered what I had said that put him on edge. His eyes stayed fixed on the road and then he nodded. It was his way of ending a discussion that he felt was going nowhere.

I leaned forward and flicked on the stereo. A CD was already loaded, and the tumultuous sounds of Carmen filled the car.

"Hmm," I hummed appreciatively, reclining back in my seat.

The opera was my favorite, as it was my dad's favorite. He had introduced me to opera as a child and our love for the art was something that bound us together. Of all of the performances we had seen over the years, both live and recorded, nothing had ever come close to beating Carmen for pure melodramatic excitement. Of that, we were always in agreement.

"A classic," he said.

"A vision," I added.

My dad turned his head a fraction of an inch to glance at me and I smiled at him. He returned the gesture but, even reserved as he was, I could see that the smile did not reach his eyes.

A few minutes later, I was standing before Cecily's front door, clasping the edges of my leather coat together to keep the cold off of my barely-covered skin. The lace top my mother and I had purchased was pretty if a touch goth, thin and delicate in a way that clung to my gently curved torso while still being loose enough for comfort. Underneath it, I wore a black camisole that did nothing to trap body heat.

Before I could ring the bell, the door flew open and a gaggle of pink-clad college juniors exploded out onto the porch.

"Happy Birthday, Sahle!" several cried in unison.

I restrained my rolling eyes as I spotted Melody and Katherine, two friends-of-friends that somehow always seemed to be around. My mood was only slightly more excited to spy Cecily's boyfriend, Jason, and his friend, Lyle. In my estimation, they were the male equivalent of the giddy but empty-headed Melody and Katherine.

And then I spied Cecily and Jenna, and my fake smile shifted into a real one.

They wormed their way through the gathering crowd—ignoring a few people who I was pretty sure asked "Who's birthday is it?"—and threw their arms around me.

"Thank you both for hosting the party," I said, still confined in their embrace. As some of my closest friends, they knew my general feeling about birthdays and parties, but they played along, happy to believe for even a few moments that I was genuinely excited to be here.

"Come in. Come in. You're all letting the cold in," another voice called from the open doorway, and I angled my head to see the fourth member of our usual group, Mer.

Pronounced "Mare," Mer was my oldest friend and the person I trusted most with my secrets. I had known her since the third grade, and we had been inseparable ever since.

While Cecily and Jenna were friends, Mer was like the sister I never had. I broke away from Cecily and Jenna to make my way over to her, and she wrapped me in her own warm embrace, the heat from the house tickling around our frames.

"Happy birthday, cupcake," she said in my ear, and I smiled into her mane of red hair. For a whole year, when we were eleven years old, she called me cupcake. Now, she only broke it out on special occasions or when she wanted a favor.

"Thanks, Mer," I replied, pulling away from her to survey the scene before me. "Let's get this party started."

The party was exactly what I expected. Music pumped from the built-in ceiling speakers. The mingled smell of musty beer and sweet icing filled the air. The heat of too many bodies packed the room.

There were probably fifty people here, I estimated—fifty people and most of them I had never met.

I also knew exactly how that happened. Cecily had always been a talker, and when she was throwing a party for any reason, it was an open invitation. That was just how she operated, and I accepted that, even as I took an offered red cup of lukewarm beer with a nod to the baseball-capped guy manning the keg in the kitchen.

"The big two-zero," Mer said, taking a cup for herself from the lineup on the counter.

I took a sip, mentally preparing myself for the bitterness before my lips even met the cup. "Don't remind me."

Mer shook her head at me with a smile. "You always have such a thing with birthdays. But you know, you're only supposed to hate them when you're older, like when they're a reminder that you're one year closer to the grave."

"They're already a reminder of that," I quipped back. "Seriously, though, I remember having a sense of dread around my birthday even as a child. It's hard to explain but there has always been this sense of imminence that I could never shake."

Mer looked at me—really looked at me. There was kindness

in her eyes as she said, "I understand, Sahl. I mean, I've never felt like that on my birthday, but I get that that's how you feel. And I get that the feeling makes it hard to have a happy-go-lucky day."

I nodded at her, shifting my feet on the white tile of the kitchen floor. I pulled my gaze from her green one to scan the room. "Where did Cecily and Jenna go?" I asked, ready to move on from the conversation.

"Cecily was having an argument with Jason before you arrived, so I'm sure she's finishing that up. And you know wherever Cecily is, Jenna is bound to be, too."

I laughed at the observation. It was true. Cecily and Jenna were practically joined at the hip and had been as long as we had known them. If Mer and I were best friends, those two were best friends. The four of us combined as a looser group of great friends but we all knew who our closest person was.

I scanned the party again. I narrowed my eyes as I looked past the beige and white living room towards the sliding doors leading to the back deck. Between the low light inside and the approaching darkness outside, it was hard to see the figures moving, but they were certainly there.

Something drew my eye right to the dark silhouette of Cecily's high ponytail at the exact moment the taller, wider silhouette that was Jason stepped towards her and raised his arm. That hand reached out and connected with Cecily's cheek, and I imagined I could hear it like the sound of a snapping whip.

I did not consciously tell my body to move but it did just that, as if drawn towards that deck and whatever was happening out there.

"Sahl?" Mer called after me in confusion. I heard her footsteps following behind as I shimmied through the mass of bodies gently swaying to the beat of the music.

I reached the glass doors that led to the backyard and flung them open. I hurried out onto the porch, dodging two people moving back inside.

The outside light was turned off, but night had not fully descended. In the half-light, I could easily make out the redness of Cecily's face as she cupped one palm to her cheek.

"What the fuck?" I exclaimed, turning to Jason as Cecily cast her eyes to the deck.

But Jason was not speaking. His eyes were narrowed and an angry scowl cut across his face.

"Sahl!" Mer called for a second time as I marched up to Jason. I probably should have thought about how this large man could strike me just as he had hit Cecily, but I had never been one to think first and act later. It was quite the opposite really—I had always been a touch impulsive when my emotions got the best of me.

And my emotions burned now with outrage and disbelief. I could almost see the haze of anger like a physical barrier between my eyes and Jason's stubborn face. I did not try to reign it in.

I walked up to him, stopping a touch too close for comfort. I looked up into his ruddy face with a scowl of my own. "I said what the fuck?"

"I don't know what you're talking about," Jason muttered, not meeting my eye.

My breath was heavy, coming quickly in and out as I stared at him. I willed him to be the tough man he was and look at me.

Almost reluctantly, his eyes met mine.

"I'll ask you again. What the fuck was that?"

"It's none of your concern."

My mouth nearly fell open. "Like hell it isn't!"

Like any good bully, Jason was drawing himself up in indignation, using it as armor to deflect any sense of wrongdoing. I could see it in his posture. He stood a little taller and his shoulders pulled back a fraction of an inch.

"Sahl, everything's fine," Cecily called from behind me, and I turned my gaze to her. Mer and Jenna were standing beside her, Jenna's arm draped around Cecily's waist.

But it was not fine—not at all.

I turned my attention back to Jason. "You think it's acceptable to hit your girlfriend?"

"I think it's none of your business what Cecily and I do," he quipped back.

"You make it my business when you hurt someone I care about."

But Jason was not listening. He stepped around me and reached for Cecily just as Jenna and Mer tightened their hold on her.

"Let's go," he told her, his wide fingers digging into the pale skin of her wrist. He pulled her as if to drag her back inside, but she would not budge.

I hated that hand on her. I hated the look of his fingers where they made deep indentations in her skin, and I wished he would release her.

He pulled his hand back, shaking it as if her rejection physically stung.

"I think it's time you leave," Mer said, her green eyes taking on a fierce light as she glared at him.

For one intense moment, the two stared at each other. No one dared move. Our breath seemed to still. The birds who sang of night's descent quieted in the trees and the whisper of the leaves froze. Even the gentle breeze seemed to stop to watch in fascination.

"Come on, man," Lyle called from where he stood by the railing. "Let's just go."

I did not know Lyle well, but in that instant I knew he had more sense than I had ever given him credit for. Leaving was the only good option, unless Jason was planning to physically beat us all to pieces.

That was the only way Jenna, Mer, or I would let Cecily go with him.

Jason looked between Lyle and Cecily, seeming to decide that ignoring the rest of us was the best course of action. Abruptly, he turned away. "Fine. This party's lame anyway."

He stormed off the deck with Lyle at his heels, but I did not move until I saw, through the glass back door, the front door to the house close behind him.

Only then did I fall back to where the three women were standing. Jenna was gingerly touching the red spot on Cecily's cheek and Mer was whispering something to Cecily in the same tone one spoke to a horse or a sick baby. We all moved slowly, quietly, shocked as we were by what had just happened.

Eventually, Cecily cleared her throat. "Thank you, Sahl," she said as her eyes met mine. "You didn't need to do that…but I'm glad you did."

She blinked against the tears that welled up, and I smiled a little at her. "Of course. No one hurts the people I care about."

She nodded. "I know."

The four of us spent the next fifteen minutes in the bathroom, fixing Cecily's hair, redoing her makeup, and patting away the tears. Even if this had not been her house, I knew Cecily would not have left. It was my birthday after all, and she and Jenna believed in nothing if not that all the stops must be pulled out for a good birthday.

Although it went unspoken, it was as if the four of us agreed to wallow in what had happened while we were in the bathroom. And when we stepped outside of that sanctuary, when we rejoined the party, we would not speak of it again—not tonight at least.

Tomorrow, Cecily had some tough choices. I knew I would be calling her first thing in the morning to urge her in the strongest way possible that it was time to leave that dick of a boyfriend.

The party hummed along without us, and if anyone had noticed what transpired on the porch, no one asked about it. I pasted a mask of a smile on my face and greeted the friends-of-friends who wished me happy birthday. I accepted a new cup of beer—this time cooler, thankfully—and sipped at it. And then Mer was calling to me from across the room, a cake knife brandished over her head.

Those partiers who knew me, or who were paying attention generally, sang happy birthday. We ate cake. We danced to whatever thumping club mix Cecily had picked out earlier in the night. And we laughed—oh, how we laughed.

I disliked my birthday but if there were anyone who could make it better, it was the three women standing around me. I glanced at their open faces as we spun around and jumped up and down and shook our booties ironically to the beat.

And I smiled my first real smile of the day. If this were twenty, maybe it would not be so bad after all.

A few hours later, I stifled a yawn and glanced at the grandfather clock in the corner of Cecily's living room. As if on cue, the clock chimed eleven o'clock, and I knew it was acceptable for me to leave.

Mer, Jenna, and Cecily all protested when I said I was heading home, but I knew they were just happy I stayed as long as I had at the party. I gave a round of hugs, a stern promise to call Cecily in the morning, and then I pulled out my phone to order a ride.

Minutes later, I slid into the backseat of a car. And a few minutes after that, the car pulled up to the front yard of my suburban home.

I closed the door of the cab as I hopped out onto the curb in front of the house. My parents were early sleepers, often going up to their bedroom by nine o'clock but here it was hours later, and the house remained lit as if they were still downstairs. They could have left the lights on for me, or perhaps it was a rare moment when they were up late to finish a movie.

It was no surprise, therefore, to find them seated on the couch as soon as I unlocked the front door.

"Mom. Dad," I greeted them as I relocked the deadbolt. "You two are up late."

"We were waiting for you," my mother said quietly. But something about the tone of her voice was off. It was too calm, too flat as if she was mastering it against nerves or fear.

I focused my attention on her and then my dad. Quiet as he was, he had always been able to communicate one thousand words with a single look or the angle of his head. His silence now rang out like a shot. He was communicating nothing, just staring at the floor, the ceiling, a spot over my shoulder—anything to avoid meeting my eye.

"What's going on?" I asked.

It was then that I spied two small bags sitting next to the couch. "Are we going somewhere?"

Despite my questions, no one spoke. Slowly, my parents looked at each other and, as if some decision had been made in that single look, my father stood and approached me.

His broad frame towered over me, his gray-blue eyes locking on my own. "Sahle, I need you to trust us. OK, honey?"

Something was wrong. My skin tingled with the knowledge of it. No, it was not OK and I shook my head, unable to say the words aloud.

But my father was having none of that. "No, honey, you have to trust us. In a moment, we're going to go on a trip. It's been planned for a long time. It's going to be difficult and a little scary, but I promise that nothing will hurt you."

"What are you talking about?" I choked out. My eyebrows had risen in incredulity. Surely, surely my father had to be losing it.

I turned to my mother for confirmation. "Mom, what is he talking about?"

She had been looking away from the two of us but when she turned back, I saw that her eyes were glassy with unshed tears. She cleared her throat before she stood. "Sweetheart, please just listen to him. Listen to us. We have to go. I know this is strange and that it doesn't make sense, but it will all make sense soon. Everything will be alright."

Of course I trusted my parents. I loved them and I knew they would never hurt me, but something in the way they held themselves, something in how they talked, told me on an instinctual level that this was not just any trip.

Something was off. Something was wrong.

But even as I kept shaking my head, willing whatever was happening to stop, my parents were picking up the two bags. My father came back to me and took my arm in his, propelling me towards the kitchen and back door.

"Can someone please explain where we're going? It's nearly midnight! Why do we have to go now?" I questioned, trying to squirm out of my dad's grasp.

"All will be explained shortly," he responded, his grip like an iron band on my elbow. "I promise."

It was the second time he had made a promise tonight and I noted it. I was going to throw it back in his face if someone did not explain shortly, and if I so much as stubbed a toe.

For some reason, though, I stopped fighting. Maybe it was the look in my mother's eyes, the way her bottom lip trembled the more I tried to pull my arm away from my father's grip.

I trusted my parents and as much as I did not understand what was happening, I made the decision to go along with it. They would not lead me into harm. They would only do what was best for me. I knew that as deeply as I knew that the sky was blue, that my body needed air to breathe and food to sustain itself.

So I let myself be guided to the kitchen, through the back door and out onto our back lawn. Once there, my parents put down the two bags.

"Sahle," my father spoke sternly. "If I let your arm go, will you please stay put?"

I simply nodded, not trusting my voice to hold steady if I responded verbally.

"Good," he said and let go of my elbow. And I did not run. I just stood there, close to my father as I had before.

A faint click to my left drew my attention and I glanced over to where my mother stood. She was holding her silver locket in her hands, the one she always wore. No matter the time of day or night, no matter if we were at the beach or sitting on the couch at home, I had never seen that locket off of her neck.

Now, she held it in her hands, cradling it like it was a precious amulet. And perhaps it was, for she opened it and I saw the miniature of the three of us that had been in that locket since I was a baby. She had often told me it was her favorite photo of our family whenever I had begged her to open the locket and show me what was inside.

To my shock, her finger now grasped the plastic overlaying the photo. She pulled it out, along with the image. Below was a small stone. It shone like off-white milk glass, and it was perfectly shaped to fit behind the image without rattling around or forcing the photo to bulge.

She shook the stone out on her palm and then closed her fist tightly around it. I watched as her eyes shut, and she whispered a series of words to herself. Then she opened her palm and the stone was alight, shimmering as if the edges were lit from within with silver dancing bands.

"Sahle," she said, turning to me. I felt her hand slip around my own and she gave my hand a little squeeze as she smiled. It was a wistful look, and I struggled to make out the emotion behind her tear-filled eyes. "Always remember that we love you."

I opened my mouth to tell her that I would, that I did, that I could never not know that. But before the words could get out, a shimmering net of light rose from the stone in my mother's hand.

It shot straight into the sky before arching over above our heads, creating a dome around us, a net of white light that shone like blood vessels in the night air.

I blinked at the sight, trying to make sense of how ribbons of light seemed to cage us in. In one blink, I was assessing the light and in the next there was nothing.

And in the next, there was everything.

journey

IT IS HARD TO EXPLAIN THE FEELING OF THAT FIRST journey. It both felt like it lasted seconds and that it stretched on for days. My body felt whole and at the same time insubstantial, as if I were a figment of my own imagination.

But what I remember most was the light, that starlike glow that seemed to be before my eyes and throughout my entire body. I was not sure whether my eyes were open or shut, whether the light merely danced before my eyes or permeated my very being. All I knew was that it had the same quality, the same ethereal shine as the stars that I used to stare up at.

Just as suddenly as the light began, it ended and the three of us were standing in a field.

"Wh-wh-what?" I stuttered as I whipped around, yanking my hand from my mother's grasp. My heart was pounding ferociously. My breath was shallow and too fast, but I could not calm it as I tracked my eyes over my surroundings, trying desperately to make sense of what had happened.

"Sahle," my mother called gently. I felt her cool hand touch the back of my arm and I jumped, spinning back to her with wide eyes.

"Sahle," she tried again, this time reaching out the hand but not touching me. "Let us explain."

I shook my head frantically. I wanted an explanation of course—no, I needed an explanation—but all I could do was shake my head. I did not know where to begin or even what question to ask. I did not know how my mother looked so calm and spoke so gently, or why my father merely hung back silently and watchfully.

I spun to him, hoping that something about this would make sense when I gazed at him. But when I looked into his eyes, I did not recognize the man staring back at me. There was hesitancy there. Not fear, necessarily, but wariness. I realized, with a shock, that it was directed at me.

"Dad?" I whispered, my voice sounding hollow to my own ears.

Instead of responding, he bowed.

"Roland," my mother murmured and I shifted my confused gaze from my father, who remained deeply bowed, to her.

"Eliza," he responded coolly. "You forget yourself. Bow."

And to my horror, my mother immediately dropped into a low curtsy.

"What?" I tried again. "I don't understand."

When no one said anything, I nearly shrieked, "Get up!"

But before they could rise, a vibration started under my feet. It grew to a rumble within seconds, and I turned from my bowing parents towards the commotion.

A dozen horses were galloping at breakneck speed in our direction. Banners streamed above the astride riders in what I thought were reds and golds, but it was hard to make out the colors in the low light.

As the riders drew closer, I blinked at the sight before me. The horses were not horses at all; rather, they were overly large zebras. Their stripes were clear as the animals cut their speed before us. One by one, each of the twelve riders dismounted and sank into bows alongside my parents.

I stared uncomprehendingly at the small crowd before me. I had no idea where I was, how I had gotten here, who these people were or why they were prostrating themselves before me.

And I certainly was not ready when one of the riders, an older man with graying hair, finally rose from his bow with a smile.

"Welcome home, Queen Sahle," he said.

3
shock and awe

I STARED AT HIM DUMBFOUNDED. "EXCUSE ME?" I whispered—or tried to. I was not sure my mouth could move enough to form those words.

"Welcome home, Your Majesty," he repeated, this time with another quick bow from the waist.

He waited a moment to see if I would respond, and when I did nothing more than stare, he continued. "I understand that this must be overwhelming for you. If you would permit me, I think it's best that we make our way back to the palace before giving explanations and introductions. You'd be most comfortable that way."

Some part of my brain told me he was waiting for me to acknowledge his suggestion, to agree or not to agree, but I could not move. My mind felt like it was frozen. I could only watch as the bowed men cast sideways glances at each other, as my parents looked up at me, as this older man waited with questioning eyes.

"Advisor," my mother's clear voice called out. "Knowing the Queen as I do, I must agree that that is the best course of action."

At my mother's voice, I settled my wide-eyed stare at her. She was still dropped low into a curtsy, but she was looking at me. A small smile touched her lips and she nodded at me once. It was the same way she used to encourage me when, as a child, I would look to her to determine whether an action was the right one.

She was trying to tell me that this was alright, that I could go with them to whatever palace they mentioned. And in the swirling sea of shock and disbelief, my mother's approval was the buoy I grasped onto. It was the one thing steady and sure.

I nodded back at her jerkily.

"Wonderful," the gray-haired man—the advisor, as my mother had called him—said. "Let's be on our way then."

With that, the small crowd of men rose out of their bows and began mounting their...zebras. I thought I had originally spied twelve animals galloping towards us, but what I had failed to notice were the three extra holstered zebras that had come with them.

Three zebras for three extra people—my mother, my father, and myself.

Unexpectedly, panic bloomed in my chest. I had no idea how to ride a horse, let alone something as exotic as a zebra, or even how to get on one. Sure, I had seen plenty of movies where the characters planted their foot and swung themselves up. I had even ridden on a horse once as a child, dressed up in a red, white, and blue cowboy hat as part of a Fourth of July parade. Before the panic could take hold, my mother was beside me once more.

"Come, Sahle. Ride with me," she whispered, her voice cast low so that only I could hear her.

And then my father was there, hoisting me onto the zebra, helping my mother up behind me, and mounting his own zebra beside us.

With the last of us mounted, the advisor moved his zebra back in the direction they had come, and the rest of us followed him.

I could feel my mother's slight frame wrapped behind me, how she led the zebra with soft words and slight tugs on the reins she held. But I was too busy staring at and through the landscape around us to question how she, who had never shown any interest in equestrian sports before, could perfectly manage the zebra beneath us.

Our path led us through a twilight-skied field. It must have been early morning for the sky was dark but, near the horizon, a glow of pink and orange shone. I am not sure how long we rode. It could have been minutes or hours, such was my confusion, my shock which made all rational conceptualization impossible. But as the sky lightened, as the sun rose higher in the sky, I could make out more of the landscape of this strange place.

From lush slopes studded with strange, meaty pink flowers, trees eventually began to rise around us. They were tall and reaching, with wispy leaves that rustled like thin silver feathers in the breeze. And as we wove through the forest on a red-dirt path, I began to hear more and more noise, like a commotion of bees buzzing softly nearby.

Suddenly, the silver trees just stopped. We had reached a clearing.

But it was not a clearing—not really. It was a city. It stretched out from the edge of the forest, rising like a twinkling sea out of the red ground as lights from windows glinted. At the far edge of the city, a tall structure rose floors above the rest of the rooflines. It had to be the palace, I thought, as we continued our journey off the forest trail and through the winding streets of the city.

Shops and houses in muted tones of brown and red plaster passed by us as our party marched on. My eyes caught on the thatched roofs, the rounded walls of the homes. These were unlike any buildings I had seen before.

Then I began to see people. Children stuck their heads out of windows. Shopkeepers came to their doors to watch us pass. Passersby in the street stopped and stared up at us.

And every person who saw us bowed.

Looking back, I wish I had made a better impression. Even if I would have been able to close my mouth and lift a hand, maybe share a small smile, anything would have been better than the gaping-fish expression that covered my face.

If they noticed my confused expression, I do not think they minded. So many smiles broke out on the faces of those we passed. Children cried out, "Queen Sahle! Queen Sahle!" Several of the adults murmured, "God and gods bless you, Your Majesty."

Their faces blurred in my confusion and before I knew it, our zebras were approaching the tall building I had spied earlier. Up close, I could see that the building was actually a circular stone wall that curved, like a protective hand around what I could only assume were the palace grounds. I squinted at the mortarless walls, wondering how the stones were held together, especially in sections where intricate patterns interspersed with standard stone sections.

Large wooden gates opened before us, and our zebras moved seemingly of their own volition. Just inside the gates was a large courtyard with stables to one side, smaller outbuildings dotted around the edges, and a tall stone staircase that led up to a huge white-walled home. It was more like a mansion really, sprawling and with multiple floors. Two trees with vibrant purple flowers sat on either side of the stone staircase that led up a monstrous wooden door, arching over the passageway.

My mother pulled our zebra to a stop before the staircase, passing the reins to a waiting stable hand. Another stable hand stepped up to help my mother dismount, but my father brushed him aside with a flick of his wrist. It was an assertive motion which showed a certain confidence I had never seen before. As he helped my mother dismount and then myself, I stared up at him quizzically as if I was suddenly meeting an entirely new person.

His features looked the same, of course—the tightly curled hair, the dark skin, the gray-blue eyes. But the angles of his face seemed to have grown sharper along with this confidence.

He turned to me as if he felt my eyes on him. "Sahle?"

"Dad?" I responded in the same questioning tone he had adopted.

Before either of us could say more, the advisor and the other riders dismounted and were making their way to us. My mother threaded her arm through mine and began pulling me alongside her, up the stone stairs.

"Your Majesty," the advisor called, coming up beside me as we ascended the top step. The doors swung open at our approach, and we stepped into a hallway of shining checkered black and white marble. "I think it is of the utmost importance that we immediately meet with the Council and get you acquainted with your new home."

I opened my mouth to speak, but my mother replied before I could form the first word.

"With all due respect, I believe Her Majesty would like to settle in before she meets the Council."

The advisor's graying eyebrows rose in surprise. "Lady Eliza, I appreciate your past role with the Queen, but it is time she stepped into her position."

"In my past role, as you put it," my mother quipped back. "I've come to know Her Majesty quite well, and I insist that she is shown to her chambers and given adequate time to rest before she begins."

With pursed lips like he had tasted something sour, the advisor turned to me. "Your Majesty, what would you prefer?"

I did not need to think to respond to that question. My head was still swimming, confusion thick and humid like a cloud that muted my hearing and blurred my vision at the edges. All I wanted was to talk to my parents away from all of these strangers and find out what was going on.

"I'd like some time to rest," I managed to say, holding my mother's gaze. She nodded her approval at me, and then we were in motion again.

We wove through hallways filled with regal paintings and towering ceilings lined by exposed beams. Animal heads—some sort of antelope primarily—and tapestries in the same gold and red I had seen on the zebras' banners hung here and there. Light filtered in from tall windows and reflected off the polished stone floors.

And in each new room and hallway, there were people. Although they were dressed in loud, multi-colored and patterned outfits, their personalities were entirely different to those I had seen outside the palace walls. Here they did not shout my name or clap and laugh as the people in the city had; rather, they sank down into polished bows and curtsies while murmuring, "Your Majesty" or "Queen Sahle."

I did not respond but just kept moving, propelled forward by the constant pressure that was my mother's elbow leading me on. But I did stare—at the light brown clothes of the ones carrying baskets of wood and trays of food and drink, at the bright dresses and coats of the ones seemingly at leisure. I guessed those in the light brown were servants while those dressed more elaborately were not.

Suddenly we were winding up and up another staircase, then another. And then we were at a large, heavy wooden door painted with a design in red and gold. As I moved closer to the door, I could finally make out what the banners and crests depicted: the same strange flower I had seen on my journey to the palace, ringed by stars.

"I took the liberty of having your chambers prepared before I came to retrieve you, Your Majesty," the advisor said. "I hope they are to your liking."

"I'm sure they will be," my mother answered for me, too aware that I was quickly moving beyond the capacity for speech.

The advisor swung the door open for us, and my mother led me into an enormous room. The ceiling reached well over twelve feet tall, arched as it was up into a point at the center. Exposed beams and a low brass chandelier hung above us, and as I stared at what looked like the underside of a thatched roof, I wondered if this room was the very top point of the palace.

The same tall windows I had noticed in the halls also lined this room, spilling soft morning light into the room. Wood-framed maps hung along the walls, and the floors were adorned with deep burgundy rugs interspersed with what looked to be beige pelts of some sort. Here and there, great-leafed green potted plants dotted corners and empty spaces along the wall.

I noticed a fireplace and two leather wingback chairs to one side of the room, and a tall wooden four-poster bed to the other. I looked longingly at the sheer drapery, the crisp sheets, and plush blankets. My head was beginning to ache and all I wanted was to lay down.

But my mother did not take me to the bed. She steered me to the seating area and gently pushed me into a seat before spinning back to the advisor.

"My Lords, if you would be so kind as to excuse the Queen. She will join you in Council soon."

In my confused haze, I had hardly realized that there were more people than my parents and the advisor with us. No, at least ten people had piled into my room and were staring at my mother and me.

I noticed my father among these men as he stepped out of the mass and turned to address them. "I must agree with my wife. Let's leave the Queen to settle in and then we can make our introductions."

He turned to me with a slight smile and for the first time since we had arrived, I recognized a little part of the dad I had grown up with. I smiled back, slightly and hesitantly, although even to my face it felt strained.

Grumbling under their breath, the men began to make their way back out of the room until only the advisor and my parents were left. My father and the advisor spoke quietly near the door, but I could not catch what they were saying.

I realized I was clutching my mother's hand—somehow I had transferred my grasp from her arm when she had urged me to sit. She rubbed my fingers with her free hand and smiled at me as she turned my way.

"Everything is fine," she said again, nearly cooing the words, and it reminded me of the way you spoke to a frightened animal—a mix of love and worry, with just a hint of condescension for little creatures that did not understand the complexities of the world. "Just try to relax. We'll explain everything soon and it will all make sense then."

I nodded even though I did not believe her. I did not think I would ever understand what was happening, where we were, or why people were calling me Queen.

I must have hit my head and started hallucinating. Or perhaps this was a wild dream, one where everything looked and felt and tasted real—so real that when you woke up, you almost swear that reality was the dream, and the dream was the truest life that had ever existed.

My father cleared his throat from across the room and I looked away from my mother and back to him. "Eliza, come along. Grimly has requested that we speak to him while the Queen rests."

"Roland, we should stay—" my mother began to protest.

"We'll be back shortly," my father interjected.

My mother shook her head. "She has no idea what is happening. She needs us to be with her right now."

"My Lady," the advisor cut in. "The Council wishes to speak to someone now. Either it is the Queen or it is the two of you together. You may pick."

My mother snapped her mouth shut, eyes narrowing. "Have you no heart? Sahle just arrived here and has no clue what this place is or what she is doing here. You'd have her left here alone, without the only parents she has ever known—with no explanation, I might add—so that we can speak with a handful of—"

"Lady Eliza," the advisor interrupted, his tone going cold and forbidding as his sharp eyes narrowed on my mother. "You forget yourself. She is not your child. She is the Queen and you will address her as such."

I stared, the words crashing into me and bouncing away. They did not sink in. They could not sink in because they made no sense.

What did he mean about me not being her child?

"Moreover," the man continued, oblivious to the utter confusion raging inside me. "While I can certainly sympathize with the Queen's need to rest after her journey, the issues of state must be addressed by someone. It must be you and your husband as Protectors if the Queen is not able to attend to them now. So, I ask you again, will it be the Queen coming to Council now or you and your husband?"

Protectors.

My brain grasped at this word, playing with the syllables and trying to make sense of the meaning.

My mother did not respond for a moment. Then she took a deep breath, drawing her shoulders back as if she were about to step into battle.

"Fine," she said curtly, and my eyes widened even further. "But I will give the Lords thirty minutes and no more. Then I will come back to the Queen."

The advisor merely nodded, but he did not leave. He looked at my father and mother expectantly. I realized he was waiting for them.

My father moved from his place across the door, coming to stop before the chair where I was seated like a rock. "I made you a promise that you would be safe. I'm sticking to that, do you understand?"

"Yes," I whispered, more so because I knew that was the correct response. Truly, I did not understand anything.

"Eliza and I will be back shortly."

At her name, I turned my gaze to my mother.

"But what is happening?" I choked out. Distantly, I realized I was in some sort of shock but, through that stupored haze, the unresolved question pulsed like a strobe light.

"I'll explain it all when we get back," she replied, leaning down to kiss my cheek and smooth a wayward curl from my face.

My father bent down and kissed my forehead. "Try to get some rest."

And then they were stepping away from me. With a soft thud, the heavy wooden door closed behind them, and I was all alone.

Or so I thought.

Soft steps echoed over my shoulder, and I turned quickly to glance behind me.

Two young women, both dressed in light brown, approached slowly. "Queen Sahle," they curtsied. "Would you like to bathe? And change into something more comfortable?"

I shook my head, hugging my arms around my torso as if I could protect myself from this foreign place by keeping these clothes on my body.

The two girls glanced at each other, and I noticed that one of them was holding a gauzy white dress of some sort.

"Your Majesty," the one holding the dress tried again. "Your clothes are dirty from the road. Perhaps you would be more comfortable if you let us wash them?"

I looked down at myself. Maybe the dress-carrier was right. I had been wearing my black lace top and black jeans but now they looked more brown than black, covered in a fine coating of red dust as they were. I had no memory of when they got so dirty, but I figured it must have been when we were riding the zebras.

Zebras.

I physically shook my head at the memory.

"OK," I whispered to the girls. "You can take my clothes to wash."

I looked around for a bathroom or some place to change but already the two girls were upon me, pulling me to my feet, pushing my shirt up over my head, and unbuttoning my jeans. I was too shocked to be embarrassed by my nakedness, especially as they also pulled off my bra and underwear.

I stood naked in the room for only a moment before they slid the white dress over my head and onto my arms. It was a night-gown, I realized, and the light material felt airy and floating.

Then they had a damp washcloth that they pulled over my hands, my neck, and my face. And then they were gently tugging me in the direction of the bed.

"I'm not tired," I murmured as my bottom landed on the downy white blanket.

I noticed the two girls glance at each other again. The one who had been carrying the dress—the more vocal of the two—said, "I know, Your Majesty. But perhaps you'd be more comfortable sitting here than on the chair?"

I looked down at the crisp white linen on the bed, the fluffy pillows in front of the polished headboard and, somehow, the next thing I knew I was laying down.

I was closing my eyes.

I was sleeping.

4

fairytales

SLEEP IS A FUNNY THING. WE ALWAYS THINK THAT noise wakes us from it—the honk of a car outside our bedroom window, the creak of a floorboard down the hallway. But sometimes, motion is the thing that wakes us.

At least, that was what I thought woke me from my slumber. Even asleep, I saw more than felt my mother stand from her chair and move towards the pitcher that sat on the table before her.

"Mom?" I croaked through my sleep-thick throat.

She turned at my voice and when our gazes locked, she smiled.

"Good morning, sleepyhead."

"Morning?" I rubbed my hand groggily across my eyes as I looked around the room. Where was I?

A soft buttery light was floating through the wall of windows behind my mother...windows that looked out over a palace ground, a city, a vast forest. And like a clap of thunder, all of the memories of yesterday came back: the alien flowers I had seen while on zebraback, the smell of warm polished wood as I had entered this estate, the confusion and fear that rendered me quiet with shocked disbelief.

I willed myself to take a deep breath through the rising panic. The sheets tangled around me felt real. This room with its off-white walls and tall monstera and ferns felt real. This place was not just some dream, and I wondered anew what was going on.

"Where are we?" I asked as I pulled myself into a seated position against what felt like at least a dozen pillows. Their softness warred with their foreignness; this was not my bed, this was not my room, and wherever we were was not my home.

My mother did not respond right away. She remained quiet while she poured what looked to be water into a glass before coming over to the bed.

The bed was gigantic—easily a king-sized bed if not bigger—but still I scooted over to make room for her in the warm spot where I had been sleeping. She sat, pulling her legs up from the floor, and I noticed that she had changed. Gone were her own jeans and, in their place, was a floor length dress in shades of blue and yellow that draped around her torso and fell to the floor in waves. She tucked these yards of intricate patterned fabric around her feet as she settled, putting her arm around my shoulders and then handing me the glass of water.

"It's a long story. Drink this first. You must be thirsty. Then I'll explain while we wait for breakfast to be sent up."

I took the cup from her, draining the cool liquid in eager gulps.

My mother took the empty cup from my hand, placing it on the side table next to her. Then she tucked me more securely under her arm. "Your father will be here in a few minutes, but I thought you and I could start without him. Sahle, I owe you an explanation…"

A myriad of quips came to mind. You think. Obviously. About damn time. But I did not say any of those. I just swallowed and waited for her to continue.

She let loose a little nervous laugh, the giggle I had heard countless times whenever she got into an awkward situation. Perhaps it was cruel of me to feel at home in her discomfort, but that moment of recognition put me at ease—or as at ease as I could be.

No matter where we were or what in God's name was happening, she was still my mother. I was still tucked under her arm as I had been hundreds, thousands of times before. And she was going to make it all make sense.

At least, I hoped she was.

My mother cleared her throat before starting. "This place, this land, is called Izwe. It's a kingdom in what we call the Alterealm."

"The Alte-what?" I asked incredulously. She could not have just said realm.

Right?

"The Alterealm," she repeated, looking at me patiently. When I did not respond to that, she carried on. "It must sound strange, impossible really. But the Alterealm is another realm, or universe, from the Humanrealm."

I narrowed my eyes. Had she lost her mind? "The Humanrealm being real life, like where we have always lived…"

But she was not thrown off by my tone. She all but ignored it as she replied, "Yes, the Humanrealm is where we raised you. It's where we traveled from last night. This realm exists above, below, parallel to that. It's not like a different galaxy, but rather another plane. Does that make sense?"

"No," I replied simply. There was no reason to pretend when everything she was saying sounded absurd.

"That's ok. It'll take time for this all to feel real. For now, just understand that while the Alterealm looks much the same as the Humanrealm, it is another dimension from what you are used to. It is possible to navigate between the realms but only certain people have that ability."

"Like you?" I asked her as I remembered the words she had spoken over the stone in her locket.

"Not me, necessarily," my mother replied slowly. "The stone I used to bring us here was primed by those with the ability to allow us to travel back to the Alterealm whenever I activated it. I merely had to say the correct words and it would transport us."

I just looked at her as if she was speaking a foreign language. "And I'm here because…"

"Because you're the Queen, Sahle," she said matter-of-factly, as if it were normal to have a crowd of men on zebras bow before me, as they had last night.

"The Queen?" I repeated. The words did not feel right on my tongue. "But how? Why?"

"How are you the Queen?" she replied, guessing at my line of thought even though my mind could not form the full sentences.

I nodded and she sighed, a sad sound like she was carrying the weight of a lifetime upon her back. Before she could begin, though, a quiet knock sounded at my door.

My father stepped inside and, seeing me awake, approached the bed with a weary smile. "You're up."

"I was just trying to fill her in on how she's Queen," my mother explained as she angled her body to make room for him on the huge bed.

Settled in the downy covers, he gave me a hesitant smile. "You must have a lot of questions."

"I don't even know where to begin," I said.

"I'd imagine the beginning is most fitting," he replied. "Eliza, would you like to tell it?"

She took a deep breath as if it would steel her for the tale. Then she began. "Twenty years ago, there was a little baby born to a great and powerful Queen and her Consort. Their names were Bekha and Otto. There was already unease in the kingdom, but the Queen and her Consort had managed to keep the kingdom as safe as possible.

"As is tradition here in Izwe, when a baby is born to a noble family, the baby is taken before a wise woman to see if there is a prophecy to be had for the child. Sometimes there is nothing the woman has to say about the child's life, not because the child will not do anything of significance, but simply because the child's future is veiled to her. Yet sometimes the wise woman can see into the child's future, and she'll set a prophecy.

"That is what happened when this child was brought before her. She took one look at the child and began speaking. She said that this child, this daughter, would grow to become the finest ruler that Izwe had ever had. She said this queen would bring unity amongst the Alterealm and peace to Izwe. It would be a peace more lasting and prosperous than any time before her.

"When Izwe's enemies heard of this child's destiny, however, they were determined to stop it. See, other kingdoms had long made profits off of the strife and conflict plaguing the Alterealm. Peace at last, and prosperity for Izwe specifically, was a threat they could not accept. And so they sent men to kill the child, the little princess…"

I looked at my mother when she did not continue and was surprised to see silent tears trailing across her cheeks.

"Mom?" I asked, lifting my hand as if to wipe away her tears. Before I could reach them, she took my hand in hers and brought it down to her lap.

A sad smile graced her lips and she began again, "The assassins came in the night. They killed any and all who stepped into their path as they searched for the princess. When they reached the Queen and Consort's chambers, the parents would not step aside and let their child be destroyed.

"They fought the assassins and held them off just long enough for soldiers to arrive. By then, the Consort was dead and the Queen was near to it. They could not stop the bleeding and she died, in the arms of her dearest friend and Lady-in-Waiting."

The way my mother spoke, the haunted quality in her voice, answered my unspoken question. This was not a secondhand telling; this was a memory. And I knew without asking that she was this Lady-in-Waiting.

"As she laid there, the Queen did not beg for her own life.

She did not fear death, even then. All she asked, as she stared up at me, was that the Princess be taken somewhere safe. So that's what I did.

"The Councilors deemed it too risky for the Princess to stay in the Alterealm. The assassins who had come were dead, but they knew there would be others. They decided to send the Princess away."

My mother looked up at my father. "The Queen's cousin, Roland, and I were asked to act as Chief Protectors. Together, the two of us were tasked with taking the Princess to the Humanrealm and raising her there until the day of her twentieth birthday, at which point she could return to claim her crown. She would take up her great responsibility and this destiny that would mean the salvation of so many.

"My darling, Sahle, that child is you. You were the little Princess that we bundled into a blanket and traveled with to the Humanrealm. You were the little Princess that we raised as our own, that we poured all of our love into, that I promised my best friend I would protect.

"You may not be ours, but Roland and I loved you from the day you were born. And even though you are our Queen, you were first our child."

I am not sure when I started crying, but I only noticed the tears when my mother wiped them away.

My mother. My mind spun on the term. I could not believe what I had heard but I knew somewhere deep, in my bone marrow, that it was true. There was much I was confused about, but I trusted my mother's words, the sincerity of her tears.

My mother. I did not mourn for a woman I had never known, a woman I had just now only known had existed, but the term kept catching in my mind. Eliza had always been my mother, at least in any way that counted, but now I did not know what to call her.

There was so much to ask but I started with the most immediate. "What do I call you both if you're not really my parents?"

I whispered, my head turning between my parents…Eliza and Roland.

My mother smiled wistfully and smoothed one of my curls behind my ear. "I will always answer to 'mother' or 'mom' from you, because I have always seen you as my own. But now that we are here, others may not take kindly to that association. At least in public, it's best if you call me Eliza, or Lady Eliza in formal settings."

I nodded. "And Dad?"

"The same goes for me," he replied. "Although, I am actually your blood. As your birth mother's first cousin, I am your second cousin and a member of your Royal House. Most call me Lord Roland, but Roland is also fine for you."

It made sense that Roland and I were related. I had always felt I resembled him, and I was right. He was not my biological father, but our shared features were not simply my imagination. The thought comforted me in the foreignness that was this strange place.

I ran my eyes around the elegant room once more—the tall plants near the wall of windows, the maps on the off-white walls, the high-arched ceilings, the polished wood and leather. My eyes snapped back to the maps. "If I'm the Queen, I must have responsibilities. What are they?"

"Don't worry about that now," Roland replied. "Just start by suspending the disbelief I see in your eyes. Try to take in the Alterealm for what it is."

But my eyes stayed glued to the maps, following the shape of the border, the symbols that meant mountains at the center. Roland reached out and squeezed one of my hands where it rested in my lap, drawing my attention back to him and Eliza.

When I met her eyes, Eliza said, "Remember what your dad told you before we traveled—we won't let anything happen to you. We may not be your true parents, but we have loved every second of raising you. We love you like you are our own, and we have looked after you like our own. We will continue to do so.

That will never change."

"Thank you," I said. It seemed like the only thing to say, in the wake of all of these revelations.

"No need to thank us. It's what family is for."

All I could do was nod, my eyes wide and disbelieving.

The two servants from last night reappeared with breakfast soon after. I learned that their names were Kaiht and Mara. Kaiht was the more talkative of the two while Mara was the quiet observer. They were twins, both with the same porcelain skin and mousy hair that landed somewhere in the color spectrum between blond and brown, but you would never mix them up. How they held themselves, the way they moved, transformed their features. It would be impossible to confuse the two.

Eliza and I had just dug into our breakfast of eggs and a porridge made of cornmeal—something Eliza called pap—when a messenger came. We were expected in Council in one hour, he told us before bustling back the way he came.

While Eliza bristled and muttered about anyone expecting a queen to do anything, we hurriedly finished our meal. Kaiht and Mara conferred with Eliza about what I should wear, and then I was being pulled out of my white nightgown and trussed up into a floor length dress of gold and red.

There was a tall mirror beside the bed, and I stood before it to see the dress. Alternating patches of gold and red lines ran down my torso and arms. The color pattern continued across a bodice that hugged tightly across my chest and waist, and then draped comfortably across my hips until it pooled at the ground.

Absent-mindedly, I realized the gown was the same color as the crest on the door, the banners attached to the zebras. I guessed they must be official colors of some sort.

"You're just a touch shorter than your mother," Eliza murmured from behind me.

I turned to glance at her over my shoulder, and her eyes were shining with tears again.

She approached me with a brush and began pulling it gently through my unruly curls, starting at the ends. I watched us both in the reflection of the mirror.

"This gown was your mother's favorite," Eliza continued as she moved onto another section of hair. "After she died, I had them keep her gowns in case you ever wanted them. I'm glad I did because you're nearly the same size she was."

Eliza set the brush down and began braiding my hair in a loose plait that hung down my back. She nestled a tall gold headband across my head as I met her blue eyes over my shoulder. Eliza smiled that wistful smile, "You look so much like her."

I did not remember the woman who had given me life, but I smiled all the same—for the memory of her, for the love Eliza felt for her. In fact, I had no idea what this mystery woman looked like except that I looked like her. "Is there a picture of her somewhere?"

"Of course," Eliza replied. "We'll pass it on our way to the Council Chamber. I'll point it out to you."

I tried to keep my smile up as Eliza led me from the room and back down the winding staircase we had climbed yesterday. We walked down more hallways that I was sure I would never remember, hallways filled with maps and paintings.

"There she is," Eliza whispered in my ear as we stopped in front of a state painting that was larger than the rest. "Queen Bekha of Izwe."

Eliza had been right. I did look like her, like Bekha. Staring back at me was an image of myself if I had been a few inches taller and with slightly tighter curls. My eyes were nearly identical, as was the line of my nose and the way my cheeks dimpled.

I could have stared up at this image of my mother forever, awed as I was by the surrealness of her. But Eliza was tugging on my hand and urging me to continue down the hall. We had somewhere to be.

Moments later, we were standing in front of a bustling chamber. The door to the chamber was shut, but I could hear the commotion from behind the closed doors: the stomp of a foot, the scrape of a chair, the buzz of dozens of voices talking all at once.

Eliza stepped up to my side. "Are you ready?"

"Ready for what?" I replied. Of course she had told me that story, but I still did not really believe it, understand what I was to do, or how I was supposed to help anything. I was just Sahle, just the twenty-year-old who had gone to a birthday party and stayed only long enough to not offend the hosts. I was the girl who dreaded crowds, who habitually made a fool of herself when her emotions got away from her.

And somehow now I was meant to be Queen?

The thought was nearly funny and perhaps I would have laughed had I not still been floating in a haze of shock and confusion. But Eliza had always known me. She saw the thoughts turning behind my eyes and she reached out and took my hand.

"Ready to be Queen," she answered, leaning in almost conspiratorially as if we were sharing a joke.

I just stared at her. "No, I'm not ready."

"You will be," she replied.

And then the door to the Council Chamber opened, and the drone of bees quieted to absolute silence as all eyes turned on me.

THE SILENCE WAS OPPRESSIVE.

It reminded me of when, as a child, my parents had taken me on a tour of caves deep within the earth. At one point our guide asked us to turn off our flashlights and try not to make any noise—not the scuff of a shoe or even a whispering inhale.

Over a decade had passed since I stood in those caves, but I could still remember the sound as if it were yesterday. The sound of silence rings in my ears even now, as pressing and real as the blast of a gunshot.

I always thought that in the absence of all noise, the human brain roars defensively, fighting against the nothingness. That roar is what I heard as all sound ceased across the Council Chamber.

I was still outside the door, still clutching Eliza's hand. Then suddenly we were in motion and the echoing of our heeled footsteps on the polished checkered floor replaced the sound of silence.

We crossed the threshold and entered the Council Chamber,

a great room punctuated by an extended ebony wood table that would easily fit twenty or thirty bodies. The same red and gold crest was hung in repeat along the tall white walls, and above the long table hung a series of brass chandeliers similar to the one in my room some floors above.

At the head of the table was a dais. A gleaming, stately chair made out of some kind of polished yellow wood sat atop it, just high enough that whoever sat there would be a single head above those seated at the table.

Eliza led me to that chair—that throne—and I realized that it was me who would take that place. For some reason, I was that all-important person.

I was too distracted to contemplate that fact, too focused on the still-silent men standing around the long Council Chamber. And they were all men, I noticed. Eliza and I were the only women here.

The men ranged from thirty to seventy years in age. Their skin tones spanned from the soft cream of Eliza's to the darker mahogany of Roland's. Their hair textures were straight and gently curled. Their eyes ran the gamut of colors. But there was something about them that was similar. It was how they held themselves, the set of a shoulder and the tilt of a head. Each had a confidence about them, a quiet sense of belonging in that chamber.

I did not have that same ease, even as Eliza nudged me gently to take my seat on the throne. I forced my eyes away from the watching Councilors.

"What?" I asked quietly, and I could hear the edge of panic creeping into the tone of voice.

Eliza squeezed my hand reassuringly before releasing it to motion at the throne. "Please, Your Majesty. This is your seat."

It was just a chair, I told myself as I looked away from Eliza and stepped up onto the dais.

It was just a chair. I moved to the throne.

It was just a chair. I lowered myself onto the seat.

It was just a chair. I lifted my head to look out at the still-staring men.

And then all hell broke loose.

If I thought the silence was loud, I was not prepared for the immediate crack of twenty-odd voices calling out at the exact same time. I flinched at the sudden noise that filled the echoing chamber.

"Queen Sahle!"

"Your Majesty!"

"My Lady!"

Unsure of what to do, I glanced at Eliza who had stepped back until she was standing off the dais but just to my left. She, too, was watching the men but she did not look distressed. If anything, she looked amused.

"My Lords," a voice I knew as well as my own called over the chatter. Roland strode forward, dropping into a curt bow before coming to stand just over my right shoulder.

"My Lords," he repeated, not willing to talk until there was silence. "May I present to you Queen Sahle."

As one, all of the men dropped into a bow. When they rose, the advisor I had met yesterday stepped forward.

"Thank you, Lord Roland. I believe introductions are indeed required," he announced. Then he turned to me, "May I have the honor, Your Majesty?"

I had no idea what was proper in this situation and so I merely nodded.

"Wonderful. Your Majesty, let me begin by introducing myself: Lord Grimly of House Kubuga, Chief Advisor to the Crown," he said, with a flourished bow at the end.

He proceeded to name each of the men gathered around the long table. I had always been terrible with names and my head spun at the thought of remembering all of these now, especially since each one seemed vitally important and many had titles to boot.

"Lord Silas of House Sephiri."

"Lord Isaac of House Indlulamithi."

"Lord Walsh of House Manje."

But then Lord Grimly paused, squinting slightly as he passed his eyes along each line and corner of the room. "We seem to be missing one Lord, Your Majesty. Although it is not surprising. He was waylaid along the coast some days ago and would have had to make the journey back to the capital in a hurry once the messenger arrived with news of your return. In any case, let us begin."

I did not give it any thought, though looking back I always wonder what it would have been like to have had that missing Lord present from the start. Would he have stood out amongst the rest, like a shimmering stone cast amongst gray pebbles at the bottom of a pond? I like to think so.

The assembled Lords took their seats, and all looked expectantly towards me.

My eyes widened as it dawned on me that they were waiting for me to do or say something. "Um, sorry. I'm not sure what is typically done here…"

Several Lords glanced at each other. Others looked down with little smirks, and to my horror I realized that it was amusement on some of their faces. They found my complete and utter lack of knowledge…funny.

I could feel the heat move to my cheeks, and I thanked whatever stars that my skin was dark enough that a furious blush would only show up as the tiniest hint of pink on my face. But still, I studied the floor, hoping that the look of the polished marble would bury my shame at my ignorance.

Roland cleared his throat from his position over my right shoulder. "It is us who should apologize, Your Majesty. We forget that you are new here and do not yet know the ways of the Council."

I closed my eyes slowly and took in a deep breath. I was so thankful for Roland, for the only father I had ever known. Even if just to rescue me from awkwardness, he was there.

"Quite right, Lord Roland," intoned Grimly. "Our apologies, Majesty. The floor is yours should you wish to address the Lords."

I opened my mouth but was unsure of what to say. The Lords stared back at me, and I felt a wave of panic crest above my head, upping the pace of my blood.

What did I say to this crowd of assembled Lords? I was their Queen, newly returned after almost twenty years away—or so they told me. I imagined myself standing up, giving a grand speech, rousing every Lord there with my fervent love for Izwe and my desire to dedicate my life to its success.

In reality, all I could do was stare out at the sea of wearily amused faces and pray that I would not make a fool of myself.

But at that moment, a noise broke through the expectant pause. The tall wooden door into the Council Chamber was still open, and from my throne I could see straight across the room and into the hallway Eliza and I had walked.

A clattering sound echoed down that hallway and at the end of it, I watched a small contingent of men turn a corner and make their way to us. Long swords clanked against their hips with each step they took, especially from the one leading the way.

My eyes scanned past him and then snapped back.

Even from where I was seated, down the hall and across the Council Chamber, something about him caught my attention. It was an awareness of him, almost a gravitational pull that kept my eyes locked on his form.

The world narrowed until only he was in focus.

He strode forward with long, powerful strides, the sword clanking with each step as if a drumbeat announced his presence here.

"Ah, Lord Anson," Grimly called as he followed where my attention had turned.

"Grimly," the newly arrived Lord replied as he made his way past the Advisor and to my dais.

He stopped before my throne and dropped into a bow. Barely

a heartbeat passed before he resumed his full height, and I heard Eliza make a tsk sound from my left.

But if his bow was too short, too casual, I did not notice. In an abstract part of my brain, I wondered if this was the most attractive man I had ever seen.

I guessed his age to be around thirty. He was tall and leanly muscled. His dark hair was tousled and windswept, a wayward lock tumbling across his forehead. Although he was tanned, it was the tan of someone who spent long hours outdoors rather than a genetic disposition to more melanin. Vibrant green eyes shone over strong cheekbones, a proud nose, a wide mouth, and a sharp jawline.

What made him attractive was all of that and none of that. It was something in the way he carried himself—some grace, some strength—that kept my eyes glued to him. Something in the way his muscles moved under the red dirt- and dust-covered dark clothes caught my attention.

I guessed that this was the missing Lord that Grimly had mentioned.

"Your Majesty," the man greeted me with an easy smile. The smile looked right on his lips, but there was something behind it in the glint of his eyes and the angle of his head that I could not place. "I am Lord Anson, Izwe's Lord of War. I apologize for my delay. My men and I were away when word of your return reached us."

He stopped speaking and stared at me, raising one dark eyebrow expectantly as I stared back at him.

When I did not say anything, Roland stepped in. "Lord Anson. A pleasure to see you after all these years."

Anson kept those green eyes on me a moment longer before turning to Roland. "Likewise. It's been too long."

"That it has. You surely remember my wife, Lady Eliza?"

Anson nodded his head in her direction. "Lady Eliza."

"Anson," she replied. Something in her tone had me turning slightly towards her. Was it distrust?

I expected this Lord Anson to try to speak with me again, to give me another chance to acknowledge his presence here, but to my surprise he turned on his heel and strode to the empty seat at the Council table.

When he was seated, Grimly started again. "Now that we're all assembled. We have some pressing business to discuss.

"I'd like to formally welcome Queen Sahle back to her home, Izwe. The entire kingdom has waited eagerly for your return, Your Majesty."

"Hear, hear," several Lords further down the table called.

I tried to smile but I feared all I managed was a grimace of discomfort.

"But now that you are back, Your Majesty, there are several topics that must be urgently discussed. First, myself and several of the Lords here have already begun making arrangements for your coronation. You are ruler by birthright, but you must also be anointed to officially wear the crown. If there are no objections, we should be prepared for the ceremony to occur tomorrow. Your Majesty?"

The room turned to await my response.

I glanced at Eliza who nodded once, encouragingly.

Looking back at Grimly and the Lords, I swallowed nervously. "OK," I managed to croak out, my voice harsh from nerves.

"Very good," Grimly said, although his tone did not sound like things were good. His eyes had tracked my glance at Eliza, my reliance on both her and Roland since I had arrived. So it was no surprise when he turned his attention to it next.

"Once you are crowned, you will fully be the Queen of Izwe. Up until now, Lord Roland and Lady Eliza have served as Chief Protectors to you, especially while you lived in the Humanrealm.

"Now that you have returned to the Alterealm, however, you will no longer need their guidance. I motion this Council to relinquish their roles as Chief Protectors upon the date of the Queen's coronation."

There was a commotion from around the table, hushed

words and apprehensive glances, as attention turned to Roland and Eliza.

But it was not them who spoke next. No, it was Lord Anson.

I turned my attention to him, still in awe by whatever quality he possessed, whatever glint in those green eyes that seemed to capture my attention.

"I've been here a matter of minutes," Anson began. "But already it is clear that the Queen has an unhealthy reliance on her Protectors—"

"Lord Anson," Roland nearly barked.

"I'm speaking," Anson quipped back with a raised eyebrow. When Roland did not continue, Anson waited an arrogant moment and then continued. "As I was saying, the Queen was a toddler when she left the Alterealm. Roland and Eliza served as protectors for all of the years since, but she is home now. I fear any further protecting on their part will quickly morph into undue influence upon the crown."

"Speak plainly, Anson," Eliza bit out from over my shoulder. My glance to her confirmed what I suspected—she was speaking through gritted teeth.

"Of course, Lady Eliza," Anson smirked. "My fear is that you and your husband have grown too comfortable with the idea of Queen Sahle as your daughter. You are not her parents, and she should not need your approval to make decisions."

"She does not know the Alterealm," Roland replied.

"That is true," Lord Anson said. "But that can be rectified. This reliance on you and your wife, though…that must be nipped in the bud."

"How dare you—" Eliza began.

Anson just looked at her with that smirk. "How dare I what? Do you not wish the Queen to be her own person? No, perhaps you wish to rule through her as you and your husband are surely doing now."

"We would never—" Eliza tried again, but Roland jumped in.

"Eliza," he said quietly. I had heard that tone a million times before. My father—Roland—was never one to yell. Rather, he grew quieter when he was upset, his tone fiercer and nearly whisper thin. He was not angry at Eliza, but he was cautioning her to stop, to not pick this fight.

I watched as Eliza looked to physically hold back her words. She snapped her mouth shut, but her eyes were glaring daggers at Anson.

I turned to look at him again and could finally place the glint in his eye. As he took his seat with that fluid grace, I realized swaggering arrogance was the opposite side of the same coin.

From further down the table, another Lord rose. I recalled that Grimly called him Lord Evan of Imfene.

"I agree with Anson," Lord Evan added. "The Queen must be given the space to make her own decisions now that she is of age and has returned to the Alterealm. Although I would like to add that since Roland and Eliza were forbidden to tell her anything about the Alterealm, she may need instruction to fully realize her role."

Lord Grimly stood as Lord Evan took his seat. "Thank you, Lord Evan. That is precisely the next point I'd like to discuss. But first, I'd like her Majesty's consent to remove the Chief Protectors of their roles effective upon her coronation."

Again, all eyes turned on me and I stared back at them. I was confused about what was happening but I thought I understood the gist of it. Even I, an outsider, could see politics at work. I knew the reason they wanted Roland and Eliza one step removed from me was because they did not want them to be able to influence my decisions.

There were too many other Lords in this chamber who wished to do that.

But I also understood that a Queen—any ruler—was supposed to rule on their own judgment. As this supposed Queen, I would need to look less to others for their approval. I understood that on an abstract level.

Yet, when it pertained to me, everything about this felt like a sick joke. With my fear and lack of understanding, a cold sweat broke out on my skin. It was hard to agree that the people I had leaned on for the last two decades should simply go away.

I forced myself to stare straight down the table, however, to not look to my left or right at Eliza or Roland. "Alright."

"That is settled then," Grimly continued. "As for the next topic of instruction, we have a proposition for Your Majesty. Full immersion into the Alterealm may take months or even years. In the meantime, it is important that Queen Sahle learns the basics of Izwe. I have taken the liberty of commissioning two trainers—one for physical combat training and another for etiquette training. Some of you may already know them: Commander Finn and Lady Lisidera."

Another Lord stood—I could not remember his name—and voiced his approval. Faint applause echoed around the table, and I suspected much of this was theater. When Grimly said he 'took the liberty' to do anything, I was sure that meant that the men sitting here had carefully orchestrated this before I arrived.

They knew exactly who would best suit my training, most likely who would help mold me into whatever they personally wanted me to be. All I could do was scream internally at my inability to do anything, to control this situation, to even understand the extent of what was being decided for me.

I tuned back into the discussion around the table as the Lords discussed this Commander Finn and his ability to hone powers.

Powers? I thought.

To my horror, I realized that I must have said it aloud for twenty sets of eyes again swiveled towards me.

"Your Majesty?" Grimly asked.

"Erm," I cleared my throat. "I was wondering what you meant by powers?"

That too-still feeling of silence sat in the chamber as the men continued to stare. Then Grimly, seeming to catch himself staring at me, too, hurried to fill the void. "Again, we forget that Your Majesty is unfamiliar with the Alterealm.

"Some individuals in Izwe are gifted with certain extra abilities at birth; however, these abilities do not fully manifest themselves until later in life, after training. Your parents both had exceptional powers, and thus we suspect you may as well. It is not guaranteed, of course. But with proper training like the kind Finn could provide, you would be able to develop any abilities that lay dormant."

I nodded at his explanation, even as my mind spun again.

Powers?

I could not even fathom what that could mean or what sort of powers I could possibly have. My mind immediately conjured images of me sprouting wings and flying, me blasting water at an enemy, me reading minds—anything I had seen in an action movie.

It was laughable, really. I was just Sahle, just a normal twenty-year-old woman.

Right?

"If we have no objections to Lisidera instructing her Majesty on etiquette," Grimly continued, "And Finn working with her for physical training, including any possible power development, then let's continue."

"I would add one point," a voice I was quickly growing to dread called out.

"Yes, Lord Anson?" Grimly replied.

Anson fixed that green gaze on me. I could almost feel the weight of it as he dragged it from the top of my head to the tip of my toes as if surveying me. "This may be a waste of Finn's time."

Hushed murmurs rustled around the room at that statement.

"Would you like to explain your reasoning, Anson?" Grimly prodded.

"Of course," Anson replied, his lips only breaking that smirk to pass words through. "At twenty years old, Queen Sahle should have some sign of power manifestation, if she has any powers at all. From her question of what powers even are, it seems like we may be hoping in vain for her powers. Perhaps we should not keep our hopes up—and waste Finn's time—by having him train a woman who is ordinary."

I felt the muscles of my jaw slacken, my mouth wanting to pop open in shock. But I willed my lips to stay shut, for my face to remain immobile even as blood rushed to my skin in the oddest mix of shame and anger.

I understood the shame. I was ordinary, and I had always been. I had never been the belle of the ball, the center of attention. I was skilled at blending into a crowd and being unobtrusive—at least until something made my emotions rear up.

It was a fact I knew about myself, a fact as unavoidable as the color of my eyes or the sound of my name. Yet I was not prepared for a man I had just met to see the truth of me so clearly. And I was certainly not prepared for him to lay it bare before these Lords.

How dare he.

Perhaps he saw my pinkening cheeks. Perhaps he saw the swirling emotions behind my eyes, locked in shock as they were on him. Either way, he saw fit to add, "That is no fault of your own, Your Majesty. Rather just that some people are born without added abilities."

I nodded slightly, still inexplicably unsettled by him.

Seeming to take my nod as agreement, Grimly jumped in. "Very well. I'll suggest to Finn that he first take an assessment of Her Majesty's powers before full training begins. We will be able to better assess the merits of training after that. The Commander can also provide fortnightly reports on Her Majesty's progress."

"Quite right," Anson said, taking his seat once more.

Grimly led the discussion on to politics of the Alterealm and although I knew I should pay attention, my mind struggled to focus.

Despite everything new and shocking and absurd about whatever this realm was, I grappled with what Anson had said.

My vision blurred as I felt tears fill my eyes, but I beat them back through sheer force of will. I would not cry in front of these men. I may or may not be a Queen but, even as plain old Sahle, I had some pride.

I focused on breathing in and out, training my gaze on a spot low on the long Council table before me. I was overwhelmed. I was reeling, and I wondered whether my numbed sense of shock and disbelief was finally turning into a full nervous breakdown.

But something Grimly said, some mention of Trina Cheile and their threat to Izwe snapped my attention back to the conversation.

"Who is Trina Cheile?" I blurted out.

All eyes turned to me at the interruption.

I thought I heard someone choke on their water down near the end of the table.

After a beat of silence, Grimly responded. "Your Majesty, Trina Cheile is a kingdom in the Alterealm. They are the chief threat to our safety."

Before I could stop myself, I asked another question. "Why?"

Again, shocked silence hung in the air. Several of the Lords looked at each other and when it appeared no one wanted to respond to the question, Roland did.

"Queen Sahle, that is a good question. Trina Cheile and Izwe have been at war for generations, primarily over access to vital resources. They are also the kingdom responsible for the deaths of your parents."

I felt Eliza's warm hand plant itself on my shoulder at this statement, a gesture of comfort as much as support in this moment of uncertainty.

I did not know what to say to that, and a niggling part of my brain whispered how did you not know who killed your family?

But I did not have to wait long for that sentiment to be echoed externally for all to hear.

From his seat, Anson made a sound that was a cross between a laugh and a snort. "Your Majesty has much to learn, it appears, if you do not comprehend the basics of your own kingdom—or who is responsible for the murders of the former Queen and Consort."

This time, my mouth did pop open, albeit just slightly—more a shocked parting of lips than a full gape.

And that same mixture of shame and anger burned hot and fierce through my blood. I was mortified but I was angry that he would lay my lack of knowledge, my ultimate naivité, out on the Lords' table as if it were something to be admired—as if it were something to laugh at.

Because that was what he was doing. Lord Anson was laughing at me.

I forced my eyes up to his. But that was a mistake. The moment I saw that mocking look, I reached the end of my tether.

Without conscious thought, I stood from the chair, shaking off Eliza's hand on my shoulder as I quickly stepped off the dais and headed for the door.

Dimly, I was aware of a great commotion, a shuffling of twenty chairs and pairs of feet as every Lord hurried to stand and bow. But I did not care. I was done here.

I did not look back as I passed the last chair, nor when I cleared the Council Chamber door, the long hallway and started up the staircase from which Eliza and I had descended before.

I did not look back as I heard Eliza call my name from a flight of stairs below, nor when I finally reached the door to the chambers I had slept in last night.

I flung it open and quickly shut it behind me with a dull thud, the door too heavy to truly, mightily slam.

And then I threw myself on that tall, stately bed and cried.

I did not care that I was still trussed up in the gold and red dress, that my little heeled slippers were still on. I did not care that Eliza was knocking at the door, asking to be let in.

The tide of shock had broken, and in its place was horror in suddenly being in this new world, shame in my complete and utter ignorance, and anger so deep I could feel it burning in my chest.

I was angry at Eliza and Roland for lying to me all these years, for not preparing me for this. I was angry at every person I had met here thus far for not telling me what I should have known to go into that Council Chamber better prepared.

But all of that anger paled in comparison to the anger I felt when it came to one man: Lord Anson. I hated that I had been so taken with him at first glance. And I hated how cruel he was, how vicious to carve me open for all to see and laugh at.

With a bitter taste in my mouth, I admitted he was right: a queen should know something of her kingdom, of her enemies, of her own self. I just hated that he alone was so adept at bringing awareness to all of my shortcomings.

As I cried out this haze of emotion, I thought of that stupid mocking smirk of his and I made myself a promise.

If I were truly a queen, I had to act the part. I would learn all I could about Izwe, its enemies, and its history. I would learn how to act and what to say. I would learn if I had any of these powers.

Because I would never let this Lord Anson make me look like a fool again.

6
determination

I LOST TRACK OF TIME THROUGH MY ANGRY TEARS. I might have been crying for an hour, or perhaps just fifteen minutes. But suddenly, I was done. My eyes were dry, and a fierce determination replaced the sadness.

I had made myself a promise that I would never look like a fool again, and I was going to do my damnedest to stick to it. When I set my mind to something, there was no alternative than to forge ahead and complete whatever was necessary. And right now, what was necessary was learning as much as possible about wherever or whatever this Alterealm was. I needed answers, and I knew exactly where to start.

I pulled myself off of the four-poster bed and approached the door, ready to march out into the palace and find a library or an academic wing that could perhaps provide the answers I so badly needed. But a little voice in my head stilled my hand as it reached for the handle of the solid chamber door.

I was not going to look like a fool. I was going to look like a Queen. And that meant I could not show anyone in this palace that I had broken down into overwhelmed tears.

Turning quickly to the tall mirror on the other side of the room, I ran my eyes over my reflection. I had thrown myself face-first onto the bed, so my hair had avoided the worst of the dishevelment. I smoothed a few wayward curls that had escaped the braid back into place, and then turned my attention to my face.

My eyes were red from my angry tears and my eyelids were slightly puffy, the lids bulging gently as if overinflated by too much water.

I groaned.

God only knew how long it would take for my eyes to look normal again.

I scanned the rest of my body, focusing mostly on my dress. It had sustained the worst of the damage—the fine silky material had wrinkled in multiple folds from where it had been crushed underneath me. I could change the dress, of course, but I did not want anyone to wonder why I had changed it.

No, I would just have to fix it. And given the state of my eyes, I had some time to kill.

I located a smaller door across the room and gingerly opened it. To my surprise, it was a modern bathroom. Because of the gowns, the palace and zebras, I had assumed this Alterealm was a different place but also a different time—one without the modern luxuries of indoor plumbing. I was quickly realizing that I should hold no assumptions when it came to this place, or anything in my life really. I shrugged to myself as I stepped up to the clawfoot bathtub and opened the tap.

The moment water appeared, so did Kaiht and Mara.

"Your Majesty," Kaiht said as both women bowed. "Can we assist you with something?"

"Erm, yes actually," I said absently as I looked over my shoulder towards the corset-like dress closure running down my spine.

Mara undid the laces of the dress and helped me climb out of it while Kaiht turned to the bath, filling the tub nearly to the brim.

Self-consciously, I realized I was again naked in front of these two women. Yet neither seemed to care. They were businesslike as they sprinkled scented oil into the steaming water. I willed myself to be queenly, to not cover myself as I walked over to the tub and lowered myself in.

A queen would not hide.

I had nearly forgotten the other reason for the bath, but remembered as soon as Kaiht moved to bundle up the discarded dress.

"Kaiht," I called. "Would you mind hanging the dress up in here? I'd like to wear it again today but I want the steam to relax the wrinkles."

She looked at me inquisitively. "Your Majesty has many dresses, should you require another."

"I'm sure that's true," I replied. "But I'd like to rewear this one in particular."

Kaiht must have thought I was crazy, but she curtsied nonetheless before hanging the dress along a narrow railing above the door.

I sat in the bath until the steam in the air cleared and the water ran nearly cold. I opened the tap and ran fresh water across my face, gently rubbing my eyes to clear them of the markers of tears.

And when I had finally climbed out of the tub, dried off, and re-dressed in the refreshed gown, I looked at myself again in the long mirror.

There, that was better.

The puffiness had gone down and my eyes almost looked normal. The whites of my eyes had lost their red tint. My dress was no longer crumpled in the front.

With a satisfied nod at myself, I turned once more to the main chamber door and pulled it open.

And I nearly tripped over Eliza, sitting as she was just outside the door.

Eliza had long-since stopped knocking after my abrupt return from Council. She had probably turned away when she realized it was futile to try to reason with me in my anger. I had assumed she left, perhaps to seek out Roland, but here she was.

Tears burned at the back of my eyes again at the sight of her here, at the knowledge that she had not left. But I breathed through it. I would not cry again, not now.

"Sahl," Eliza said, jumping to her feet and enveloping me in a tight hug. "Are you alright, sweetheart?"

I closed my eyes at the endearment. It was a balm on my nerves, this familiar moment where she was once again my mother and I her child.

"I'm alright," I assured her, pulling away after a few heartbeats.

She ran her eyes over me, as if to say she did not believe me. And if anyone would be able to see through my lies, it was certainly her.

"You've been crying."

"How did you know?"

Eliza smiled sadly and put her hand on my cheek. "Sahle, I've known you for twenty years. Even if no one else notices, I always will."

I smiled back at her because she was right. She was my mother in every way that mattered, and she would always be able to read me like an open book.

"I can't let them know," I told her. "I looked like a fool in that Council Chamber, and I can never do that again. A Queen wouldn't do that."

Eliza watched me, not saying anything. She finally nodded.

I continued, "I want to learn all I can. I want to be prepared next time. I know I'm getting trainers to help me, but I want to start now."

"Where would you like to begin?"

"The prophecy," I stated assuredly. "I want to start with knowing exactly what this prophecy says about me."

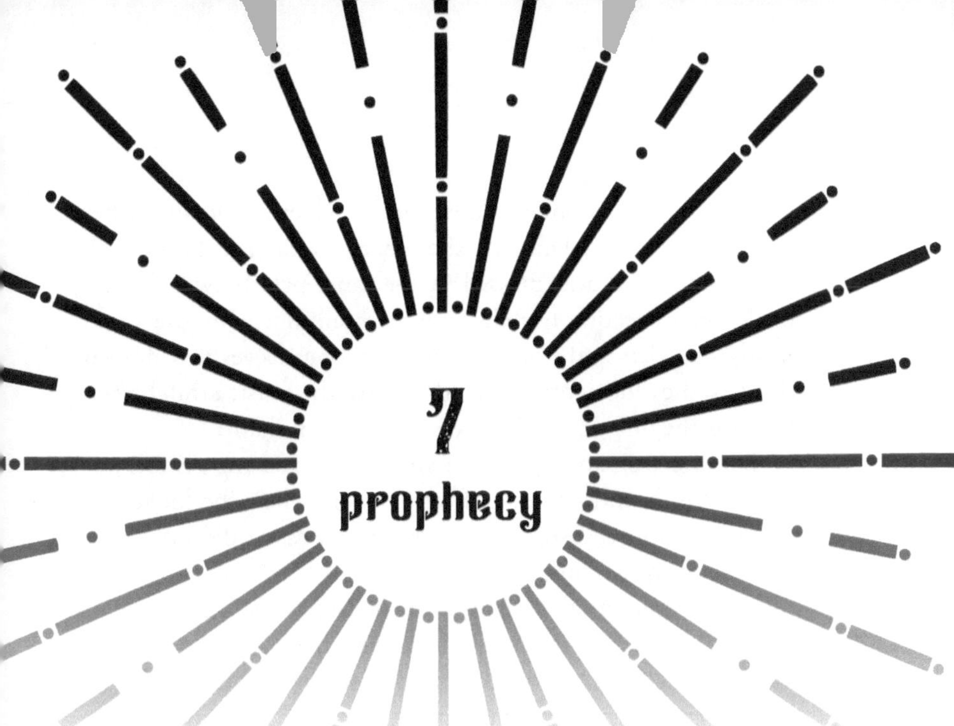

ELIZA, ALONG WITH A CONTINGENT OF GUARDS QUICKLY becoming my shadow, wasted no time in leading me to a library deep in the underbelly of this great estate. We must have taken a back route, or perhaps I was the only person keenly interested in books. We saw only a handful of servants, Lords, and Ladies on our way. They bowed and stared, of course, but I kept my head up, my eyes trained on a spot ahead of us in the hallway. I would not quake. I would not look down.

The library itself was equally vacant. Tall pillars rose between the stacks, veritably holding the weight of the palace off of the precious books nestled into its underbelly. Rows and rows of leather-bound books stretched as far as the eye could see on dark wooden shelves, illuminated by flickering candles housed in hanging chandeliers.

I spied a number of servants who I assumed were librarians, given the cart of books they were reshelving. Eliza urged me to sit at a low wooden table near the center—at least I thought it was the center—of the library before she began speaking to one of these individuals.

She returned moments later with an elderly woman on her heels. Like Kaiht, Mara, and the other servants I had observed, this woman was also dressed in the same pale brown cloth. I could only describe her clothing as monk-like. The dress was nearly shapeless and floor length, with long sleeves that draped down to the older woman's hands. Across the waist, a thin brown belt was the only thing that gave the material shape.

But the woman's eyes were what transfixed me. There was such warmth and genuine affection there when she looked at me. I found myself smiling at her with an ease I did not think possible in this strange place.

"Your Majesty," the elderly woman said as she bent stiffly in a bow. "My name is Ruth, and I am the Chief Librarian in Izwe. Lady Eliza tells me you would like to learn about your prophecy."

"That's correct," I confirmed, my voice barely louder than a whisper. "I'm not sure how these prophecies work, but is there a recording of it somewhere that I could hear or read through?"

Ruth smiled again. "No one would expect you to know how it all works. You have been in the Humanrealm, after all."

It was such a simple statement, but the truth of it hit me like a thunderclap. Even though it had only been a day and a half since my arrival, I had been worrying about not knowing everything about Izwe and the Alterealm. I had been ashamed at my ignorance, but Ruth was right. How could I know any different?

"You seem surprised, Your Majesty," Ruth inferred. "While the Council of Lords likes to pretend that they know everything, they in fact do not. Their individual power comes from their performance—their ability to convince each other of their knowledge and competence. In that place, there is no room for ignorance.

"But here, in this domain, ignorance is opportunity—so long as the keeper of it is willing to acknowledge one's lack of knowledge and rectify the situation. I believe you are."

"I am," I stated, a little transfixed by this woman. How she had known that the Council of Lords had sent me reeling, I did not know. But I was grateful for her ability to see my internal struggle and make me feel that it was not something to be afraid of.

"Good," Ruth said before turning on her heel. "Then let's show you your prophecy."

Eliza and I followed her deeper into the library, until we reached a spiraling staircase that led down. Around and around we turned until the stairs met a stone floor. Ruth led us through another hallway, a maze of dimly lit shelves and books punctuated by the smell of well-worn pages, crinkling leather, and candle wax. It was one of my favorite smells in the world, and it reminded me of libraries back home—a smell of promise, knowledge, and generations of scholars pouring long hours into impassioned research.

At the far end of this underground room, Ruth stopped at a wide table where a half dozen scrolls had been set down. One scroll sat unrolled in the center of the table, and I turned my eyes to it eagerly.

I was impatient and Ruth's smile told me she knew it. "Would you like to take a seat, Your Majesty?"

I glanced from her to the scroll, not wanting to take any more time than necessary in unearthing what this prophecy actually said and what it could mean for me. Eliza had given me the main points when she told me her tale about my parents, but I needed to know the unabridged version.

Yet, not wanting to be rude to this woman whom I already liked, I sat on the edge of a wooden chair before the table. Eliza and Ruth sat in two others nearby.

"I see you've already noticed the prophecy scroll," Ruth began. "Before we read through it, I'd like to give you some context. Lady Eliza may have told you that this prophecy was pronounced soon after your birth?"

Ruth looked at me for confirmation, and I nodded in response.

"Good. That's correct. Most noble parents elect to have a prophet assess their child but not every child will have a prophecy attached to them. As you know, you certainly did.

"At every prophetic reading, there is the prophet, the child or some personal effect to represent the child, parents or other witnesses, and a scribe. The scribe records each prophecy on a scroll which is then stored in this underground room."

"The parents don't keep it?"

Ruth shook her head. "They are welcome to come here and transcribe a copy for themselves but, no, law in Izwe dictates that all original prophecies must be kept here in perpetuity. In any case, let's look at yours."

Ruth reached out with both hands towards the scroll and gently lifted it towards us. Despite the scroll being as young as I was, she handled it like a curator would, balancing the weight of the scroll on her palms, moving it slowly in our direction.

She placed it down in front of me, and I leaned forward to get a look at it.

"Most prophetic scrolls are not as ornate as this one. But, of course, you were then a princess and the heir to this kingdom. Therefore, your parents had this one gilded in gold."

I noticed immediately what she was referencing. Along the border of the scroll there was a finely painted design. I leaned closer still to make out what it was: an interlinked pattern of whorls and stars, punctuated by leaves and those strange pink flowers I had seen on my ride to this palace and on the crest of Izwe. At the very top, these interconnected miniature images met and encircled a crown.

"They're protea flowers," Ruth noted, having seen my attention snag on their image on the scroll. "The official flower of Izwe."

"It's beautiful," I murmured.

"It is," Eliza agreed. "I remember when your parents commissioned this to be done. Even in a mock-up form, it was stunning."

I nodded absentmindedly as I tore my eyes from the border

and turned to the words centered on the page.

"If you will allow me, Your Majesty, I will read the prophecy."

"Yes, thank you," I said, even though I could very well read it myself. But something in my chest was tightening in anticipation. My breath was speeding up. And it felt less overwhelming to have Ruth simply read it aloud.

Ruth cleared her throat and began.

"Behold this child, this daughter of Bekha.
Only through the Father can the daughter become.
She alone can bring true harmony to Izwe, and to the Alterealm.
In white light, she will stop all wars.
With her heart, she will forge a kingdom and a legacy.
Behold the commander of lions, the leader of jackals."

Ruth looked up at me as she spoke those final words and I met her gaze. "What do you think, Your Majesty?"

But I did not know what to think. When I asked to be brought here, I expected the prophecy to answer all of my questions, to explain what I was doing in this place, to cast some light that led to an overarching "Ah-ha!" moment.

Instead, the only thing the prophecy did was make a few grand statements. I certainly appreciated that there was nothing ominous within it—in fact, it seemed remarkably positive—but it was not necessarily helpful.

And right now, in the chaos that was figuring out who I was in this brand new land, I needed it to be helpful.

"I can see that you're disappointed," Ruth said quietly. "May I ask why?"

I tore my eyes away from the scroll and looked at her, at the gently wrinkling skin at the corners of her eyes and the way her mouth curved up in just the barest hint of a comforting smile.

"I don't know," I said simply. "I wanted it to explain more, I guess."

"More of what?" Eliza asked.

"Who I am, what I'm doing here, how I'm supposed to act. This is just a vague proclamation that I'll do important things. I want to know how."

Ruth smiled then and, to my surprise, she reached out and patted my hand where it sat dejectedly atop a fold of my skirt. "You won't find the 'how' in prophecy, Your Majesty. But you can take comfort in the knowledge that your destiny is greatness. No matter how unsure and uncomfortable you are now, that won't matter one day.

"As for that 'how,' like I told you before, this library is a place of answers, of knowledge for those who are willing to see ignorance as opportunity. I hear you are to have trainers assigned to you to assess your powers and to teach you court etiquette. You and I both know that there is more that you want to know.

"If you can spare a few hours a week, I would be happy to provide you with the resources for you to teach yourself the history of your family, your people, and their enemies. The Council may also provide instruction, but you may wish to supplement it with your own study. That information is all here, if you have the willingness and patience to learn it."

I did not need to think about it; I was nodding before Ruth finished speaking. I needed answers and, more than that, I needed to figure things out on my own. Ruth was offering me both. For that, I was so grateful.

I turned my hand so that I was gripping hers. "Yes, thank you Ruth. I would appreciate your help."

She tipped her head in my direction, that soft curve of a smile still on her lips. "Of course, Your Majesty. It would be my honor."

I wanted to start learning right then and there but Eliza insisted that I come back to the library the following day. Although I grumbled, I knew she was right. It had been a taxing day with the Lords and my tears, I mused as I tucked myself back into my downy bed that night.

The next morning, I rushed through a plate of fluffy eggs and toast, half listening as Eliza and Roland mentioned something about a ceremony. Then I was clattering across the worn floors of the library in search of Ruth, a small retinue of guards at my heel. I found her seated in a leather chair beside one of the tall pillars on the main floor, a book balanced in one hand.

She smiled at me over the corner of a page, a knowing glint in her eye that told me she understood well my anxiously excited energy. "Good morning, Your Majesty. Back here early, I see."

"Yes, I'm eager to get to work," I responded, smoothing my hands over the front of my dove gray dress. "If it's not too much trouble for you."

Ruth took one more sip of what looked to be red tea before putting the mug down on the table beside her. She rose to her feet with a bow. "Never, Queen Sahle," she said. " Please follow me."

I bustled behind her, clumsily navigating corners in my bulky, floor-length gown. What ridiculous clothing, I grumbled to myself as I nearly caught the wide, patterned skirt on a chair leg.

Ruth and I wandered far into the library but instead of taking the spiral stairs that led to the prophetic basement, we went up. Two floors later, we stepped off the stairway and made our way through the stacks.

I turned my head this way and that to try and make out the names on the thick leather spines atop the shelves. I caught just a few words of each title as we moved past them. *Naval History…Peace and War…Political Developments of…*

I supposed we were in the history and politics section of the library, and I realized with a start that this is exactly where I needed to be even though I had not communicated my exact wish to Ruth.

"Your Majesty," Ruth called, catching my attention. She was standing before another library table, the mirror to the one she, Eliza, and I had sat at yesterday, a few floors down.

I moved over to the table. A small selection of books had been set out and I ran my fingers over them as I read the titles:

Royal Lineages of Izwe.

A History of the Royal Family.

A Brief History of Izwe.

"How did you know?" I asked as I turned my eyes to Ruth.

She raised a single eyebrow at me. "That Your Majesty would want to start with the Royal family history? It was a lucky guess."

I nodded. Perhaps it was not such a stretch for her to assume that a woman suddenly ripped from her world and thrust into a new one would want to know who she was and where she came from. But still, I was grateful that Ruth was able to read my mind. Being understood felt good in a moment when I felt so out of place.

"Well, thank you," I said awkwardly, still standing at the table's edge.

"Please sit, Your Majesty," Ruth directed.

And I did just that. I sat, arranging the wide skirts around me, and then held out my hand to accept the first book that Ruth passed my way: *Royal Lineages of Izwe.*

She nodded at the cover. "I would suggest starting with this. There have been several royal lines throughout this land's history. Your line is the most recent, so you'll find it in the final chapters of the book."

I turned the book on its edge to assess the inches of thick pages, and I was grateful anew that Ruth was directing me to the end. It was not that I did not appreciate reading. I did—in fact it was one of the things I enjoyed most in the world—but I was too rushed, too anxious to understand this foreign place to sift through the entire tome.

I needed the summary. I needed only the critically vital pieces of information so that I could make sense of everything immediately. Details and superfluous historical linkages could and would come after.

"Thank you, Ruth," I said as I looked up at her from my seat.

"It's my pleasure, Your Majesty," she said with a curtsy. "I'll be two levels up if you need anything. Otherwise, enjoy your reading."

I watched her head back down the passageway until she turned a corner and I could no longer see her form. Then, I turned back to the book.

Taking a deep breath, I opened the book to the table of contents, searching for the page number of the final chapter.

Page after page of *Royal Lineages of Izwe* detailed how, over the course of nearly 300 years, my family had retained the crown of Izwe. The crown had been contested before that and a brief war was eventually fought over it. Won on a battlefield in such fierceness no one could challenge the results, the crown was placed upon my ancestor's head and his line was cemented in history.

The book made a brief mention of "social and structural changes" this Royal House had ushered in, but it did not go into detail. What it did explain was that a series of my male ancestors had ruled, each more prepared and cunning than the one before until, finally, my mother had inherited the throne.

I was already seeing that the Alterealm, foreign as it was, was not so different to the real world—or the Humanrealm, as those around me called it—in one clear way. Women were not typically in positions of power here either. I had not spotted a single woman on the Council of Lords, and it seemed Eliza was only admitted because she was in my company.

Yet my mother, the only royal child, had broken tradition. She, too, was young when she ascended to the throne. Her father had died when she was seventeen years old, and she was named Queen six days later. A son would have been named King right there, at the bedside of the deceased former King. But Izwe had never had a female monarch and the Council of Lords debated the ramifications intensely.

They sat in Council day and night for nearly a week, and on the morning of day six they came to a majority decision that my mother's crown was rightfully hers. She was crowned the following morning.

With a start, I realized that many of the Lords who voted against her rule would still be on the Council. I read about certain Lords whom I had been introduced to, and I noted their ages. Grimly had been 116 then…making him 136 now.

I reread the passage, sure I had misunderstood it. The man looked no more than sixty to me. But no, the number "116" was clearly printed on the worn page. The thought boggled my mind.

How old was Eliza, then? And Roland? How old was Ruth with her white hair?

I asked Ruth about this when she came to check on me. Patiently, she explained that age worked differently here compared to what she knew about the Humanrealm. The average lifespan in the Alterealm was double what it was in the Humanrealm, and while it was uncommon for someone to reach the age of two hundred, it was not unheard of.

I thanked her, wide-eyed and shaking my head in disbelief. I filed it away to contemplate later.

Yet the thing that made my brows lift the highest was the mention of powers. The Lords had discussed it casually before. They told me I would have a trainer to assess my abilities and perhaps hone them, but I let the ramifications of that pass over me at the time.

Now, paging through the books, each passage on different rulers also noted whether they possessed magic or not. I flipped through the rulers in my line, noting that each had some form of magical ability, including my mother who apparently was able to will things into existence.

There was a small note on my father, barely two lines that explained how he had come to marry my mother and what magical ability he had: minimal, it seemed. But still, if I was truly who everyone here said I was, they would expect me to have magic, as well. In fact, I could not find a single ruler in my line who did not have magic.

I leaned back in my chair dejectedly. I did not have magic—whatever that looked like. Of that, I was certain. Still, I could feel the weight of all of the expectations laying heavily on my shoulders.

I feared there was nothing to do but disappoint the Lords, Eliza, Roland, everyone.

I turned to another book, curious about the "social and structural changes" my ancestors had brought about. *A History of the Royal Family* and *A Brief History of Izwe* had descriptions in spades.

My eyes widened as I read them—how the ruler who won the crown for my Royal House was not just any man. He was a foreigner. One passage explained,

On the Ninth of May, a ship of metal came out of the sky. Inside was Manelesi the Conqueror and his family, along with animals never before seen in Izwe: striped horses, birds with feathers that flamed pink, deer with pointed antlers, great cats with fur the color of golden sand. Manelesi stepped out of the metal ship, took off a great glass helmet, and knelt on the red ground of Izwe. He proclaimed that this land was promised to him and those who had traveled with him. The locals did not appreciate this proclamation, especially the ruling House at the time. That ruling House was called Warbeck, but would go on to be known as Ingonyame under Manelesi's rule.

Manelesi's rule was a time of great transformation in Izwe. He had brought cuttings of his native plants like the silver tree and the protea flower, as well as two of every kind of native animal including the zebra, lions, flamingos, hadedas, and insephe that have become synonymous with Izweian flora and fauna.

He also transformed the nobility by better organizing the ruling class into twenty Houses, each with an animal as its emblem. For his own Royal House, he chose no animal to represent it. His House

was not part of the twenty Houses of nobility. It existed apart and above it.

Manelesi and his wife looked noticeably different from the nobility and peasantry of Izwe. Their skin was dark as night. Their hair curled in tight coils. Their eyes were a vibrant blue-gray. Over generations, as the children of the Houses began to marry with the children of the royals, darker skin became a mark of how close one was to royalty.

Today, neither the royal family nor the members of the Houses are as dark as Manelesi and his wife but this social metric remains. The members of the royal family continue to be darker than those of the Houses, and have more features similar to Manelesi and his wife…

The description went on, but I let my gaze float over to where my hands held the book open. The caramel skin that had always marked me as different, that had always been a little out-of-place in my white bread, suburban upbringing, suddenly took on a new meaning.

Apparently here, this was important. Here this was coveted.

I shook my head at the implications as I thought through the people I had met in the Alterealm thus far. There really was much to learn about this place, and I was coming to see that everything I knew from the Humanrealm was going to be turned upside down.

Eliza bustled into the library at some point. It may have been midday or perhaps early evening; the lack of windows in this cavernous den of learning disguised the true time. I wondered if the scholars and architects who had created this refuge had planned it that way. Set apart physically and visually from the world, you could almost forget anything else existed besides the books piled high in front of you.

Yet, Eliza's arrival immediately ripped apart that illusion.

"Sahle! There you are," she exclaimed. Her chest heaved up and down as if she had been running laps around the palace. And perhaps she had, I thought, as I looked at her flushed cheeks and the hand she pressed into her side.

What was equally as notable was her outfit. Eliza stood before me in a gold and red gown similar to the one I wore yesterday. It shone in the low light of the library as if the silk itself was made of liquid metal.

Her blonde hair was piled atop her head and threaded through with clear gems of some sort that equally shone. Her neck and fingers were studded with matching stones. They looked like diamonds, but my rational mind disregarded that. There was no way the woman I had known my whole life—who had shunned extravagance like it was the plague—would be draped in diamonds nearly from head to toe.

Eliza reached out her hand, still trying to master her breath. "Up!" she prodded between inhales. "Come!"

I rose immediately, taken aback by the frantic rush she seemed to be in. "What's the matter?"

"Do you not remember the Lords saying your coronation is today?" Eliza said, as she grasped my palm and began pulling me away from the table. I sent one longing glance back towards the stack of books and the safety of my newfound reading nook. Then I turned my attention to Eliza.

"Sort of...I was a little overwhelmed by everything, so I don't remember the particulars."

Eliza nodded quickly, setting the little gems in her hair swinging. "I'm sure, sweetheart. I understand. But you are being anointed this evening and Kaiht and Mara have been in a state trying to find you in time to get ready."

"How long can it possibly take to get ready?" I muttered under my breath. I had never been one to primp and pluck and apply makeup, and I certainly did not plan to change that no matter who I was or where I was now.

"Oh Sahle, you just love to needle, don't you," Eliza muttered in turn. I bit my lip to keep from laughing. "As Queen," she continued. "You'll be expected to be made up and dressed in ceremonial attire. That could take a bit of time."

"Sure," I responded, my eyes glancing towards the windows as we surfaced from the library's depths. "And when exactly is this coronation?"

"At sunset," Eliza responded, also glancing at the windows and the lengthening light there. "So you'd better hurry."

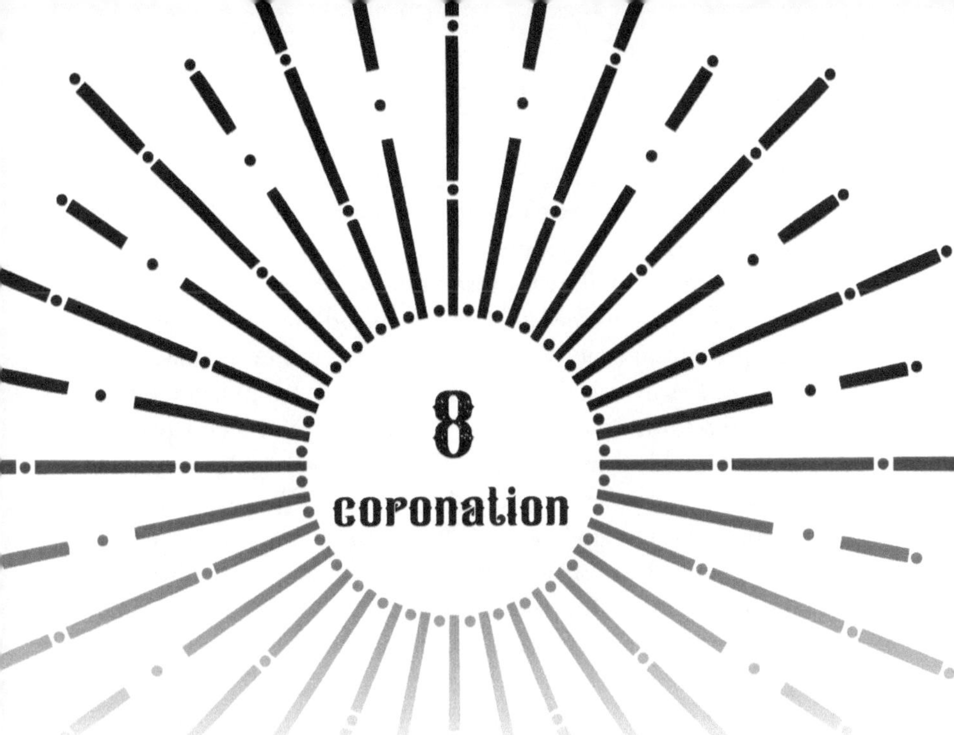

8
coronation

ELIZA HURRIED ME OUT OF THE LIBRARY AND BACK into my chambers in the highest reaches of the palace. We burst through the doors and my eyes widened at the number of people already in my chambers.

Kaiht and Mara were there, of course, fluffing material in tones of glittering gold. Roland sat in a wingback chair, equally resplendent in a formal jacket and pants in the same red and gold pattern as Eliza.

There were several other people I had never seen: a woman who was laying out an array of jewelry, a man who was unboxing some sort of wide glimmering headpiece, young palace servants who were polishing what looked to be solid gold slippers.

"Hurry, hurry," Eliza replied, pushing me gently at the thronging mass. Before I had a chance to greet Roland or ask any questions, I was being pulled into the bathroom where floral-scented steam already rose from a full tub of bathwater.

I shed my clothes and jumped into the water gladly. Someone rubbed soap through my curls, and then some sort of conditioner or lotion. Someone ran a comb through my hair while another buffed my skin with a sponge.

Washed and polished, I rose from the water like Venus from her shell. My skin smelled like jasmine and the towels that were wrapped around me were warm and soft and oddly made me think of freshly baked bread. Eliza returned and pulled me half naked back into the bedroom; I noticed Roland had departed, the strangers had turned away. Then the towel was gone and in its place was a gown of gold satin, so thick and matte it seemed to both reflect the light and swallow it in the same moment.

The gown had a structured neckline that sat low, parallel with my collar bones. Thin sleeves hugged my arms just off of my shoulder in a way that made a scooping, seamless line across my chest.

The bodice of the dress fit snugly over my breasts and waist before widening out in a bell-shape to the floor. As I watched the dress be fitted to me in the mirror, I saw Kaiht and Mara pick up the trailing fabric that hung from my back. Like a cape, an additional layer of the gold material hung over the back of the dress and fanned out like a cathedral train behind me. It swept the ground as I turned to get a better look at it, and I figured it was at least six feet in length.

Eliza and Mara turned to my hair. With quick fingers they began to twist the strands so that they created crisscrossed patterns that spanned my head and trailed off into two braids down my back. They wrapped these up and around my head and pinned them in place, transforming my usually thick and voluminous mane of curls into a neat web of braids.

"Your Majesty," the man with the headpiece said, bowing low at the waist. In his hands, he held the object in question—a gleaming circle of gold as wide as it was tall. Designs were carved into the metal, and I squinted my eyes to make out what looked like constellations of stars dotted here and there.

The man approached and held the crown in place along the back of my head as Eliza and Mara used an array of pins to attach it to the braids. I tried to glance at the mirror. I wanted to see how this headpiece sat, but the woman with the jewelry approached first.

After a bow of her own, she turned me to her and then attached a collar of solid gold around my neck. To my wrists and forearms, she slid on snug gold bands. She placed a single gold ring—a signet with the letter I—onto my pinkie finger. Then she bade me close my eyes. I felt a soft spray of some type of liquid hitting my eyelids, the bridge of my nose, and the arch of my cheekbones.

"Your Majesty, may I ask that you keep your eyes closed?" she murmured, close to my face, just as I was about to open them once more.

I nodded before what felt like a paintbrush touched my face. The soft bristles brushed the middle of my forehead, several single points along my cheekbones and chin, and my lips.

I flinched when something spritzed over the exposed skin of my chest. "Apologies, Your Majesty," the woman said. "It's only perfume."

I smelled it then—more jasmine and something else that was rich and smokey and promised pleasure.

From near my ear, Eliza spoke with an odd catch in her voice. "You can open your eyes now, Queen Sahle."

And I did. I opened them to find Roland back in the chambers, his eyes wide and—if my own did not deceive me—shining with unshed tears. Eliza's hands were clasped in front of her red- and gold-clad chest, her lined eyes large and adoring. Kaiht, Mara, the jeweler, and the crown-wielder had similar expressions.

"What?" I said dumbly, suddenly uncomfortable with the weight of the gown and crown, the force of their shining gazes. I shifted my stance and heard the thick rustle of the gold satin against my legs.

Eliza reached out to grasp both of my arms and turned me back towards the full-length mirror. "See for yourself, Majesty."

The woman in front of me was not me. I blinked, and she blinked. I turned my head to the side, and she did the same. But it could not be me—this golden goddess who stood staring back.

The dress was the same one I had seen before but the crown, the gold jewelry, and the makeup transformed me into something I did not recognize. The headpiece sat along the back of my skull like a wide, ornate disk that radiated outward and lent the effect of a halo. The makeup looked like golden paint had been finely sprayed in a band across my eyes, nose, and cheekbones. Then, larger golden spots had been painted on in a series of dots across the apples of my cheeks, the bridge of my nose, and my eyebrows. And through the paint, my own gray-blue eyes shone like silver moonbeams in a sea of sunlight.

A similar line of gold dots ran vertically up from the base of my chin to the underside of my lips—lips that were painted a brilliant scarlet that drew the eye there. The lips in question parted of their own volition, exhaling in wonder.

"Wow," I murmured.

"You look beautiful, Sahle," Eliza said.

"You look like a Queen. Like your mother," Roland added.

For the first time since my arrival just days ago, I looked in the mirror and believed them. The woman before me was the Queen everyone was expecting.

I just could not square me, Sahle, with this woman.

I shook my head to clear my disbelief and disassociation. "I don't know what to say."

"You don't need to say anything," Eliza answered, stepping up to me and clasping my arms once again. "But it is time."

I took a deep breath. And then I let her guide me to the door.

My exit from the palace was the quietest walk through the palace I had yet experienced. A few servants bustled here and there,

84

casting furtive, curious glances towards me as my retinue and I made our way to the great entrance doors. Yet, we did not come across a single courtier in the wide hallways. Our footsteps on the checkered marble echoed in the unusual stillness.

"Where is everyone?" I asked Eliza, who kept pace beside me.

"At the ceremony hall, of course," Eliza replied with a smile. "You'll see them soon enough."

We left the palace's main door and descended the stone steps to find a carriage made of interspersed yellow and ebony wood, polished and shining almost as bright as the fabrics Eliza, Roland, and I wore. Kaiht and Mara helped me into the carriage, tucking my long train around me. Eliza and Roland followed, and then we were off.

The quiet did not last, not as the gates to the palace grounds opened to a veritable sea of zebras and mounted men. They were soldiers, I guessed, by the swords strapped to their waists, by the matching mahogany brown uniforms and two-horned helmets.

But if the horns caught my eye, my attention was immediately stolen by the city as I once again drank in the thatch-roofed round buildings that made up the majority of the city's architecture.

Our carriage stood still a moment and then with the bleat of some horn, we set forward. The clip of hooves before and behind us made me think the soldiers had formed some kind of large, parade-like accompaniment. I fumbled with the glass at the carriage window until it slid open, and then I craned my neck out to see.

"Sahle," Eliza hissed at the same time the crowd of people roared. It was not the soldiers alone making the deafening sound around us but also the townspeople. They lined the streets, kept back only by the zebras around us, and their cheers rose as they caught a glimpse of me.

For a split second, I considered waving. Surely that is what a Queen would do, right? But I was a chicken. I was afraid of whatever was happening, still wrapped in disbelief about if this realm were even real or if at any moment I would wake up from this exceptionally detailed dream.

I quickly pulled my head back inside the carriage.

"Sahl," Roland said this time. His admonishment was clear in his tone. "I know this is overwhelming, but please don't stick your head out. It's a safety issue."

"But what is all of this?" I said stupidly. They already told me—this was my coronation.

Roland seemed to know this. He smiled patiently—a smile you would use with a child who was just not old enough to understand complex ideas—before replying, "On the way to a coronation, it's customary for the Vikela, the Queen's Guards, to accompany you in a sort of parade to the ceremony hall. That's what you're seeing around us now. If you heard the horns, there's a marching band at the start that announces your approach to the ceremony hall."

"Alright," I nodded, turning back to the window though I did not try to stick my head out again. "Where is this ceremony hall?"

"It is in the center of the city. We should be there in ten minutes or so," Roland answered. His eyes also tracked the city that swept by us. I wondered if he had missed this place when he was in the Humanrealm all of those years.

Streets lined with jacaranda trees caught my attention. A gaggle of squawking hadedas winged overhead, and their chatter reminded me of a question I had for Roland.

"This place," I began hesitantly. "I was reading that Manelesi arrived hundreds of years ago with animals, a distinct culture, traditions. From that description and from what I've seen in the last few days, this"—I motioned outside the carriage windows—"looks strangely like photos I've seen of Africa."

Roland nodded, his brow puckering thoughtfully as he considered my words. "I often thought the same. The first time I saw pictures of Africa, especially Southern Africa, it reminded me of home—so much so that I even asked Eliza if we should relocate there."

He smiled at Eliza adoringly, taking her small hand in his larger one. "But we felt our town was the safest place for you so we never seriously considered it. Yet, I do wonder if growing up there would have made your transition to the Alterealm simpler."

"Nothing would have made this simpler," I said quietly. From further ahead, the horns sounded again, and the crowd answered with ululations and cheers.

"True," Eliza added as she watched me with bright eyes.

Roland continued, "Anyway, yes, the closest thing to compare the architecture, the wildlife, the nature of Izwe, is to imagine if Africa had colonized Europe at some point in history. The mix of language, traditions, and culture is an approximation of what Izwe is today, in Humanrealm terms."

"It's beautiful," I murmured as I caught sight of a wide bunch of calla lilies lining the road.

When the roar and bustle of the crowd began to press in on us even in the enclosed carriage, we finally stopped. I felt my eyes widen in anticipation. But then Roland was taking my hands in both of his. Eliza reached out and squeezed my knee through my gold gown.

"Sahl," he said. "You have grown into the brave woman and Queen we knew you would be. We have always loved you and been proud of you, but especially so in this moment."

I glanced between him and Eliza, too overwhelmed by the noise outside, the weight of their teary gazes, the feel of the heavy gold atop my skin. Dimly, I felt like I was gazing down upon this scene as an observer. It could not be happening to me. I was just Sahle.

Roland knocked on the top of the carriage and a man in a dark, military tunic and horned helmet opened the carriage door from the outside. Immediately, the sound of stomping hooves, the beating of drums, the shouts and calls of the crowd, the melodic notes of the horns rose another notch. It warred with the feeling of incredulity, and I felt overwhelmed by the assault on my senses.

I watched in the same numb disbelief as Eliza and Roland got out of the carriage first. Then Roland reached back for me, shouldering my weight as I navigated out of the narrow doorway with gown and crown.

I did not think the roar of the crowd could intensify but it did. My gaze swept across the sea of curious, eager faces before I let Roland turn me towards what had to be the ceremony hall. As Eliza had said, it was sunset, and the sky was bathed in red so deep and lustrous it was nearly the same scarlet of my painted lips. It was unlike any sunset I had witnessed. I stared at the garnet sky in wonder before my gaze lowered to the grand building before me.

I had never seen a building like it. I had expected some form of the plaster-walled, thatch-roofed buildings that seemed to make up the city, but the ceremony hall was something else entirely. The roofline was a series of raised peaks and low valleys crafted out of seamless white plaster. It looked like the rolling waves of the sea floating freely above the ground.

Roland tucked my arm into his elbow and drew us closer to the building. Only then did I see that there were indeed walls on this alien building. They were made of glass, and I wondered to myself how glass alone could hold up its churning roofline.

I did not have time to dwell on those thoughts because the moment we entered through the towering glass doors, the moment we stepped onto the long raised aisle, the roar rose another level still.

Yet this time, it was not just the crowd. No, it was also the courtiers, members of the Houses and their guests who packed the ceremony hall from door to far wall.

There were so many faces, so many colors and patterns of headdresses, skirts and jewels that I felt my eyes would cross trying to spy people I recognized in the crowd. I gave up and focused my eyes ahead of us.

Each step we took was amplified by the sound of drums that kept time with our pace. Notes from a marimba of some sort overlaid the drum beat in a boisterous, energetic song. And the same horns from the parade blared above it all, a beckoning call that urged me forward, forward to an elevated glass dais.

Roland led me up the dais' steps. There, a series of men stood, clad in vibrant gowns of red and yellow. And in the center of them sat an unassuming chair.

One of the men stepped forward and the music abruptly ceased. "Esteemed residents of Izwe," he called, voice booming through the great space. "We come to the ceremony hall today to witness an auspicious moment: the coronation of our sovereign, Queen Sahle of Izwe."

From the corner of my eye, I saw Eliza step up to my other side and then she leaned in to whisper as the man continued on about the pride and lineage of Izwe. "Don't be frightened Sahle," she breathed. "Just follow whatever the Masters tell you to do."

I looked at her and gave the slightest nod before I looked back at the man speaking, the Master.

He continued, "It has been decades since our last ruler sat on the Izweian throne. Today, we anoint the next in that line. Today, we welcome Queen Sahle home to Izwe."

A chorus of applause and shouts swept through the ceremony hall and then the Master was reaching out to me. I let him take my hand and he led me to the chair. I sat at his gentle prompting as three of the other Masters approached.

One held a bowl and the other two held my hands. Closing their eyes, they said a prayer or benediction of some sort. The words were in a language I did not understand though the pacing reminded me of the Lord's Prayer, a sort of rhythmic, worshipful meditation said aloud. Once done, they dipped their fingers into the bowl.

Red paint coated their hands. They began to draw symbols across my fingers and bare arms. They continued up my chest and up the edges of my jaw until their fingers met what I imagined was the gold paint that spanned the top half of my face. They did not paint over the gold line from chin to lip, but they did wipe their hands across my lips. I tasted something metallic and salty.

Then the men drew back, and the drums alone began to beat once more. The Masters bowed and then Eliza and Roland were bowing, and then in a wave moving out from the dais to the door, the crowd bowed.

"Rise, Sahle of Izwe," the first Master called from his place of supplication. "Rise as rightful Queen."

I hesitated for only a moment. Then I found my feet.

I rose from the simple wooden chair and, as soon as I did, a warmth tingled across my skin everywhere the Masters' red paint touched. A bright flare lit my peripheral vision, and I looked down at my hands. I realized it was me who had lit up exactly where the red paint lay.

I gasped.

But as soon as the light that coated my skin flared, it disappeared. And the red paint went with it, seeming to sink into my very flesh. I turned my right hand over, blinking at what had been painted skin. It was once more unmarked.

The Masters rose, Eliza and Roland rose, and the gathered crowd rose. Their clapping and hollering rang out as the marimbas and horns joined in. All eyes fixed on me.

And I stood there, still as a statue, unsure of what had just occurred. But Roland was there once more, Eliza behind us.

"Congratulations, Your Majesty," Roland said quietly as he took my arm again.

I stared back in shocked silence.

I watched my hands the entire length of the carriage ride back to the palace, though the people continued to fill the streets and the zebras marched around us. None of it seemed as vital as the utter strangeness of what had just happened. I was not sure if it was my imagination playing tricks on me or whether I could see the outline of the Masters' paint like a faint reflection glinting under my skin.

"You did well in there, Sahl," Roland said from the carriage seat across from me.

When I did not respond, Eliza asked, "Sahl, what are you staring at?"

"Do you see it? The pattern or symbols or whatever the Masters drew on me…it's like I can still see them in my skin from certain angles."

Roland looked at Eliza and then back at me. "There's nothing there, honey. The symbols sink into your skin during the ceremony and anoint you as ruler."

"Hmm," I murmured. Perhaps my eyes were playing tricks on me. "What was that in there—the paint, the Masters? And that light? It looked like the light of that dome or whatever it was the night we came here."

I watched Eliza nod from her seat across from me. "That's right. It was the same light. The Masters are what they'd called priests or clergy in the Humanrealm. They helped imbue the talisman I used to create the dome the night we traveled. They made it right before we left the Alterealm with you, with the express purpose that it would bring us back on your twentieth birthday.

"The Masters lead Izwe's religion, and that religion is intrinsically linked with magic. You mentioned Manelesi earlier—how he is your ancestor and the first King of Izwe—but what you may not have learned yet is that Manelesi was also a god who brought magic to the realm. His family alone had magic yet over time, through intermarrying with the Houses, some of the Lords have been able to wield varying amounts of magic.

"The Masters are different, though. They are not from Manelesi's line, nor are they related to the Houses. They are simply conduits. They can access the magic for ceremonial purposes, but they do not have magic."

I tried to suspend my disbelief about my ancestor being a god even as my brow furrowed. Instead of asking about that, I focused on the Masters. "I don't understand. How does one have and yet not have magic?"

"It's as if they're stewards of it," Roland jumped in. "As long as the Masters serve, they are allowed access to the magic for limited purposes. They can only use their magic in the service of Izwe, and they permanently lose all access to it if they leave service."

"So then their magic allowed the paint to sink into my skin?" I asked, looking again at my now bare fingers.

"First of all, it was not paint," Roland replied.

Eliza grimaced. "Unfortunately not."

Suddenly the metallic taste on my lips made more sense. I opened my mouth, as if to pull my lips further away from my tongue.

Roland continued. "Before the coronation, the Masters ritualistically chant and pray over an oryx. Then the animal is slaughtered, and its blood is captured to use in the anointing.

"But you can stop doing whatever you're doing with your mouth now. The magic either accepts or rejects the one being anointed. If it accepts, then the blood sinks into your skin and becomes a part of you. It's no longer there—just the makeup."

I looked at him skeptically, even as I scrubbed at my cheek with the back of one hand. It came away with the faintest glimmer of gold but no red. "What an…interesting ceremony."

Eliza chuckled even as Roland freed one reluctant grin. "Interesting is one way to put it," he replied. "Ancient, powerful, binding. Those are all other, more appropriate descriptions for the importance of the ceremony."

"Yes, well. It was certainly something," I said simply.

The carriage stopped moments later, and we were headed back up the stairs of the palace. This time, courtiers filled the space—and I wondered how they had managed to beat us back to the palace.

They lined the stone steps up to the palace doors. They lined the hallways and they filled the large room we entered.

"This is the Great Hall," Eliza said in my ear as she nodded at courtiers she knew milling about in the space. Like most of the palace, the room had off-white walls. Exposed beams hung from a ceiling that towered several stories high. Chandeliers of wood and brass hung from these beams, lit with what looked to be real candles. Paintings lined the walls. A head of a horned antelope was mounted in one place, the head of a wildebeest in another.

Towering French doors were open to what looked to be a series of balconies along one wall. Long tables ran lengthwise down the room, and a head table sat up near the fireplace. I knew without being told that was our table—helmed as it was by an ornate throne at the center.

I thought we would head directly to the table. I hoped Roland and Eliza would deposit me into that throne and let me fade into the background. But of course I was mistaken. Roland and Eliza did lead me towards my seat; yet, they took every opportunity to stop and greet courtiers who caught their eye.

"Your Majesty, it is an honor," one woman wrapped in purple fabric said over my hand.

"Congratulations, Queen Sahle," a young man with burnished red hair said with a raised eyebrow as he tracked his gaze across my lips. I clamped them tighter together.

It was a whirl of faces and bright fabrics, and I was all too thankful when Eliza and Roland finally allowed me to sit. I slumped into my seat in the least ladylike way. I heard Eliza scoff from beside me.

"Really, Sahle, we were just greeting people. It's not like we ran a marathon," she said under her breath.

"It does feel like it."

Roland laughed from my other side.

As soon as we sat, the same music from the ceremony hall started again. I turned my head from side to side to spy the drums, the marimbas, the horns, but I could not make out where the musicians were seated.

"They're behind the walls," Roland said, guessing at what I was looking for.

"Behind the walls?"

"Yes, there are hidden alcoves within the walls of this room where the musicians perform."

"Why? What's wrong with them being out in the open?" I replied, confused why anyone would not want to see the skill of those who had such control over an instrument.

From my peripheral vision, I saw Roland shrug. "It's just how it's done here. Music is important in the Alterealm, but it's more prized as something to be heard and not seen."

"Noted," I murmured as Roland handed me a glass of wine from a passing servant's tray. I took a sip at the golden wine, surprised at the sweetness that instantly coated my tongue.

"It's very sweet," Eliza noted. "It's called konstans. It is the typical wine grown in Izwe and it's made from passion fruit."

"Passion fruit?" I exclaimed, eyeing the gold liquid with much more interest now. I had always loved passion fruit.

"Passion fruit," she confirmed with a smile.

I took another sip and Eliza followed suit. Then she turned her eyes to the crowd of people that thronged the hall. There were so many of them and I could tell by their curious glances and pacing that they all wanted to approach us.

"Why don't they come up to the table?" I asked.

"It is seen as somewhat improper to approach the head table unless for a ceremonial purpose—"

"Like what?" I interjected.

If Roland thought anything of my interruption, he did not comment on it. "In a few moments, Lord Grimly will begin the formal part of this evening. Each of the twenty Izweian Houses will be presented before you and will swear an oath to you. They will approach your table and kiss your ring after they've said that oath.

"The Vikela will swear their allegiance. After that, if you would like to speak to anyone, you would call for them or you could approach them. But it is not typical to interrupt you here or to lobby you for anything when you are at the high table."

I nodded, hoping I understood. There were few things I hated as much as making a fool of myself and I was doing that time and time again in this new place, it seemed.

Lord Grimly materialized from one of the balcony doors a few moments later and he approached the head table. With a bow to me, he turned to face the courtiers who swarmed like hungry locusts around the room. The music stopped.

"Lords and Ladies, I welcome you to the coronation banquet of Queen Sahle of Izwe—"

Cheers swelled again and Grimly waited until they died down before he continued. He turned to me, though his voice remained projected for the entire hall to hear. "I know I speak for all of us when I say your kingdom has waited for this moment for two decades. We would take this opportunity to greet you and present the Houses."

As if rehearsed—and it may have been, for all I truly knew about Izwelan coronations—a number of courtiers split from the main contingent and formed an orderly line. Grimly stepped to the side as the first small grouping approached.

"Presenting House Ngwenya," Grimly said as a courtier in a white and yellow formal dinner jacket bowed. The woman next to him, dressed in the same pattern, curtsied simultaneously. They remained low to the ground though they lifted their voices in what was almost a chant.

"Queen of Izwe, Queen of all Houses, we swear to you this oath: Loyalty, fealty and obedience to you is our gift. Long may we serve. Long may you rule."

They stood and approached me, their eyes curiously meeting mine. I remembered what I had been told and held out my hand with the ring. Each of them took my hand in turn, kissed the ring, and then backed away bowing.

The next couple approached.

"Presenting House Isibankwa," Grimly called. And again the couple bowed and curtsied, the hems of their brown and silver clothing sweeping the floor.

They, too, said the same oath and kissed my ring where it sat on the pinky finger of my right hand. And then there was another couple and another. I did all I could to keep track of the names. I remembered a handful of the House names from my initial study, and I made a mental note to look up which animals these names correlated with next time I was in the library.

"Presenting House Nkwe."

"Presenting House Ndlovu."

"Presenting House Sephiri."

"Presenting House Kgathla."

There was one House I was waiting for, one House that stuck out to me from my history lessons: Ingonyame, the former rulers. Granted, they had not ruled in centuries but, still, I was exceptionally curious. I waited House after House to catch a glimpse of the family.

"Presenting House Ingonyame," Grimly finally called. My eyes immediately narrowed, the history instantly forgotten, as the one person I could not stand in all of Izwe strolled towards me.

Lord Anson…of House Ingonyame.

He stood, dressed in a blue coat so dark it was almost black. Gold thread ran in some embroidered pattern across the chest and scrolled on the pockets. Beside him was a woman in the same style of dress. I guessed that she was a sister or a cousin, such was the closeness in the texture of their hair, the planes of their faces, the green of their eyes.

Those eyes in question locked on mine as Anson bowed and approached my throne, lithe as a lion.

Because I could not help myself from being petty after our interaction in the Council Chamber, I held my hand out to the woman in blue first. She kissed my ring and backed away. And only then did I turn my attention to Anson.

He had not missed my slight and he smiled knowingly at me, one eyebrow raised. But he did not take my hand, held out as it was in his reach. No, he paused and, with a smile, swept his eyes over me from head to toe.

I bristled at being stared at and my lips set in a tighter line. But after a moment, after he noted my distaste, he at last took my hand and bent over the ring.

The kiss lasted less than a second, but I felt it like an electric current skittering across my skin. I pulled my hand back quickly and tucked it in the folds of my golden skirt. And as Anson bowed again and turned away, I rubbed my hand until the tingling stopped. And I wondered why it had happened. And I wondered why I was imagining things.

More and more courtiers were presented from various Houses. Finally, Grimly presented himself beside an elderly woman in the same orange that Grimly was adorned in. "Presenting House Kubuga."

They said the same oath, kissed the ring and backed away. And when I looked back up at the courtiers, there was no one left in the line.

I heaved a sigh of relief.

"Twenty Houses," Roland muttered next to me.

"It felt like more," I replied under my breath.

Yet as soon as I said that, a distant shuffling alerted me that this was not over. The Vikela were next, I remembered, as a sea of soldiers entered the Great Hall. They were dressed in the same uniforms from earlier: deep brown, formal tunics helmed by rows of double-breasted buttons, and dark metal helmets that each had two horns sweeping skyward like some sort of short antlers.

There must have been at least one hundred soldiers, I estimated, as they packed the center of the hall. Only three of them approached the high table and, as the three knelt, the rest followed suit.

"Your Majesty Queen Sahle," the eldest of the three said. "The Vikela presents itself. We vow to protect and serve as faithful soldier-servants to Izwe. May the God and gods strike us down should we fail."

Each of the soldiers raised a hand to their chest and pounded it in a repeating, synchronized three-beat rhythm. They continued this, looking at the floor and not me.

Roland leaned in to whisper quietly in my ear. "They will not approach you or kiss your ring like the members of the Houses did. You must tell the soldiers to rise when you see fit."

"Rise," I said instantly. I did not know how long the court would expect this to go on but I felt shamed at having men kneeling before me, beating their chests and waiting for me to let them stand. No matter what coronation had just happened, I was still just Sahle from the suburbs. No one kneeled before Sahle from the suburbs, nor would I ever want them to.

Hearing my word, the soldiers rose. They bowed as one and shuffled out.

Music and laughter thrummed through the hall again and then servants began filling the long tables with platters of food. From my seat at the head table, I spied long haunches of some type of roasted meat. Trays of vegetables and slivered garlic passed by, the savory smell wafting my direction. Steaming breads, soups, and sauces arrived next. Finally, platters of fruits and cheeses arrived.

Before I could ask how this worked, the courtiers had found their seats and servants were bringing smaller trays of each dish to me directly. Roland and Eliza told them what to heap onto my plate, and then they were urging me to eat.

I nibbled at each dish, surprised at how fragrant and fresh the food tasted. I sipped at my wine, amazed again and again how sweet the flavor was.

And once more, I wondered what in the world this place was.

Roland and Eliza were chatting with each other over me, but I did not mind. I had nothing to say. I just stared at the food, focused on putting the fork into my mouth with each bite, and reminded myself to breathe.

I noticed Grimly had taken a seat further down the head table. The two Masters who had painted my hands were seated beside him. And with a start, I spied Anson, as well.

What was he doing up here?

I looked away before he could catch me watching him and turned again to look out at the crowd. These were my courtiers, apparently.

Sometime after the food was consumed, the music changed, and the servants returned to clear away trays. I had long since given up finishing the food on my plate—against my natural inclination to not waste. I took another sip of my wine and leaned back against the tall chair. My headpiece made a quiet clanging sound as it knocked the sturdy wood.

"Tired, Your Majesty?" Eliza asked as she swallowed a bite of meat.

"Exceptionally," I replied, and it was not a lie. From the balcony doors, I could see the sky. Sunset had long passed, and the night was dark and filled with stars.

I yawned without meaning to.

"The end of the meal is the official end of the coronation festivities," Roland said. His knife and fork sat discarded on his empty plate. "If you would like to return to your chambers, that is perfectly fine. You just let us know."

I nodded. I was ready but I did not want to do anything wrong. "Are you sure it's OK?"

I looked from one to the other and they both nodded. "Of course," Eliza supplied. "We were here for your mother's coronation, remember. She left right at the end of dinner and no one thought anything of it. Isn't that right, Roland?"

"That's correct," he confirmed with a smile. "We'll walk you back to your chambers."

"Thank you," I said to them. "I'm ready if you are."

And with that, the three of us stood.

The music stopped instantly.

The chatter and motion in the hall paused.

"It was her Majesty's honor to dine with you this evening. She will retire and she bids you all continue the celebration in her honor," Roland called, pitching his voice so that it could be heard by everyone present.

He looped my arm into his elbow once more and led me down the long ballroom and through the doors that led to the hallway, the staircase, and eventually my own domain.

"Thank you," I said to both of them as soon as my chamber door closed behind me. "Thank you."

They left me soon after, having secured my promise to go straight to bed once I washed the paint from my face. But I did not do that. Instead, I stared in the mirror at the gold woman.

I had no notion of the time, transfixed and frighted as I was at what looked back at me.

This was not Sahle. This was Queen Sahle, and she was not me.

I WAS SIPPING WHAT MARA HAD CALLED RED ROOIBOS tea in my chambers two days later when a note arrived from Commander Finn, the man the Council had selected as my physical and magical trainer—whatever that meant. It said we would meet the following morning at seven o'clock. I promptly wrote back and said I would be there at ten o'clock.

An hour later, another note arrived with a single number written: "8."

I stared at that number, shocked that this Finn character would dare contradict me. It was not that I thought I was too important or special. I definitely did not see myself like that, not now, not ever. But I had been told time and again that I was Queen, that my word was law, and I had begun to test the limits of this in innocuous ways.

So far, I found that servants obeyed my commands regardless of how silly, and courtiers and servants alike dropped into bows whenever I entered a room. I could even shut the Lords up with one word.

Yet here some man named Finn was bargaining with me.

I liked it. It felt good and typical and normal, and so I wrote back: "9:30."

Unsurprisingly, another note arrived on my bedside table mere minutes later: "8:15."

I tried my luck again with a crisp "9."

And to my shock, the next note that landed on my table said, "As Your Majesty commands."

I smiled to myself as I set the note down next to the mug of tea. I thought I might like meeting this Finn, and I could already picture him as a curmudgeonly old man with enough experience and personality to not balk at the idea of talking back to a Queen.

You can imagine my shock, then, when I arrived at what they called the training grounds—an area within the palace walls designated solely for the Vikela—only to find a young man. I looked around, craning my neck for the crotchety old soldier I was meeting and the young man watched me with a curious look on his face.

When I finally looked at him directly, he bowed deeply but rose with a smile. "Can I help you, Your Majesty?"

The sun at its midmorning angle hit the man's bound hair in a way that made the blonde strands glint silver. His eyes were a piercing blue, his nose straight and proud and the correct size to balance a strong jawline.

I scanned over the rest of him quickly, assessing who this might be. He was dressed in the usual brown of servants and soldiers, although the cut of the man's outfit marked him as someone ready for training. A fitted, sleeveless tunic draped over the clearly-present lines of toned muscles on his shoulders, chest, and legs. And even from thirty paces away, I could see the dips and crevices of skin over taut muscle on his bare arms.

He was definitely a soldier.

I refocused on his face and was surprised to see the smile still there. "I'm looking for a man named Finn. I'm supposed to meet him here at nine o'clock."

The man's smile cracked wider, showing a set of well-formed teeth. I had the distinct impression that I was speaking to a life-sized version of a Ken doll.

"You've come to the right place," the man said. Then, gesturing to himself with a vague wave of a hand, "You've found him."

"What?" I said, my mind desperately trying to match the vision of the trainer I had imagined with the man before me. "You're Finn?"

"At your service, Your Majesty," Finn said, dropping into another bow before righting himself and coming towards me.

"Thank you for arriving on time, even if it's later than I would have preferred," he continued. He stopped a few feet away, and I could see the slight breeze pick up wayward strands of his hair as they curled softly around his ears.

My eyes narrowed at the statement. "We'd be here at ten o'clock if it were up to me."

"Thankfully, it's not," he responded, the smile in his voice the only thing stopping me from gasping out loud at the impertinence.

"Ugh," I said, somewhere between a sigh and a grunt of frustration.

The noise only seemed to make his smile grow wider. But then he dropped his gaze from my face and to my body. It was not a lecherous look. No, it was assessing.

He ran his gaze over my arms and chest, my waist and the swell of my hips under the flowing green dress that I had chosen to wear. That was where he stopped.

"You're in a dress," he remarked, blandly.

"It would appear so." I self-consciously smoothed the draped skirt over my hips. I had always hated being stared at and assessed, and becoming Queen of Izwe had not changed that.

"Why are you in a dress?"

I looked at him, my mouth nearly hanging open in surprise. Except for the clothes I had worn to the Alterealm—and had not seen since—I only had dresses in my wardrobe. I did not think I owned a single pair of pants.

So what did he expect me to wear?

Irrationally, I could feel the skin of my face prickling in anger and embarrassment and defensiveness. "Finn, that's your name right?" I began rhetorically. When he did not answer, I carried on, "Do you know how many days ago it was that I was ripped from my own reality and brought here?"

He looked at me a moment before answering. "No, Majesty."

"By my estimation, it was a week ago. A week ago, I was living a normal life in the Humanrealm. And then suddenly, I was hurtling through God knows what or where or when. I was suddenly here, and people were telling me that I now live in a new realm. Not a new city, or a new country. A new realm.

"I barely even understand what that means, but now I'm expected to be a Queen and to lead people. To lead a nation of people. So I'm sorry if I did not think through my wardrobe for the perfect outfit this morning. Since arriving in this…place, I haven't given much thought to what proper workout attire might look like."

My vision felt narrowed by the time I closed my mouth, and I could feel my heart beating as it did when adrenaline flowed through my veins. I was upset, but mostly I was annoyed and overwhelmed and embarrassed. My outburst had caught me off guard. Everything I had said was true, of course, but I realized that I really must be at the end of my tether if I was ranting and raving to a complete stranger.

To his credit, Finn did not argue back. He merely looked at me—really looked this time—and whatever he saw there made him apologize. "I'm sorry," he said, inclining his head forward in a way that was not a bow but still showed deference.

"What are you sorry about?" I replied, too frustrated to take this olive branch he was handing me.

He shrugged, his strong shoulders drawing up towards that golden hair. "You're right, you've been through a lot and sourcing proper training attire is low on the list of things to figure out."

I nodded once in acknowledgement, equally mortified and annoyed.

"Perhaps we can start there," Finn suggested, motioning to a bench on the side of the packed-dirt training ground. I walked over to it, kicking up wisps of red dust in my wake, and sat in a huff.

Finn sat next to me, the width of a third person separating us—so much space, in fact, it seemed like Finn would topple off the edge of the bench should a strong wind blow. It was a strange way to sit but maybe that was just something else I did not know. Perhaps he did not want to or was not supposed to be too close to me.

"I apologize," Finn began. Then, turning to me, he extended his hand. "Let's start again. I'm Finn, and I'm a Commander of Your Majesty's Vikela. I'm the one the Council of Lords has asked to assess and train you."

"Assess?" I asked. The Council had mentioned taking stock of my skills and I was eager to understand what exactly that meant.

"Well, yes." Finn's eyebrows rose up. "I'll naturally have to assess what your current understandings of combat, both physical and magical, are at present and then work from there."

I chuckled at that. "My 'current understanding of combat'? I don't think you understand. I've never so much as taken a Taekwondo class."

"A tikwon-what?" he replied with confusion.

"Exactly," I muttered.

Finn looked at me a moment more, then shook his head as if casting aside whatever bewilderment was clouding his mind. "Well then we'll start from the beginning," he said.

"OK," I replied hesitantly.

"And that means with a proper outfit."

"Great," I sighed as Finn stood and made his way towards a series of buildings that ringed the training ground. I followed him when it became clear he was leaving the area, not just moving around.

Finn entered one wooden building that was more of a hut than anything. In fact, all of these buildings were more like huts, what with their round forms, brown plaster walls, and thatch roofs.

It was a shock after being in the castle. I had come to expect everything in Izwe to be the marble, polished hardwood, and white walls of the palace that loomed above us. Yet here, just outside of the doors of that grand manor, were buildings that looked more like mud huts.

They were put together in a rustic way that made me look twice. They were elegant—all gently sloping edges and rounded curves—but they were still sparse, unadorned structures that seemed so at odds with the finery just yards away. Was this how everyone lived?

I turned my head to watch a small group of soldiers come out of one larger plastered structure and then break away in fare-wells to separate ones. Another group came out of the same large building, several soldiers in their servant-brown still chewing.

The cafeteria, I reasoned as I watched one soldier burp and absently rub his distended belly.

I glanced up to find Finn watching me again, one hand braced on the handle of an open door to another thatched hut. I hurried after him.

Six curved windows allowed light into the structure so my eyes hardly needed time to adjust to being inside, even when Finn shut the door behind us. Large storage cabinets lined the walls and Finn stepped up to one, pulling open a cupboard door and immediately rifling through the contents.

From where I was, I could see clothing. I could not make out what kind but from the color I would guess that these were extra soldiers' outfits.

Finn's quick rifling stopped suddenly, and then he was pulling two pieces of brown clothing out of the closet with a little backward kick to shut the door behind him.

"These ought to fit you," he said, handing me the shapeless brown garments.

I took them hesitantly, turning them over and holding up each piece at a time to get a better look. "What are they?"

"You have seen pants before?" Finn said, a joking edge turning the corners of his mouth up.

"Yes…" I fixed him with narrowed eyes, before glancing back at the outfit.

I could see now that there was a pair of brown pants and, cut from the same cloth, a tunic similar to the one that Finn was wearing except that it had sleeves.

"You're fine in what you're wearing now, Your Majesty," Finn continued. "But please come dressed in these from now on."

When I raised a questioning eyebrow at him, he added, "I promise you they'll be more comfortable."

"Fine," I answered simply.

"Good," Finn nodded. "That was step one. Now the real work begins."

Since I did not have any physical abilities, Finn was determined to assess my magical abilities. And despite my constant protests for the last few minutes, he did not believe me when I said I had none of those either.

"It's not possible," he said, shaking his head in disbelief. He leaned back and crossed an ankle over the opposite knee, seated as we were back on the training ground bench. "Magic is like any other genetics. It runs in bloodlines. Both your mother and your father were from magical lines, which means in all likelihood you also can wield magic."

"I understand why you would think that," I responded calmly, and for what felt like the tenth time, repeated, "But I can't do any magic."

Finn's eyes crinkled at the edges as he narrowed them at me. "Have you ever tried?"

"Tried what? Magic?"

"Yes," Finn gave me a look that said obviously. "Although you might not have consciously thought of it as magic. For magic wielders, the first uses of it are generally not purposeful. Maybe you wished for the rain to stop and it did, or you wished for someone to shut up and suddenly they were overcome with a coughing fit. You could almost chalk it up to coincidence but it's timed a little too perfectly."

I shook my head. "No, never."

But Finn fixed me with a disbelieving look. "I doubt that."

Even though I shook my head, I did try to think through my twenty years of living and any instances that could match what he was saying.

My mind jumped to a time when I was maybe thirteen years old. I was walking down the road when a kitten darted into the road. It was a busy intersection, what with people making their way home after days out and jobs worked. I remembered being so afraid for the kitten, so instantly concerned for its life, but I was old enough to know that I myself would be killed if I rushed into the traffic.

As I watched, fear and horrified anticipation rising in me like a tide, all four directions of the intersection's stop lights turned red. There was a moment of confusion as the drivers looked at each other, not sure what was happening or who had the green light. And then understanding dawned on them as all of the red lights began to flash: the lights were broken and the intersection was now a four-way stop.

But in the time it took for the drivers to realize that, and then begin the cautious progression through the lights, the kitten had carried on across the road. It scurried the final foot to the curb, pulled itself up and over the concrete ledge of the gutter, and disappeared into the shrubbery on the other side. I remember letting loose a sigh of relief that it made it, and then I continued on my way home.

Yet traffic lights went out all of the time in the Humanrealm.

It was serendipitous. It was not magic.

I shook my head at Finn again. "Well I'm not lying to you, so I guess you'll have to believe me when I say I haven't done anything like that."

Finn made a noise in his throat somewhere between a grumble and a snort, then stood from the bench abruptly. "Fine. Let's try it then."

When I balked and stared at him, Finn continued. "Come on. Up you get. Stand here facing me."

I rose from my seat, absently brushing the back of my skirt where I had sat on the rough bench. I took my place exactly where he pointed, facing him and about five feet away.

"Now, hold out your hands," he instructed. "No, palms up."

I did as told, my arms extended out from my body with my hands facing the sky.

"Close your eyes," Finn continued. "And try to feel the air."

"The air?" I questioned incredulously.

"Yes. All magic is an interplay of the world around us and our own bodies—our needs and wants. If you can feel the air, you can start to break down where the world ends and your body begins. That is the place where magic happens."

"Do you have magic?" I asked, even if it was deflection.

I could not see his reaction with my eyes closed but the question must have thrown him off because he hesitated before answering. "No."

"What makes you qualified to teach me this then?" I quipped. I was well aware that I was acting like a petulant child, but I was past the point of caring.

But even if I could not see the smile on his face, it was clear in his tone of voice. "Focus, Your Majesty."

I rolled my eyes behind my eyelids, and I wondered if he could see the movement. If he did, he made no indication.

Try as I might, I could not feel the air.

I could feel the skin of my palms and how they warmed as the rays of the sun glanced off them. I could feel where I was, but I could not push myself to see the other side of it—where the air ended and I began.

After a few moments, Finn's voice cut through my futile attempts. "What do you feel?"

"The sun," I responded, closing my upturned hands as if to capture the spools of golden light in my fists.

"What else?"

"That's it. I can't feel the air."

"Then you're not trying."

My eyes snapped open at that and I glared openly at Finn. "Not trying?"

"No, Your Majesty."

My annoyance was climbing to new heights, and for the millionth time in the last few days here, I realized that it stemmed out of embarrassment.

I was supposed to be a queen, and a mythical one at that. I was supposed to be powerful and magical and world-altering, according to some prophet who said as much when I was born.

In reality, I was none of those things. I was Sahle—plain old Sahle. Even if I wanted to be the Queen they all imagined, I simply was not. And I felt like every time I interacted with someone, I was letting them down.

I dropped my balled up fists to my side and looked at Finn. He stared back at me, not cowed by the anger that was visibly swirling in my eyes.

"Let's try something else," Finn finally said when it became clear that I was done talking to him.

I folded my arms across my chest and said nothing. I waited for the instructions, the next futile activity that would shame me anew.

"Close your eyes and hold up your hands like before. Good. Now, you said you can feel the sun. What does it feel like?"

I took a breath, willing myself to focus even though I wanted to scream. "It makes my palms feel warm."

"That's what your palms feel like," Finn corrected. "What

does the sunlight feel like?"

He was right. That was again what my own self felt like. But like the air before, I could not feel what the sun was like—only its effects on me.

"I don't know," I finally replied, my eyes still shut.

"OK, but you can feel the sun's effects on your palms. Can you grab the sun?"

"Grab the sun?" I repeated, confused.

"Yes," Finn confirmed, and his voice moved as he spoke. He must be walking even if I could not hear the crunch of his boots in the dust and gravel of the training ring. "Visualize the individual rays of the sun like ribbons laying in your hands. Then try to tug on the ribbons."

While I appreciated the visual, I could not see any imaginary sun ribbons. And I sure as hell could not pull them.

With an exasperated sigh, I opened my eyes and dropped my hands to my sides once more. "I can't."

"You keep saying that," Finn replied, now standing on the opposite side of me.

"Because I mean it."

"No, because you refuse to try," he said with a smile on his face.

And just like in the Council Chamber with the Lords, a wave of anger and embarrassment rose up in me. Before I knew what I was doing, I was turning, my skirt snapping in the ruby dust behind me.

"Your Majesty?" Finn called, jogging the three steps it took to catch up with me.

I stormed out of the training ring with Finn on my heels. "We're done here."

"We're done when I say we're done," Finn said quietly back to me.

I had just made it to the stone steps that led up and out of the unpaved soldiers' grounds and back to the palace. On the first step, I spun to face Finn. He was standing on the ground and with me boosted up, we were the same height, our faces barely a foot from each other.

My chest heaved and, spitting like a cat, I said, "No, we're done when I say we're done. Or is that not true? People keep telling me I'm the Queen, yet now some random soldier can tell me what to do?"

To his credit, Finn did not seem disturbed by my anger. He looked me over from my head to my feet and then bowed formally. "Of course, Your Majesty."

I did not stay to watch him rise, silhouetted against the round huts of the soldiers' grounds as he was. I did not say anything else. I was done here.

I took the smooth stone steps two at a time, holding my skirts nearly up to my knees so as not to trip. All I wanted to do was be alone.

I had told the Council I had no magic. I had told Finn I had no magic. Yet over and over again, they asked me to prove it. It was like they wanted to make a mockery of me, to cut me open and assess the extent of how disappointing of a Queen I truly was.

And oh, was I a disappointing one.

10
abandon

AFTER MY OUTBURST IN THE TRAINING RING, I HEADED back to my chambers. I needed space to breathe and collect my thoughts. My blood was up from my interaction with Finn, that newly familiar mix of outrage and shame swirling in my veins.

But when I opened the door to my chambers, hoping for peace and solitude, there was a visitor waiting for me.

"What's wrong?" Eliza said, hopping up from her seat in one of the wingback chairs before the fireplace.

I shook my head, collapsing in another chair beside her. "Everyone has such expectations of me and all I'm doing is disappointing them."

Eliza approached, placing a hand on my hair and stroking it gently so as not to disturb the strands lifted into a high bun. "Tell me, sweetheart."

I told her about the training grounds, Finn's admonishment of my outfit, my lack of magical abilities and, of course, how I had stormed off in anger when I could not do what Finn asked.

At this, Eliza chuckled. "You always have been a tad petulant."

"Thanks…" I said though it came out as more of a question. Was she trying to make me feel worse?

"I just mean that it does not surprise me. Even as a small child, you wanted to be good at everything you did. If you were not, you refused to do whatever task—whether that be drawing a picture or riding a bike.

"You have never liked to feel like you are unworthy. I can imagine that's what you're feeling now, and have been feeling since we arrived. But it will pass. Sahl, you've been here for such a short time. As you become more acquainted with the Alterealm and more at home with your role, this sense of failure will go away."

Tears brimmed at my eyes unbidden, and I blinked rapidly. I was tired of crying. Eliza saw how my eyes filled up, though. Eliza saw everything.

She took my hand in her own and tugged on it gently. "Come."

I rose on her insistence and she guided me over to the bed where we perched on the edge, side by side. She looped her arm around my shoulder, pulling me to her. I felt a little kiss on my temple.

"I know this is hard now, but I promise you that everything will be alright, Sahl. You are exactly what Izwe needs."

"What if I'm not?" I sniffled.

"Now you're just feeling sorry for yourself." Eliza was quiet for a moment before continuing. "But, Sahle, I do have to tell you something…"

Something in her tone had me drawing back to look her in the eye. "What is it?"

She took a deep breath and shut her eyes. Then she determinedly fixed those blue orbs on me. "Roland and I are leaving."

I blinked at her, unsure of what she meant. "Leaving? Leaving where?"

"Leaving the palace, sweetheart. We both feel it's best that we stay at our country home for a bit. It will give you some time to settle into the palace, meet new friends, focus on your task."

"You two want to leave?" I asked incredulously. I knew Eliza. She had been a mother to me for twenty years, and I could not imagine under any circumstance that she would abandon me in a time of need.

Had I truly never known her? I knew I had. I might not have known the real details of her past, or mine, but I knew the person underneath. I knew her kindhearted soul, how she had held my little hands as a child and whispered comforting words to me when I had nightmares.

You could not fake caring like she cared, and so I knew there was more behind this. Eliza would never leave me, floundering as I was, unless she was being forced.

I saw it in her eyes now as she looked away. She did not know how to answer my question. Her throat bobbed as she swallowed heavily.

"That's ridiculous," I said, my voice low and angry. "You're not leaving because it's what you and Roland want. Who told you two to go?"

"Sahle, it's our choice," Eliza said quietly, still not meeting my eye.

"Bullshit!"

As if my anger shocked Eliza out of her avoidance, she turned to me and took my hands in hers. "Listen to me. This is what has to happen. As you heard in the Council Chamber the other day, there is a discussion around the idea that Roland and I have too much influence. We raised you. We're parents to you. Certain people—" she looked at me knowingly, "—are concerned that we will try to rule through you, that your relationship with us will make it so that our desires become your desires.

"They are not entirely wrong, Sahle. We are close to you, and anyone close to you becomes influential to you. Roland and I must step back to show them that we are allowing you to be your own person now."

"Did they order you to go?" I asked, still caught in my outrage that anyone would order Eliza and Roland to leave me. Did they not understand that these two were the only people I had here?

Eliza shook her head. "No. No one ordered us. It was a suggestion. Roland and I thought it over and decided that while neither of us want to be away from you, it may be for the best while you get your feet under you."

Even through her reasoning, I struggled to process what was going on. I still did not believe the Alterealm was real. That I existed somewhere else from the world I had always known. That my dearest friends were nearly a figment of my imagination. That everything I knew about life and society and culture was suddenly useless, alien that I was in this new place. And now, Eliza and Roland, the only people who provided continuity between these two lives, were also going to disappear.

It was too much.

I stood from the bed. "So that's it? You're just going? You're leaving me here, alone?"

I could see the pain swirling in Eliza's eyes. This was hard for her. "Sweetheart, it's temporary, and we won't be far. The estate is only an hour's ride away so we can visit often."

I scoffed. "Sure."

"We will visit often, Sahl. Roland may need to sit in on the Council for you some days, so he'll be here. I will come and see you as much as I can. We love you, and we won't abandon you."

"Fine" I said, turning to the wall of windows so that Eliza could not see the devastation on my face.

I heard Eliza's sigh of resignation behind me. She knew there was no reasoning with me on this. I would be upset, and they would still leave, and the only thing to do was accept that.

"We're leaving tomorrow evening. Before that, I've organized a tea with several of the court Ladies, some old friends of mine, some influential people that I felt you should meet. Please join us. It will be good for you to meet others here."

"What if I don't want to meet anyone?" I snapped.

"Then you can sit here alone day after day and wallow in your loneliness," Eliza said, bluntly. I gritted my teeth. "Or you can take this one step at a time. You can begin to truly meet your court and form some relationships. The kind of life you have here…it's up to you, Sahle, to create it. And you have to start somewhere."

Rather than respond, I tracked a group of what looked like flamingoes flitting past the windows. I watched them twist mid-air before shutting my eyes.

Flamingoes.

I did not have the mental space to contemplate the absurdity of living in a world where flamingoes flew past as readily as pigeons once did in the Humanrealm. It was so strange, so foreign—just another moment where I realized once more that this was not my home.

I shook my head as if it would physically clear the thought. And then I refocused on Eliza. I was angry she and Roland were leaving but I also knew she was right. I had to meet people here—both for my own sense of community and the need to know the court if I were to rule it. I took a breath, trying to think past my hurt before responding.

"When is this tea?"

"Tomorrow at three o'clock, if that suits you."

"I thought I was merely a guest," I responded through tight lips.

Eliza approached me then, turned me by the shoulders, and put her hands on either side of my face. "You are never merely a guest. You are the Queen, Sahl, and tea will be served when you arrive."

Eliza left soon after. She and I were not sure what to say to each other after our conversation about her impending departure. I could not shake the feeling of being abandoned, and I knew she could not shake the guilt.

I was not making it easy.

It was still early in the day—lunch had not yet been brought to me—but I did not know where to go or what to do now. I should go to the library and keep reading about the history of Izwe, but the thought of having to face curious courtiers as I made my way there turned my stomach.

Everyone kept telling me I was Queen, and if that were truly the case then perhaps I could have the library brought to me if I could not bring myself to go to it. I wrote a note to Ruth, asking for a few of the books I was studying to be sent to my rooms, and sent it with one of the Vikela posted outside my door. Then I waited.

An hour later, I answered a tentative knock to find a wizened librarian holding a stack of four books: two on the geo-political history of Izwe, one on its economy, and another on its natural resources. I thanked the librarian, taking the books from his hands, before retreating back to my chair.

Mara eventually brought a plate of food, and I looked up from my books long enough to thank her. Then I turned my attention back to the stack, turning page after page as I absorbed as much factual knowledge as I could.

Sometime later in the day, another knock at the door sounded and Kaiht answered it. She handed me a sealed note from the messenger.

Your Majesty Queen Sahle,
It is a great honor to be appointed your teacher in court etiquette. I hear through Lady Eliza that we will both be attending tea tomorrow. Perhaps we can speak then and come to an agreed upon meeting time? I look forward to making your acquaintance.
Yours,
Lady Lisideria

I sighed, refolding the note after reading it a second time. There was no avoiding this, though. I needed a better understanding of court etiquette as surely as I needed to know the history and politics of this place. I had hope that once I knew enough, everything would grow less foreign.

Still, I was not excited about the prospects of more lessons, more intensified moments of being shown exactly how little I understood. I knew it was for the best, that each moment in training would reap benefits when I was next with the court or the Council. But it was unpleasant, and I shuddered just thinking of the Council Chamber.

I tossed the note in the fire, not bothering to write back to Lisideria. I watched the paper crinkle in the intense heat before alighting in a pattern of black char and red embers.

Tomorrow would come soon enough.

WHEN I AWOKE THE NEXT MORNING, STILL TRYING TO push the news of Eliza and Roland's departure from my mind, the training gear Finn had given me was neatly folded on one of the wingback chairs in my chambers. I stared at the brown pile as I sipped my tea.

I was not surprised.

I had forgotten all about the clothes in my abrupt departure from the training grounds, but Finn had not. And now they were here, crowned with a folded note. The word "Majesty" was scrawled across the front in a neat hand.

I picked up the note and scanned the brief words. *Round 2. 9am…if it pleases Your Majesty.*

I rolled my eyes but could not stop the slightest smile from curling on my lips. I had to give it to this Finn character. I had been anything but pleasant yesterday, yet here he was trying again. Perhaps he was a bit of a masochist, eagerly waiting for me to bristle at him again.

Or perhaps he just liked to push. Still, I could see the humor in his pushing, and it was a welcome change to the hidden derision most of the court treated me with.

Glancing at the clock on the wall, I hurriedly finished my rooibos and a bread roll smeared with butter and some sort of yellow berry jam. I was going to be late if I did not hurry. And we could not have that.

Thirty minutes later, I was standing in the training ring. The wind softly mussed the coiled strands of my hair, loose and gravity-defying as it was. I tugged at the high neck of the training tunic. It was made out of some type of linen or, I thought derisively, canvas. It was thick and sturdy and could possibly be its own armor. It was the brown that all soldiers and servants wore, and for some reason I found that funny.

The Queen, hair unbound and dressed in soldier-brown. If only the Lords could see me right now. I was not sure this is what they had in mind when they sent me to train with Commander Finn…

The tunic was formed in a type of wrap that had a three-button closure on the top left of the chest. Both the tunic and the matching pants were a tad too loose to be called form fitting, showing the shape of my body while allowing free movement.

I widened my stance experimentally and was pleasantly surprised that the pants did not pull, despite their stiff material. I would much prefer a pair of spandex yoga pants if I had to do a workout but, alas, they did not seem to have spandex in the Alterealm.

"What are you smirking at?" Finn called, as he approached with two swords. I noticed a second later that neither sword was made of steel, but rather wood.

That was probably best, if I were being honest.

"Just thinking about spandex yoga pants, and wishing I had a pair of those right now."

"What are spandex yoga pants?"

I laughed, despite myself. I should have been embarrassed to face Finn after my temper tantrum yesterday, but I was not.

He had merely nodded at me this morning and asked me if I were ready to try again. He listened to my confirmation and that was that—no mention of my storming off.

I was grateful.

"In the Humanrealm, they had this material that was stretchy and tight. It felt like a second set of skin so that when you moved, the material stretched and moved with you and you didn't even know it was there. Most people used it for sports, some people for lounging around."

"Hmm," Finn mused, fixing his gaze on the brown pants I was wearing now. "Are those not comfortable?"

"They're fine. Maybe it's just that I haven't worn pants in a while."

That made him laugh, and his face broke into a wide smile that showed straight, strong teeth. "I would imagine there are few pants in the royal wardrobe."

"None that I've seen so far."

"Well then, let's put these to good use." He handed me one of the wooden swords. "Today we're going to try something different. We're going to get you started on physical combat training."

I was surprised by the weight of the sword, balanced as it was in my hand. Even though it was only wood, it had a definite heft to it, and I knew my arms would be shaking by the time we were through today.

"Heavy?" Finn asked, observing my focus on the sword.

"Yes."

He shifted his own weapon from one hand to the other with such ease it could have been made of paper. "That's the point of these training swords. They weigh more than steel swords so that you develop your muscles."

"And so you can get used to the feel of it without killing yourself?" I guessed.

That earned me another smile from Finn. "Precisely. And that, in a nutshell, is your first swordsmanship lesson: getting your body acquainted with the feel.

"Hold the sword in your right hand and bring your feet hip-width apart," Finn directed. I followed each of his prompts, my leather lace-up training boots anchoring me into the packed red earth of the training ground.

"Good. Now, lift your right leg."

I looked at him a moment to see what he meant by that and he demonstrated, holding his right foot out wide and clear of the ground by a few inches. "It doesn't have to be high. I just want you to see how the weight of the sword affects your balance. And how your body compensates."

I followed his lead and lifted my right leg so that my foot dangled two inches from the ground. I found a focal point—a discolored bit of plaster on one of the huts just outside the training ring—and I focused on that as I took a breath in and out.

"You have good balance," Finn said, nodding his head in acknowledgement. "That will be a benefit to you. Is it as good on the other side?"

I shifted my weight so that I was balancing on the left this time.

"Great. Now lift the sword but stay on that one leg."

I did, moving a bit too quick as my confidence got the best of me. I felt my balance begin to teeter before I was actually moving, and I had to throw my weight back into both feet before I tumbled over.

My tottering did not seem to phase Finn, though. He pointed towards my left foot with his dummy weapon. "See, that's what happens when you hit the limits of your balance with the sword. Let's reset and try it again."

We did the exercise a few more times, adjusting for the position of my legs and arms, which side held the sword and how far I could reach and maneuver before I lost control.

"Very good, Your Majesty. Your balance will be helpful as you keep learning. Now, let's put the swords away and do some push-ups."

"Excuse me?" I said, not expecting that to be the next thing that came out of Finn's mouth.

He smiled at my shocked face as he took the wooden sword from my hand. He discarded both dummy weapons at the edge of the training circle before continuing. "I wanted to see your balance but it's clear to me just from these initial exercises that one of our main tasks will be general fitness. You have limited arm strength, and we need to build it if you'll ever wield a sword well."

I glanced at my arms, cloaked as they were in the brown fabric. "How can you tell I don't have arm strength?"

"If your arms were stronger, you would have naturally held the sword higher in those exercises. You didn't. Ergo, that's where we will start every training session."

"With a workout."

"Exactly." Finn's smile had not lessened, and I suspected he was enjoying watching my discomfort. "Let's start with ten push-ups and see how you do."

"Here?" I asked, looking at the fine red dust and gravel under my boots.

He shrugged. "Why not?"

Sighing, I dropped to all fours. The gravel bit into my knees and palms where the weight of my body pressed into the ground. I looked up at Finn once more, and then rose in a plank.

One push-up.

Two push-ups.

Three…push-ups.

On the fourth, my arms began shaking. And by the sixth, I could barely lift my body back up. I let my body collapse into the dust on what should have been my seventh, and I could almost feel the smirk on Finn's face even though all I could see, from where I laid on the ground, were his boots.

"That's what I thought," Finn said.

I craned my neck to look up at him. "It's been a while."

"I'd say so. That settles it. Each training day—whether we're doing magic or swords—will start with a two-mile run and fifteen push-ups."

"Fifteen!" I exclaimed. I could barely do seven, and he had just seen the proof of that himself.

"Yes, fifteen. It's something to strive for." He chuckled at the look of outrage that I was sure danced across my face. "Cheer up, Majesty. It'll be fun."

"Doubtful," I muttered.

"Sorry, I didn't catch that," Finn replied, cupping his hand behind his ear in mocking pantomime.

"Nothing," I said into the gravel, stirring up little clouds of dust with each exhale.

But Finn just smiled. "Great. Let's go."

We ran for what felt like forever. It had been several years since I had last gone for a jog. In high school, I used to enjoy running and I had been an active participant on our school's track and field team. I was never a prize-winner; I was always too slow to really be competitive. Yet, I did enjoy the rush and the challenge of running.

I focused on pulling back that feeling of enjoyment as I chased after Finn through the tall purple-blossomed trees that ringed the palace grounds. I knew I could run, but it was a struggle to keep up with his pace. Still, I tried, and my breath grew more and more labored with each step I took. When my throat and lungs burned and I could go no further, I stopped.

"Keep running," Finn called from several paces ahead of me.

"I can't." The words came out rushed, sandwiched between two gasps. I dropped my hands to my knees and hunched over, my head hanging loose from my shoulders.

Finn turned and came back towards me, jogging in place as he looked at my crumpled form. "Pull yourself together and run."

I glared up at him. "I…can't," I repeated.

He was not even winded as he replied, "'I can't.' Those seem to be your favorite words."

My mouth hung open as I looked at him, and then my eyes narrowed. "How dare you?"

And then he laughed. He laughed.

I saw red, deep and rich as the ground beneath my feet. Once again my embarrassment and shame flamed to life under my skin. Before I thought about what I was doing, I was walking away.

Winded as I was, I was not moving very fast but the adrenaline of my outrage urged me forward. I huffed as I marched away from Finn.

Just like yesterday, Finn came after me. This time, though, he grabbed my arm and pulled me to a stop.

I looked down at his hand where it rested just above my elbow and then raised my gaze to his. "Take your hand off of me."

He did not move the hand. If anything, his grip grew tighter. "You're not leaving."

"I'm done here."

"No, you're not."

"How many times do we have to have the same discussion? I am Queen, and you do not tell me what to do."

"Listen up, Queen. You're right. I can't command you, but I can urge you to stay. I've heard about you at court, with the Lords, with the courtiers. I've seen you out here in the training grounds. You're in the habit of running when things get challenging. You run when you're uncomfortable, when you're out of your element, when you get embarrassed by your ignorance."

I bristled at the word ignorance, but I knew it stung because it was true. I could have flares of anger and temporary shows of bravado but, at heart, I was a runner. I always had been. And he was perceptive enough to notice it after such a short time knowing me.

Finn continued. "Let me give a word of advice, Your Majesty. You can't run from the Alterealm and your commitment here.

I'm not saying it has been easy for you, or that it will get easy any time soon, but you owe it to yourself and to your people to give it more than a temper tantrum when you get uncomfortable. You can't throw up your hands as a leader."

I stared at him, suddenly feeling deflated. My anger was gone like a candle hastily snubbed out and, in its place, I felt disappointment in myself.

Finn seemed to see that change in me, too, for his tone became kinder then. He let go of my arm. "The thing to do is to fight that impulse, Your Majesty. Each time you do, and each time you're able to face the hardship head on, will make the next time easier."

When I did not say anything, he asked, "Do you trust me?"

I scoffed at that, still holding his gaze. "I barely know you."

"That's true," Finn replied with a nonchalant shrug. "But from what you know of me, do you trust me?"

I thought about his notes to me, his willingness to call me out, his uncanny read of my character, even the fact that I felt comfortable enough around him to act like a brat. And I was surprised to find that I did trust him, or at least the part of him I was coming to know.

He alone had treated me like a fully-fledged adult here, even with his needling and poking. Annoying as it was, there was a part of me that was coming to appreciate not being handled with kid gloves.

I nodded. Then I shrugged. "I guess."

"I'll take that." Finn smiled again and brushed his blonde hair back from his forehead. The sun hit the edges of it and made him look like an angel with a luminescent halo.

He was anything but an angel.

"Let's keep running," he said. He turned on his heel and jogged off, and I noticed that he did not look back over his shoulder to see if I was following or not. He was leaving that choice up to me—to stay or to leave, to power through my discomfort or to give in to my impulse to bolt.

But I would not do it today. As much as my legs ached and my lungs burned, I started jogging again. Even if it took me all day to go the two miles, I would finish it.

Finn was right, I begrudgingly admitted. I was and had always been accustomed to fleeing when things got tough or awkward, but I could not rely on that any longer. Not here, not with whatever I was supposed to be doing as Queen. I needed to face what made me uncomfortable.

Jogging after Finn, his broad back growing more and more distant, I had to admit that I held a respect for the Commander. He was too uppity, but maybe his brusqueness was exactly what I needed.

I glared at his back as he sped up, evidently hearing me behind him. Ugh.

I amended my thoughts: a grudging respect.

We ran for God knows how long and when my legs were jelly and I felt like I would never move them again, Finn let me stop, drink some water, and head back to my chambers. We would meet again the next morning—and every morning after that, he reminded me.

I wandered back up to the palace, let Kaiht and Mara help peel me out of my sopping training clothes, and soaked in a bath for the better part of an hour. I paged through a few of the books Ruth had sent from the library and, before I knew it, it was time to join Eliza and her friends for tea.

I had been dreading this ever since Eliza invited me, but I put on a brave face as I dressed in the gown Kaiht recommended for the occasion. The fine fabric was cream and the protea flowers I had seen on my initial arrival to the Alterealm were embroidered across the bodice and the front of the skirt. They trailed across the fabric in a pattern that made me look as if I were draped in vines.

Kaiht placed a low, unremarkable headpiece on my head—more a heavy headband than a crown. It was made of silver or white gold alone and had no stones. I smiled at it, and its casual implication. It was something that still signaled I was Queen without being ostentatious or flashy.

Apparently tea was the most relaxed occasion in the palace—apart from training.

With a deep breath to steel my nerves, I left Kaiht and Mara in my rooms and headed for Eliza's chambers. I knew where they were, but I had not been to them yet. My Vikela trailed me, my ever-present shadows, as I made my way down the surprisingly busy hallways that lead to various courtiers' chambers.

When I finally made it through the crowd, I realized that most of the hubbub was about me. A guard posted at Eliza's door was admitting ladies to the tea off of a short list of attendees. Some tried to reason with the guard, explaining that Eliza must have just forgotten them when she put it together or that there must be some other sort of miscommunication for why their name did not grace the invitation list.

I smiled at the attempt, knowing that Eliza had made this a small group on purpose so that I could be introduced to members of the court slowly and comfortably.

The woman trying to talk her way past the guard shuffled out of the way as I approached. Of course, the guard did not need to look up my name on his list. Everyone knew who I was, and that I had free rein here even if this tea had not been set up in my honor.

The women quieted suddenly, their protests dying on their lips. And as one they bowed and parted, forming a pathway from me to the doorway. "Your Majesty," several courtiers murmured. I gave them tentative smiles as I passed by and entered Eliza's rooms.

"Ah, Queen Sahle!" Eliza called as soon as the guards shut the door behind me. She was standing beside large windows nearly equal in size to the ones that adorned my chambers, and she straightened a platter of tea sandwiches before bustling to my side in a flurry of vibrant purple skirts. They were nearly identical in shade to the flowering trees outside.

She kissed my cheek, and I closed my eyes at the too familiar scent of lavender that she always wore. "I'm so happy you came."

I nodded at her as she pulled back. "Thank you for inviting me."

She looked at me—really looked at me then—and raised her eyebrows at my formality. "Please, Sahl, don't be angry with me."

I glanced away, unsettled as always by how well Eliza knew my mind. She had been my mother for so long, she could anticipate my moods and interpret a single thought by the tilt of my head or the tone of my voice.

Now, I was sure she could feel the tension in the air between us, as I could. We were awkward with hurt feelings and things left unsaid.

I drew my shoulders back. I understood why she was leaving. I truly did, but I could not shake the feeling of abandonment. She was my mother in every way that mattered, and she was just going to leave me to the wolves in this palace?

I tampered down that line of thought quickly. This was no place for it to grow.

"I'm not angry," I said quietly. I pasted a small smile across my lips as I turned my gaze from her to sweep the room.

"I know you, and I know you're upset even if you're doing your best not to be."

"If you know I'm doing my best, then let's leave it at that," I bit back, a slight edge rising in my voice despite my best efforts to be calm. Several of the courtiers had begun to pay attention to the tightness between us, and the last thing I wanted to do was have this discussion in front of an audience—not that this discussion would even be productive.

Eliza and Roland were leaving without me. It had been decided and nothing I did or said now would change that.

Eliza watched me a second longer, and I could see hurt and love churning together in her eyes. Then she took my hand, threaded my arm through hers so we were hooked together at the elbow, and pulled me in the direction of the courtiers.

Four women had already arrived, dressed in finery that complemented the colors Eliza and I were adorned in. They had been seated on little wooden chairs and woven cushions scattered around the sun-bathed room, but they had risen to their feet upon seeing me.

Now they sunk into bows as Eliza steered me towards them. Eliza made quick work of introducing them, one by one.

"Mary of House Kgathla," Eliza motioned to the eldest of the women, her gray hair swept back and pinned simply, up and away from her ears.

"Sybil of House Ndlovu." Sybil was approximately Eliza's age and shared her coloring. She smiled with a warmth that immediately endeared me to her.

"Genevieve of House Inyathi," Eliza announced as the woman, perhaps just a few years older than me but with startling red hair, bowed in acknowledgement.

"Lisideria of House Nkwe," Eliza said at last, motioning to the last woman there with purpose—my soon-to-be etiquette tutor. I noted that she was not in the same House as her father, Grimly of Kubuga, and assumed her husband must be from Nkwe.

Lisideria nodded at me, her dark eyes shining intelligently. She was short and slim in a way that made her look childlike. Although she was several inches shorter than I, the wrinkles at the corners of her eyes marked her as close to middle age.

"It's a pleasure to meet you all," I said, even though meeting courtiers was the last thing I wanted to do.

"The pleasure is ours, Majesty," Mary replied. "Your entire court has been looking forward to your return for a long time."

I smiled at that, unsure of how to respond. I certainly had not been looking forward to my return and, if I could, I would gladly go back to the Humanrealm and forget all about this place and my supposed duty here.

"May I offer you some tea, Your Majesty?" Eliza said, jumping in before the silence could stretch into awkwardness.

"Erm, yes. Thank you, Eliza."

Eliza untangled herself from me and went to check on the refreshments while I stared at the four women before me. Grasping at the only thing I knew of them, I turned to Lisideria.

"Thank you for your note yesterday," I said, as I nervously threaded my hands together in front of me. "I look forward to our lessons."

Lisideria bobbed in a curtsy. "It is my honor to serve you, Your Majesty. I can imagine how out of place you must feel, not knowing the customs and etiquette of Izwe. I hope I can help put your mind at ease by sharing my knowledge."

"Me, too," I replied with a genuine smile. "Did I hear that Lord Grimly is your father?"

"Yes, Majesty."

"Hmm," I replied vaguely, not yet sure if I felt that was a fortunate fact or not. Then I turned to the others. "Please, feel free to sit."

"After you, Majesty," Mary replied, motioning with her hand towards the low chairs and pile of cushions near to the windows. Like in my own chambers, reaching green plants were situated periodically around the windowed wall and I immediately thought of the jungle—the tones of wood and green playing against the buttery light that filtered through the glass. I sat on a plush beige cushion, thinking the older women might like the easier-to-navigate chairs.

"Oh please, Queen Sahle," Lisideria exclaimed. "Surely you'd like a proper seat?"

I looked up to see four shocked faces staring down at me. But I simply shook my head, smoothed my skirts out around me on the floor and smiled. "I'm fine here, but thank you. Please go ahead."

The four women traded glances and then gingerly sat on the cushions beside me. Not one picked the taller chairs, and again I wondered what etiquette I was missing.

No time like the present to find out, I figured.

"Lisideria," I called, turning to the small woman now on my left. "From an etiquette perspective, is there a reason why you four should not sit in the chairs?"

They darted a look at each other quickly, and so I added. "Truly, I don't know. I'm curious."

Lisideria inclined her head. "In Izwe, it is tradition for the monarch to take the highest seat. That is why your chair is mounted on a dais in the Council Chamber, and why your throne is elevated in the main hall.

"The same would apply here. It would be…customary for the monarch to take the tallest chair while the rest of us sat on lower chairs or the floor cushions."

"Ah," I said, leaning back and placing my weight in my palms. "I understand, although perhaps some traditions are a little silly?"

Again, the Ladies looked at each other. Mary's lips pinched together in discomfort.

"It is how things are done here, Your Majesty," Lisideria said simply and with a sort of finality that did not welcome questions.

Before I could respond, Eliza was back with tea. Or rather, Eliza was back accompanied by a servant bearing a platter with dishes of tea. Steam rose from the rooibos as Eliza passed a dish to me first, and then to each of the women in order of how she had introduced them. I wondered if there was a hierarchy there, too.

I would have to ask Lisideria about that tomorrow, for I feared Mary might have a stroke if I questioned her elevated rank next.

"Thank you, Eliza," I said as I gripped the dish. "And thank you for serving," I said to the servant.

Eliza had been tittering away with Sybil. Lisideria and Genevieve had been noting something about the wood grain in the polished floor. Suddenly, the soft chatter stopped.

I looked to the servant who stared back stunned, then bobbed and departed swiftly. I turned to Eliza with a raised brow. None of the other Ladies said a word. They just stared.

Slowly, Lisideria leaned in with a stage whisper, "Before you ask, Majesty, we're all staring because it is uncommon to thank the servants. It is their job, and no thanks are required."

The other Ladies chuckled, but I glanced at Eliza. Eliza did not smile but stared at me with a look that urged me to be nice.

I thought about telling them that there was no harm in saying thank you, that perhaps it would be the thoughtful thing to do for those who fetched us tea, served us meals, helped us dress. Instead, I continued to stare at Eliza, trying to reconcile all of the small kindnesses I had seen her bestow to those considered "below" us in the Humanrealm. I could not square that thoughtful woman with the rigid one before me.

It seemed I had much to learn about the ways of Izwe, including things that were utterly preposterous.

Genevieve stirred her tea delicately and then rested the spoon on the edge of the saucer beneath the cup. "Her Majesty is a bleeding heart!" The others tittered daintily, and Genevieve continued, "It is very admirable, but it is unnecessary, Queen Sahle. The servants were born and bred for their duty. They live to serve and the only thanks they need is our continued maintenance of them—we clothe them, feed them, tend to them when they are ill. That is how we show thanks. Anything else, any extra would be…superfluous."

"Quite right," Mary agreed.

"Superfluous?" I ran the word over my tongue, as if testing it for faults—and there were many, used in this context.

But Eliza, knowing me as she did, cut in before I could say more. "Lady Lisideria, I am sure you are excited to work with her Majesty on all of the finer points of court life. Did the two of you decide on a time to meet?"

"We did not, Lady Eliza," Lisideria responded. "Though I'm sure I can accommodate anytime that suits Her Majesty."

"Might I suggest that you two meet daily, over lunch perhaps?" Eliza added.

I narrowed my eyes at her.

"If it pleases Her Majesty, of course."

All eyes turned to me.

Just in the brief conversation we had had over our barely cooled tea, I wanted to carve my eardrums out with the spoon laying untouched in my tea saucer. I could hardly imagine what daily lunches with Lisideria would be like. I might accidentally spill my drink in her lap, or stab her with my fish fork. The sky was the limit, depending on whatever ridiculous ideas she spouted.

Still, I smiled and nodded. It was becoming my signature move—smile and nod, smile and nod.

"That would be lovely," I replied evenly over the lip of my tea cup.

Eliza stared at me knowingly and I stared back.

Tea carried on much the same. At one point, two more courtiers arrived, equally dressed in soft muted colors, equally as chatty, equally as horrified by the prospect of taking a chair higher than me.

Eventually, upon my insistence, Eliza sat on the highest chair but glared at me all the while. And I made sure to thank each servant who brought us tea cakes, the biscotti-like cookies the Ladies called rusks, refills of our tea or cream to mix into it.

I knew I was being difficult. I was antagonizing these women on purpose but I could not bring myself to care. Where I came from, thanking a server was normal, expected even. Anything less would be considered rude.

I might be in an entirely different realm, but it did not change my personality overnight. I still had manners—whatever they counted for here—and I would say thank you as long as I felt it was right.

Simpering courtiers be damned.

Thankfully, the Ladies began to depart as soon as the cakes and tea sandwiches had run out. Each made their excuses beautifully, bowing and remarking on how their husbands would be requesting their presence, or how their children would be needing them. I had no clue whether this was true, merely the custom of departing in Izwe, or whether they were running from me as soon as it was socially acceptable.

And honestly, I did not really care.

The last to leave were Lisideria and Sybil. I bid Lisideria goodbye as she rose lithely from her floor cushion.

"I will send word of our first lesson, Your Majesty," she said with a curtsy, and then she was gone.

I turned my attention on Sybil, who had leaned closer to Eliza now that the others had left.

"You're right, Eliza," Sybil remarked, running her gaze over me as if to read my secrets. "Her Majesty is delightful."

Eliza laughed and squeezed Sybil's hand briefly before turning to me. "Queen Sahle, I've waited so long for you to meet Sybil. She is my distant cousin, and we grew up together in House Ndlovu. She was a dear friend before Roland and I went with you to the Humanrealm."

I looked at the two women and I could see it: the ease of decades of knowing each other, a bond so concrete that twenty years apart meant nothing in the span of a lifetime. I wondered if the two of them had spent hours sitting around on cushions like these with my birth mother. I wondered if the three of them had been inseparable, much like my own friends, Mer, Jenna, and Cecily, had always been for me.

"Eliza is like a sister to me," Sybil added. Then, with a smile, "And, if you will allow, Your Majesty, so was your mother. That makes me your adoptive aunt in a way..."

Seeing the joy in Eliza's eyes tugged at something in me. She had a life before me. She had close friends, family, and a happy home. But when my mother and father had died, she and Roland had left everything behind to keep me safe in the Humanrealm.

I had known all of that for weeks now, but suddenly it felt real. This interaction, seeing this relationship that had been taxed and survived—all built and stretched and contracted around the shape of my being—opened my eyes.

And for the first time since I arrived at tea, I was truly glad I came. I reached out, offering my hand to Sybil. "If I am delightful, it is due entirely to Eliza's and Roland's parenting. It's a pleasure to meet a relative of…the family."

I wanted to say "of my mother" but I knew I could not. Even here, even with family friends, it would not be acceptable to call Eliza my mother. I had a mother, a celebrated one, one who made me Queen on her untimely death.

Sybil squeezed my hand gently before letting go. "I know Eliza and Roland are departing today for their estate. That must be hard for you. If you need anything when they are away, Your Majesty, please feel free to come to me."

I glanced at Eliza and the easy contentment in her eyes told me that I could trust Sybil. So I nodded. I nodded and said, "Thank you, Lady Sybil. I appreciate that."

Sybil climbed to her feet, dropping a quick curtsy to me and then to Eliza. As she walked to the door, she turned back. "Your Majesty, I can only imagine how difficult adjusting to this life must be, but I just wanted to say that you're doing a good job."

"Thank you," I replied with wide eyes, surprised to hear praise from any of the women I had shocked by thanking the servants.

"Thank you," Eliza echoed.

Then Sybil was gone and the servants returned and the discarded dishes of tea and platters of cakes and sandwiches were cleared away. When all that was left was me and Eliza, she wrapped me in another fierce hug.

"We have to go soon. Would you like to say goodbye to your father?"

I swallowed. "Of course."

She called a servant to fetch him and within minutes, Roland was there.

"Sahl," he said simply, wrapping me in a hug that felt exactly as his hugs had always felt. For a split second, I could pretend that we were back in the Humanrealm and I was just leaving for class or a quick trip to the grocery store. This hug could mean nothing more than that—nothing more than "see you later."

But this was not the Humanrealm, and this was not "see you later." This was Roland and Eliza leaving me alone in this palace with people who had no idea of the woman I had grown into, and no notion of the life I had lived for the past two decades.

"I'm sorry," Roland whispered into my bound hair, and I felt tears prickle behind my eyelids. I squeezed my eyes shut, willing the tears away.

I would not cry. I could not cry.

Eliza approached us and Roland shifted so that one arm wrapped around her and the other around me. The three of us clung to each other.

I breathed in their scents: the lavender, sunshine, and grass smell of Eliza, the musky sandalwood cologne of Roland. And although I could not say it, I willed it to the universe that I loved these two people, my parents in all the ways that mattered.

I pulled away first. "I know," I said, rubbing my eyes as if it would help keep the tears in.

"You're going to be alright, Sahl," Eliza said from Roland's side. "Work with Lisideria and Finn, and Ruth even. We'll be back soon."

"I should go," I said finally.

"OK," Eliza replied. She gave me a final kiss on the head and Roland did the same.

"We love you, Sahle," Roland whispered so quietly it was barely audible, as if saying it aloud would cause scandal across the court.

I nodded, unable to bring myself to say any more. I just needed to go, to get out of their chambers where their love and resentment choked me. I just needed to be alone. And so I left, composing my face into a neutral mask and hurrying back down the hallways to my own room.

Once again, I retreated into what was quickly becoming a sanctuary. Only when the guards had safely sealed the door behind me did I say aloud what I did not have the strength to say to Eliza and Roland in person.

"I love you, too."

Hours later, commotion from beneath my window drew my attention and I approached the glass cautiously. Eliza and Roland mounted zebras and departed from the palace, their few possessions pulled behind them in a carriage. I wondered why they had not invited me to see them off; there were certainly enough courtiers below me, waving furiously in farewell.

But then I remembered for the millionth time that my mother knew me. Her hug, her kisses, and Roland's whispered "I love you" had been their goodbyes. They knew I could not watch it in a crowd. I could not face the actual moment when my parents galloped away from me, and so they had made their farewells in private.

I shook my head as their forms retreated further and further away, and then were entirely swallowed up by the round huts of the city and silver-leafed forest that ringed it. They knew me so well.

I loved them for it. I missed them already. I wondered when they would come back, and I was angry with them for leaving.

I also understood.

This was my moment to grow into a Queen in my own right, without their influence. I just hoped I would be a Queen they could be proud of.

12

yesonto

WITHOUT ELIZA AND ROLAND IN THE PALACE, THINGS felt quieter and lonelier. I mulled over the time we had had together in the Alterealm, and I realized it was up to me to explore the world they had barely scratched in their explanations.

Weeks after my coronation, I still felt the phantom tingles of the Masters painting across my face. I could still taste the metallic tang on my tongue. I let this fixation on the ceremony pull me in the direction of the church.

It was not called a church, though. No, without knowing who to contact, I had sent a note to Ruth asking her where I would find the Masters. Her note in return read:

> *Your Majesty,*
> *I'm surprised they have not already reached out to you. As Queen, you are integral in the ceremonial aspects of our nation. If you are apt to seek them out, you can find the Masters at their place of worship and meditation. It is called the Yesonto. Ask your Vikela. They will accompany you.*
> *Ruth*

I folded the note as I finished reading it. I sounded out the word, Yesonto, letting my mind adapt to foreignness of it. Then I approached my chamber door.

"Excuse me," I said to the two guards stationed just outside. "I'd like to go to the Yesonto. Can you take me there?"

I hated the way my voice shook, the way I sounded so unsure of what I was asking. Surely the Queen would command and not ask. Surely. Yet it was not in me to demand as if my word was more important than anyone else's. I wondered if I would ever become comfortable with that idea.

"Right away, Your Majesty," one of the soldiers replied as he rose from his bow. He turned down the hallway and, with a slight backward glance to the safety of my chambers, I shut the door and followed.

I was not sure where the guards would take me, and I let them wind me down series after series of staircases. We made our way past laughing, painted courtiers who greeted me with flourishing bows, and then we were making our way out of the palace itself. Gravel crunched under my feet as we walked down a long path through verdant, lush gardens.

At the end of the path, rising out of the greenery, stood a single white-washed plaster building. It was round in shape, much like the buildings in the city outside of these walls. Rondavels, I reminded myself—that's what everyone had called these round structures. This one was taller, though, and clear windows took up a significant portion of the curving walls. I thought I could make out a faint glow from within the building, through the glass, but I was not sure. It could have easily been the midafternoon light's reflection.

"Your Majesty," the guards murmured as they opened solid wooden doors and gestured me through.

Inside, I paused to let my eyes adjust to the darkness. Candles strewn across the perimeter and gathered at the center of the structure were the only light within the rondavel.

In the dimness, I did not make out the Master who approached on silent feet. I nearly jumped when he spoke from over my shoulder. "Good afternoon, Your Majesty. You honor us with your presence."

I raised my hand to my chest in an effort to still my beating heart as I turned to face the man. "Master, I did not see you there."

As my eyes adjusted, I recognized him as one of the three Masters who conducted the coronation. His graying hair gave away his advanced age, but that was his most identifiable attribute. Something about the set of his features, his medium height, his average build was decidedly unmemorable. Unbidden, I thought he was the sort of person who could be a spy, the sort of person who could blend into a crowd.

He bowed. "Apologies, Your Majesty. I did not mean to startle you. Let me introduce myself. I am Master Edgar, the lead Master in the Yesonto of Izwe."

My poor heart had returned to a normal rhythm, and I extended my hand to the Master as if to shake his. He looked at me in question and, remembering that was a Humanrealm gesture, I dropped it quickly to my side. "It's a pleasure to meet you, Master Edgar."

Edgar inclined his head. "I have been preparing to write to you, Your Majesty, asking you to join us. Yet here you are, before my letter could be delivered. Can I help you with anything in particular?"

"No," I replied quickly, suddenly unsure of myself and my desire to come here. "I...I heard from those in the palace that I would have a role in the church...I mean, the Yesonto. I was curious about that, and thought I would stop by."

"Of course. It would be my pleasure to explain more. If it suits Your Majesty, we could take a seat near the devotion while we discuss?"

I was not sure what a devotion was, but I nodded anyway and let Edgar lead the way up the aisle that led to the central grouping of candles in the middle of the building. Long cream robes swung around his bare feet with each of his steps, and his short gray hair rose over a red capelet that covered his shoulders and upper body.

While I expected to see pews, instead wooden chairs were set up in a series of concentric circles. The circles grew smaller with fewer and fewer seats as we walked, until the cluster of candles rose up as the central point, the eye of the Yesonto's storm.

The sound of scuffling feet and hushed voices were the only noise in this sanctuary as other Masters in the same long robes moved from place to place along the perimeter of the chairs.

When I turned back to Edgar, he motioned to a place directly before the candles. "Thank you," I said, as I lowered myself into the offered seat. He took the one next to me.

"What would you like to discuss, Your Majesty?" Edgar asked as he folded his hands in his lap and studied me with a patient, curious face.

"As you know, I am new to the Alterealm and to Izwe," I began. "I'm just trying to get a grasp on my role in this place. I know I'm the Queen, don't get me wrong, but when I heard I would have responsibilities here, no one explained what they would be.

"I guess what I'm really trying to say is that I'd hate to have a certain role or responsibility but not know I had that role or responsibility, if that makes sense. If the Queen should be doing something in the Yesonto, then I'd like to know what so I can be prepared and do a good job."

Edgar nodded patiently through my rambling explanation. "Thank you for taking an interest, Your Majesty. I apologize if my lack of communication has given you cause to worry. I was merely hoping to give you time to adjust before we asked for your presence here."

"I understand," I replied. A flickering candle caught my eye, but I forced my focus back to the Master.

"From what you say, it seems to me that there are two things you are truly asking. The first is for more of an explanation of the Yesonto generally. And the second is how you fit into it."

I caught myself leaning forward slightly, happy to be understood by this man. "Yes, that's exactly right."

Edgar thumbed his chin in thought. "Very good, Your Majesty. If you'll bear with me, I'll gladly provide you with more information.

"The Yesonto of Izwe is what you might call the head church of Izwe. It sets by example the ceremonial and religious life across the kingdom. It is based on the core belief of the God and gods—"

"God and gods?" I interrupted, surprised that both could exist within the same religious system.

"Yes, Your Majesty. Manelesi, the Great One, your ancestor, was not just the first King of Izwe. He was also the God of life, the one creator, who brought magic to the Alterealm and blessed us with it in Izwe. He is God. Below him are lesser gods: the goddesses of fertility and harvest, the gods of warfare and the hunt, among others.

"God and his lesser gods are the center of our world. They influence life across the realm, and we honor them through Yesonto worship and ceremony. Notably, we acknowledge their influence on the wheel of the year and the passing of the seasons with high holidays. We celebrate the arrival of Manelesi, the fertility rites of spring, the start of the harvest season, and the descent into winter each year. We also share in a daily meditation service before the devotion," the Master said as he gestured at the assortment of candles burning before us.

"The devotion burns continuously at the heart of the Yesonto to signify our unending belief in the God and gods; the daily service takes place at sunrise each morning."

Edgar paused momentarily and, seeing I had no questions, continued with his explanation. "As for your particular role, you, as Manelesi's heir, are the living link to the Great One. Through your living line, power remains in Izwe. As such, it is traditional for the monarch to play a key part in the high holidays, as central moments in the ceremonies involve you."

I wanted to shake my head at what Edgar said. It seemed each time I spoke to someone in Izwe, the tales surrounding my birth and family grew wilder. I took a breath and tried to take Roland's advice. Suspend your disbelief, he had said. And boy, was I trying.

"And if I am not there?" I asked, thinking through the practicalities of Edgar's words rather than the larger concepts. For nearly twenty years, there had been no living link to Manelesi in this realm.

Reading my mind, Edgar smiled. "The last years have admittedly been a challenge with you in the Humanrealm. We have had to be creative to make the ceremonies work as they are supposed to, but I believe the people understood the intention behind the changes. Regardless, we are very happy to have you here once more."

"And what about the daily services?"

"The monarch is welcome to attend, though it is not required. There is no role for you, per se, since it is simply a quiet meditative hour around the devotion candles. Your mother attended some though not all mediations, for example."

I nodded at his words, turning my head once again to take in the peaceful low light within the Yesonto. The rich glow of flickering candlelight intertwined with the shadows of the chair backs, and I tried to imagine Bekha in this space, eyes closed and hands clasped. I wondered what a moment of quiet here had meant to her.

"Thank you for the explanation, Master Edgar. It is very helpful," I finally said. "I'm sorry but I don't know when any of the high holidays will happen. Will you please send word to me when I am needed? And what I will need to do?"

Edgar inclined his head once more. "Certainly, Your Majesty. The next holiday is not for some time yet, but I will be sure to give you ample warning."

"Thank you," I said again as I stood. Edgar followed suit.

"I look forward to seeing you soon, Queen Sahle. If I or any of the Masters can be of service to you, please do not hesitate to let us know."

I smiled at him as I took another look around the still room. "Will do."

I met Lady Lisideria of Nkwe for lunch one afternoon. She had sent word through my Vikela where lunch would be set up and so I followed the guards there. We made our way through the halls of the palace until we arrived at a wide hallway that was bathed in sunlight. The walls in this section of the palace were all glass and it reminded me distinctly of a conservatory made of shining crystal. Round wicker tables lined the windows, and I spied Lisideria seated midway down the hallway.

Two other small groups were seated at nearby tables, and they stood and bowed as I passed. Lisideria did the same when I reached her.

"Your Majesty, I trust you had a pleasant morning."

It had been anything but pleasant, actually—my mind seeming to forget and then remember anew that Eliza and Roland had truly left me in this vast, echoing palace. That and another day of huffing and puffing to Finn's workout.

But I smiled and nodded all the same as I took my seat. "It was lovely. Thank you."

Lisideria raised her hand to snap her fingers at a servant, and then she sat after me. "Thank you for joining me for lunch, Queen Sahle. I am most delighted to be working with you and instructing you on proper Izweian etiquette.

"I have been giving some consideration to the best way for us to begin. I sometimes provide similar etiquette lessons to new arrivals at court but, of course, your case is different—you having absolutely no experience with the Alterealm at all.

"As such, I have divided the outline of my instruction into four sections: general expectations of the Queen, Council etiquette, court etiquette, and servant etiquette. Shall we begin with the general expectations today?"

A servant arrived carrying tall glasses of what looked to be lemonade. I took a sip before replying. "Sounds good."

"Wonderful, Your Majesty! It is important to remember that you, the Queen, are the highest member at court..."

Lisideria launched into a monologue, explaining, in short, that I was above everyone in Izwe. Anything I wished for, I could have. Anyone who annoyed me, I could have killed—and she was only half joking when she said that.

My word was law, and the only thing that should guide my hand was my own conscience and, arguably, the precedence of previous monarchs. Tradition and custom were very important in Izwe, Lisideria explained, and the monarch typically had an eye to what had been done in the past in order to inform his or her decisions in the present.

Given that my knowledge of past Izweian history was limited, I wondered how that would work but I declined to share this thought with Lisideria. I smiled and I nodded.

Servants eventually brought platters of fish and rice. A tray of salad arrived, as well. We ate as Lisideria prattled on and I asked clarifying questions every few minutes, just to show I was listening.

"You mentioned that I am supposed to sit in the most elevated chair. What if the chair options are all equal?" To which Lisideria responded that it was acceptable for the Queen to be on equal seating, like now, as long as no one sat in a higher seat.

"I'm meant to always have some sort of headdress. Does it need to be a crown or would a hat also do?" To which Lisideria responded that a hat would only be acceptable in extreme situations when no crown, headband, or tiara was available.

I questioned her about my training with Finn, particularly the soldier-browns I wore in place of my gown and my lack of headdress. She pursed her lips at that. "I shudder to think what the Council was thinking, asking you to undertake such barbaric training with a soldier!"

The last word was whispered, as if it were scandalous. I blinked, forcing myself to not roll my eyes.

"Perhaps they fear external threats to my life and wish for me to be able to defend myself?" I replied around the thin tines of my fork in what I was sure was a very undignified manner.

Lisideria scoffed, eyes focused on her plate as she spooned more greens to it from the larger tray. "That is what the Vikela are for."

I shrugged as I took another bite of lemony fish. I did not particularly relish the training and the sore muscles it caused, but I was growing to enjoy my time with the Commander. He was cheeky and, for the few hours I was at training each day, I could almost forget that I was here in the Alterealm as its Queen.

Lisideria explained that I should never be in pants.

I should regularly have new dresses ordered and fitted so that I could stay up with the latest fashions.

I should bathe daily with scented oils.

My hair should never be loose but pinned up.

I should always have an escort or guard with me. I declined to tell her that I often went to the training grounds on my own.

I should host regular dinners for the courtiers with entertainment so as to keep the court lively.

I should take care to speak to different courtiers so as to not show too much favor to some. I declined to tell her that I did not speak to any besides the Council, when necessary, and Eliza and Roland.

I should "keep only to myself," as she put it, by which I took it to mean I should not be dating…or do anything that went along with dating. I definitely declined to tell her that, if she was hinting at my virginity, that ship had sailed some years ago. It seemed the Alterealm was more conservative than the Humanrealm, and suddenly all of Eliza and Roland's rather prudish lessons growing up made more sense. And because of their modesty, I had always kept whatever dating I did very quiet.

Finally, as the servants removed our empty plates from the table, Lisideria noted with a very careful air of casualness that I should pick Ladies-in-Waiting. I smiled into my glass of lemonade, thankful for my ability to be able to read between the lines.

I wondered if Grimly had set this up. Perhaps he suggested her for the role of etiquette instructor simply so that she became useful to me. And then, when she mentioned the idea of court Ladies, she would naturally be up for consideration—indispensable as she was.

"I have no need of Ladies," I replied evenly.

"With all due respect, Your Majesty, it is tradition for the Queen to select women from the Houses to serve you. It is a great honor for them, and it would allow you to get to know the courtiers better, as well as our ways."

I fixed her with a patient look. "I understand. As I said, I have no need of Ladies. Kaiht and Mara serve me quite adequately now. But I'll take it under consideration for later."

Lisideria did well to keep her emotions in check. I could see that she wanted to try to bring me around to her line of thought. She bit her tongue instead.

She was good at following the guidelines she had laid out: my desires were law here.

"Lady Lisideria," I said as I stood abruptly. "I thank you for your time today, and your knowledge, but I should be going."

Lisideria hurried to stand, as well, bobbing in a curtsy. "Of course, Your Majesty. It is my honor."

"Same place tomorrow?" I asked her as I folded my napkin and placed it on the chair.

"Yes, Majesty, if it pleases you."

"It does," I said with a smile. It was only a half-lie. I surveyed the glass room once again, taking in the sunlight, the small bistro tables with their wicker chairs. The setting did please me even if the conversation did not.

"Have a nice day," I said in farewell. My guards melted in from the sides of the room, seeming to appear out of thin air with each step I took from the table.

As much as I was amused and annoyed by Lisideria's etiquette lessons—and scheming—I was also grateful for them. I did not plan to follow half of the rules she laid out, but it did help to know what the expectations were of me. At least I would know how I was offending the courtiers and servants when I did something they perceived to be wrong.

I chuckled to myself as I made my way to the cool palace underbelly that was the library. None of Lisideria's rules could force me to bathe when I did not want to or put certain oils in my hair. I was still my own person, even if I was Queen. They— the courtiers—and I had to remember that.

Still, a coolness was settling over me. It was a feeling of understanding, of certainty finally taking root. Thus far in the Alterealm, I had been avoiding the Lords and Ladies, avoiding really anyone who was not Eliza and Roland.

Now, Eliza and Roland were gone. And as much as I found solace in my meals alone in my chambers, the contented chatter of Mara and Kaiht in the background, I knew Lisideria was right. I had to try to at least engage the courtiers.

Passing through the palace as I was now, many were about. Even in the weeks since my return, the courtiers never tired of staring at me. I was the new, shiny toy, just retrieved from the Humanrealm. I was a mystery, something to be puzzled out.

But they had also quickly learned that I was not particularly effervescent. I did not return their smiles or their bowed heads. I did not approach them to laugh and chitchat over glasses of wine. I looked right through them as if they, too, were paintings on the palace walls.

Today, though, I nodded. I made eye contact. I even uttered a few "Good afternoons" to some kind-looking courtiers. They all stared back at me shocked, and I shrugged internally.

I guessed that it would take longer than a day for them to come to trust me.

Reaching the library doors was like making it to safe shores, a sanctuary for the refugee soul within me. I hurried through the timber door frame and let out a deep breath I did not know I was holding in.

If nothing else, this column-lined library was a place of safety.

"Majesty," a voice called to me immediately.

I turned to find Ruth standing a few yards away, two books in her hands. "Ruth."

"Lovely to see you, Queen Sahle. I was just about to put out a few more books that I thought you might enjoy seeing."

I smiled, the expression coming naturally to my cheeks. Ruth always seemed to anticipate exactly what I needed. "Thank you. Are those the books? I can take them."

"No, no. I'll walk with you." She gestured, urging me ahead.

I set off with her at my heels. "How has your day been, Ruth?"

"Very much the same as always, Majesty. And yours?"

"Very much the same as always, except that I began taking etiquette lessons with Lady Lisideria over lunch."

"Hmph," Ruth intoned, more a sound than a word. "Lord Grimly's girl."

"I don't know if I would call her a girl, but yes."

"I remember her as a nuisance child, years ago, running through the library and knocking down stacks of books. To me, she will always be a girl."

I laughed at that image—the prim Lisideria being a wild child who easily defied the rules she seemed so bound by now. "I think she's very much changed. Now she lectures me on what is and is not proper."

"Hmph," was again Ruth's only response.

We reached my usual seat two floors down and Ruth deposited the books on the table. I scanned the covers quickly and then looked up at the librarian with one raised eyebrow.

"Magical history?"

"Of course, Your Majesty."

"Why of course?"

Ruth blinked at me as if I had lost my mind. "You have made good progress on your historical and social studies. Yet I know that you are also expected to realize your magical abilities. You have not yet."

"I have no magic," I replied automatically.

"You must," Ruth said simply, like she was reminding me that the sun rose and set each day or that the moon controlled the ocean's tides. It was not an opinion. It was a fact.

"People keep telling me that, but I have never had any abilities."

Ruth watched me a moment more before nodding. "In time you will. Until then, it would be prudent to learn as much as possible about magical abilities in Izwe. I'd recommend starting with these two books, and then you can let me know if you'd like to continue on from there."

I did not have the heart to argue with Ruth. She had been such a godsend to me, cloistered away in the quiet calm of the library. If she urged me to read these books, I would.

And so I sat down and opened up her first book. I paged through a history of the greatest magic-wielders—those who could command the weather, control the tides, cause earthquakes to shake the ground. Those were the ones they called elemental. Then there were the non-elementals, the ones who were able to read minds, to influence others' thinking, to effect changes that made no more logical sense than the mere wish of the magic-wielder.

Both sets of magic seemed strange, untamed and uninhibited, as if the wielder could affect everyone in this realm and the next just by wishing something into being. That was true power and the idea of it scared me. No one should be able to command such things.

But apparently my mother had, and many others in my line. I shook my head at the thought.

The book also described a third set of people who were not called wielders but still had some amount of access to magic. The Masters were listed among this group and, as Roland had explained to me, they were individuals who were keepers of magic as long as they served the temple. They used the magic for rituals and worship but, almost like flipping a switch, they immediately lost the ability to channel the magic when not in the service of the temple.

I chuckled to myself, imagining the Masters in the Yesonto ruling the universe during their nine-to-five job and then being boring, normal people the moment they clocked out.

I traced my finger over a line in the book about a lesser category of magically gifted people. This final category was unique as they did not have any ability to wield magic or steward magic. Yet, some could sense the presence of magic in magically altered objects or places. Others could feel the power within a person, no matter whether that person was using magic or not.

Finn's face immediately popped into my mind. That first day of training, he told me he did not have magic—in fact, it seemed no one but the royal family and the highest of Lords did—so it had to be the reason the Council selected him to train me. Of course, he was more than qualified to train me physically as a commander, but I had questioned time and time again why a man seemingly with no magical abilities of his own was so confident in what existed within me.

Flipping past a few pages, I came to a genealogical tree and began to recognize names of the Lords and Ladies I had met. I thought it was a giant family tree of all the households but upon closer inspection, I realized the tree did not depict each member in each generation. Rather, it included each House and the notable magic wielders within it.

Going back several generations, there would be dozens of names listed under each House. With each subsequent generation, however, the names dwindled so that there were only a handful of magic wielders a few generations ago. Now, there were one or two names listed in each House in this current generation of Lords.

Lord Anson of Ingonyame was listed among them, as was Lord Grimly of Kubuga. Two other Lords were listed though I could not put their faces to the names printed before me. Interestingly, each of the Lords mentioned had a grade next to their name—one.

I flicked back a page or two, looking for a key to the grading system before finding it. Five was the highest grade and denoted exceptional abilities to control elemental or non-elemental magic, while one was the lowest and denoted magical abilities typically as minor as being more persuasive or being able to warm water. Certainly nothing like commanding storms or forcing a human to act a particular way.

I paged forward again and looked at the grading for the earlier magic-wielding monarchs and Lords. It was a veritable sea of fives and fours, then midway down the chart were lots of threes and twos. Now, with the current Lords, there were ones.

I turned a few more pages until I found my own magical lineage chart stretching from Manelesi to my mother, Bekha; I was not on the chart as its production predated my birth. The sprinkling of fives and fours reigned down the page, generation after generation. My mother's own grade was five.

How had my own family managed to retain magical powers while the Houses lost theirs with each passing year? I shook my head for what felt like the millionth time today. It did not make any sense, though I did now realize why everyone was so convinced that I would have magic.

I quickly discarded the books on magic. There was no point in learning more than I already had. I knew the basics of elemental and non-elemental magic. I understood, through Ruth's explanations and the charts, that magic had become exceptionally rare in Izwe over the years, growing more and more scarce with each generation. I had heard Master Edgar explain the link between magic and religion in the Yesonto. And I knew a history of the most famous magic wielders.

But the idea that I should have magic itched. I did not have magic. I did not have magic. And so I put aside the concerning idea.

I turned my attention to the history of Izwe, the Alterealm and the geopolitical interactions. This included a history of Trina Cheile, the conflict between that nation and Izwe, and how the Alterealm had once split into allied groupings to wage wars over land and resources.

In the last seventy years, in particular, it seemed the conflict had grown more intense. Trina Cheile, like all nations in the Alterealm was losing magic as quickly as everyone else. While I thought this would make everything safer, it seemed to have had the opposite effect.

The loss of power made the nations jumpy, afraid of their new weakness, and much more likely to fight each other. I still pinched myself most days, not entirely believing that this world I was living in was real. But especially when I read passages that all but yelled how dangerous this world truly was, I felt like I was moving through a nightmare.

I wished I would wake up, safe in my bed back in the Humanrealm with Eliza making pancakes and Roland reading the newspaper on the porch. This had to be some sort of sick dream, because I was certainly not equipped to deal with the shambles that was Izwe.

The longer I read, the more the words began to shift and dance before my eyes. The letters started to blur with my fatigue, and I was vaguely aware of the library attendants beginning their evening ritual of closing the space for the night.

It had been a long day, filled with my ever-present resentment about Eliza and Roland, my training with Finn, my first lesson with Lisideria, and now my studies. Perhaps it was time for me to go back to my chambers.

I marked my place in the second book, then rose from the table heavily. This was enough for today, and I could digest the facts about magic with a glass of konstans in hand and warm water pouring over my body.

A bath sounded exquisite, even those oils Lisideria was telling me I must use. I stacked my books neat on the table and pushed my chair in precisely. I would come back tomorrow to continue and I would come right here.

AS THE DAYS CONTINUED TO PASS IN IZWE, I FELL INTO A routine.

The days I awoke before sunrise, I forced myself to climb out of bed and join the Masters and worshippers in the Yesonto. I struggled to believe in the tale of Manelesi being a God and me somehow his living representative, but still I took a seat before the eternal candles. I clasped my hands. I bent my head in supplication.

I did not know what others prayed for during the stillness of daybreak, but I prayed over and over for understanding: understanding of my place in this new world, understanding of these people who felt so foreign, understanding of Eliza and Roland's need to put distance between us, understanding of my role as Queen, understanding of my supposed power and how to harness it.

The mornings I arose too late for the Yesonto, I began my day with training. At nine o'clock, I arrived at the training grounds in my soldier-brown outfit, minus a headdress much to my delight. Finn instructed me to run, to jump, to do push-ups, to ride a zebra, to balance and strike with the wooden sword. And eventually, when I had stopped complaining—internally and externally—he handed me a real sword.

To this day, I can remember the feel of the metal in my hand. It was lighter than the wooden training sword, but I could feel the intensity of the weapon. It was an awareness that this item could and would kill given the person wielding it and their intent. It was deadly and beautiful, cold steel folded into an excruciating edge.

Of course, we did not spar with each other. I would be much too clumsy, and probably take an eye out or a limb off Finn. Instead, Finn set up a series of dummies shaped like people. He dressed them in various things: soldier tunics, bright gowns, winter coats, armor. He taught me what it would take to pierce each one.

Something in the way I wielded the weapon must have eventually made Finn confident in my abilities because one morning, I arrived at the training grounds and there were no dummies set up.

"Offering yourself up as today's practice doll?" I joked as I wrapped my wrists in the braces I had taken to wearing. I realized early that my wrists were weak, the narrow and delicate bones unable to withstand the weight of a full soldier's blade. Finn assured me that I would gain strength in time and, until then, I wore my braces.

"Something like that," Finn replied, handing me my usual sword and taking up another for himself.

My mouth popped open. "I'm sorry, what?"

Finn just smiled at me, dropping into a fighting stance with the sword pointed in my direction. "Come now. Give it a try for real."

I stared at him, unable to sort through the overwhelming flood of reasons why this was the worst plan Finn had ever had. Finally, I managed to get out, "I…that's not a good idea."

But Finn laughed, his blue eyes lighting up as he took in my shocked demeanor. "Probably not, but I can't have you poking at dummies forever. Eventually you have to learn how to actually face someone who fights back."

"Yes, but surely I'm not ready."

He shrugged. "Ready as you'll ever be."

"I'm serious, Finn," I said, my shock turning to actual concern. I lowered my sword, the weight pulling the blade down to the scarlet earth.

Finn seemed to understand that. He stood up out of the fighting stance and came towards me, his legs moving in a grace that all soldiers seemed to possess. "I know you are," he said gently. "If I didn't think you were ready, I would not hand you a real sword. You are competent—much more so than you realize. You're ready."

He wrapped his hand around my own where it limply grasped onto the sword. Squeezing my fingers into the grip firmly, he repeated, "You're ready."

He let go of my sword and dropped back into his stance. With one hand, he motioned me to come forward. "Let's do this."

I took a breath and sent a silent prayer up to the heavens. As much as Finn could tease and push, I had a soft spot for him. He was one of the only people in this world I actually liked. It would be a shame if I killed or maimed him.

I dropped into the mirror fighting stance that Finn was in, my knees bent and ready to spring forward or backward, side to side.

Finn nodded. "Good. Now, come towards me two steps but do not swing your blade yet."

As I stepped forward, Finn stepped back in equal measure.

"See, it's like a dance. Your steps direct my steps. You move towards me, and I move backward. Now, step back as I come towards you."

I did as I was told, trying to force my feet to mimic what Finn's had done moments before.

"Good." Finn smiled and I almost believed it would be this simple. Then he said, "Now swing your sword at me as if you would chop off my head."

"Finn!"

And of course he laughed, a carefree and lovely sound that reminded me of the lower register of church bells. He was enjoying this too much.

"You're not going to hurt me. I promise. Just try."

And so I did. I came forward swinging my sword. Finn blocked it with his own in a quick slice upwards, and the impact reverberated through the sword, my hands, and up the bones of my lower arms.

"Gack!" I shrieked as my hands immediately loosened on the handle. The sword fell to the packed training ground, kicking up a small puff of red dust. I looked from it to my hands in shock.

This time, Finn roared his laughter. His wide mouth broke open and he let his head fall back in mirth. He even wiped tears from his eyes at one point, I noted. I shook my hands to stop the tingling and then placed them on my hips in disapproval.

I left the sword lying on the ground at our feet.

"Quite done yet?" I snapped.

He wiped his eyes one more time, a final chuckle sneaking out. Then he took a deep breath and turned highly amused eyes on me. "That was just too good."

"Well, I'm glad someone's enjoying themselves."

"I think you are, as well, Your Majesty."

"Not right now."

"No, I suppose that's true. How are your hands?"

"They're tingling," I replied shortly.

Finn looked at them, and then gave an infuriating shrug. "That's what happens when you hit steel on steel in full force. It's not pleasant but it happens, and happens often on a battlefield. I wanted you to feel it now, early in training, so that you come to know the feeling and not react...like that...when it matters most."

"I understand," I said past tight lips. "A little warning might have been nice, though."

"No warning on a battlefield, Your Majesty."

And then I picked up the sword and tried again.

Over the course of the hour, he taught me basic sword swipes—some I had learned on the dummies and a few new ones that required a live participant to practice. He also taught me some basic blocks and evasive maneuvers, and he wisely told me that these were the most important things. These would be the moves that saved my life, not the strikes.

The sun was high in the navy sky when we finally wrapped up. Sweat was pouring down my face, and I could feel the rivulets running along my neck and torso under the thick training clothes.

I unwound my wrist brace as Finn returned the swords to their rack. "Good work today," he said.

"Thank you," I replied as I pushed a stray curl out of my sticky face. I felt good. My arms felt like jelly and the ghost of too many sword impacts still flitted along my nerves, but my soul was content. I had accomplished something today, and I was enjoying a little taste of pride after such a long time of being embarrassed and ashamed of everything I did in the Alterealm.

"Have time for a bit of magic practice?" Finn asked, a wicked gleam in his eye.

I knew he was joking, but I scoffed nonetheless. I unwound the last layer of my wrist brace and, tucking the material into my pocket, turned and began my walk back to the palace.

"Don't push it," I called over my shoulder.

I thought I heard a quiet laugh, and it brought a smile to my own face.

If training was a regimented part of my morning, then my lunch with Lisideria was a regimented part of my afternoon. I joined her in that solarium, sat on the same wicker chair, and poked at an assortment of salads, meats, and soups while she prattled on about what was and was not proper in Izwe.

After our initial conversations about the general expectations for an Izweian queen, we worked our way through Council etiquette. Lisideria explained how the Council functioned and how the twenty Lords who served on it were representatives of their respective Houses, which oversaw specific regions of Izwe almost like counties. While most of the Lords sat on the Council for that purpose alone, several of the Lords held powerful, coveted roles including Lord Grimly as Chief Advisor and Lord Anson as Lord of War. There was also a Senior Council made up of representatives of the five strongest Houses: Nkwe, Kubuga, Ingonyame, Ndlovu, and Inyathi. I noticed her own glowing pride as she named Kubuga, her father's House, and Nkwe, the House she had married into.

Lisideria also explained what my role was in Council meetings, specifically that I was there to oversee and pass judgment on important topics but would not be bothered with items of lesser importance. Thus, while I was always welcome at Council meetings, they would invite me to specific sessions as needed. I would have the final say in any matter but the Lords were there to serve as my advisors, to offer up different perspectives according to the regions they governed, and to air their own opinions on matters so that I could make the best decision. I should, in turn, listen to their perspectives but know that I would always be the most important voice in the room.

That entire topic only took five lunches to get through. Then we turned to courtier etiquette. Lisideria went into greater detail about the hierarchical structure of nobility in Izwe—much of which I had already read in the library, but I was happy to have a refresher. She also explained the more technical aspects of how to address Lords and Ladies by their proper titles, and how they should in turn address me. This took her three lunch sessions.

And finally, my least favorite topic that Lisideria covered: servant etiquette. This only took her two scandalizing lunch sessions to get through, and it covered all sorts of topics such as how the servant staff of the palace were to act, what we as nobles should expect of them, what they as servants should expect of us, and what was fitting for a servant to do versus for us to do for ourselves.

That conversation made me ill, and I pushed away my salad of some sort of pulses and chopped greens before my plate was empty.

"Remember, Your Majesty, they are not our equals. They were born to lesser, and they are lesser," she concluded, taking another hearty bite of her meal.

I placed my fork down gingerly and when the server came to refill my glass of water, I smiled at the brown-clad young woman. "Thank you."

Lisideria turned sharp eyes on me, and I saw the reprimand there even if she did not dare voice it to her Queen. "Your Majesty is too sweet."

"No," I replied shortly. "I'm not. I was raised to acknowledge people who do things for me. The servant brought me water when I was entirely capable of doing it myself. She should be thanked."

"Again, this is what they were born to do."

"No one is born to serve," I snapped. I had bit my tongue through both days of this lesson, but I finally lost hold on my temper.

"Most are, Your Majesty. It is their destiny just as yours is to be Queen. That is the way of the world. You can put a servant in a fine gown, but she'll always be the help. You can put a queen in a servant's uniform, but she'll always be a queen. It's unshakable and unchangeable. It's something in the blood."

My own blood was beginning to boil, and I was conscious of the itching that had started at my chest. "Lady Lisideria, so what you are saying is that the parents one is born to determines everything about a person including their inherent worth?"

Lisideria looked at me as if I was asking if the sky were indeed blue. "Yes, your Majesty…"

I shook my head. "So no one born to a 'lesser' family could possibly amount to anything? They might not have skills or intelligence akin to ours, or even greater than ours? And for that matter, no one born to a noble family could be useless and stupid and not worthy of being here in this palace?"

When she did not respond, I could not help but continue. "I seem to remember something from my lessons about my own family not being of the ruling class. House Ingonyame were born to be rulers but, when Manelesi arrived, he took the crown by force. By your logic, was he born to usurp a crown or was he a mere upstart who got lucky in reaching above his station?"

If my eyes did not deceive me, then a faint blush had sprung upon Lisideria's sallow cheeks. "I'm not sure I understand, Queen Sahle," she said slowly.

"Of course not," I muttered. Then, clearing my throat, "Your logic may be the thought here and now, but that is not the thought from where I was raised. There, in the Humanrealm, there are class structures, but it is also accepted that regardless of where you were born and who your parents are, you can make whatever life you want through merit. It is hard, yes, but the possibility is out there.

"And that possibility, that hope, is everything. To be told from birth that either you have made it or you have not…that, Lady Lisideria, is ridiculous."

Lisideria had sat and listened to my protests silently, but I could see the thoughts swirling in her eyes. It was the look of a parent waiting for a child to get through the worst of a tantrum before jumping in to calm or chastise. "Again, Your Majesty is most kindhearted. But the Alterealm is not the Humanrealm, and it never will be."

"Of course," I said stiffly, smiling. I grabbed a crusty piece of bread from the basket between Lisideria and myself and took a bite—anything to fill my mouth and stop me from calling her a whole host of names.

She was a perfectly fine woman, to be sure. But she was a product of her environment. She was like all the rest of the courtiers here: arrogant and inflated by their own supposed superiority. It sickened me each time I saw it so blatantly. I knew right then and there that if I had my way, I would change this in my time as Queen.

Sure, history should be respected. Family lines were important. But if I came across a man or woman with skills I needed, I would elevate them to whatever position based solely on their use to me, not because of who their father was.

A change like that had to start somewhere. And the fight for that would be brutal—I could already hear the Councilors' outrage echoing from the misty, distant shores of the future— but I would do it. I promised myself that as I smiled at Lisideria and chewed on that bread.

I promised that.

Study should have been a regimented part of my afternoon. Unfortunately, it was not. Too many competing interests warred for my time—Eliza's insistence through her letters that I have tea with various courtiers, wardrobe fittings to better assess which of my mother's gowns needed to be altered for me, Council meetings in which I sat like a wallflower and occasionally offered "yes" responses. Always yes.

And when all of those tasks were done, I retreated to the rows of books that I so loved. A part of my mind did wonder why none of the Lords, Eliza, or Roland had insisted on my being taught the history, geography, and politics of this realm. They only seemed concerned with my ability to wield a weapon, and I wondered what that said about me and their plans for me.

I had to be my own teacher, it seemed.

That was fine with me. While I did not know the particulars of this place, I was smart enough to realize what I was missing. And so, I spent hours in the library reading everything I could get my hands on. I had poured over family trees and lineage charts for the royal family at first. That had led me to several books on the history of Izwe, maps of the kingdom and the Alterealm broadly. Now, I was looking into the political structure of Izwe and our enemies.

I firmly believed that every paragraph I read would help me feel more grounded in this place. I absorbed facts, dates, and names. I stored them like little seashells in my pocket, clinking around like a child who has spent all day out at low tide. One day soon, they would be useful. One day, I would make a piece of art with my gathered seashells and the whole would take form as something new entirely.

I just hoped that, whatever that "whole" was, it looked like the shape of a Queen.

Ruth remained an incredible help. She seemed to know the progression of my study, and she supplied the next logical book exactly as I was ready for it. Perhaps that was the librarian's gift—to know and anticipate the mind of a researcher—but I was grateful nonetheless.

While I learned that the official policy of the library was that court members must come there to read rather than borrow books, it seemed Ruth made an exception for me. No one would think to say no to their monarch; yet, it felt like Ruth would have given this special consent to me regardless of my station. I liked to think that she recognized a curious soul when she saw one, and that she understood that I needed to be alone with my thoughts when delving into delicate topics.

I continued to request certain books be brought to my rooms when I did not have the time to spend in the library. And some days, when the library became too much, when the glances of passing courtiers grew too heavy on my crown, I carried a few important tomes back to my chambers. Granted, those who frequented the library were some of the kinder ones but, still, solitude felt better at times.

However my afternoons varied, I always moved into night in the same way. I joined the courtiers for dinner in the Great Hall, hurriedly picking at my plate of food while the courtiers sent me furtive glances from their own tables. Without Eliza and Roland in residence, Grimly often sat beside me at the head table—along with the four other members of the Senior Council. I pointedly refused to speak to Anson, not that he particularly cared to speak with me. He never engaged me in conversation past his usual, "Good evening, Majesty." Each day I nodded, waiting for him to take his seat two chairs down from my throne, and then I returned my attention to my food.

As soon as it was polite, I retreated back to my chambers. Sometimes Sybil caught me on the way out of the Great Hall to say hello or to ask after my welfare. I always greeted her warmly. I always put on my most convincing smile as I told her I was fine.

And in many ways, I was fine. I was adapting to whatever this place was with a speed that even surprised me. Still, I was most comfortable curled up in the wingback chair before the fireplace, my books on my lap and scattered around me on various surfaces.

Sometimes I poured a glass of konstans, that passion fruit wine. Sometimes I poured another. Other times, I sat with nothing but the books and the light of the fire illuminating the important words on the page.

Sometimes I cried when reading about a particularly brutal campaign. Other times, I seemed to see past the words until the words took shape like a movie in my mind and I could envision my mother as a young girl being trained to be Queen as I was now, my father courting a blushing seventeen-year-old, my parents sitting at the same Council table I sat at.

And I realized why this learning was so important to me. It told me about my kingdom, about the expectations that were placed upon my shoulders, but it also taught me about who I was. It brought my parents, their parents, and their parents before them to life. And through knowing them, I began to know myself just slightly. I began to understand the importance of the crown and why so much had been done to protect me, hide me, and bring me back.

While I was coming to understand the context of my crown and my prophecy, on the one hand, it did not mean that I wanted or could truly wrap my head around my role in it. Just as I knew that my body needed oxygen to breathe, that my heartbeat kept blood pumping through my veins and arteries, I knew I did not want to be Queen.

I had not wanted this life. I had not asked for this life. I had not been raised for this life. And so while I learned and while I understood, it did nothing to make me want my crown. This juxtaposition warred within me, day after day as I sat before the fireplace.

I wondered, lifting my head from one of the books to take a sip of wine, did that make me a monster or just a petulant brat?

WHEN I ARRIVED AT THE TRAINING RING, I WAS SURPRISED to see Finn seated on a bench. These days, we had fallen into a routine of running first thing and so I had grown used to arriving at the training ground amidst the jumping and stretching and general warming up that Finn did before he set off.

I instantly narrowed my eyes in suspicion. What did he have planned?

"Good morning, Majesty," he called innocently as I crossed the training ring and made my way to him.

"Morning, Finn. How did you sleep?" I replied with a sugar-sweet smile.

He saw right through me, the suspicion and false niceness. His answering smile said as much. "Oh, very well. Thank you for asking. Now, if you would be so kind, please come and take a seat beside me."

I looked at the seat and then back at him. From somewhere over my head, one of the hadedas called its trumpeting caw. "Are we not running?"

"I thought we'd try something a little different today."

"Like?"

"Like some more magical training."

My answering huff was drowned out by Finn. "Before you get all twisted up about it, just hear me out. I have a few more exercises that I want to try with you. These might be the things that unlock whatever gifts you have."

"I don't—"

"—have any magic," Finn finished for me. "Yes, I know, I know. You've said so before."

"So why are we wasting our time with it this morning?"

Finn smiled again, a genuine one, one that communicated his goodwill and his belief in me. "Just humor me. OK?"

It was hard to say no to such a hopeful expression, to the smile lines that bracketed his wide mouth and the crinkled skin at the corners of his eyes. "Fine."

"Good!" Finn said, and I think he was truly surprised that I gave in so easily. "Come sit."

I sat heavily, already knowing that I was going to be a failure. I did not have magic, as I kept repeating to anyone who would listen. I was just Sahle, now Queen Sahle, but definitely not Magical Queen Sahle.

Seeing me settled on the bench, Finn began. "Last time we tried this, you stormed off in frustration. Promise me that no matter how annoyed you get, you'll stay this time?"

"Fine," I muttered, looking at my hands with the teensiest bit of embarrassment. I really could be petulant sometimes.

"Great. We tried sensing the air and sun last time—"

"And pulling at sun ribbons," I added.

Finn smiled knowingly at me. "Yes, and pulling at the sun. Today, I want us to try and feel. Most magic is elemental— people draw on the earth or the air or the water to channel their gifts. For them, visualizing is often the best way of harnessing their power.

"But, for some people, magic is internal. It's like a heartbeat or like one's thoughts. It's inside you and the force of your emotions or your desires cause a reaction—a magical reaction. Since we did not have much luck with the elemental activities last time, I thought we'd try this different approach."

"Alright," I replied wearily. At least he was not asking me to visualize the air again. Still, I was already dreading my all-but-guaranteed failure.

Finn's voice cut through my internal chatter, urging me to focus. "Close your eyes, and try to calm your mind. Just let whatever is swirling around your brain clear."

I followed his lead, closing my eyes, but I struggled to do what he asked. I had always been terrible at meditating. I tried again now, my thoughts bouncing around like a squash ball ricocheting off the walls of my mind.

After a few seconds, Finn continued. "Then, I want you to think about a time when you were afraid. What did you feel? What did your pulse do? How did your skin feel?"

I cracked one eyelid open. "My skin?"

"Yes, your skin. Magic wielders sometimes report feeling their skin glow or shiver or tingle when they feel strong emotions. Have you ever felt anything like that?"

"No," I replied reflexively. But unbidden, my mind pulled up memories like the time I had dropped an ice cream cone as a child and grew so angry and sad that it felt like my skin itched. Or the time, more recently as a college student, when a professor called on me and I had been entirely zoned out, not tracking the conversation even slightly. My shame had felt like a razor blade across my chest and neck.

"No," I repeated.

"Sure," Finn said, and I could hear from his tone that he did not believe me. "Think about the first time you came to train with me, and the anger that made you storm off."

I thought back to that moment, and to my shame and fury over the magical practice in particular. I scowled, my eyes still closed.

"Try to feel those emotions again. Feel that futility and anger and embarrassment. Then magnify it."

But I was not trying. I had opened my eyes as Finn talked. I looked at him, observing him even though his eyes were still shut. And I was amazed. He had seen through me so quickly, so easily, even on that first meeting.

"I can feel you not trying," Finn called, and I instantly closed my eyes again before he could open his to find me staring.

"Sorry," I murmured.

"Focus on those emotions. Once you have them, try to heighten them. Live the emotions again. Feel the anger and the frustration and the embarrassment. Step back into it."

Oh, that I could do. I had felt nothing but anger and frustration and embarrassment since I arrived here in the Alterealm. Those emotions seemed to now be a permanent part of my personality, hovering just under the calm surface but ready to break free at the slightest provocation.

I delved into them, feeling them anew as I thought about my humiliation in the Council Chamber that first meeting, Anson's words to me, the courtiers' disapproval. I felt my face heat with the force of the emotions. Angry tears burned at the back of my eyes.

"Now, see if you can feel the emotions. Not with your mind but physically. Can you feel your skin tingle, your fingers twitch?"

I thought about that. Maybe I felt my skin? I was aware of it, like it was pulled taut over the sinew and muscles beneath it, like it was pulling closer into me to protect me.

Or maybe I was imagining it all because I did not have magic.

"I don't know...No."

"Let's focus on that 'I don't know.' You feel something. That's why you didn't say 'no' right off the bat."

"Well then 'no.' I don't feel anything."

"You blush when you get angry. That's a feeling. And you're blushing now. What does that feel like?"

I crinkled my nose but left my eyes shut. He was peeking.

"Hot."

He made a short back-of-the-throat sound. "Be serious, Majesty. Think about your face. A blush is when the blood comes to the surface of our skin. It happens to everyone but for non-elemental magic wielders, they can feel the blood like a living life force. What do you feel beyond heat?"

My cheeks seemed to itch but I knew that was just my reaction to being watched. I could feel Finn's eyes on me, glancing over the low bridge of my nose, the rounded apples of my cheeks, the dusky shadows beneath my lashes.

"Just heat, and I can feel you watching me." I opened my eyes and met his gaze. "But then everyone can feel when someone is looking at them."

"That's true," Finn agreed. "Close your eyes again."

"Hmph."

"Delve back into those emotions. Think back to your first day at the Council Chamber, when you fled because you got embarrassed by your lack of knowledge."

"How do you know that?" I snapped. "You weren't even there."

"No, but I heard all about it from the Vikela in the room. People talk, Majesty."

I pursed my lips in disapproval. It was normal, but I still did not like being the object of people's gossip.

"Something made you jump from your seat and flee. What was that feeling?"

"Embarrassment, as you said," I bit out.

"No, what did it feel like in your body?" Finn corrected.

I thought about it, really thought. I had not made a conscious decision to stand from my seat on the dais that day. I had simply moved when my body told me to move. It was like a live wire had gone off inside me, the emotions propelling my limbs.

"I just wanted to get out of there."

"You're not listening to what I'm asking," Finn chided.

I cracked my eyes open. "I am listening. I just don't have any magic to tell you about."

Finn opened his eyes as he exhaled in a loud puff. "You do, Majesty. I might not have magic, but I can sense it in others. I have been around plenty of magic-wielders, enough to know when it's there and when it's powerful. You have it. You just refuse to give it a chance."

"That's ridiculous," I replied.

"It's not. Your father had minor elemental magic. Your mother had major non-elemental magic. Both should flow through your veins. You keep denying it but one of these days, you won't be able to. One of these days, you'll see it clearly and it will be unmistakably magic."

"Sure," I replied. My palms had grown sweaty, thinking about my most horrific moments in the Alterealm. I wiped them on my training paints.

Finn stood from the bench. "Well, if you won't work on your magic, then I guess we'll have to go for a run."

"I guess so," I replied, happy to be doing anything else besides trying to coax something that was not there out of me.

"After you, Majesty."

I turned from Finn and set off at a quick clip. Running was not my favorite thing, but anything—*anything*—was better than trying and failing again and again at magic.

From that morning on, my training with Finn shifted. While we always ran, always wielded some weapons, we also spent at least a few minutes practicing magic. Well, trying to practice magic was a more apt way of describing what we did.

Every day without fail, Finn proposed a new magical exercise. I tried, tried again, and failed utterly and completely. And once I had thrown my tantrum, repeated that I did not have magic— and, on my touchier days, threatened to go back to the palace— we moved back to physical training.

Where I was failing with the magical training, I was improving with the physical. I could now wield a sword fairly well. I could block Finn's attacks when we sparred, and even land a few of my own mock-blows every now and again.

Finn seemed pleasantly surprised at how my swordsmanship was coming along. And I was proud of myself, for the first time since arriving in the Alterealm. Here was something I was actually succeeding at. Here was someone who was not entirely and eternally disappointed in me.

Finn's smile when I bested him lit up a part of me that had forgotten what contentment was like. It made me…happy.

As I progressed, he pulled out more and more diverse weapons: a spear, a bow and quiver of arrows, a double-pointed shield, a mace, a battle ax, a set of daggers. I always seemed to be better with the sword than anything else, but I grew to enjoy the feel of the weapons in my hands, the heft of them balanced against my strengthened muscles.

In between bouts of magical attempts, swordplay, and physical fitness, I asked Finn about military strategy. He was young for a commander, he explained. Although he was forty-six years old—the equivalent to late twenties in the Humanrealm, I guessed—he had been a commander for nearly four years, during which time there had thankfully not been any full-out wars. However, he still had studied battlefield tactics at the officers' training that was required of all soldiers progressing up to Vikela leadership posts.

I would never understand the strategy as he did, but I drank in his top-level overviews of how battles were waged, won, and lost, how soldiers fought singularly and as a company. I asked about our enemies, and he told me as much as he could.

I knew that I would always have military advisors who would explain this to me, if and when the time came. But still, I was grateful to Finn for imparting to me whatever bit of knowledge he could. It helped me feel more prepared for whatever was coming.

And something was coming. Maybe I asked those questions because I knew it then, on some subterranean level. Maybe it was just inevitable, now that I was twenty and in the Alterealm. Our enemies knew the prophecy as well as I did, and they would come for me.

In either case, some voice in my head urged me to ask those questions of Finn and to drink in his answers. A day might come when I needed that knowledge.

THE MASTERS SENT WORD ONE DAY THAT THE SPRING high holiday would take place the following week. My presence was requested with the briefest of explanations that I would be "involved," barring my express refusal.

I tiptoed the next morning to the Yesonto to ask exactly what this involvement would entail. Somewhere between the dozens of bowed heads in meditation, the peaceful glow of the devotion, and the calm face of Master Edgar, I accepted his vague, "It is nothing, Your Majesty. A mere pinprick."

Yet now, sitting before my mirror on the morning of the holiday, I wondered what that actually meant.

"Have you seen these holiday festivities?" I asked Mara as she pinned my hair into a circular braided halo around my head. She added little yellow, pink, and white flowers periodically, held in place by sharp pins.

"No, Your Majesty. Well, I've of course been to recent holiday festivities, but if you're asking have I seen the proper version where the monarch takes part, then no. I was a small child when your mother passed—may the God and his gods rest her soul."

"Hmm," I mused. "But people are excited about this?'

"Oh yes, Majesty. The entire city has been talking about this for weeks now. They cannot wait to see you, and to have the old traditions back."

Mara finished with my hair after tucking a veritable bouquet amongst the braids in place of a crown. Then Kaiht helped me dress. She had picked out a light gown of gauzy yellow and green. The colors reminded me of the landscape I had come to associate with Izwe. While I usually wore little satin flats in the palace, the shoes Kaiht laced me into today were ankle-high leather boots. I wondered at the need for such sturdiness.

Mingled curiosity and worry remained my companions as I let the Vikela lead me out of the palace and to a carriage at the base of the palace stairs. I rode alone in the carriage to the center of the city and, only when the carriage stopped, did I stare in wonder around me.

Every surface in the city was covered in greenery and flowers. People—courtiers and city residents alike—thronged the square I stood in. I recognized a few palace faces as the crowd dropped into a bow before me.

"Rise," I said, as loud as I could to ensure this massive crowd could hear. They heard; as one the crowd rose and Lady Sybil wandered to my side.

"Your Majesty," she said with a smile in greeting. "You look marvelous."

I self-consciously ran my hands across my skirts, feeling the rough grain of the tulle-like material on my skin. "Thank you. It's strange to be without a crown."

Sybil laughed, threading her arm through mine. "Oh, don't worry, my Queen. No one will mistake you."

That was not my concern. Rather it felt nice. It felt normal to once again have the weight of a crown gone while moving about in public. Without it, I could almost pretend I blended into the crowd. I could almost pretend I was free, a normal girl in a festival square. For that was what this was, I realized as I looked around.

A maypole of sorts, complete with streaming rainbow ribbons, stood at the center of the square. Around it and scattered throughout the large space were vendors selling roasted nuts and trinkets, games for children, musicians setting a jaunty tune with their marimbas and little mbiras. Young people in small groups laughed and whispered conspiratorially into each others' ears. Women balanced babies on their hips while their husbands drank from horn cups.

It looked for all the world like a county fair, and the familiarity made me smile.

"What are you grinning at, Queen Sahle?" Sybil asked.

I turned my attention back to her. "Nothing. This just reminds me of home—I mean my old home in the Humanrealm."

"Really? That's surprising."

"Well, large groups of people tend to be the same no matter where they are. A party is a party here or in the Humanrealm."

"Fascinating, Your Majesty," Sybil replied with an encouraging look. "I wonder if Eliza and Roland would agree with you. Such a shame they could not attend today. I'm sure you'd have liked their company."

I nodded. "Yes, maybe they could have filled me in on what I should be doing. The Masters were very vague in their description of the day."

"Well, I can help you with that! Your role today is chiefly to enjoy yourself—"

I barked out a laugh. Several curious people turned towards the sound.

"Aside from that," Sybill continued, patting my hand where it rested on her forearm. "Your other duty is to open the festivities with a rite called the Umnikelo. The Masters do this by making a small cut on your hand and dropping some of your blood into the vat over there."

She pointed to a large, clear tank of what looked to be water before continuing, "Your blood is that of Manelesi's, the Great One, and sharing it with us is your blessing on the spring, symbolically. Those who seek blooms in their gardens, fertility for themselves or a family member, luck in a venture's beginnings are welcome to drink from the vat—"

"To drink my blood?" I interrupted again. Surely I had misunderstood Sybil.

"Yes, Your Majesty. Your blood is power and by drinking it, the people may share in the potential of that."

I involuntarily shuddered. "That's…interesting. And that's it?"

"Then there will be dancing and music and feasting. They'll expect you to dance, so you're forewarned."

I looked at the tips of my leather shoes where they peaked past my skirt with each stride. The sturdiness made sense now.

"Thank you, Lady Sybil," I finally said. Sybil opened her mouth to say something but, before she could get a word out, Master Edgar stood before us with three other Masters. Gone were their red capelets; their yellow robes were all that they wore. I said a quiet farewell to Sybil before following them as they led me towards the vat of water so ominously positioned in a central, raised spot on the square. The crowd hushed as I stepped up to the vat, the Masters beside me.

"People of Izwe, children of the Great One, welcome to the Spring Holiday," Master Edgar began, raising his arms as if to embrace the sky. "We are gathered today to honor the wheel of the year with a ritual too-long put aside: the Umnikelo."

Cheers and applause and stomping rang out, even as I tried my best to keep my face neutral.

"For twenty years, we have gone without this gift from the Great One as our Queen lived in sanctuary. Now she is back and can renew our sacred ritual, this gift of power from the almighty Manelesi. Your Majesty, if you will?"

Master Edgar held out his hand to me and I placed mine within it. A hush fell over the crowd as another Master handed Edgar a citrine-encrusted blade.

"This may sting," Edgar whispered to me. I took a breath and nodded, and then he drug the blade along my palm.

Bright pain bloomed across the skin and tingled down the length of my fingers. I sucked in my breath and willed myself not to be a baby. I would not cry at a little cut.

Little cut, little cut. I repeated that to myself as Edgar turned my hand and let the blood trickle in droplets into the vat.

I averted my gaze as I felt a strange swish of vertigo. A group of Lords stood clustered nearby and they inclined their heads as I made eye contact. The only one who did not was Anson. He looked at me unflinchingly, unmoving, and I could not puzzle out the tension on his face.

Edgar closed my fingers around something soft and I turned my attention back to him. "Hold pressure on that," he said, leaning towards my ear. I glanced down to see a white napkin in my hand.

He quietly continued, "The last thing to do is for you to say, 'I share the gifts of my power, my blood, freely. May the festivities begin.'"

I repeated his words loudly to the people as I held the cloth napkin against the wound. The crowd applauded, whooping and hollering. Their excitement was palpable in the air and I wondered at these people, this tradition. What was it to have such exhilaration over drinking my blood. I had no power and thus my blood was no more potent or unique than any of theirs. Still, as the beat of the music rose, the people queued before the vat.

I moved back to allow them space, but I watched, fascinated and horrified at the sight in equal measure.

"Queen Sahle," a low voice said from beside me. I turned to find Anson.

"Lord Anson," I replied, wondering when he had left the group of Lords I had spied him with just moments before.

A lock of his dark hair fell across his forehead as he looked down at my cut hand. "Hold pressure on that to stop the bleeding."

"Yes, thank you. I know," I replied shortly. I might be young, but I certainly knew how to take care of a cut.

"Good. Then you should dance, Your Majesty. Your people will accept no less," he said. There was a twinkle in his eye and if I had not already heard that I should dance from Sybil, I would expect he was pulling a prank on me. How silly a Queen could be made to look, twirling around with the commoners—or something equally ridiculous to him.

"So I've been told."

Anson raised a brow. "You are very informed today, my Queen."

The day was too fine, the sun too warm, the festivities too exuberant to let Anson bother me. Still, I could not stop myself from quipping back, "As opposed to every other day?"

But Anson did not voice his confirmation. He merely, frustratingly smirked and bowed before strolling away. I was left looking after him, the lone person dressed in dark colors at this springtime festival of pastels. I shook my head.

I spied Lady Genevieve's red hair in the crowd moments later. A Lord had just fetched fresh drinks and Genevieve passed me one of the horned cups filled with konstans. I thanked her as she rattled on, complimenting my flowers, remarking on the material of my gown. I was distracted, though. I struggled to tear my eyes away from the never-ending queue of people drinking from the vat.

There was so much water and so little actual blood mixed in that it gave a strange, murky pink look to the liquid. It reminded me of the fluid left at the bottom of a chicken packet from the grocery store.

I swallowed past a wave of nausea that roiled in my stomach.

"…Your Majesty?" Genevieve asked, and I realized I had completely missed her question.

"I'm sorry. What did you say?"

She gestured towards a gathering crowd at the center of the square. "Only if you'd like to dance? The music has shifted, you see, and the dancing is about to begin."

"Certainly," I replied, though I was anything but certain. I did not know how to dance besides a basic two-step I had relied on at Humanrealm parties and the odd dance clubs my friends and I had managed to sneak into. "Will you also dance, Lady Genevieve?"

"Oh no, Your Majesty. I am not one for dancing. I have the feet of a hippo."

Despite myself, I laughed. "The feet of a hippo? What does that mean?"

Genevieve chuckled along with me. "Do they not have that phrase in the Humanrealm?"

"Not to my knowledge," I replied. I imagined a stout hippo attempting a waltz and I snorted at the image.

"Oh, yes. It's a saying here. It's how you'd describe someone who is uncoordinated."

"Good to know," I mused.

The music did indeed shift and I turned my attention to the dozen women who circled around the maypole. I did not recognize any of them and so I assumed they were city residents rather than courtiers. It was hard to tell by outfit today as everyone donned their most colorful attire.

As the music sped up, the girls clasped hands and twirled, hooting and hollering at certain intervals when the music purposefully quieted. The faster they turned, the more the crowd clapped. Then, on a crescendo, the girls broke apart and each found the hands of others in the crowd. Willing or not, they dragged the new dancers to the pole and began circling again.

I clapped along with everyone else, surprised that my face naturally turned up in a smile. This was fun, and I realized I had found nothing else fun since I arrived here weeks, months ago. I took another drink of my wine, draining it to the bottom of the horn, before turning to Genevieve.

"Would you mind returning this for me?" I asked her.

"Of course, Your Majesty."

Then I moved closer to the revelry, letting the excitement in the air pull me forward. The notes of the music wrapped around me like a warm cocoon.

The music built once more and the girls spread out, looking for new people to join the fray. One spotted me on the edge of the dancing and approached with hesitant steps.

"Your Majesty," she said, sinking into a shy curtsy. "Would you like to dance?"

I nodded at her. I was not entirely sure what I was getting myself into yet nodding felt right. This felt right and natural, as if my cells knew the beat, as if my body had danced this dance before. I gave her my uninjured hand willingly and she led me to the dancers as cheers erupted anew. It seemed everyone was happy to see me get involved.

I followed the girl's lead as she pulled me into the linked circle around the pole. And then we were moving, circling and dancing and running and laughing. My breaths came in quick succession, yet I did not care, not as I giggled at someone's flamboyant twirl, not as I decided to spin away and return to the circle on my own.

I let the dancers, the music, the energy of the festival flow around me and through me. A sort of giddy exhilaration settled under my skin as I danced. Wisps of my curly, frizzy hair escaped their braids and whipped across my face. My long skirts snapped around my ankles with each turn and twist. I was sure a few flowers had dropped from Mara's updo and been crushed under boisterous feet. But I did not care.

I spun and spun, until the faces of watching Lords and Ladies blurred. I spun and spun until I felt at one with the men and women and children in the circle. I spun and spun, laughing and happy.

17
this is not a drill

I WAS SEATED AT MY USUAL TABLE IN THE LIBRARY SEVERAL days later when two soldiers approached.

Long before they stopped in front of me, my head had snapped up at the sound of their distant movement. Their weapons clinked with each step they took, their boots echoing on the flagstone floors and past the stacks.

I was ready for them when they rounded the corner that led to my underground table, and I held my head a bit higher. I felt my own guards draw in a touch closer to me out of an overabundance of caution.

"Your Majesty," the soldiers said in unison as they bowed. "We've been asked to escort you to the Council Chamber immediately."

"Why?" I questioned automatically. Something in the seriousness of their tone, the unprecedented nature of sending soldiers to fetch me, had my senses on high alert. As if I could scent it on the wind, I knew that something was not right.

"We were simply tasked with bringing you to the Council. We have no other information, Majesty."

I nodded. It was stupid of me to ask them in the first place. The Lords would not have sought to justify themselves to the soldiers.

I stood. "Let's go then."

My guards fell in step behind me. The soldiers walked a step ahead of me. And our contingent left the library in a great clatter of swords, scuff of boots, and the swish of my own long gown.

Several of the librarians and assistants craned their necks to see what the commotion was, and then abruptly bowed upon seeing me. I nodded at them, trying to spread a small smile across my lips. But my insides were growing cold with wondering what this was about.

Was it Eliza or Roland? Was there an accident? Something had happened—of this I was sure.

We made our way through the back stairs and servants' hallways rather than the main halls. I was grateful for that. I did not trust my nerves in my current state to not snap at a courtier who stared or snickered at me.

And then we were entering the Council Chamber. There was no need to open the doors for they were already thrown open. I was not the last person here. Lords were streaming in on either side of me, bowing perfunctorily as they squeezed past.

"Your Majesty, my Lords. Please, if you will be seated, we have urgent business to discuss," Grimly intoned from his spot near my seat far at the other end of the room.

My guards left me to walk on my own and I made the long journey to my dais and then my yellowwood perch. I knew the Lords were waiting for me to begin and so I waved my hand in a vague "go ahead" gesture.

Grimly nodded. "I've called this special session to discuss a piece of intelligence we've just come upon. Our informants outside of our borders tell us of whispers of an imminent attack."

Murmurs and intakes of breath broke out along the chamber, and Grimly lifted his hand to silence them. "Nothing has happened yet," he said, raising his voice to be heard. "But we must take this tip-off seriously and put in place any necessary precautions now to protect our Queen and our nation."

"Me?" I said, genuinely surprised to hear Grimly utter those words. I could understand protecting the people but what did I have to do with it?

Grimly bowed again as he turned towards me. "Yes, Queen Sahle. The threat has been made against your life as well as the people of Izwe."

I felt my mouth hang open and I willed it closed. "Why would they threaten me?"

"Why did they kill your parents?" a voice answered from midway down the ebony table. I shut my eyes in dismay, all too aware of who had now entered the conversation.

"Excuse me?" I replied, hoping that my will to be calm was translating over to my voice.

Lord Anson stood, leaning one arm casually against the back of his tall wooden chair. "I asked, 'Why did they kill your parents?'"

I just stared at him, unsure of the response he was looking for.

And of course Anson smiled cheekily. "Since you are unaware, let us educate you, Your Majesty.

"Your parents were killed by our enemies in an attempt to get to you. They hoped that by killing you, they could prevent the prophecy from coming true—a prophecy that spelled out Izwe's prosperity and one they understood as a threat.

"Your parents' deaths were just a happy byproduct of that attempt. Without them, you are the only heir to this kingdom. By killing you now, they could remove the threat of the prophecy, and also cause anarchy as our country grapples to name a new monarch.

"So you see, Majesty, killing you is the ultimate goal for them. It is one in the same with the destruction of the Izweian people. Does that make sense?"

My lips had pressed themselves together while Anson spoke. I willed them to relax now. I did not want him to see how he irked me, how his every word felt like needles pressing in on me.

He was insufferable, and even more so now that he was right. He was putting it in very pointed terms, but he was right nonetheless. My death would be a multifaceted prize for our enemies.

I did not trust my voice and so I merely nodded at Anson. Another Lord saved me from having to speak, though.

A blonde Lord by the name of John of House Isibankwa stood from his seat and turned his youthful face to me. Anson sat to allow him the floor. "Majesty, if I may…your safety is of the utmost importance. Anson puts it bluntly but everything he said is true. Your death would be the greatest prize to our enemies. You are valuable to us, as you are to them.

"Accordingly, I believe we need to increase our protective measures here at the palace. The Queen must be well tended to, and any unknown entities must be prevented from entering our sanctum."

Nearly all the Lords gathered around the table nodded. Another stood, although I did not know this one's name.

"My Queen, I would also urge you to relinquish your training temporarily while we investigate this threat," he said.

Several Lords agreed—I could tell by the nods, the several rounds of "hear, hear."

"And the reason for that request, my Lord?" I replied.

I was surprised to feel myself grow defensive about the training. For all that I complained, I had come to relish the time I spent on the training grounds with Finn. I was convinced that I would never wield magic, despite Finn's continued attempt to coax it out of me. But I might very well manage a weapon with some amount of skill, and that could be the exact thing that saved my life if and when a threat came for me.

John Isibankwa responded, "It is much simpler to keep you safe within the palace walls. The entrances are controlled. Guards are posted at nearly every door. Outside in the training grounds, there are limitless ways to get to you—"

"Aside from the fact that I am surrounded by soldiers?" I interrupted.

The Lord bowed. "Of course, Your Majesty…Still, I do not know if we can risk the life of our Queen on the mere fact that the Vikela are around."

"Then ask Commander Finn to guard me when I am in the training ground. Or better yet, set up a perimeter of guards so that no strangers can enter the grounds when I am within."

Grimly stood up to add. "Would you accept guards stationed in the training ring with you?"

"No," I said shortly. And I meant it. My training time was embarrassing and occasionally bloody and bruising. The last thing I wanted were witnesses to my ignorance and incompetence, even if they were other soldiers. "I do not need spectators in the actual ring with me. A perimeter around the soldiers' barracks themselves will do perfectly fine. They can secure the area and prevent anyone entering or exiting who shouldn't be. I don't have to see them."

I thought I heard a sigh from down the table, in the vicinity of Anson's seat. I pretended it was my imagination. I thought about calling him out, but instead I cleared my throat and spoke calmly. "I know several of you may disagree with me, but this is what I am asking. I consent to the increasing of guards at the training ground, but I will not have more people than I already have following me around. I do not wish to feel like a prisoner. I trust you can respect that and maybe even understand that.

"As for the people of Izwe, what can be done?" I looked from one Lord to the next, and none seemed willing to be the first to speak. "Anyone?" I called.

Anson rose once more. "Queen Sahle, Izwe is a vast kingdom. There is a limited amount that can be done to secure it—"

"And so you're suggesting we do nothing?" I quipped, my voice rising despite my best efforts to keep it level.

Anson arched one eyebrow, seemingly surprised that I had interrupted him. Then he smiled. "No, Majesty. Yet I would urge you to understand that all of your soldiers deployed could still not protect every region of your kingdom. There are too many people, too many assets, too many cities. Unless you yourself would like to protect them with your magical abilities…"

My eyes cut straight to Anson and I could feel my hatred for him bubble up. How dare he.

I knew the Council had been receiving progress reports from Finn. I knew that each Lord here must know exactly how ineffective I was with magic—so much so that ineffective was not even the correct word.

No, I was useless, unable, incapable. Ineffective implied that potential was there; I had no potential. Because I had no magic.

My cheeks flamed, and I thanked the Great One for blessing me with doe-brown skin. The embarrassment would have otherwise clearly shown lobster red across my face. My hands clenched the smooth wooden arms of my chair and my body tensed as if I would jump up.

A part of me wanted to. Half of my brain immediately envisioned myself flying down the length of the table, grabbing Anson by the collar, and slamming his arrogant, chiseled face into the Council table. The other half of my brain focused on my breathing, willing each inhale and slow exhale in an attempt to regain my composure.

"My Lord, this is hardly the time or place to—" an elderly Lord began.

"Perhaps you are correct," Anson said curtly, silencing the elder. "Excuse me," he said, though his eyes glowed with mirth even as he bowed in apology and resumed his seat.

I blinked again, telling myself to breathe. This was not the time or the place to get angry, just as that elder Lord was saying. I turned my attention to him now. I did not recall his name, which was hardly a surprise to me.

"My Lord," I addressed him generally. "Please remind me of your name."

The elder stood slowly, as if each limb needed a few seconds to settle into the new position. "Marcus of House Inyathi, Your Majesty."

I nodded, forcibly pushing down any embarrassment I felt at needing to clarify who he was. "Thank you, Lord Marcus. What do you think about the defense of Izweians? I would like to hear your opinion."

Marcus looked at me but if he was surprised, he did not show it. "Majesty, I would recommend deploying as many troops as can be spared to key locations: cities, important resources like bridges and mines and water reservoirs, major border crossing sites. We cannot protect everyone, but we can provide troops and resources to the most necessary sites."

I listened closely, thinking I understood his logic. Still, I wanted to be sure. "And why those resources?"

"Every life is important, Majesty, but as a government we can only protect so much. A husband can protect his wife, but the same man cannot singlehandedly protect an entire water reservoir from being poisoned. That is where we come in. We must look after the collective needs and resources and allow our people to fend for the individual."

"It's not perfect," I replied, mulling over his words in my head. "But it makes sense."

"Thank you, Your Majesty," Marcus of Inyathi replied.

I shifted my attention back to the Council's leader. "Grimly?"

"Queen Sahle."

"I motion to follow this Lord's plan. If we have limited resources, I believe this would be the best use of it. Can I entrust you and the rest of the Lords to deal with the logistics of deploying soldiers to these sites?"

Grimly bowed his head. "Of course, Your Majesty."

"And Anson," I called, unable to help myself. "Perhaps you can lend your own magical abilities to the task. I understand that yours are nearly as effective as my own."

For the first time, I heard snickers and disbelieving held-back laughter from the Lords.

I took in a deep breath and then I rose from my seat and slowly made my way down the length of the Council Chamber. I walked directly towards Anson, the heels of my little satin shoes clipping on the floor as I approached. I could feel my skin crawl as he looked at me, his eyes narrowing. And for a moment, I thought I saw that wicked humor still swirling behind those green pupils.

I stopped right next to him, and he held my gaze with his own. Then he grinned and I knew I had to walk on before I did something I would regret.

He was insufferable and I wished I could smack that cocky look off his face.

Instead, I simply walked on. My skin tingled again, and I knew his eyes were on me, probably glaring in the same way I had glared at him.

And for the millionth time I wondered what I had done for him to hate me so.

IN THE NEXT DAYS, I RECEIVED WORD THAT TROOPS HAD indeed been stationed at key locations in Izwe. This included border crossings, water reservoirs, grain stores, mines, major arterial roads, and more.

As much as I knew Grimly was right—we did not have the soldiers needed to protect every citizen in Izwe—I worried about them. I had spent hardly any time outside of the palace grounds. I had met few actual residents of Izwe apart from the soldiers, servants, and courtiers here. Still, I felt like I could picture them out there, living quiet, comfortable lives in their modest rondavels. The nameless, faceless Izweians led the sort of life I had always wanted for myself. If I were being honest, I envied them most days, as well as feared for them.

I was forgetting what it felt like to be normal.

After word came of the threat, the palace had felt on edge. Servants seemed to move faster, getting from point A to point B as quickly as possible. Courtiers spoke more in whisper than word, casting furtive glances over their shoulder as if someone would be standing right behind them with a knife.

Yet as days turned into weeks, I could feel the palace shifting back into a sense of normalcy. The relaxation of the courtiers almost made me believe the threat was something I had imagined, some dream I had had where I once again sat in the Council Chamber and made a fool of myself.

I had those dreams often.

The courtiers and servants might have forgotten about the threat. But there was one group who had not forgotten: the Vikela. They were trained to be on alert, to meet an attack head on, and I continued to feel their anxious, restless energy every time I went to the training yard for a lesson in combat, magic, or zebra riding.

The number of soldiers stationed at the palace had not lessened. I knew Grimly would not allow that, not with me in residence, not to mention himself and the other Lords. It was not a reduction in soldiers I felt each time I trained with Finn; rather, it was a sense of displacement that seemed to hover over the soldiers' barracks. Their minds were far from the palace, out on would-be battlefields of water reservoirs and border crossings. They worried about and envied, in equal measure, their soldier-brethren there on the frontlines.

Finn told me as much one morning. We were sitting in the soldiers' mess hall with wooden cups of water in front of us after a particularly grueling run.

"Make the water boil," Finn said, nodding to the carved cup resting on the table in front of me.

I snorted, picking up the water and taking a sip. The earthy smell of the mess hall's thatched roof complemented the cool, clear liquid on my tongue. "Like I could."

"You know, your biggest problem is that you undermine yourself. You're convinced that you can't do something before you even try. With that attitude, you'll never learn your magic."

"I don't have any magic," I said again, for what felt like the millionth time.

Finn drank a sip of his own water. "You keep saying that, but it's nearly impossible. Both your mother and father had magic of some sort so it's almost a certainty that you do, too."

"Maybe I'm an anomaly."

"Maybe you're just stubborn."

I rolled my eyes. He was not wrong. That was the thing about Finn—he seemed to be able to see right through me. It was both unnerving and nice, and I realized that despite our bickering, we had formed a sort of friendship through our training.

I looked at him a moment, taking in the blond hair swept back from his face, the high eyebrows, and the strong jawline. "Do you think we're friends?"

He choked on his water, his eyes darting to mine. "Friends?" he asked incredulously.

I refused to let his response sway me. "Yes, I was just thinking that, as much as you're annoying, you might be the only person I genuinely like here in Izwe."

He watched me a moment more before smiling a little. "That's high praise coming from you, Your Majesty."

I snickered. "Maybe."

"I am your trainer, first and foremost," he continued. And then, with only the slightest pause, "But yes, I like to consider us friends, as well."

"You're the only one I let treat me like shit," I quipped back.

"I don't treat you like shit," his eyebrows rising in complete shock.

I laughed at his appalled face. "No, no, you don't. I...just thank you for being a friend. I feel like I need all the friends I can get these days."

"With the threat?"

I took a contemplative sip of water. "Yes, all of the waiting and uncertainty...it's exhausting."

Something in Finn's eyes told me he understood even before he opened his mouth. "For us, too. I'm sure you can feel it here, in the barracks?"

I turned my head to survey the other men sitting at various tables scattered through the hall. "Yes, it feels like a pall over the entire soldiers' grounds. Do the men worry for the other soldiers? The ones on guard now across Izwe?"

"Yes," Finn replied, looking at the cup he was cradling in his hands. "Most of these soldiers came from other areas. They were the best in their cohort and so they were sent here to join the Vikela, to guard the palace and serve the Lords—and now you. So the men stationed out there, looking for any threat, are their family and friends."

I had never thought about the reality of my orders, that I would be putting soldiers' lives on the line by trying to protect the people and resources of the broader kingdom. I was beginning to understand how every decision I made had its own set of unintended consequences.

"You're feeling sorry for them," Finn said, accurately reading my face.

I nodded. "I was so focused on protecting the people that I did not think about who would be doing the protecting."

Finn caught my gaze with his own and held it. "Don't feel sorry about that. We soldiers chose this life because we want to serve. That means putting ourselves in danger in defense of the crown and the kingdom. At the same time, we can still miss and mourn our brothers, and worry for those on the frontlines. Those two things can exist simultaneously."

I was not sure I would ever truly understand that, deep in my bones. I was not a soldier, and though I spent time here with them each day, I would never be one of them. Still, I nodded. "I get that."

"No you don't," Finn responded, reading me once more. "But you don't need to. Just trust me when I tell you it's one thing you should never worry about. Protect your people, use your soldiers. That's what we're trained to do."

"Thank you," I said, smiling slightly at him.

"Anytime, Your Majesty. Now, shall we try again with the water?"

I ignored that and downed the rest of my water in a single gulp.

Each day after, I waited with baited breath for some word to come. I ate my breakfast of pap with an ear turned to the door for a messenger. My hands constantly twitched with anxious energy.

I felt the waiting like pressure behind my eyes, and no matter how many times Eliza and Roland wrote and told me that an attack was not guaranteed, I worried. They urged me that intelligence and whispers were often wrong, and that even if it were true, our troops were stationed broadly. My soldiers were well trained and ready to take on a challenge.

I should not worry. That was what they told me in each letter.

But Eliza and Roland also knew me well. They knew I would worry, and so they sent little bobbles to distract me: a pressed flower similar to my favorite white and purple daisies from the Humanrealm, a small unpolished gem they had found while walking at their estate, a "coupon" for a one-night stay at Maison Eliza—the name they had jokingly adopted for what I understood to be their small country manor.

I appreciated their notes and the earnest love that flowed out of them, and they did distract me for a while at least. But what I found worked even better was spending time with Finn.

The training helped, our banter helped, even forgetting that I was Queen for a few hours as I tried to beat him to a pulp helped. I was grateful for that and grateful for the start of our friendship. I tried to focus on the silver linings of the moment even while I sat on edge.

AS I DUG INTO A CUT OF GUINEA FOWL AT DINNER, I mulled over the patterns of chitenge cloth on display. The courtiers were always dressed in the brightly colored and busily patterned material, cut into traditional gowns, breeches, and waistcoats. It was the most fascinating combination I had ever seen—squarely landing somewhere between a Lagos fashion show and a historical reenactment from the 1700s.

But in all the time I had been in the Alterealm, I had looked upon these outfits mockingly. Their brightness and boldness had always been ostentatious, but I purposefully tried to look past that knee-jerk reaction now and rather see the intricacy and effort.

And the outfits were intricate, and they were clearly chock-full of effort both by those who designed the attire and by those who had to carefully walk, sit, and move to keep it on their bodies.

I smiled into my cup at a nearly-neon yellow jacket that whizzed by me as two courtiers danced. It was certainly a sight to behold, even if I had no plans of my own of rushing out and purchasing a gown in that color.

Finishing the downy yams on my plate, I set my fork aside and stood. As always, the music stopped whenever I moved but I signaled the musicians to carry on. I was not leaving. I merely wanted a few moments in the cool evening air.

I could see the shine of the stars even through the glass doors lining the Great Hall. The stars, so bright and luminous in the jet sky of Izwe, called to me as all the stars had called to me before. I let them guide me past the spinning courtiers who paused and bowed at my approach, past the servants pouring glass after glass of bubbling konstans, past the trays of sliced meat that never seemed to empty.

The stars were more glorious and, fixated as I was on them, I did not notice the balcony was occupied until the echo of my heels caused a dark head to turn to me from the railing.

For a split second, I contemplated marching back inside. I had no desire to chit chat with anyone, let alone with this man. But Anson's stupid lips had already turned up into that smile I was coming to know too well. That teasing glint quickly replaced whatever contemplative look had been in his eyes just moments before.

I had never known when to fall back from a challenge, and so I did my best to pretend I had not hesitated. I squared my shoulders and walked on, pointedly ignoring the way his gaze tracked me, pressing in on my profile as I, too, settled against the railings with my hands balanced over the edge.

"Good evening, Majesty," Anson said, his voice like a whisper on the wind.

"Anson," I nodded to the distant hills and silver trees. I had no desire to meet his eye.

"It's beautiful out here."

"Yes." He was right, but that did not mean I had to say anything more than a single syllable in reply.

Silence stretched between us for the space of one, two, three heartbeats. I lost count after the tenth, the awkward tension radiating in such a way that made all purpose of spending a few peaceful moments on the balcony useless. Just as I was about to go back inside, Anson cleared his throat.

My eyes shifted to his form unbidden, shocked as I was by that sound. There was something uncertain in it—something almost…nervous. And that was not an emotion I had ever associated with Anson.

He had turned slightly, angling his body so that his hands still dangled over the edge of the railing while keeping me in his sight. I quirked an eyebrow at the expectant face looking back at me. "Yes, Lord Anson?"

"I did not say anything," he replied simply, innocently. Too innocently.

My eyes narrowed. "No, you did not."

His smile widened, quirking up a touch higher on one side.

But if I was not in a mood to be heckled by him on most days, I certainly was not today. Despite the ever-present threat to Izwe, it had been a good day filled with the tiniest bit of hope and acceptance that I was finally settling here. I finally had a friend. I was making some amount of progress in my understanding and my training. In a small, infinitesimal way, I was coming to accept that this was home.

I did not need Anson to ruin it.

I stepped away from the railing and made to turn before Anson's voice sounded again. "I did not say anything, Majesty, but I was planning to."

I crossed my arms and waited. I did not see the point in wasting more breath asking why or what.

Anson seemed to realize that, because he did not hesitate much longer before finally coughing up what he had to say. And it was like coughing up, just like a cat coughs up a hairball. He looked pained and uncomfortable as he bit out, "I wanted to apologize for my words about your magic in the Council Chamber."

I stared at him, willing my jaw to clench rather than drop open.

I was utterly flabbergasted. Granted I had not known Anson for long, but the little I did know did not lend me to believe he was a man who ever ate his words or felt the smallest hint of regret for them, especially not when it came to humiliating me.

I shook my head—some motion to focus on as I tried to rein in my surprise—and met Anson's gaze. "That's something I never thought I would hear."

Anson nodded at me knowingly. "I will admit I often find it difficult to own up to my mistakes."

"Shocking," I muttered under my breath.

His eyes shown in what was either anger or amusement, perhaps both. It was hard to make it out clearly in the shadows of the balcony, illuminated as it was by the stars and the distant glow of the Great Hall.

"Yes, well, the Council hears often about your work with Commander Finn. We understand you are still unused to this realm and the concept of magic, but you are trying—when it suits you—" he added with a pointed look.

I rolled my eyes, not bothering to hide the gesture. If this balcony was suddenly the Sahle and Anson safe space, then I was glad to do my part in making it as honest as possible.

He continued, "To imply that you could not protect the realm was uncalled for—"

"Thank you," I interrupted.

An open-handed gesture that said, "Of course," was the only response before he carried on. "You may be young and naive, unskilled and—"

"Hey!" I called, cutting off whatever twist in the conversation he was taking.

"Just wait," he replied. When I clamped my lips together in a way that sufficiently ensured him I was done interrupting, he smiled and pointedly added, "ignorant…But you are trying to remedy that. And that's all we can ask of you."

I bit the inside of my cheek as I looked at him. He was like a snake, beautiful and shimmering black in the moonlight, but not something you wanted to lose sight of lest it bite.

"Thank you?" I asked, unsure what to do with these convoluted words.

"Is that a question?"

"Was that an apology?"

"Certainly," he answered simply, like there was nothing more straightforward that had ever been spoken.

"Hmph," I muttered, not entirely convinced. But who was I to look a gift horse in the mouth? From this man, I was surprised that the notion of an apology was even possible for him to grasp. And so, for the first time, I gave him the benefit of the doubt. "Then the 'thank you' is a statement, not a question."

He inclined his head in an approximation of his ironic bow, and I scoffed. His eyes glinted.

Before I knew what was coming out of my mouth, I was speaking. "For what it's worth, I apologize for what I said about your magic."

It seemed to be his moment to be caught off guard because the smile dropped from his lips instantly. "Oh…no apology necessary, Majesty."

I clasped my hands in front of me, glanced down at them before I replied. "I think it is rather necessary. I may not understand everything about this realm, but I have the distinct impression that one's magic is a touchy subject, especially for the Lords."

When I brought my gaze back up to Anson, he was looking at me in a way I could not place. It was like he was trying to puzzle me out, see inside my skull, or make sense of a foreign language I had just spoken.

"Perhaps I'm mistaken," I added, suddenly unsure of myself.

He blinked and the look was gone, replaced once more with the unaffected expression he wore when not all-out mocking me. "No, you are correct. It is a touchy subject, as you put it. Many families are sensitive to the perception of their magic slipping through their fingers."

"But not you?"

He leveled a sly smile at me, "Majesty, I thought you were keeping up with your studies? Surely you should know that I still have mine."

I took a breath, willing myself not to rankle at the teasing tone. "I am and I do know. That's why I said what I said, what I just apologized for."

"Ah, yes," Anson replied. "Then what do you want to know?"

My mouth did drop open now, and I contained my annoyance as I watched him notice it and smirk. He was spinning me around on purpose, confusing my words and making me sound like a blubbering idiot. I wondered why that surprised me. This was Anson, good old Anson, no matter what he had said or done in these few minutes on the balcony.

"I was going to ask what your power is. In one book in the library, magic wielders were given a grade to denote how powerful they were. You were graded as one. I'm curious what that means, what you can do."

"Tsk, tsk, tsk," Anson admonished as he lazily moved towards me. With each step, it seemed a tangible web of tension built in the space between us. Unconsciously, I took a step back. "That's something your book didn't tell you then, Majesty. It's frightfully rude to ask a wielder what they can do."

A pace away, I watched as his gaze dropped and then swept slowly from the hem of my gown, over the swells of my hips, the dip of my waist, the valley of my collarbone, and back to my confused and quickly-becoming-infuriated eyes. I clenched my hands as if I could squeeze away the weight of his look.

"One day, you'll understand exactly why that is," he said quietly.

Before I could ask what that was supposed to mean, he turned and walked quickly back through the doors to the Great Hall.

I stared after him until his dark form melded into the mass of colorfully clothed courtiers. And I wondered what it was that Anson could do—what it was that he did not want me to know.

20
unexpected

"LEFT, RIGHT, LEFT, PARRY. LEFT, LEFT, RIGHT."

Finn announced the steps as we moved through the motions, the sounds of our swords crashing together its only accompaniment.

We had been at this constant sword training for weeks, and I was beginning to tire of its monotony.

"You're not focusing," Finn barked as he nearly struck my arm with his weapon. A lock of his blond hair fell across his forehead as he lunged at me, a look of annoyance in his blue eyes.

While we usually trained each morning, our training routine had begun to grow more haphazard of late now that Finn and the soldiers were performing more active drills and watches. I was happy to be flexible and train around their schedule whether it was early morning or later in the afternoon like today. Besides, the Izweian sky was glorious in the afternoon. The sun glinted through the clouds, bathing the sky in paint strokes of pink and orange as it moved ever closer to the horizon.

But we had been at this for hours. My arms burned as I held off another strike from Finn, and my feet scrambled in the loose red dirt of the training ground as I barely spun out and away from another blow.

"I'm trying," I ground out past my gritted teeth. Sweat dripped down my forehead and I could feel wayward strands of my hair stuck to my neck. I did not dare wipe at the sweat or lift my hair free. Finn would take it as another sign of weakness.

"You are trying," Finn agreed as he stabbed at my right side. "You're just not doing a very good job of it."

"Excuse me?" I gasped at him as I countered his strike with one of my own.

Finn's answering smile was mischievous. "I apologize. You're just not doing a very good job of it, Your Majesty."

"Ugh!" I exclaimed. I knew Finn was baiting me, trying to use my outrage to keep my focus on him. He knew me well, and he understood that I had an unhealthy dose of pride and stubbornness.

Finn swung again at me, the muscles underneath his tunic bunching and relaxing as he moved. It was not the first time I had noticed such things, of course. Finn was an attractive man, strong and well-built in the way of those who worked with their bodies for a living.

"Your Majesty, I said focus."

I did not have the mental capacity to wonder whether he caught me staring at his arms, not as another blow was aimed at my thigh and I had to jump out of the way.

I stumbled and nearly fell on my face in the red dirt, but I managed to pivot on one foot and keep my balance at the last second. I knew Finn had expected me to fall. He planned that maneuver to get me covered in dust and chastise me about my clumsiness.

But this time I did not fall. This time, I could use his plan against him.

Before he could track that I had caught myself, I swung around on him. I threw out my blade not at his left side as would be expected from this angle but from below, as if I would gut him from groin to navel.

I saw the shock on his face, followed quickly by his pleasure that I had outsmarted him. He was too fast, though, and he jumped up and away before my sword could come close to actually cutting him.

"Well done, Your Majesty," he panted.

I was not done, though. I had always been a good student, obstinate and determined to do an exceptional job. In the Humanrealm, that usually translated to things like studying extra hours for a test. Here, it applied to combat training with Finn.

I was a Queen who had many enemies. I always had guards with me these days, but so had my parents. I was all too aware of where that had gotten them. There would be a moment when I needed to count on my own abilities to save my skin, and every second I pushed myself with Finn upped my chances of coming out of that moment alive.

I was on the offensive now, spurned forward by being able to outsmart Finn. I was determined to show him I would not be underestimated.

I lunged forward, swiping my sword at belly height in a way that made Finn jump back again. Left, right, left. I kept up my assault as I pushed us towards the other end of the training ground, swords clashing as we went.

The far side of the training ground was ringed by the tall, purple-flowered jacaranda trees. Finn and I often took breaks from practice there, sitting in the shade of the vibrant canopy.

Now, I wondered how I could use the trees to my advantage. If Finn wanted to see me focus, I would show him just how focused I could be.

Finn monitored my attacks as I steered us towards one of the large jacaranda trunks. I felt the change in him instantly as he went from merely fending me off to using my distraction of the offense to his benefit. I just did not know what he had in store yet.

We reached the ring of trees, and I lunged forward as if to skewer Finn directly through the sternum. As quick as I moved forward, Finn stepped sideways. I spun to follow him as he moved behind me and, as I turned, I realized my mistake.

In two steps, Finn had me caged between his body and the jacaranda's trunk. There was no space to swing a sword but it did not stop Finn from lunging, this time with the sword up and horizontal against my neck.

Distantly, I felt my back collide with the scaled bark behind me, then the cold steel of Finn's sword placed against the thin, exposed skin of my throat.

I stilled.

I knew Finn would never actually hurt me, but it was human instinct to cow when the bite of a blade pressed into such a delicate area.

My chest rose and fell quickly. My heart beat in double time, adrenaline pumping through my veins at both the exertion and the animal reaction to the threat.

But my gaze was locked on Finn's. His blue eyes blazed with a single-mindedness that made him the fighter he was.

He was so near to me. The front of his tunic brushed across my breasts every time his chest rose with an inhale. His breath blew across the bridge of my nose and the arch of my cheeks with each rapid exhale.

I could feel the heat of his body radiating mere inches away, and I had an impulsive desire to know what his skin would feel like pressed against my own. And suddenly, the animal instinct in me shifted. I was not afraid of Finn's sword. It had been forgotten in the blue of his eyes.

To this day, I wish I knew what went on in Finn's head at that moment. Could he see my sudden interest in my eyes or scent it on my skin, as close as he was? I will never know but, as if he read my mind, his lips were suddenly on mine.

His mouth closed over my own in a fierceness that took my breath away. The sword he held at my throat clattered to the ground and then there was no space between us. Finn's chest was pressed against mine, his thighs pushed into my own, holding me against the trunk of the tree as his hands swept up my sides, my neck, and to the edges of my face.

He cupped my face between his palms as his lips skated over mine. His tongue teased the seam of my lips and I opened for him with no reluctance.

But just as his tongue met my own, it was as if a shock ran through him. In an instant, he jumped back, putting a good foot of space between us.

"Your Majesty," he whispered, and I saw a dawning horror on his face.

"Finn," I said, reaching out a hand to him from where I was still pressed against the tree.

But he stepped another foot away.

"Your Majesty, my deepest apologies. That was entirely inappropriate," Finn said, averting his eyes from my face and to the ground. I noticed his cheeks had the faintest stain of pink and I wondered, in a remote part of my mind, if it was from the kiss or the shame he was feeling now.

And I realized that I did not want his apologies. In fact, I hated them.

Ever since I had arrived in this God- and godsforsaken place, I had been treated like a child, albeit one also feared for the implicit power my birth had given me.

I wanted to feel normal. I wanted for one moment to just be a woman, an ordinary woman who could enjoy a kiss with an ordinary man without any more repercussions than the possibility of a broken heart.

I wanted Finn to stop apologizing and kiss me.

I knew it was uncouth and improper. I could already imagine Eliza and Roland reprimanding me over even the second of a kiss that had just occurred. I could see Grimly, Anson, and the rest of the Lords losing their minds over the Queen of Izwe locking lips with Finn, the soldier.

But I did not care. I had spent the last months ashamed at my ignorance and frightened of my power, overwhelmed at learning the customs of this new land and alone with not a single true friend.

I wanted to feel good, to feel wanted. I wanted to have something entirely my own in this world where I had nothing.

It was simple. I wanted Finn.

"Finn," I said again, and this time I stepped forward.

Finn's only response was to bow and stay bowed, his eyes fixed on the red dust swirling around our feet. I strode the few paces that separated us.

From his lowered position, I watched his blonde hair gently stir in the breeze. I ran my eyes over the line of his shoulders, muscled and broad. I laid my hand on one arm and squeezed it lightly.

"Please rise."

Finn slowly unbent, standing before me with the straight back of a soldier, his eyes trained on a distant point just past my head.

"Look at me," I said quietly, for I could not stand the idea of someone being afraid to face me—especially when that someone was my friend.

A heartbeat passed and then his gaze shifted to mine.

I could see fear in his eyes, discomfort and fear. But I could also see an inkling of that desire still swirling in their blue depths, and it emboldened me.

I stepped closer to him and watched his breath catch as he tracked my movement.

"I don't want your apologies," I whispered as I took another step.

When Finn did not back up, I took the last step into him. My heart was beating a mile a minute and my skin felt tingly, like a live wire had sparked across every inch of it.

Our bodies rested against each other, and I reached up with one hand to cup Finn's cheek.

"I don't want your apologies," I repeated, so close now that his breath was again on my face, his heart beating next to mine where our chests met. "I want you to kiss me."

Finn's gaze sharpened and he glanced at my lips, then back to my eyes. "It is most unwise, Your Majesty."

"I know," I agreed. "But I don't care. I'm an adult, and I enjoyed your kiss. Will you answer a question honestly, regardless of the fact that I'm the Queen?"

Finn looked at me a moment and then nodded.

"If I were just a regular girl, would you have stopped that kiss?"

"No," he said without any reluctance.

"Would you want to kiss me again…if I were just a regular girl?"

"Yes," he replied.

"Then kiss me," I whispered as I leaned my face up to his.

But Finn was not ready. He did not back away from me or tell me no, but I still saw the warring emotion on his face. "What of the Council?"

"Fuck the Council," I said without a moment's hesitation.

Finn laughed, and I could not stop my lips from turning up into a mischievous smile.

"They won't like it," he said, even as his hands made their way to my waist.

"I don't care what they like," I replied, even as my hands found their place on his chest.

"They'll think it's wildly inappropriate," he whispered, even as his face lowered to mine.

"Then it'll be our secret," I murmured, even as his lips brushed against my own.

And then all thought and words were forgotten as Finn's tongue picked up where it had left off just moments before.

FINN'S KISS BURNED THROUGH ME, AND I FELT ALIVE.

The feel of his hands on my waist, my hip…the feel of his chest, his shoulders, the edge of his jawline under my hands…it consumed me. I was a live wire, crackling and sparking in pure feeling. And I wanted to chase the feeling as far as it would go.

Despite the relatively quiet life I had lived in the Humanrealm, I was not unaware of what I was doing. I had dated—albeit briefly and quietly—and I had slept with several men by my fateful twentieth birthday. I knew what I was doing, and I knew what I wanted from Finn.

I did not articulate this, but such is the way of bodies; we have always moved and kissed and spoken through our actions. I spoke to Finn through the angles of my hips, the catches in my breath, the small gasps of pleasure that broke past our interlocked lips. And he understood what I wanted without me having to speak the words.

Late in the day as it was, many of the soldiers were in the mess hall or relaxing in their rondavels. Still, we moved unassumingly through the soldiers' compound, our hands momentarily to ourselves, our faces composed and blank, even with our blood humming in our veins.

Finn led me to one of the huts, and I guessed it was his own personal residence. With a quick glance left and right to make sure no one saw us, he pulled me inside and shut the door.

I had never been inside a soldier's rooms before and, though I was curious what these little round houses were like, I did not care to explore it at this particular moment.

Because in this moment, the instant the door was shut and locked behind us, Finn's hands landed on me once more.

This time they were more insistent, daring to reach further south to cup the swell of my bottom and up to brush the sweep of my breasts. I moaned under his ministrations, and suddenly I needed more.

I found the buttons of his training tunic and undid them in a rush, my shaking fingers making it hard to remove the sturdy cloth loops from each one. Each freed button bared more of Finn's chest, and I took it in like a starving man consuming food.

I had seen Finn move, and I knew the lean muscle under his tunic would be defined. It was not so much a shock, then, to see it fully; but it was a fulfillment, a moment of seeing exactly what I had pictured in my mind's eye whenever I noted a particularly complementary angle of Finn's body under the training tunic.

His shirt shed, his hands reached up to unbutton mine. He paused as his hands grasped the first button, and I felt his fingers shake slightly against my collar bone.

"Are you sure?" he whispered, his voice thick and husky in the dim light of the rondavel.

"Completely," I said back to him as I dislodged his hands from my own clothes and began unbuttoning them myself.

Finn watched me, his eyes following my fingers as I pulled each button free and then shrugged off the tunic. I did not waste time in unhooking the snug training bra and stepping out of the training pants. The last to go were my underwear, and I tossed them aside, too, before meeting Finn's gaze.

I could feel his eyes on me like a warm touch as he drank in each angle of my naked skin. I wondered what he saw when he looked at me. Was I just a woman? Or did he see a Queen, bared completely?

I did not have the wherewithal to be nervous or uncertain, not as I stepped towards him again. He did not move, and I knew then that he was seeing his Queen. He was hesitating because he was thinking logically.

I wanted him to think illogically.

I took his hand and raised it to my lips. "Finn, you're thinking."

He swallowed audibly and I watched the column of his neck tremble. "I am."

"Do you want me to put my clothes back on?" I whispered, taking one of his fingers into my mouth and sucking the pad.

He let out a low hiss at the sensation. "No."

I let the finger go as I looked up into his eyes. "Then touch me."

And it was the last encouragement he needed.

Hands moved across my bare skin, squeezing and teasing. His mouth found mine again and we drank hungrily from each other.

Then I felt something behind my knees, and I realized we had moved across the room to the bed. I let myself collapse backward onto the mattress, dragging Finn with me. He landed between my legs, and I thought that was fortuitous.

That was exactly where I wanted him.

I helped ease the pants down Finn's hips, and then he was as naked as I was. Cradled between my hips, I could feel the swell of him pressing into my soft skin. I shimmied slightly until he was positioned at my opening.

He stilled and his gaze caught mine. I held it for a split second, before recapturing his mouth with my own. And as I ran my tongue over his lower lip, he pushed into me in one startling thrust.

I cried out, the feel of him stretching and filling me exactly what I wanted. He withdrew and thrust again, and this time he caught my mouth, the sweep of his tongue timed with the motion of his body.

We moved together in a frenzied tangle of limbs. Our gasps and moans filled the space of the small rondavel as we hurtled towards completion. I could feel it building in me, a tightening that swelled and swelled until, when I thought I could not take it any longer, it broke like the crest of a wave.

My own release spurned on Finn's, and he thrust twice more before spilling into me with a gasp of his own.

He laid his forehead on my shoulder, careful to keep most of his weight on his arms so that he did not crush me. I felt the brush of his exhales come quickly along the curve of my shoulder and I shivered.

"Are you cold?" he asked abruptly, pulling his head up to look at me.

I smiled at him and shook my head. "Not at all. You?"

He shook his head, beads of perspiration shining across his forehead.

We stared at each other for a few moments, both unsure of what to say. Then, with another kiss, he pulled away from me.

He did not go far. He merely turned onto his side on the bed, and I followed suit so that we were both looking at each other.

"That was unexpected," he said after a few more seconds of silence.

"It was," I said, stretching and flexing my limbs.

"What now?" he responded, and something in his voice made me refocus my eyes on him.

"What do you mean?"

"I've just slept with the Queen of Izwe—"

My snort was loud enough to interrupt him. He paused, glancing at me, and I took the opportunity to speak. "You might as well call me Sahle. We're certainly familiar enough for that now."

His eyes narrowed slightly, and then he continued. "...the Queen of Izwe, and I can't imagine that everything now just continues on as before."

"Well, no," I replied, adjusting the position of my arm where it held up my lolling head. "It means we can do this whenever we want."

Finn balked at me, his mouth opening wordlessly.

I allowed myself a chuckle before scooting closer to Finn once more. I traced the line of his jaw, the slope of his cheek with my fingers. And then I placed a firm kiss on his lips. "We're both consenting adults. I quite enjoyed myself, and I hope you did too. I see no reason why we can't do this again, if we're both willing."

"But the Council," Finn said, repeating what he had said before in the training ring.

I rolled my eyes and gave him the same response. "Fuck the Council."

"You keep saying that, but you have no idea what will happen if they find out about this."

I shrugged, as if to disregard the words. But I did want him to understand. "Finn, since coming to the Alterealm, this is the first moment where I've done what I wanted for me. I enjoyed myself and I hope you also did."

His sated smile was answer enough.

"The Council won't like it, but they don't need to know about this. If we're discreet, it can be our secret...assuming that you'd like this to happen again," I added as a pang of self-doubt hit me.

He seemed to see that flicker of doubt, because he scooted closer and looped his arm around my waist. I was pressed into his chest when he spoke next. "Of course I'd like this to happen again. I'm not hesitating because I don't want you."

He guided one of my hands down to the rapidly growing evidence of that as he spoke. "I do, as you can see for yourself. My hesitation is for you. You are a Queen and people will not like the idea of you bedding a soldier."

"I don't care," I answered flippantly.

"I know you don't now," Finn said, placing a kiss on my

forehead. "But you might regret it one day. I'd hate to be the cause of hardship for you."

I understood what he was saying and I saw the logic in it. I had certainly heard Lisideria loud and clear that this was not how a Queen behaved. But I could not bring myself to grasp onto sense, to swear this would never happen again.

It felt too good—not just the physical act of it, but the agency implied in the act. In this bed with Finn, I was my own person. I was making my own choices. And I had missed that these last months.

I told Finn as much and he nodded thoughtfully. "You're looking for something of your own," he confirmed.

"Something that's mine and mine alone. Will you be that?"

His gaze locked onto mine and he did not respond for some time. My heartbeat was in my ears, and I was suddenly nervous. I itched to pull the blanket at the foot of the bed over my nakedness, bared as I felt to him in that moment.

But then he smiled, a radiant show of white teeth across his fair face. His golden hair fell lazily over his forehead and I brushed it back into place with my free hand.

"Yes, I'll be that."

At some point, hours or days later, I peeled myself from Finn. My skin was sticky with my sweat and, if I were being honest, his as well. We had had a fierce workout and then…two more workouts in his bed.

I smiled to myself as I shimmied into my pants.

Finn had not needed any encouragement the second time around. After his words of concern for me, and my response that this is exactly what I needed and wanted, he seemed to understand.

He had shown me just how willing he was to be mine.

"Headed back to the palace already?" Finn asked sleepily from his pillow.

He had dozed off after our second round, and I had enjoyed watching his face ease in sleep, the feel of the strands of his blonde hair across my skin as I ran my fingers through it gently.

But slowly, oh so slowly, I had watched the light that crept past the edges of the shaded windows grow dark. My guards and anyone else who happened to be keeping track of my whereabouts might not blink twice at my being in the training grounds; it would be noted if I were absent for dinner.

I rebuttoned my tunic and then stood from the bed. "Already?" I chuckled. "It's near dark."

"Did I sleep for so long?"

I smiled at him, as I leaned forward to brush a finger along his jaw. "You did, and I enjoyed watching you."

Finn glanced at the window and, finally believing me, sat up. "Let me go out first and check that the men are not hanging around."

"Sure," I nodded. That was probably the smartest course of action. People would definitely notice if I walked out of Finn's rondavel.

Finn pulled his own pants and tunic on. He was moving quickly, but I still caught a broad expanse of back and thigh and I inadvertently flushed as I thought about the feel of that skin on mine.

I shook my head. If I were going to go back into the palace now and pretend that nothing had happened, then I needed my thoughts to stay far from those intimate memories.

I cleared my throat.

"Huh?" Finn asked, turning to me as he pulled on his boots. "Nothing."

If Finn were curious, he did not ask any further questions. Finished tying his boots, he moved to the door and cracked it open. I moved with him.

"Stay here a moment," he whispered to me as he slipped outside, pulling the door shut behind him.

I stood still, wondering what or who he saw out there. Then I heard the deep chuckle of male laughter and I realized he was trying to herd whichever dallying soldiers elsewhere.

I thanked my lucky stars I had not just rushed out, as I had initially planned to do. I thought it would have been nice of me to let Finn keep dozing, but now I realized that I could never depend on that. I needed him to navigate through the soldiers' quarters, especially if we were doing…this.

A thrill shot through me—the excited adrenaline rush that strikes when you know you are doing bad. Well, not bad necessarily but something unexpected, something out of the usual, something frowned upon.

And this would definitely be frowned upon.

The door cracked open, and Finn beckoned me out with a wave of his hand.

I followed him, craning my neck to peek around the corners of the door, left and then right. Seeing nothing, I hopped out and pushed the door closed behind me.

Now, who was to say Finn and I were not just chatting in the soldiers' quarters? It was one thing to be caught leaving his rooms. It was entirely another to be wandering the training area as I did regularly.

"Come," Finn said. I noticed his hand twitch, rising upward a fraction of an inch as if he would clasp my hand or take my arm. But he caught himself, letting the fingers relax at his side with effort.

"Not here you don't," I teased as I passed him, just a hair closer than I needed to.

Oh, this was going to be fun.

I could hardly stop my lips from curving up into a wicked smile as we wandered through the soldiers' training grounds and then mounted the stone steps that led back up to the palace.

At the top of the steps, in front of the palace doors that led back inside, Finn stopped and bowed to me fully.

"Until tomorrow, Majesty."

"Until tomorrow," I responded, struck by the sudden shift in the air.

I glanced over my shoulder and saw the two guards standing watch at this lower palace door. Then I caught the smooth movement of another four guards as they materialized from the perimeter they had established around the training grounds while I had been there.

Ah, that was why Finn had taken on his formal tone.

"Good night," I said quietly, turning away while he was still bowed.

I could feel the guards' eyes on me until they too dropped into their bows. And as soon as they did, I looked back to find Finn watching me.

I could not make out his eyes this far away and in the darkening of twilight, but I knew his gaze was on me and it sent a shiver up my spine.

I smiled to myself as I passed the guards.

I kept smiling as I made my way through the palace, enjoying seeing the courtiers' shocked gazes as they spied me wandering through their evening revelry in the clothes of a soldier.

It was not a shock that I was training, and I was sure they realized that I did not train in my gowns and crowns. I realized that it was always, without fail, a surprise for them to see me pass through so unassumingly in this outfit.

But something about their open-mouthed faces, which they so quickly tried to hide, lit a little wicked giddiness in my chest…much like the giddiness I was floating on for other reasons now.

I made it back to my room without anyone stopping to speak to me, although for a moment I thought Lord Anson might try.

I had noticed him just outside the Great Hall, sipping at a goblet and speaking to another Lord as I passed by. Out of the corner of my eye, I saw him lower the goblet and take a step in my direction as if he would approach me.

But either I was moving too quickly or he simply reconsidered that action. He stopped and raised the goblet to his lips once more, choosing to track me with his eyes instead.

No matter. Not even Anson's constant needling could annoy me right now.

The Vikela opened my doors for me as I approached my chambers and I thanked them as they shut the doors again behind me.

And then I let the full glow of my happiness out. I felt the smile stretch from my teeth to my lips to my eyes, and I could not control it any longer.

I giggled to myself as I launched myself on my bed. I clutched the downy blanket up to my face. It felt like joy was radiating out of every pore and I laughed audibly, the sound echoing around the room.

When had I last laughed and smiled with such happiness, I wondered? Oh, I had enjoyed the spring high holiday to be sure, but that momentary spinning, dancing joy paled in comparison to this. This joy was large and decadent, rich as the deepest melted dark chocolate.

And illicit as it was, it was mine and mine alone.

I was doing something that made me happy, and I allowed myself to collapse onto my back, smiling like a fool at the sheer white fabric that draped across the four-poster bed's canopy.

Sometimes you have to make happiness for yourself.

22
hesitate

I PRACTICALLY SKIPPED INTO THE TRAINING RING THE next morning. I had not been able to wipe the stupid grin off my face since the moment I woke up.

Surely much of it had to do with the oxytocin flowing freely through my veins, but I was equally aware that a large part of my happiness came down to having a secret, especially one as indulgent as this.

This thing with Finn—whatever it had been—was something I had picked. It was something I wanted, rather than what someone told me I must do.

In the face of doing it, I got to quietly and secretly rebel against everyone in Izwe telling me who I must be, how I must act. I knew it was petty of me. All of the guidance and explanations and rules had been laid out with the best of intentions. Yet, I was tired of living up to the near-impossible standards of a Queen. I wanted something for me and me alone. And this was it.

This whole situation really was a win-win.

My sense of elation slid to a halt the moment I faced Finn, though.

The sun was beating down on us out of the deep blue sky, and I shielded my eyes with a hand to my brow. "Good morning?" I asked, suddenly unsure of myself.

It was not anything he said or a particular look he gave me; it was the set of his shoulders, the fine lines around his too-casual mouth.

There was something wrong.

Finn bowed formally to me, casting his gaze to the ground. "Your Majesty. Good morning."

I stared at him, at his averted eyes, and willed myself to take a deep breath. This was certainly not what I expected.

I was not sure exactly what I had expected to find in the training ring this morning. Perhaps arms extended wide for me, a deep kiss, or at least a smile that promised more later. I certainly did not expect the frigid and all-too-tense man in front of me.

On uncertain feet, I stepped closer to Finn. I placed one foot in front of the other slowly, like I was a curious child approaching a deer who had come to graze.

"Finn?" I asked quietly, when I had made it in whispering distance.

His eyes did not meet mine. "Yes, Your Majesty?"

"Is something the matter?"

"No, Your Majesty. Let's be on our way with the training."

My mouth popped open. He was doing this…he was going to avoid what happened between us.

My slight movement seemed to catch his attention and he finally shifted his gaze up to mine for a heartbeat before moving it away just as rapidly. Before I could question him, demand an answer, or yell in frustration, he turned and began jogging away.

"This way, Your Majesty."

I watched him for a moment, completely flabbergasted at what had just passed between us. Then, shaking my head, I set off into a run.

I would figure this out. I would make Finn talk to me, even if I had to catch him first.

Finn stayed two paces ahead of me for miles. Every time I tried to increase my pace, he sped up on instinct. And each time this happened, I felt my temper rise higher and higher.

I was quickly growing frustrated. I did not like to be ignored, and I certainly did not like pretending that there was nothing between us—no matter how inconsequential and purely physical it had been.

The least Finn could do was acknowledge what passed between us less than twenty-four hours ago. If he wanted nothing else from me then that was fine. That could be the end of it.

But I would not pretend.

With determination in my veins, I sped up my pace once again. Once again, Finn increased his until he was even further out in front of me.

Abruptly I stopped. I planted my feet into the ground, threw my hands onto my hips, and breathed in and out in gasping breaths. My cheeks burned in frustration, and I bit out in part yell, part gasp, "Finn!"

Smoothly, he continued running in place as he turned around. "Yes, Your Majesty?"

I stalked to him, my cheeks burning in frustration. "Don't do this."

Still running in place, infuriating though it was, he responded calmly. "Do what?"

"Uh!" I nearly shouted between breaths. "You're ignoring what happened between us. Or have you already forgotten?"

That seemed to bring him back to earth because he stopped running in place. His eyes quickly tracked the space around us, and I could almost see the physical calculations he was making about the distance between us and any other soldiers or palace-dwellers.

His eyes landed back on me. "Keep your voice down."

My eyes widened. "I will not—"

"Queen Sahle," he said. The tone of it, the intensity of it, quieted me instantly. "I remember perfectly what happened between us, but we are not having this conversation right now where anyone could overhear. No one else can know."

"OK…" I replied, the fire in my veins quickly extinguishing.

His only answer was to begin running again.

"Uh," I gasped out again as I launched after him. I sped up my legs, pumping my arms to urge my body faster.

When I finally pulled up next to him, my stride momentarily in pace with his longer one, I bit out. "Fine…I understand…the secrecy. But why…do I…feel a…tenseness…between us?"

"You're imagining it," Finn replied, barely winded.

"I am not!" I reached out and grabbed his wrist, forcing him to stop and spin towards me.

We had reached the forest surrounding the palace and it was my turn to quickly scan our surroundings to make sure no one was nearby. "I'm not," I repeated. "You're regretting what happened."

He did not say anything for a moment, and I let go of his wrist as I doubled over, placing my hands on my knees as I sucked in as much air as possible.

"It should not have happened," Finn said quietly, so quietly I was not sure I heard him at first.

I peered up at him from my hunched position. "Was it not good for you?"

He scoffed. "Hardly."

"Hardly good?"

It was his turn to be exasperated. He spun around, his back turned to me as he spoke. "That's not what I meant." His arm lifted and maybe he scrubbed his hand over his face; it was hard to see from my position behind him. "I enjoyed it very much, Your Majesty. But it was inappropriate of me to engage you in that way."

Feeling more in control of myself, I stood up fully now. "You said as much yesterday."

"Well, yes."

"And we still slept together."

"Yes, and I should not have allowed that to happen."

"Allowed it to happen?" I repeated incredulously. I stalked over to him, moving until I was face to face with him. "This was not a one-sided situation. I'm not a child. I had just as much agency in this as you did, and I chose it. I wanted it."

His eyes closed tightly in an extended blink. When he opened them again, I could see the turmoil warring in their depths. "I know, but you are new to this world. You do not know the ramifications of your actions."

"I know," I replied, shaking my head vehemently. "But I don't care."

My words seemed to shock him. "You don't care," he repeated slowly.

"No, I don't. You tried to convince me this was a bad idea yesterday, but it didn't work then and it's not working now. I'm an adult and I chose this. I wanted it. You chose it and you wanted it in that moment. That's as complicated as it needs to be."

It was his turn to shake his head. "If only it were that simple…"

"It is that simple," I insisted. "I'm sorry that you regret it."

"I didn't say that," he replied gently, his eyes finally deigning to meet mine.

For a moment I stared at him, unsure of what to say to not spook him again. But he continued of his own accord. "Your Majesty, you're a beautiful woman. As a man, I enjoyed myself immensely, but regardless of what I felt, I am also a commander of the Vikela. As a commander, my highest honor is to serve the crown. I should not have done anything to compromise it."

I shook my head again. "You didn't compromise anything."

"How can you say that? What happened between us is clearly forbidden."

"I don't care," I said again. Again he stared. "How many times do I have to tell you that I don't care what anyone might think? This is one thing I chose for me—the single thing I've chosen for me since I came here. I won't apologize for it, and I won't feel ashamed of it."

As if tracking the direction of my thoughts, Finn said somberly, "It can't happen again."

I took a step into him, close enough to feel his breath blow across my face. "Is it Finn saying that or the Commander saying that?"

The column of his throat shuddered as he swallowed thickly and gazed down at me. I looked back at him, all earnestness and honesty in my eyes for him to see.

"The Commander."

"Mm-hm. And what does Finn say?"

To my surprise, Finn raised a hand to my face. He brushed away a curl that threatened to fall into my eyes. Then he placed his palm along my cheek. "That he's not done with what we started."

A slow smile spread across my face, and I allowed myself to step into Finn fully now. I cautiously threaded my arms around his neck, careful to feel for him tensing under my grasp. When his hands landed squarely on my hips, I relaxed. I had no interest in forcing Finn to do anything he did not want to do. I knew it was a fine line between duty and his own desires. I was sensitive to that, even wanting as I was.

"I'm glad to hear that," I said, looking up at him from my lowered lashes. "You know how I feel about this. And I'm not done either, assuming that's alright with you?"

He did not hesitate this time but nodded. "It'll have to remain a secret."

"Of course."

"We'll have to be careful," he continued.

"Certainly."

"We have your crown to think of, the Lords, your reputation."

"So you've said," I said flippantly. "I thank you for caring, but will you just kiss me already?"

His smile was wide before he bent his head towards mine. Against my lips he murmured, "Yes, Your Majesty."

23
a perfect world

THE FEELING OF FLOATING ON A CLOUD STAYED WITH ME for weeks—so much so that I nearly forgot the rumors of an imminent threat to Izwe. I would wake from sleep with the same stupid grin on my face and I would move through my breakfast and dressing as if in a dream. Then on a typical day, I would bow my head in the Yesonto, head to the soldiers' grounds to train, have lunch with Lisideria, spend time in the library, and pretend—sometimes very convincingly and other times not— that nothing had changed.

But everything had changed. The sun seemed brighter. The hadedas seemed to sing more enchantingly. Each leaf and blade of grass seemed softer and greener, dotted in morning dew and with a fine mist floating above it.

I was not in love. No, I had been in love before, and I knew what that was. This high was much like it, but I recognized that it was more selfish. It was a happiness of feeling like me after months of being a stranger to myself.

I tried not to dwell on the whispers of my mind, the ones that asked me if I was using Finn. He looked at me so earnestly when we were close, his body moving alongside mine. We did not always find time to sneak away each day but, when we did, it lit another fire in me.

His touches were like food, his kisses like warmth and shelter. And if we could not be alone for days at a time, his furtive glances—held just a touch too long, with just a touch too much knowing—sustained me. Those looks were like the enveloping scent of freshly baked cake, a promise of the splendor to come.

I could see that despite his initial hesitancy, he wanted this. He wanted me. When I sat alone at night, curled before my fireplace after a long day of stolen glances and suppressed smiles, I wondered whether I really wanted him, or if I just wanted freedom…

I told myself it did not matter. And it did not matter, for I was happy, and the sky was a brilliant blue, and even the gossiping, nosy courtiers looked beautiful in the gowns that had once looked so gaudy to me.

The world was perfect, until suddenly it was not.

It had been a long day of training, both magically and physically, and I was tired. As usual, nothing Finn or I did ever helped me push into whatever magical well I might have within me. Finn was convinced it was there, shimmering like a gold pool just beneath my skin. He claimed he could sense it stir in me when I grew angry or afraid, but I did not believe him. I did not have magic.

My physical training was coming along much better. Once I moved past my own unwillingness to look stupid, I had been able to commit to the work properly. I would never say I was an expert, but I could certainly hold my own in a swordfight. Finn was also teaching me the basics of hand-to-hand combat, how to defend myself when only my fists were an option, how to unbalance an opponent with a sidestep, how to bring a man down with the force of my knee.

That was coming along a bit slower, but I did wonder if it was because we always got distracted. Held close together, squirming as we tried to off-balance each other, it was not uncommon for us to abandon the lesson and retreat to Finn's rondavel for a training break.

The thought alone made goosebumps run up my skin, despite the warm bathwater I was currently sitting in. I ran my hands along my arms, massaging the sore muscles after the long training session.

It has been almost a week since the last time Finn and I had snuck away to his hut, and I could feel the call of it like a whisper at my ear, beckoning me back. But we had been busy, and our training had been serious.

The threat to Izwe still hung over us. Before, our training had seemed theoretical. If I threw a fit and grew frustrated at my own inability, it was annoying but fine. I would most likely never need these skills.

But now, with the threat always looming nearby, the need for me to be able to defend myself, to fight, and to command others to fight was real. If I did not master that, it could hurt more than me—if a threat ever materialized.

I dunked my head under the water, hoping the warmth would drive away that thought. Despite being in the Alterealm for nearly six months, I still had moments when I felt like my existence in this realm was not real. I could almost believe every-thing that had occurred since my twentieth birthday was a bad dream, my overactive imagination playing tricks on me. Perhaps I would wake up any moment, ready for another day of college classes with Mer, Jenna, and Cecily. And the idea that Izwe had enemies could be just part of that dream.

Pushing my head back past the surface of the bathwater, I blinked at the sudden sounds from within my rooms. The door to my bathing chamber was closed, but I could hear the raised voices of Kaiht and Mara as they spoke with someone—a man, I guessed, by the pitch of the muted words.

A moment later, Kaiht and Mara were opening the bathroom door and approaching with my towel.

"What is it?" I asked, instantly alert as I saw the two women's faces. Their usual happy smiles were gone, replaced instead with weary eyes and cheeks that were too pale.

"There is a messenger for you, Your Majesty."

"Now?" I looked down at my half visible naked body through the soap-murky water.

"Now," Kaiht said, and the touch of urgency that marked that single word had me moving.

I climbed out of the tub, sloshing bathwater here and there, as Mara wrapped the towel around me. I patted myself dry as Kaiht fetched my shift and dressing gown. I pulled on the shift, the dampness of my skin making the long sleeves stick. I contemplated going out to see the messenger in just that, but thought better of it when I caught my reflection in the mirror. The wide-necked shift clung to my wet skin and showed off the swells and dips of my body.

I reached my hands out to Kaiht for the dressing gown and pulled the heavy, wide-skirted overdress on, as well. I tied the cord at the waist to keep it shut, though the low V-cut of the dressing gown showed off more skin than I would usually like. There was no time to dwell on such inconsequential things, though. Not when I was out of the bathroom door and walking towards the messenger in a hurry.

Seeing my approach, the messenger instantly straightened from where he was leaning against the front door of my chambers. He bowed quickly, though deeply, and then said the words I never wanted to hear.

"Your Majesty, there has been an attack on Izwe."

The air seemed to rush out of me. My ears rung, hollow and echoing.

I stared at the messenger, unable to respond. Had I heard him correctly?

He continued. "Your presence is being requested at the Council Chambers. Immediately."

I continued to stare, the shock of the moment wrapping itself around me. Having delivered his message, the man bowed once more and then departed. My guards entered moments later, standing on either side of the ajar door. It was clear that I was meant to go with them.

My heart was beating in my throat as I made my way down the stairs that led from my room, and then down the long echoing hallways of the palace. Courtiers in various states of undress were crowded around in small groups, and I could feel more than hear the somber hush that blanketed the palace tonight.

Everyone was caught in the spell of uncertainty—a sick cloying mix of nervous anxiety, dread, and a thin wisp of excitement. No one wished people harm, of course, but there has always been a certain natural reaction to tragedy that rises up within us, as if our bodies respond to excitement, whether good or bad. We yearn for it subconsciously.

I could feel the edge of excitement tingling on the periphery of my worry for the people of Izwe, and I was ashamed of it. I smashed it down.

With the hallways clear, the usual music and revelry of the palace evenings wrapped up tonight, it seemed a shorter and quicker walk to the Council Chamber than usual. We made it there in a few minutes and I found I was the last to arrive.

Like the courtiers outside, the Lords were in varying states of undress. Some had obviously gone to bed already and been roused from their beds, such were the shifts and dressing robes they, too, donned. Others were still in their rainbow-colored clothes from the evening, looking a touch worse for wear after several glasses of konstans.

In the general disarray, not to mention the promise of horror that I was sure would descend when Grimly began his report, I did not care about being in my shift and dressing gown either. I was slightly annoyed to realize that my hair was still wet, limp curls hanging down my back and dripping. But I had bigger things to worry about than messy hair.

"My Lords," I called over the din of voices as I entered the room. The men dropped into a bow as I made my way to my usual seat.

"Queen Sahle, thank you for joining us so swiftly," Grimly replied for the Lords. He took his seat as well. "As I'm sure the messenger informed you, there has been an attack."

"I've heard."

"Good. Here is what we know."

Grimly proceeded to explain that a town called Ukuwela on the border of Izwe and Trina Cheile had been attacked early this evening by a gang of soldiers. They were not our soldiers, and they flew no banners of their own, but it was clear by witnesses that they were not from Ukuwela. Their manner of dress and their speech was Trinaian.

From midway down the table, one Lord interrupted. "How many were killed?"

Grimly glanced at him, clearly annoyed by the interruption. But seeing my interest in the question, he resigned himself to answer. "Forty-three."

My sharp intake of breath was lost in the mirrored sounds of many of the Lords.

"And damage to property?" another Lord asked.

Grimly's mouth compressed into a thin line. "Substantial."

More chatter erupted from the table, and a Lord gesturing rapidly with his hands caught my attention. He was sitting beside and in deep conversation with a man in a dark shirt tucked into pants, but no vest or jacket. Even with his back turned to me, I knew that dark hair and the cut of those casually-clad shoulders. I had spent too many months loathing them.

Lord Anson.

The man gesturing wildly stood and Anson sat back, his hands steepled with index fingers touching and pointed to the sky. I ran my eyes over Anson's dark shirt, how it was open at the throat and all the way to the top of a barely-visible pectoral muscle.

I averted my gaze before I could think too much on that, or why I was staring at that hateful man.

"My Queen," said Anson's friend. "I humbly ask for your leave. I have family in the border region, and I have not had word from them."

Several of the Lords looked offended, but this Lord continued. "Please, Your Majesty, it is imperative that I go to them and make sure they are alright."

I glanced at Grimly and the rest of the Lords. I could tell by the set of their mouths, the tension in their jaws that they disapproved of this pleading. I understood this Lord's need to go to his family. But how many Lords had family there? How many would beg to leave, if I allowed this one?

I addressed the entire table when I spoke. "My Lords, who else has family in the region?"

I felt all twenty sets of eyes fix on me before a few tentative Lords raised their hands. Looking around, I spotted three additional Lords.

"And is this immediate family?" I questioned.

"Yes, Your Majesty," two replied. One shook his head.

I could live without two Lords, I decided.

"Very well. The two with immediate family have my permission to leave to take care of their families. You, sir—" I called to the one who indicated that he had extended family only in the area of the attack "—if you would like to step out to write a note which these two Lords can carry, that would be acceptable. But I need you here. I need as many of my Lords as possible to help us decide our next move."

All three Lords stood still for a moment and then bowed deeply. Although they tried to hide it, I could see the look of relief on their faces. I only wished I could do more for them.

"I pray your families are safe and unharmed," I said in their direction before waving my hand in a vague gesture of dismissal.

When the three had gone, I turned back to Grimly.

"With all due respect, Queen Sahle, we could have used their expertise about the area to assess the damage and plan a recourse," he said.

I looked at him a moment, not surprised to know that he was incapable of understanding the Lords' concerns for their loved ones. "Lord Grimly, those Lords are no good to me if they sit here, not paying attention and simply wondering about the welfare of their wives and children. They will not be of use until they know their families are safe, so there was no point keeping them here."

A few murmurs of agreement echoed down the table and I saw, annoyingly, Anson give me a little smirk.

"As you wish, Your Majesty," Grimly continued, turning to a map of Izwe that was pinned to the wall to my left. "Back to the subject at hand. It is all but confirmed that Trina Cheile is responsible for this attack. They have made threats before and now they have acted on it. What do we propose to do about it?"

"Invade!" one young Lord cried from the opposite end of the table, and I rolled my eyes along with the rest of the Lords. From everything I had overheard in Council these last months, we did not have the resources or the information to take any such action.

"Send in covert missions to figure out what they are planning next," another Lord offered.

"Launch a counterattack akin to theirs," a third called.

My eyes refocused on Anson as he smiled at that. "No, my Lords," he called, sounding bored. "Launching a counterattack would simply be an act of revenge."

"And what's wrong with that?" the Lord who had proposed the attack responded.

But Anson, flippant as always, shook his head and laughed. He lazily stood from the chair, the open edges of his shirt again catching my eye. "My Lords, even as Lord of War, I caution you not to rush into anything. Tempers are high and blood is hot right now. Forty-three Izweians are dead, and that is unacceptable.

"But we must be calm and measured in our response. And that begins with collecting as much information as possible to try and figure out why they attacked in the first place. Only then can we know their minds, their rationale and, perhaps, what they have planned next."

"Spoken like an old hat," one Lord muttered from across the Council table.

Anson turned on him, whip-fast as an adder. "What was that, Lord Lionel?"

The Lord Lionel in question smirked in a way that could rival Anson's favorite expression, and I worked to keep an inappropriate giggle from rising up in my throat. This was not the time…

But Lionel was not afraid of Anson. Oh no, he stood and faced Anson with a smile. Then he said, "I said, 'spoken like an old hat.' Taking our time and doing our research sounds like something you would say, after nearly sixty years of twiddling your thumbs."

"What's that supposed to mean?"

"Just that you think the world has forever. Perhaps we must move quicker."

I watched, fascinated, as a muscle ticked in Anson's jaw. He clenched his fist for a mere second and then, with an effort even I had to admire, he was sitting down and not rising to the challenge.

Grimly neatly disregarded this near-violent interlude but grasped onto the words spoken. "I quite agree with Anson. This is the first attack, but it is hardly the last. We must find out as much as possible if we are to figure out how to prevent the next."

"And the next may be much closer to home," Anson added with a pointed look at Lionel, who merely shrugged noncommittally.

"Your Majesty, what say you?" Grimly asked.

But before I could respond, the Council Chamber doors swung wide and three men entered. Immediately, my eyes flicked to one of them: blonde, tall, with a chiseled jaw and deep blue eyes.

Finn.

The three Commanders dropped into a bow upon seeing me at the head of the table. When they righted themselves, I could feel their eyes on me—or at least one set of eyes.

I was freshly aware of my state of undress, the damp hair falling down my back, the way my breasts hung free underneath the dressing gown and shift. I felt naked, and as if Finn could see this.

I thought I saw his eyes widen slightly at my outfit, but it could have been a trick of the light, dim as it was this late in the evening in the Council Chamber. Only the golden glow from a dozen candles illuminated the darkness.

No Lords offered the Commanders seats, nor did the Commanders expect to be offered them. In their soldier-brown, they were clearly beneath these resplendent Lords. I held in my shudder of disgust as Finn and the other two found a place to stand at attention along a wall.

"Thank you for joining us, Commanders," Grimly called to them. "We are just discussing our next course of action and the Queen was about to share her thoughts."

All eyes in the room turned to me and I swallowed, hoping that my nervousness did not show on my face. I spoke in front of these Lords all the time, but I had never been here, commanding this chamber while Finn looked on.

Finn and I had established a sort of hierarchy with him as my teacher and me as his student. And out there on the training ground, it was entirely possible to forget I was Queen, to forget that I commanded him and his soldiers and the Lords seated on their gilded chairs now. Perhaps that was why we had formed an attachment—I loved the feeling of being normal again when I was with Finn.

Yet now…now I was showing who I truly was. He had shown hesitancy to kiss me, to lay in bed beside me, because of who I was but I had always responded with "what ifs." What if I were just a normal girl? What if I were not Queen? I had encouraged him to forget the power I wielded and just interact with me, kiss me, hold me for me, Sahle.

But here he was, standing before me while I commanded court. There was no escaping this harsh, bright reminder that I was truly Queen.

Distantly, even as I opened my mouth to speak to the Lords, a private, hidden part of me wondered if Finn would ever come to my bed again.

"I believe that we do need more information. Rushing to action now will not do us any good." At the sound of annoyed murmurs and sighs, I held up a hand and continued. "I know this disappoints many of you, but I cannot in good conscience send in soldiers to lord-knows-what.

"We must know as much as we can: who exactly was involved in this attack, what their motivation was, what their next plans are. Until then, we are just acting on revenge because we want to feel like we're doing something. Recklessly risking more Izweians is not the correct course of action here."

Most of the Lords around the table were nodding and murmuring their assent. I felt a wash of pride flow over me. I was proud that I had spoken my mind, and it seemed to be the right decision—if mass consensus was any indication.

I glanced at Anson involuntarily and was surprised to see a genuine smile pasted on his face. For once, he looked… approving. I stared at him, not able to believe this turn of events. But then he lifted a mocking brow and winked at me, and all my illusions were gone.

I turned from him in a huff, hearing Grimly call my name.

"Very good, Your Majesty. The Senior Council will make plans with the assembled Commanders."

"Thank you," I said, nodding once at him.

I could feel the lateness of the evening pressing in on me, and I stifled a yawn before it could embarrass me.

Lords not members of the Senior Council began to stand, and I took it that I was also excused.

"Please keep me informed of all developments, Lord Grimly," I said, rising from my seat. I stepped down from the dais, holding my dressing gown in front of me so as not to trip. But two steps from Grimly and I was spinning back to him with an idea. "I would also like to visit the families of those lost."

Where once there was discussion amongst the retreating Lords, there was now silence. It was as if my statement had stunned them completely and I rolled my eyes internally at their reaction.

"Excuse me, Your Majesty?" Grimly asked, standing to address me.

"I said that I would like to visit the victims' families out on the border town. Would you be able to arrange that?"

Grimly stared at me, slack jawed. "Whyever would you want to do that, Your Majesty?"

My forehead wrinkled in confusion. Why would I not want to go, see the damage, comfort my people? I said as much to Grimly, too aware of the other Lords listening in.

"It is simply not done in Izwe," Grimly said at last. I could see from his expression that he thought that was the end of the discussion. It certainly was not.

"That's fine if that is how it was once done. But I am Queen now, and I would like to provide my people comfort by going to them in this time of need, by offering my aid. Whether you agree with my wish is not up for discussion. I would like you to plan the journey as soon as it is safe to travel."

I could tell Grimly hated being lectured to by me and surprisingly I felt no happiness in talking down to him even if he had treated me like a child since my first moment in Izwe. No, I was simply too tired and too worried about what the future might bring for my kingdom, too concerned with being there for the people suffering. And Grimly was not one of them.

I did not wait for a response but simply continued my walk down the Council Chamber. Lords bowed as I passed and Anson even tipped his head in acknowledgement. Perhaps my eyes were playing tricks on me but I thought I spied approval in his eyes once more.

I shook my head to clear that thought and then I was passing Finn, his gaze burning into me, roving over the exposed skin of my face, my neck, my chest. I purposefully did not look at him or the other Commanders. I just walked past, eyes trained on a fixed spot ahead of me.

The last thing we needed was for someone to read into a look between Finn and me. Not now, not when everything was going to hell in Izwe.

I was out of the Council Chamber, down the palace halls, and back to my rooms nearly as quick as I had come. I thanked the guards for escorting me before closing the heavy door and sitting down in one of the wingback chairs before the fireplace.

Kaiht or Mara had added a piece of wood recently and it popped, emitting a luminescent cloud of glowing orange sparks. I leaned my head back until the wet curls compressed against the back of the chair.

This was real. Until now, the threat of violence, the idea of my parents' murder, even this entire realm had felt like a story made up for dreamers. But now…now people were dying. Families were being torn apart. People were losing their homes. And it was all because of a feud my family started generations ago.

This was real.

I stared at the fire and kept staring. There was no time, no notion of the passing of minutes or hours in the night. There was just the darkness seeping in from the tall, wide wall of windows that overlooked the forest. And there was just me, staring at the slowly burning fire and wondering what it would take for me to bring peace.

That had seemed like an idea, a myth, some part of the prophecy that was more theoretical than actual. But now…now I had to play a part, and that part was doing everything I could to never let the people of Izwe suffer again because of me and my family.

I thought of all the embarrassment I had felt, all the times I had thrown a fit and stormed out. I thought of all the annoyed expressions and hurled jabs from certain Lords. For the first time I understood it. I was meant to be the one, brought in from the Humanrealm, who could save them all. And up until now, I had been nothing but a disappointment.

I let my head roll to the side, feeling shame but a new type of shame—the shame of a person who consciously did too little, too late. I could never let that happen again. I could never again not try. I owed it to my people to take this seriously and be, if not the Queen they were promised, then at least the best Queen I could be.

And I promised myself right there, sitting before the fire with my wet hair staining a damp spot into the leather of my chair, that I would try. I would try.

A knock on the door roused me some time later. I had not been asleep, but rather in a sort of weary trance as I watched the flames nearly burn out. I was going to try but I doubted I was capable of what it would take to save this kingdom. I was just Sahle.

I had not seen Kaiht and Mara since I left for the Council meeting, but Kaiht materialized just as I was rising to answer the door. She motioned for me to sit back down and I obliged, my body feeling too heavy and tired to hold itself up.

I fixed my eyes on the fire once more, but Kaiht's intake of breath had me whipping around in alertness.

"Commander," Kaiht said with the barest of bows. He was above her station after all but not far, especially when I was in the room. "Do you have a reason to be knocking on the Queen's door in the middle of the night?"

Before Finn could answer, I was up and moving towards the door. I grabbed Finn's hand and quickly pulled him into my room, stopping only to glance down the hallway before soundly shutting the heavy door. My Vikela were noticeably absent.

"What are you doing here? And where are my guards?" I whispered to him. There was no one to see us but Kaiht though, so a part of my brain did wonder why I had whispered.

"I told them I would take their place," Finn replied, neatly avoiding the first question. He shrugged like this was not anything remarkable and then his gaze slid to Kaiht.

And I understood.

Finn was saying not to make a scene before Kaiht. He was saying to act like our normal Queen and Commander selves even here.

I glanced at Kaiht. I was surprised to see pointed eyes look back at me, and I realized a moment too late that I was still holding Finn's hand from when I pulled him through the door.

"Kaiht…" I began but was not sure what to say.

"There is no need, Your Majesty," she said in a hurry, raising her hands as if to placate someone about to become unreasonable. "I've known that you and the Commander have been…involved for some time now."

I stared at her, open mouthed. "What? How?"

But Kaiht merely smiled and shrugged. "The way all servants know things. I guess I should say that I've suspected for some time now, not that I've known. I spend a great deal of time with you, Your Majesty, and I've seen how you act when you come back from…training—" she glanced at Finn with a pointed smile "—and how you act when you haven't spent time with him for a while. I also clean your clothes, which tell remarkably a lot about a person, I might add."

I could feel a blush creeping over my skin, thinking about what evidence she might have found of our relationship.

"Kaiht," I said, dropping Finn's hand and taking hers. "Please, this has to be a secret."

I could feel the pleading in my eyes, the way my shoulders bowed forward in supplication, and I saw that Kaiht noticed it, too.

She shook her head, her brows drawing together in a confused earnestness that was so unlike her. Kaiht was always the talkative, whip-smart, wise-cracking version of the sisters, but now she looked at me solemnly and seriously. "Your secret is safe with me. And Mara. We have not said a word to anyone about our suspicions, nor do we intend to, Your Majesty. You have nothing to fear from us."

I let an audible exhale out past my lips and then squeezed her hand once before letting go. "Thank you, Kaiht. That means the world to me."

"It is nothing, I assure you," Kaiht replied, her eyes shifting to Finn. "You, on the other hand…I hope we can trust you to keep this quiet. No one needs to know about you visiting the Queen in her chambers, even if she does sneak down to the training grounds from time to time."

I felt Finn's energy shift more so than saw it. He stiffened and bristled at being talked down to by Kaiht, and I grasped his arm before he could say anything scathing. He was not a man who appreciated having his honor questioned. I knew that.

"Finn would never do that," I said, but Kaiht was still staring at Finn. Finn stared back at her, and I had the impression that a silent conversation was taking place between them.

What were they saying? What did two servants of the crown, both loyal in different ways, warn the other of? Was it a competition for who was most eager, most servile? The thought nearly sickened me for I never thought of either of them like that. They were my companions, in different ways certainly, but companions just the same. I would even hazard to call them my friends, though I knew they would be uncomfortable with the title.

Kaiht seemed to make up her mind about Finn, for she nodded her head suddenly and broke her gaze from his. "Alright," she said at last, turning to me. "Can I fetch you something to drink, Your Majesty?"

"Umm…" I mused, unsure of what the protocol should be in this situation or why Finn was here to begin with. Did he have news to share?

"The Queen will have a glass of konstans," he said, responding for me in a way that made Kaiht's eyebrows raise even higher than they already were.

"Do you speak for her now, as well?"

"What?" Finn spluttered. "I was merely suggesting—"

"It sounded awfully like you were telling us both what the Queen's wishes were."

"I would never presume—"

"Stop," I cut in quietly, although it had the necessary effect. Both of them ceased talking instantly.

I raised a hand to my brow and pinched the bridge of my nose. I knew they both meant well but their pissing match was too much for my frazzled mind. "Can I please have a glass of wine, Kaiht? Actually make that two—one of those is for Finn, if he plans to stay and drink it."

"Certainly," Finn responded, eyes still trained on Kaiht who made a small huffing noise but retreated to fetch our glasses.

"Please sit," I motioned to the chairs before the fire and Finn sat in the one I had left unoccupied before.

Kaiht wordlessly handed us our glasses as we settled into the comfortable leather upholstery. "Thank you. That will be all," I said quietly. She bobbed a quick curtsy and promptly excused herself with only a slight second glance at Finn.

I sipped at my glass for a moment before looking at him over the rim. "What was all that about?"

"What do you mean?" Finn asked, taking a sip and then setting his drink aside.

"You and Kaiht seemed to be at each others' throats."

"Oh that. She's just worried about you."

I stared back at him, curiosity getting the better of me. "Why do you think that?"

"I can tell," he replied simply. "She loves you and is loyal to you. And me being here…it risks your safety and security. That's why she was acting that way."

I could not help the little flare of jealousy that sparked within me at these words. "And you know this how? Are you two friendly?"

Finn laughed then, the expression crinkling the skin at the corners of his eyes. "No. Hardly. I just know her type. A good servant is hard to come by and when you find it, you hold onto it."

"Her," I corrected. "You hold onto her."

"Of course. I apologize, Your Majesty."

I took another sip of my wine, not entirely sure what to make of that. But it was too late, and I was too exhausted to contemplate anything. Instead, I asked the question I had been wanting to the moment I saw his outline at my door.

"What are you doing here, Finn? Do you have news?"

But Finn merely picked up his wine again, running his finger thoughtfully around the circular base. "No, unfortunately not. The Senior Council and the Commanders met for maybe an hour. But without any further details, it was a futile meeting. We rehashed what we already knew and agreed to meet again in three days—sooner if details arise.

"And then I came here. I had to see you, to see if you were alright after everything you heard in the Council Chamber tonight."

I watched him closely. While a part of me was happy that he had come to check on me, another part of me was less so. It was unlike him to put me at risk, and that was exactly what he was doing by coming here. "You could have been seen, you know."

Soft as I said it, I am sure he heard the rebuke in those words. "I was careful."

"I'm sure. But still, it's risky coming here."

"Would you like me to leave?" he countered, setting down his wine again and turning his knees so he faced me square on rather than half angled to the fire as he had been.

I set my wine down with a sigh. "No. I don't want you to leave. I just want you to be careful," I told him.

And then I rose and walked to him.

He sat back, already anticipating what I would do, and I marveled anew at how well he knew me, my body, and the way my mind worked.

I perched on one of his knees. "I'm sorry I'm not myself tonight."

"I wouldn't expect you to be," he said, laying a hand on the side of my face. "That's why I came."

I nodded against his palm, before turning to lay a kiss against it. Then I caught his eye. "I'm alright. Shocked, but alright. I just can't…can't believe this is real."

His brows furrowed in the firelight. "What do you mean?"

"I…I…" I did not know how to explain it and suddenly my legs felt restless, as if I could not speak while sitting still.

I stood and moved towards the fire, pacing more than anything.

"Queen Sahle?" Finn called softly, and when I turned to him, I realized he too was standing.

I shook my head, not sure I had the words to explain what had gone through my head tonight. I had to try, though, for Finn to understand.

"A handful of months ago, I was just torn out of the Humanrealm and dropped here into the Alterealm. I was told I'm Queen and that there is some huge, important prophecy about me. And everyone has such expectations for me.

"But what if I'm not the one? What if I'm not the Queen that this nation needs? I'm just Sahle, just an ordinary girl who went to her twentieth birthday party and ended up hurtling through the stars and into a new realm.

"I have no right to be a Queen, no right to rule a people. I can hardly take care of myself, let alone have the responsibility of taking care of a kingdom!"

Finn was quiet while I ranted and only when I paused to take a breath did he insert, "You can because it's your destiny."

My destiny.

I let the words sit before me like some type of movie screen, showing me at different ages and choices, different decision points in life. "And what if I don't want it?"

But Finn was having none of it. He shook his head sharply and then moved to join me before the fireplace. "Stop this."

"Why?" I asked and the word came out more of a whimper than the angry, frustrated cry I meant it to be.

Finn knew me. He was the first to see through my habit of storming off, my bursts of temper and embarrassment, my resistance to making a fool of myself. And I was sure he understood the helplessness that coursed through my veins now.

His gaze softened and he took my face in his hands, meeting my eyes with his sharp blue ones. "You think you're ordinary but you're not. You're extraordinary. You think you're not fit but you are. You have a presence, a surety, a good head on your shoulders, and a strong moral compass. That's more than most rulers ever have. This is your destiny, Queen Sahle, and it's yours for a reason."

His blind faith touched a hopeful, wishing part of me. Tears blurred my vision and I did not try to stop myself from drawing an inch closer into his chest. "I don't want it. I just want to be Sahle."

He stroked a hand down my back. "I know...But someday this will matter. Someday you'll want this. And when you do, know that you're enough and that you're capable. You're the Queen we need."

I had no words in reply. I knew I did not deserve such unearned loyalty, and I knew, too, that Finn would fight me if I said as much.

I merely nodded. I was done talking about this. I was too tired, too weary. And so I let my head fall forward until it rested on Finn's shoulder.

24

ukuwela

IT WAS WITH MINGLED DREAD AND RELIEF THAT I FINALLY received a note from Grimly several afternoons later as I sat in my chambers with an Izweian novel—a classic work, I was told.

I unfolded the note quickly, hardly pausing long enough to thank the messenger before he slipped back out the door. I scanned the words.

The trip to the victims would take place tomorrow, and we would leave at dawn.

I had many questions but was unsure who I should even ask. Eventually I gave up and decided that Grimly or whomever accompanied me would surely tell me what I needed to know during the journey.

With that, I settled back into my novel, though my mind kept wandering to what I had heard of the attack: forty-three lives lost, property damaged, families ruined. I eventually gave up reading and asked Mara and Kaiht to run a hot bath.

I sat in the water, letting the steam rise in clouds around me, and I anxiously wondered what I would be walking into the next day.

Brilliant dawn came soon enough, and I was dressed in a chitenge-patterned navy blue riding habit, with another low crown similar to the one that I had worn to tea with Eliza. I made it out to the yard just as the sun crested over the horizon. I was the last to arrive, it seemed, and I quickly made my way to the zebra that was waiting for me, dressed as it was in Izweian livery.

"Good morning, Your Majesty," Grimly called from the front of the small crowd of zebramen.

I turned to him as I situated myself on the saddle. "Morning, my Lord. Morning, my Lords," I added as I spied several other Lords also astride. Of course, Anson's dark head turned to me and his smile reverberated through me.

"I'm surprised we have such a large party," I continued, eyes narrowing at Anson in particular. "There was much resistance to the idea of visiting the area of attack."

Anson, having seen my expression, took it upon himself to be even more infuriating. He drew his zebra closer, just a few feet from mine. "We were most concerned for Your Majesty's safety."

"I'm sure," I replied through tight lips. Movement in my peripheral vision caught my eye and I turned my attention to the right just as a small company of men in soldier-brown arrived on zebraback.

"Apologies for our tardiness, Your Majesty," a welcome voice called from the group. I smiled at the richness of that tone, one I knew and appreciated.

"That's quite alright, Commander," I replied, willing my face to remain composed. Finn bowed his head in return, and I felt heat blossom across my cheeks.

I turned my gaze away before I could make a fool of myself, like a schoolgirl fawning over her crush. With Finn close at hand, this was going to be a long day in front of the Lords. I needed to get control of myself.

"That's our entire party," Grimly said from the front of the group, closest to the palace gates. "Shall we be off?"

"Please," was all I had to say, and then we were galloping away.

It would take us roughly three hours to arrive at the border town that had been attacked. It was called Ukuwela, and it was the closest Izweian town to Trina Cheile along our western border.

To get there, our party of roughly a dozen traversed the roads that led from the palace to the surrounding city and then further into the forest and wilderness that made up much of Izwe.

Kaiht had come with me as my escort, meant to assist me with my outfit, fetch me water, or any other menial tasks the Lords would feel were beneath them. But I was happy she was here as we rode side by side, her on a slightly shorter zebra and me on one of the tall beasts reserved for royals and Lords.

I had seen so little of Izwe in the months since my arrival that I drank in every sight and sound I could. Flamingos and hadedas winged above us as we rode. The sky shone even more brilliantly blue outside of the city-ringed palace grounds. A curious mountain range ran parallel to us in the east, rising out of the ever-present red dirt of Izwe, and I wondered at the middle of the peaks. It was a flat plateau that looked curiously like a tabletop.

Kaiht was all too happy to answer my questions or provide names for the landmarks, flora, and fauna I noted. She explained that the mountains I saw were called the Hoerikwaggo Range and the flat table was itself named Hoerikwaggo. Legend had it that a fearsome monster lived in the cave system below it. Part elephant and part snake, it made its nest amidst an underground lake system lined with diamonds.

250

Some travelers had wandered below to seek those riches, never to be seen again. Others had heard rumors of the creature's wisdom, old as it was, as old as the stars and the planets itself. If travelers had gone into the cave to seek out that wisdom, Kaiht did not say. But I caught myself looking at that flat-topped mountain and wondering what secrets lay beneath it.

As we moved further and further from the curious mountain, my attention moved back to the strange yellow-green shrubbery that seemed to blanket all of Izwe. I had seen the same landscape upon my arrival: the thickly-petaled pink flowers called proteas, the tall trees with thin silver leaves.

Kaiht explained to me that this landscape was very typical of Izwe. It was a big country, as I had seen on the maps I studied, but it was not geographically diverse except for the mountain range that ran through the middle.

The proteas with their thick, artichoke-like petals were hardy and resilient, closer to small trees than flowers really. She told me that they varied in presentation depending on what part of Izwe one was in. Sometimes they looked like little sewing pins stabbed into a pincushion. Other times, they were thinner and whiter with a green undertone.

Kaiht pointed out the silver trees. I thought they were aptly named, colored as they were in a sort of green that played off the sun's rays in bursts of shimmering metallic reflections. And of course, Kaiht mentioned the jacarandas—those trees whose leaves looked like palm fronds, whose purple clustered flowers provided the vibrant color to the Vikela's training grounds and the palace entry yard. I knew the name of that tree already, and I spared a quick gaze at Finn's back in memory of the first kiss we had shared against a jacaranda trunk.

In return for her information, I told Kaiht about the United States of America, and how across fifty unique territories spanned razor-toothed mountain ranges, red canyons, serene desert moonscapes, spiraling redwood forests, soft and unending farm fields, and white sand beaches.

She shook her head, amazed. "I could never imagine such a place," she told me. "This is all Izwe is—the silver trees and the red dirt. It is beautiful, don't get me wrong, but it's just this."

I nodded as I cast my gaze around once more. She was right: it was beautiful in a stark, alien way. The silver trees seemed to be the predominant tree near the palace, but the further we rode west, the foliage began to shift to more slender barbs that reminded me of pine needles.

We rode in the center of the entourage. It was a better location from which to be guarded, Finn had explained as he had passed us early on. I had smiled and nodded, unwilling to converse with him at length as I felt the weight of the Lords' eyes upon us. He had smiled back, and then made his way to the front of the group—a skilled shepherd leading his ambling flock.

And, of course, midway through our ride, Grimly sidled up to me and began offering details about Ukuwela and the Ukuwelan people, as well as new evidence about the attack. I listened intently, determined to drink in as much as I could before we arrived. I was ashamed to realize how little I knew of this city, and I did not want to show as much ignorance when we reached its gates.

"Unfortunately, the number of deceased rose to forty-four yesterday. An elderly man died of wounds he sustained in the attack," Grimly explained as he flicked away a spot of road dust that had settled on his pant leg.

"That's awful," I murmured, swallowing against the sudden thicknesses that seized my throat. I would not cry—not now, and not in front of the people of Ukuwela. They had enough to worry about. I did not need to add the discomfort and confusion of how to soothe a sobbing Queen.

"It surely is, Your Majesty," Anson said as he pulled his zebra in stride with mine on my other side. His tone was arrogant as always, but there was an edge of humor in it that poked at me like a pebble in my shoe.

I whipped angry eyes towards him. "Is there something funny, Lord Anson?"

"Of course not," he replied quickly, with a half bow, seated as he was on his powerful zebra. "I was merely agreeing with you that it is terrible. The residents of Ukuwela have faced many such attacks over the years."

My eyebrows raised in surprise. "They have?"

He nodded. "Unfortunately, with the proximity to Trina Cheile, they have always been the easiest way to make a statement to the broader Izweian community."

"Why do the families stay then?" I mused aloud. I could not imagine myself staying in a place where it was not a matter of if but when the next life-threatening attack would come.

But Anson had an answer. He always had an answer—that peacock of a lord. "It is their home, Queen Sahle. Why do families stay in fire-prone forest villages, or along ocean fronts that flood year after year and cause immense damage? I believe that some people have a connection to the land under their feet, and surviving what occurs there is part of what home is. It becomes part of who they are."

I turned my head to fully look at Anson, and I hoped my mouth was not hanging open entirely. I had never heard him be so thoughtful, but there it was. He was not condemning them; he was sympathizing with them in a way that made me wonder if he himself had a personal connection.

"Do you have family in Ukuwela, Lord Anson?"

"No, fortunately not," he replied quickly, scanning the forest around us rather than looking me in the eye. "But I have experience with folk who are attached to the land on which they were born and will never leave, regardless of what comes."

"I see," I replied. "It reminds me of the Humanrealm, where people rebuild in the path of fire or buy a new home in a tornado zone. I have always wondered why they don't just move away, but I guess it makes sense. Their people are there. It's their home, and all they've known. So they make do with whatever comes."

"Quite right, Your Majesty," Anson replied. And then that quirking mouth was back, and I braced myself as he opened his mouth once more. "It's astonishing you're learning so quickly, Queen Sahle. This will surely be an instructional trip for you."

My eyes rolled of their own accord.

I was done with him, especially how he seemed to watch and be kind to me in one moment yet tease and loathe me in another. It was infuriating and I wanted nothing to do with it, especially not today.

"Quite right, Lord Anson," I mimicked. And then with a lift of my hand that communicated clearly that he was dismissed, I said, "If you will excuse me, gentlemen."

His answering look was sharp and clever, and I quickly broke his gaze to glance around for Kaiht. She was riding behind us. As Anson and Grimly moved towards the front of the entourage, Kaiht took her place once more at my side.

"He's always a pleasure, that one," she muttered, eyeing the back of Anson's head. I fought back a humorless chuckle.

"I think he enjoys goading me," I replied with a scowl.

"Oh, most definitely, Your Majesty," she replied quickly—too quickly. I narrowed my eyes.

"Why do you say it like that?"

Kaiht shrugged but replied still. "It's common knowledge in the palace that Anson argued vehemently for leaving you in the Humanrealm. There were others who shared that opinion, but he was the loudest. He was the instigator. It was ongoing for all twenty years you were away. Each time the topic came up, he would again say that you should be left where you were and not retrieved."

I blinked at Kaiht without really seeing her. My mouth had gone dry, my ears empty and ringing.

I knew Anson did not like me, but I wondered what had inspired this level of malice. Did he merely want power himself, or was there something deeper that influenced him to discredit me from the time I was a baby?

"I had no idea…" I said numbly, turning to stare at his broad back, clad in a dark charcoal riding coat.

"He gave up his protests about six months before you returned. But even if he stopped talking about it, it was there."

"Why do you think he was so opposed to me coming back?" I asked her. If anyone might know, it was Kaiht—trained as she was, with ears that seemed to hear between the palace walls and collect all sorts of knowledge.

"I don't know, Your Majesty," Kaiht replied sadly, and I could tell from her tone that she genuinely wished she did know. "But whatever it was, it must have been significant enough for him to spend nearly two decades arguing his point."

"Hmph," I snorted. "Charming."

We rode on in silence after that. I did not have enough information to contemplate what Kaiht had shared with me, nor did I have the patience to consider it. I was too focused on the day ahead of us. I filed it away, with a strongly underlined mental note to find out whatever I could later.

Grimly came up once more to alert me that we were nearing Ukuwela, and then the pine forest began to thin. Within another thirty minutes of riding, we began passing little farms and villages made up of familiar thatch-roofed rondavels. Another twenty minutes and the mortarless stone walls of a small city became visible over the crest of an immediate hill.

We rode on and as we reached the summit, the city of Ukuwela spread out before us. It was beautiful. Its soft brown homes and residences were topped with thatch reeds that were nearly black. The walls around the city were made out of the same gray stone our city gates were made of, it seemed. And again I spied the intricate designs and yet the lack of visible mortar.

As we approached the city walls, the guards who manned the city's gate needed no introduction of who I was. Seeing my livery, the entourage with me, and my own low crown that glinted silver in the morning sun, they immediately bowed as our party neared.

The tall doors opened and we were admitted to the city of Ukuwela, where a congregation of our approximate size awaited us.

"Queen Sahle, it is an honor to meet you," a woman with graying hair said as we stopped before the group. She stepped out from the center of the small crowd and curtsied low, her muted green gown billowing out around her. "My name is Aurora, and I am the Governor of Ukuwela."

I nodded, putting the face to the name. Grimly had told me that Ukuwela alone had the only female Governor—the term Izweians used instead of Mayor to denote the leader of a particular city. These Governors were not Lords. Oh no. No Lord would stoop so low as to be a Governor.

The Governors were elected by the people in a democratic vote that was held every two years. Aurora, in her fourth term, was beloved in Ukuwela, even if no other Izweian region could understand the appeal of a female ruler.

"Governor Aurora," I replied, as one of the soldiers approached to help me dismount. Righted again on the ground, I moved to her as she bowed. "It is a pleasure to meet you. I've heard much about you."

Warm brown eyes caught mine knowingly. "Likewise, Majesty."

Though her dark hair was graying, her fair skin was smooth. Her back was straight, her shoulders strong. She held herself like the Queen I wished I was. And in many ways, she was more of a Queen than I could ever be. She had stepped into this role as the local sovereign amidst protest about her sex, and she had fought every day to prove to her city—as well as the rest of Izwe—that a woman was equal to rule as any man.

I was not nearly as accomplished as this woman, and I respected and admired her immediately. I could feel her cool confidence, tinged with curiosity, as she watched me. I knew instantly that this was someone I wanted to be friends with.

Behind me, the clanking of Lords and soldiers dismounting sounded. Aurora motioned for me to follow and I fell into line beside her as we began our tour of Ukuwela.

But no matter how much I liked Aurora, wished to speak to her and glean insight from her, the reason I was here stood strong and looming like a giant elephant just over my shoulder.

I cleared my throat before saying, "Governor, my sincerest condolences for those lost in the attack. How have things been since?"

From my peripheral vision, I saw Aurora nod. "Thank you, Majesty. It has not been easy, but we are managing. Attacks like these have happened before, though this one was the most destructive and deadly. It is a hazard of being the closest settlement to Trina Cheile, after all."

"Of course, but that does not make it right that this city suffers time and time again," I said.

"No, Your Majesty, it doesn't," she replied wistfully, and I could almost hear the prayers she said each day for the safety of her city and all the souls who lived within it.

Standing just inside Ukuwela's gates, the city looked whole. The sounds of thousands of lives being lived floated to me on the breeze. The mingled noises of market sellers, zebras walking on stone cobbles, children laughing as they played in the streets, laundry cracking as it was being shaken out—it all mingled into the bustling background noise of any city anywhere, Humanrealm or Alterealm.

Aurora led me deeper into the heart of the city, and I began to see evidence of the attack clearly.

We stopped before a stately, white-walled building and Aurora pointed at the jagged glass where windowpanes had once been. "The attack began here. This is our City Hall, and there was a full staff of city servants working when the explosion went off inside. Luckily, Trina Cheile had misjudged where the workers actually were during the day because only three were in the immediate vicinity of the blast."

"And the three?" I asked, a cold ball in my stomach.

"Dead," she replied without flinching. I envied her matter-of-factness in the face of such horror. The bodies had long been buried. The fires had been put out. Yet the acrid smell of smoldering rubble still lingered in the air, cloying at the back of my nostrils.

"From there, it was a coordinated attack. The explosion brought many guards to the center of the city, leaving the gates sparsely manned.

"You entered through the east gate, Your Majesty, but the gate that faces Trina Cheile on the west was where they broke through. They used some kind of magic to will the gate open and no matter how many soldiers tried to close it, it would not budge."

I blinked at that. I had been told that magic was rare in the Alterealm these days—hence why everyone was so keen for me to have magical abilities. It was a shock that our enemies could command such force.

"And you did not see who it was wielding magic?"

"No. Whoever it was was not actually here, we believe— which makes it all the more concerning."

"Why?"

She stopped and turned to me then, to better look into my eyes when she spoke the words that chilled me to my core. "Because it is one thing to wield magic in person, when you are right there with the object you're influencing. It is an entirely different situation to be able to command magic, elemental and non-elemental, from a distance. That sort of power is…problematic to say the least, especially in the hands of our enemies."

I nodded slowly. I could see it: how a magic-wielder with enough power could wreak havoc across Izwe without ever leaving the safety of Trina Cheile. It was a terrifying thought, and the futility of being at the mercy of such a wielder was enough to send a physical shiver down my spine.

We continued our walk, and I glanced over my shoulder to see Kaiht directly behind me, followed by Finn and the other soldiers, then the Lords with Grimly and Anson leading. They were all silent, and I could see clearly that this news had struck them as much as it had me. Kaiht's eyes were flat, drained of their usual brightness.

We stopped at several more buildings before rounding towards the west gate facing Trina Cheile. At each place, Aurora told me how many had died in the explosion or fighting that took place there. I made a mental tally and realized that we were not even a quarter of the way through the death count. Already the horrors she spoke of were substantial.

The wooden gate itself had not been repaired, and for some reason that shocked me. Rationally, I knew that the attack had only occurred a few days before. I had not expected the City Hall to be rebuilt in that time, nor any other areas that had been damaged. But something about the gates made me shudder.

Perhaps it was because they were the clear pathway to Trina Cheile. Their broken and unhinged doors looked like a welcome mat, a banner flown behind a small airplane inviting our enemies to come on in.

"The gates have not been fixed," I said limply, as I stared at the broken wooden doors that once would have shut so immovably.

"No, they have not yet," Aurora confirmed. "It was the hinges that were affected by magic, so we've had a series of magically gifted people try and analyze what occurred."

"I see," and I did. There were several people with bowed heads leaning over the area where the gate met the sturdy stone walls. We approached slowly, and I watched as they suspended their hands over the gnarled hinges.

Each person had their eyes closed. Some were humming or rocking. Some were sitting in silence, focusing on the task at hand.

Aurora and I—and our entourage—stayed only a few moments before moving on. We did not want to disrupt the important work. And if what Aurora told me was true, these people were some of the only people who were magically gifted left.

"Do they all have magical abilities?" I asked Aurora as we wandered away, weaving through curling alleys and long boulevards alternately. The marks of fighting were present here along our path, and I wondered how many soldiers had swung weapons. Was that gouge from the impact of an arrow's tip? Was that slash the result of an enemy soldier's swipe?

"Yes and no. None of them can perform magic, but they have enough of it in their blood that they can sense the magic that opened the gates."

A thought occurred to me—selfish as it was. "Can they also sense people who are magical?" I glanced back over my shoulder as if to see the small grouping of magic-sensors, even though many buildings now stood between us.

But Aurora shook her head, glancing quickly at me and then away. I thought I spied the slightest smile on her lips. "Some magic-sensors can, but not this group. They can sense magic's effects but they cannot sense if someone has the ability inside them."

She did not say, "And so they would not be able to tell you if you have magic," but I could see in her eyes that she knew why I had asked. I thought of Finn's words to me so many weeks ago—that he could sense magic within me. His own ability to feel magic must be different from these workers' then. I shook my head, not willing to go down that line of thought at the moment.

But the thought that did stay central in my mind was that Aurora knew. She understood exactly what I had meant with my question—she, someone miles away from the palace. Did all of Izwe know my struggle as the magicless Queen?

Aurora and I walked on in silence, the muted whisperings of the Lords, Commanders, and servants becoming a sort of background chatter behind us.

My mind was racing through a million lines of thought. I was taking in the architecture of this Izweian town, kept as I was most days in the palace. I was thinking about the magic-sensors. I was wondering who or what could command power from Trina Cheile to open the gates of Ukuwela.

We rounded another corner and I stifled my gasp as I gazed out at Ukuwela's market square, or what was left of it. I had never seen the market before but I did not need to have a comparative image in my mind to understand the sheer magnitude of what had happened here.

"Yes," Aurora said, either seeing my reaction or hearing my gasp despite my best attempts to keep it under control. "This is where the majority of damage was sustained. And the majority of the loss of life. Thirty-one people were killed here, most of them vendors or other salespeople."

I cast my gaze around me, taking in the charred remains of what had once been wooden market stalls, wagons full of produce, and small store fronts.

Aurora continued as we came upon a small crater in the ground. "As you can see here, there were several explosions detonated in this location. Those explosions killed those nearby instantly. Others were injured by the debris that rained down, like the elderly man who died this morning."

"Number forty-four," I murmured to myself.

But Aurora nodded. She had heard. "Exactly. We fear more may yet die. The wounds are serious."

To the right of the market, several stalls stood unburned, if a little tattered and worse for wear. "Were these not affected?"

"Not in terms of the explosions," Aurora replied to me. "They did get jostled and torn and generally roughed up in the fighting, but they were out of the way of the worst of it."

I nodded, my gaze landing on a young woman who was sorting vegetables onto a scorched but still whole shop cart in that portion of the market. "Are the vendors still selling their wares?"

"Oh, yes," Aurora answered with a smile of pride. "Most of them have seen attacks before. They do not let it stop business for long."

"And this young woman?" I indicated to the vendor laying out a row of what looked like carrots.

Aurora glanced at her before lowering her eyebrows in either sadness or disapproval. I could not tell which. "That's Cassandra. Her mother and father were the vegetable sellers here, but they were both injured in the attack. Both later died."

I heard Aurora, and before I could think about what I was doing, I was heading towards Cassandra.

Cassandra must have noticed my approach in her peripheral vision for she looked up at me, then back down to the carrots she was sorting. Then she did a double take, nearly dropping the bunch of carrots she was holding. She caught them in an expert swipe, and then reached up to smooth a wayward strand of blonde hair behind her ear.

"My Lords and Ladies," Cassandra said quietly in greeting as we neared. She bowed her head, looking at me quizzically as if trying to make out who or what I was.

"And Your Majesty," Aurora murmured in Cassandra's ear as she took her place beside the girl, behind the vendor's cart.

Cassandra's eyes snapped to mine, and then she truly did drop the carrots, their thickly knotted orange flesh making a decided slap on the cobbles as they hit the ground.

If Cassandra curtsied, I did not notice. I was too busy immediately stooping to pick up the discarded vegetables. I righted myself and handed them to her. "Here you go."

Her eyes bulged as she looked from the vegetables in my upturned hand to my face and back again. "Erm, Your Majesty, I apologize."

"There is nothing to apologize for," I replied, lifting the carrots an inch higher. "Here."

Cassandra hesitantly reached out and grasped them. Then she curtsied several times, bobbing once, twice, and a third time in quick succession. "Again, my apologies."

I leaned towards her slightly and whispered, "Again, no worries."

We—Queen and saleswoman—stared at each other for a few more moments before I realized that she was waiting for me to take the lead and speak.

I cleared my throat. "Governor Aurora tells me that both your parents were killed in the recent attack."

Her eyes quickly shifted from my face, and she blinked several times in a flutter. I recognized that motion—the attempt to hold back tears when they threatened to fall. "Yes, Majesty."

Lisideria had told me not once but twice what would be expected of me on this trip. I was to be seen. I was to listen. I was not to talk to the commoners, as she called them. I was not to allow them to touch me, or engage with them in any other way than one would abstractly engage with a landscape—noting it and letting it pass by.

Lisideria told me and I remembered her instruction, but as if I had balled up her words like paper and chucked them in the fireplace, I threw out her advice. Instead, I moved around the vendor's booth so that I was standing side by side with Aurora and Cassandra. And then I reached out and squeezed Cassandra's arm.

Cassandra's eyes widened, and her eyes tracked where my fingers grasped her as if in awe.

"I am very sorry for your loss," I said to her. And I was sorry. Cassandra could not have been much older than I was and she, too, was without parents. Granted, she had known hers. She had memories with them and had been raised by them, whereas I had nothing but the state portraits hung in the palace by which to remember my own biological parents.

Still, I understood what came with that loss: the grief and the wondering about what life could have been with them still in it.

I let go of her arm and then moved back onto the other side of the vendor's cart, the shocked chattering of the Lords forming a sort of low droning behind me. I was sure they were displeased by my being so familiar with Cassandra, but I did not care.

I did not know how to be in this space of death and sadness without showing my own sympathy. It was what I would have done in the Humanrealm, and it was what I did now.

A small crowd was gathering in this central marketplace and I turned towards the gurgling sound of their voices. Aurora followed, introducing me to the people of Ukuwela as she went.

When we reached a couple, she paused and I saw her face pinch in a way that told me this next introduction would be painful.

"Majesty," she began. She took the hand of the woman, then that of the man beside her, before continuing. "These are the Toars. They were here shopping for clothes for their new baby when the explosions occurred…"

I looked at them—the pinched face that Aurora wore, the empty eyes that the Toars both had—and I knew before Aurora said her next words.

"They lost both their newborn and their two-year-old child."

The woman's frame seemed to quake with hearing the truth spoken aloud, and without thinking, I reached towards her. I enveloped her in my arms, her head cradled in the nook formed by the intersection of my neck and shoulder.

"I am so sorry," I whispered to the woman who clung to me. "I'm sorry."

I could feel her nodding, even as she continued to grasp the back of my riding habit for support. And I did not blame her. I did not have children and had never known that sort of love, but I could imagine what the loss of it would do to a person.

I squeezed her once more before the woman seemed to remember herself and pull upright. "My apologies, Majesty. I do not presume…"

"Speak nothing of it," I shushed her, as I handed her to her empty-eyed husband. He bowed to me before looping an arm about his wife's waist and steering her away. I watched them melt back into the crowd like two sleepwalkers, and my heart ached for their souls.

From behind me, pressure on my lower back made me turn. Finn.

"Are you alright, Your Majesty?" he said quietly, his lips barely moving as if he thought he might frighten away these grieving people.

But I smiled at him, a sad little smile. "I'm fine."

Finn did not remove his hand, and I felt the pressure faintly pushing me away from Aurora and the gathered crowd. I trusted Finn, trusted his instincts as a soldier, so I allowed him to steer me away from the anguish that was nearly overwhelming in this marketplace.

"Still, it is best to not get too close," he whispered close to my ear as I broke back into my entourage's circle.

I nodded, looking into his clouded eyes. I wondered if he was as affected as I was at seeing the state of Ukuwela. But before I could think about asking, I broke the connection and looked away.

I had to remember where we were. I had to remember who was around us.

Whatever our relationship was, it was subterranean. It was a secret. It would never be suitable to show that any connection existed between us, besides the one of trainer and trainee— espccially not here before all of the Lords.

I cleared my throat quietly as I took a step away from Finn, my gaze surveying the market square once more. As if I felt its pull, Anson's gaze caught mine immediately.

While most of the Lords were busy inspecting the charred remains of vendors' carts, the explosions' craters, or speaking to other citizens near us in the market, Anson was watching me.

I held his gaze as if I could communicate my question through a look alone. Why are you staring at me?

He raised his eyebrows a moment before glancing to Finn and back to me. And then he winked.

If I thought no Lord had noticed the moment between Finn and myself, I was mistaken.

Cold washed over me in an instant, the feeling of horror that accompanies a dreaded moment come to pass. I felt my throat constrict and my eyes widen.

Anson knew. Or at the very least, he suspected something.

But just as quickly as his knowing smile had appeared, it was gone. He looked away, turning to Aurora who had said something to him. I watched his profile as he nodded at whatever Aurora said, and my mind ran a thousand directions at once.

Was I imagining things? Had Anson meant something else with his look?

I wanted to pretend that the moment had not happened. I wanted to believe that I had misinterpreted his look, that I was imagining things. But I knew better. I knew Anson.

I wished I could be angry, that my temper could flare but all I felt was fear. Of all the Lords to suspect that there was more between Finn and me, he was the worst. He hated me and would use anything he could to undermine me.

To approach him would raise even more suspicion. There was nothing I could do, no way to confirm his look without sealing my fate. And so I squared my shoulders, took a breath, and tried to refocus my eyes on the marketplace before me.

Yet my eyes kept landing on Anson's profile. I kept willing him to meet my gaze again. I thought I could divine some sort of answer in his look, some sort of awareness of what he might do with his knowledge. But he studiously avoided my line of sight, taken as he was with whatever Aurora was describing.

I told myself to breathe, in and out, in and out. Anson had no proof even if he did suspect something. Anson did not know anything about Finn and myself. Anson could not hurt me.

I told myself all of this, even as Kaiht approached and began to ask me questions, even as I pretended to be paying attention. But mostly, what I told myself was that my life would be so much easier had I never met Anson of Ingonyame.

Aware as ever of the logistics, Grimly made us wrap up our trip to Ukuwela soon after. More citizens had come to the market to greet us and I waved absently to them as we made our way back to the gate from which we had entered.

Aurora and her staff escorted us back to the zebras, and then we were mounting for the return journey to the palace.

"Thank you," I said to Aurora from my saddle, standing as she was near the head of my zebra.

"You're most welcome, Your Majesty," she replied with a curtsy. "The people were heartened by seeing you here today."

"I wish there was something more I could do."

Aurora nodded, her eyes taking on that wistful look I had come to associate with her, even after such a brief acquaintance. "We all do. That is why we are in public service."

"You speak as if I chose this," I said, offhandedly, wrapping my zebra's reins around my hands.

But Aurora just smiled. "Didn't you?"

I looked at her, unsure of what to say. Of course, I had not picked this life. I would be back in the Humanrealm in college, studying English literature if not for the Alterealm. I would not be a Queen. I would not have the weight of a kingdom resting on my shoulders.

"I don't think so," I replied.

"I do," Aurora said. And then she was turning away, my protests lost on deaf ears. I had not chosen this life, so why did she think I had?

For all three hours of the journey back to the palace, our retinue inched along in silence. Absently I felt my tall, stately animal moving its muscles under my legs, but my focus was on my fear. A little voice in the back of my mind still worried about what Anson knew but there were two larger, looming fears that took precedence.

I was afraid of what I had seen today. It was tragic and brutal and heartbreaking. I had read about battles and attacks, seen films depicting wars but I had never myself smelled the scorched rooflines or clung to a family member left behind. It was beyond anything I had ever seen in the Humanrealm, and it left me waxy with shock.

But most of all, I was afraid of my dawning realization that I alone had the power to prevent a tragedy like the Ukuwelan attack from happening again…or not. As Queen and leader, I would ultimately chart a course for what happened next, the outcome of which could be even more attacks and death than what I had witnessed firsthand today. I was the ruler here. I was the one who made decisions about this kingdom's safety.

It was up to me to protect the people of Izwe. And it was up to me to suffer alongside them for my failures.

I wiped at an angry, sad tear that threatened to loose itself from my eye. I had to do better. I had to be better.

Being a good queen was not just about me. It was not a game. Every bit of Izweian history I learned or cultural understanding I gleaned would help me be the best Queen I could be.

Every bit of training I mastered or—God forbid—magic I developed would make me that much more powerful of a ruler. It was up to me and, for the first time, with the smell of fresh carrots still lingering in my nostrils, that was crystal clear.

As we rode through the landscape of Izwe, I understood like I had never before understood. I would spell out the ruin or salvation for a nation of people. This was larger than me. This was more important than me. I owed it to all of these nameless, faceless people to do more than try. I had to succeed and succeed quickly.

And that thought chilled me to the core.

I did not have to ask Finn to come to my chambers upon our return. He simply knew I would want him and so he came.

I needed to speak to him—about Anson's look, about my fear that we might be found out. But I also needed the nearness of him, his quiet strength and calm after the day of visceral horror we had faced.

I thought I was shaken after hearing about the attack but seeing the rubble, smelling the lingering scent of charred buildings and bodies made it real in a way I could not have predicted.

I answered the door myself and pulled Finn to me instantly.

I did not say anything for a few moments, nor did he. But then I felt his hands move in slow circles on my back, then my shoulders. He placed his two hands on my cheeks and pulled me away slightly to gaze at my face.

"How are you holding up?"

"Just a little bit shaken," I replied with a weary shrug. I heard Kaiht and Mara bustle around somewhere behind me as I pulled away.

"I'm sure. I've seen sites like that a hundred times, but it never gets easy. Let's get you a drink."

We walked to the sitting area before the fire. He took a tumbler of what looked like whiskey from Mara's outstretched hand and placed it in my own.

"Thank you," I called to both of them. Then I took a healthy sip.

I let the whiskey burn a path from lips to stomach, preparing myself for what I needed to say next. "I need to talk to you, Finn."

His eyes instantly became alert, cool and blue and cutting. "What is it?"

"I think Anson knows."

Finn did not respond for a moment. He took a sip of his own whiskey. "Why do you say that?"

"He saw you escort me back to the group today. He saw the way we spoke to each other and looked at each other. And then he caught my eye and winked."

"That could mean anything. You know how Anson is."

I shook my head. "Yes, but something about this was different. I can't explain how he knows but he does. I'm sure of it."

Finn took another sip before responding, as if he were debating whether to say the next words. "Should we not see each other anymore?"

"What? Why?" I exclaimed, nearly losing grip of my glass.

"Your reputation and security are the most important thing to me, Queen Sahle. If putting an end to this is what ensures that, then we must do it."

"No," I said with a note of finality. I was not willing to entertain that. I had given up too much already, and I was not prepared to add Finn to the list.

"Queen Sahle…" Finn said with a sigh.

"No," I repeated. "You're my choice. I'll not let Anson scare us."

Finn stood and refilled his glass. He looked into the blazing fireplace, his broad back turned to me. "And if he should tell Grimly or the other Lords of his suspicion? You could be ruined."

"We'll deal with that if and when it happens. Until then, we just need to be more careful when we're in public."

Finn did not say anything, and I could nearly see the thoughts swirling in his head—the reluctance, the desire, the loyalty. He did not know what to say or what to do, torn as he was between heart and mind.

But I did. I knew what I wanted and I was just rash enough to follow through with it.

I walked to him, discarding my glass along the way. I stepped between him and the fire, forcing my smaller form into the space between his arms.

The feel of Finn's body next to mine was all I wanted to focus on, and so I let my mind wander there instead. As it had been and would continue to be, thoughts of Finn were the perfect escape from my reality.

I angled my face up at the same time that Finn leaned down, also caught up in the pull between us. And as our lips touched, I knew we were done speaking for the night.

His hands drifted along my waist, pulling me into his body in earnest. I could feel the hard muscle of his soldier's body under his clothes and the feel of it echoed tightly, deep in my belly.

Our lips danced together for a few moments, an interplay

between the soft cushion of my own and the firmness of his. And then his tongue brushed the corner of my lips, asking for entrance.

I allowed it, opening for him as I tipped my head back further. He tasted me, sweeping his tongue against my own, my teeth, the roof of my mouth. It was pure ecstasy, the feel of him claiming me this way.

I wanted more.

I moaned into his mouth as my tongue responded in kind, toying with his and darting past his opened lips. I ran my hands down to where his tunic met his pants, and I began pulling up the tunic's hem.

He pulled back briefly. His eyes cast around the room as if remembering suddenly where we were. "Are you sure?" he asked, even once his eyes fixed on my tall four-poster bed. He had visited me here before, but he had never stayed.

"Yes," I replied, running my hands on the bare planes of his stomach. "It's fine."

"I don't want to compromise you," he said, an echo from before, even though I could still see the desire swirling in his gaze.

"You're not. Or rather, you already have been," I smirked. "You being here? It changes nothing."

He looked at me a moment longer, and seeming to make up his mind, took my mouth again.

His motions were wilder this time, as if he knew exactly where this kiss would end. And he did. I had all but told him my intentions, and I had meant them.

Without further delay, I pulled his shirt over his head and he untied the knot that held my dressing gown closed. Unbound, he slipped the gown over my shoulders and let it fall to the floor.

He ran his hands over my shift-clad arms and then around my back to grasp my hair. "It's wet," he said in between kisses.

"I was in the bath just before you arrived," I told him as my hands made their way to the waistline of his pants.

"You have the most beautiful curls," he murmured as I drew my hand lower, feeling the hard length of him eager to be freed.

I obliged, unclasping one button and then the next until his pants were sagging on his hips. I pushed them to the floor, my mouth suddenly dry as the length of him sprang free. I grasped him in my hand and his hips jerked towards me automatically.

I smiled against his mouth. "So eager."

And I could feel his answering smile. "Always, Your Majesty."

I stroked him as he hurriedly pushed the shift from my shoulders. When it too landed in a puddle on the floor, he pulled away from me to take my breast in his mouth. My hand stilled, distracted as I was by the rippling sensations echoing from my breast to my core. I moaned and he moved his attention from one breast to the other.

His hands ran the length of my bare waist and over the swell of my hips, completely naked before the glow of the fire. Then one hand dipped between my legs and a sound between a moan and a growl passed his lips when he felt the wetness there.

I did not need to tell him I wanted him. He had proof of it at his fingertips, and it seemed to urge him on.

He tore his mouth from my breast and recaptured my mouth, biting my lower lip as he pushed me gently but insistently towards the bed. I let him, for I wanted to go there too, and we tumbled into the thick sheets together.

He pulled himself over me, positioned so that his hips were wedged between my own. And in a single fluid movement, he seated himself inside me with a shuddering breath.

I could not contain my gasp at the sudden intrusion, the exquisite feeling of being filled and stretched. He set a quick, deep pace, coaxing me towards release with each thrust.

I felt it building in me, but I was not ready yet. I stilled him with a hand and when he met my gaze questioningly, I pulled at him as if to roll us over.

He knew what I wanted, even without me vocalizing it. It was a product of our training together as much as it was a product of our sleeping together; we knew each other's bodies almost as intimately as our own.

He rolled us in a smooth motion so that he was laying on his back and I was astride him. I grasped his hands to help me balance, and I rose and fell in an aching rhythm.

"Queen Sahle," he murmured, and I caught his gaze, looking down on him.

His blonde hair was splayed across the pale fabric of my pillow, and the sight of him here in my bed—illicit as it was—after all of the days of us sneaking through the training ground was enough to tip me over the edge.

I cried out, and Finn clasped a hand over my mouth. The gesture was oddly dominant, and the feeling of him taking control heightened my release.

As the final thrums of my climax waned, Finn did not drop his hand. No, with one hand over my mouth and the other clasped on my hip, he pumped upwards once, twice, and once more. Then he found his own release.

His head tilted back on the pillow as he spilled himself in me. My own moans were smothered by his fingers and I was grateful for the hand that still covered my lips.

Opening his eyes, he seemed to only now notice the hand held to my face and he lowered it. I pulled myself off him, sticky with our mingled sweat, and laid down on my side in the crook of his arm.

The night seemed to press in on me now, the memories of Ukuwela and the fear of Anson trying to intrude on this moment. And so I leaned down to grab the covers and pulled them up and over our heads.

The weight of the world could wait a little while longer. Because here in my bed, with Finn and me slick with our exertion, nothing else existed. It was just us, and I was just Sahle.

I was happy to pretend.

ASLEEP AS I WAS, I DID NOT HEAR THEM ENTER.

In some distant part of my consciousness, I am sure I heard the creaking of the heavy wooden door as it was pushed open. It was like those moments in the middle of the night when you are suddenly wide awake without knowing what sound or feeling woke you. All you know is that something pulled you from the deepest of sleeps, a niggling feeling of half-memory in your consciousness that you cannot quite grasp. That was what it was like to suddenly pop open my eyes and see Roland and Grimly staring at me.

To be fair, they were not necessarily staring at me. Rather, their gaze was locked on the bed I was laying in, and on the man who was sound asleep in it.

Roland, Grimly, and I stared between one another and the sleeping form of Finn. And then, as if a thunderclap cracked overhead, multiple things happened at once.

I sat up and pulled the covers more securely around my naked form.

Grimly let out a wordless noise of disbelief likened most to a squawk.

Roland withdrew his sword in a fluid motion that made me wonder why I had never seen the warrior in him all those years he had pretended to be my father.

Finn opened his eyes and moved quickly to angle his body in front of mine in a protective stance.

"Get up!" Roland shouted, and I was not sure who he was speaking to. Since there was no "Your Majesty" tacked to the end of the order, I figured it was aimed at Finn.

But Finn did not move from his place in front of me, one hand on my thigh as if to push me back from the unsheathed sword.

I saw Roland's gaze narrow in on that hand, its possessive placement, and then Roland lunged.

He was at the bed in one second, pulling at Finn's arm in another.

I had been training with Finn for some months now. I knew what he looked like when he was fighting earnestly, and when he was holding back. Right now, I knew he was letting Roland control him. He was not limply going along, but he was not resisting either.

He allowed himself to be pulled from the bed, his nakedness all but forgotten.

"How dare you!" Roland snarled at him. His beige skin was pulled tight, the bones standing out starkly.

"Dad!" I yelled, momentarily forgetting that he was Roland now. I wrapped the sheet around me and hopped to my feet.

Finn did not answer in words, but rather bowed deeply to Roland.

He might be seemingly unaware of the sword Roland was clutching at, but I was not.

"How dare you!" Roland yelled again as he stepped into Finn, pulling the bowed man up and nearly touching their noses together. "She is the Queen of Izwe, and you dare touch her!"

Finn did not say a word, just kept his eyes averted from Roland's. I knew he could fight if he wanted to. His sword was with his clothes on the other side of the bed, but his fists were nearly as deadly.

Yet Finn would never do that. He would never fight Roland even as Roland yelled in his face and threw insults at him. Roland was too important to me. Hurting Roland would hurt me, and Finn would never do anything to deliberately cause me pain.

Which meant it was up to me.

If I had to hear Roland yell "How dare you!" one more time, I thought I might burn up in indignation and embarrassment. I stepped between the two men just as Roland opened his mouth again.

"Dad…Lord Roland," I said quietly, placing a hand on the arm that held his sword. "Please let me explain."

In a logical part of my head, I knew I did not need to explain. I was Queen and I had every right to order Roland and Grimly out of my chambers this instant.

But another part of me—the part that had lived as Roland's daughter for two decades—still saw him as my father. And that meant I owed him an explanation for what was going on. That meant I needed to do some explaining. That meant I needed the disappointment to lift from his eyes.

As if it was physically difficult, Roland pried his gaze from Finn and shifted it to me. He raised his eyebrows. "Explain? What do you mean to explain?"

I took a breath. At least Roland was taking the bait, moving his attention to me even if he was skeptical of it.

"Roland, Finn is here because I asked him to be here."

I hardly got out the words, before a choking noise from behind me sounded. I swiveled in time to see Grimly lower himself into one of my wingback chairs in a hurry. Apparently, the thought of the Queen in bed with someone was enough to make a Lord faint.

Roland did not look much better, I noticed, as I turned my attention back to him. "You what?" he managed past gritted teeth.

The anger and disappointment in Roland's eyes made me want to cower. I instinctively felt my shoulders begin to hunch forward, a subconscious attempt to make myself smaller. But mid-slump, I stopped myself.

I was Queen, and while I felt I owed Roland an explanation, I would give it while standing tall and not flinching away. I had created this situation, this reality. It was up to me to face it now.

I took a deep breath and pulled my shoulders back, lifting my chin a fraction of an inch. "I said that Finn is here on my invitation. So, if there is anyone to question, it's me."

Roland stared at me a moment longer. "Did he force you?" he asked, his voice dropping an octave as he leaned slightly towards me.

"No!" I gasped, horrified. "Why would you think that?"

Roland glared at Finn, tracking his eyes across the still naked form of the soldier standing at attention just feet from us. "It's the only explanation I can think of."

"Well perhaps you need more imagination," I quipped back, my own anger getting the better of me. "Finn would never do something like that."

"And how do you know?"

"Because I know him. We've been seeing each other for months now."

Another little gasp from the seating area had me spinning back to Grimly. "Lord Grimly, you are dismissed," I said simply.

I did not watch Grimly go but I heard his shuffling feet as he got them under him. I heard the creak of the door as he opened and shut it behind him.

But I could never dismiss Roland. I needed Roland to understand.

The man in question was staring at me, his mouth slightly agape as if I had said the most horrific thing to have ever been spoken. "Months, Sahl?"

With Grimly gone, I guess we were back to informalities. "Yes, Dad."

"Why?"

I knew Roland was just trying to understand this situation, but that one word lit a fire in my soul. Like a match that brushed along a powder keg, my carefully held emotions exploded.

"Why?!" I very nearly shouted. "How can you ask that? Do you have any idea what my life has been like since I came here?"

When Roland did not reply, I continued, "No? That's fitting since you and Eliza left me here alone in this palace. Well, I'll tell you. It's been hell—pure hell. I've been tossed into this world without any preparation, and I've been expected to hit the ground running, to know everything there is about the Alterealm and about Izwe. About how to be a ruler!

"It's been lonely and frightening and humiliating. But the one thing that hasn't is Finn. He's the one true friend I have here, and the only person who doesn't make me feel stupid for trying to figure out what is going on around me.

"And this—" I waved a hand in an approximate gesture between me and Finn "I did not plan this. Finn actively discouraged it, in fact, and told me it was inappropriate—"

"That knowledge didn't seem to keep him from your bed," Roland interjected.

I paused. "It would have, but I told him I did not care about the appropriateness of it. I believe my exact words were 'Fuck the Council.'"

Roland's gray eyes narrowed at that, and mine did too. He may not be my actual father, but I knew where my will came from. I was convinced it was a learned behavior from this man.

We stared at each other another moment, and then Roland flicked his eyes back to Finn. "Get some clothes on."

"Sir," Finn said simply, before breaking from attention to search for his pants.

I did not turn to watch Finn but kept wary eyes on Roland.

"Sahle," Roland said, his voice a touch gentler now. "This is bad."

I swallowed, some of the wind going out of my sails. "I know."

Roland nodded, contemplating. "If I had come here on my own, I would have been able to keep this quiet. But now that Grimly has seen it, it will be all over court within hours. The Lords will want answers."

"I thought I did not answer to them," I said, a statement that was really more of a bluff than anything.

Roland laughed without humor. "Oh Sahle, you are Queen but who you sleep with and when is a matter of the Council. They will not like that you've taken it into your own hands."

Roland holstered his sword, shaking his head. Then he turned to Finn, who was back standing at attention—this time fully dressed, weapons and all.

"Soldier, back to your post."

"Yes, my Lord," Finn said immediately, bowing once more.

I watched as he made his way directly to the door. He did not glance at me or reach out in a gesture of goodbye.

It took me a moment to process this. I knew having Grimly and Roland in my chambers had thrown our usual routine out the window, but a part of me was hurt that he would not even glance back at me.

It was irrational, but I wanted a goodbye, a moment of caring, especially in the wake of what had just happened.

As Finn reached the door, I called out. "Finn?"

He paused for a moment, his hand on the handle. He turned back to me.

And then I ran the distance between us, all but hurtling myself into his arms. He held me for a moment, his arms warm and solid where they touched my bare skin above the thin sheet. I felt him press a kiss into my mess of curls, and then he was pulling away.

"Your Majesty," he said, bowing once more. Then he was gone, the sound of his booted steps receding down the marble hall.

Before Roland and I could say another word to each other, the servants' door burst open. And there was Eliza, red-faced and doubled over as if she had just sprinted all the way from her country manor.

"Eliza!" Roland called in alarm as he rushed to her side. He took her arm to help her stand up and, as she righted herself, she stared straight at me.

"I…just heard…" she said between gasps. "You and…Finn? Sahle…how…could you?"

26

summons

IT WAS NOT A SURPRISE WHEN I RECEIVED A NOTE ASKING me to join the Council in their session the next morning. It was phrased as an invitation, but I knew what it was: a summons. Despite being Queen, I was about to be reprimanded.

After bursting into my chambers, Eliza had told me as much in between random curses and gasps of outrage. It had taken her at least an hour before she had stopped swearing.

We had talked through what happened, and as uncomfortable as it was to go into the details of my relationship with Finn with the people I knew as my parents, there was no getting around it. I was surprised to hear Roland actively defending me when Eliza blurted out obscenities, but perhaps Roland had just had more time to wrap his head around the idea of Finn and me.

In the end, both of them had hugged me and told me that it would be fine—after the summons.

Grimly had taken no time in telling everyone he could what he had seen in my chambers. That was how Eliza had learned so quickly. In the wake of my trip to Ukuwela, she and Roland had come to the palace to provide support. She told me she had been having an early morning tea with Lady Sybil when Lord Grimly passed, mumbling about the Queen and a soldier. I was sure it took mere minutes until even the lowliest of shoe shiners and stable boys were clued in.

This relationship would cause an uproar. Of that, we were all in agreement. As Eliza explained, Queens were meant to be chaste. It was not explicitly stated in some Izweian code of conduct, but it was more of an unsaid expectation. As far as she knew, no Queen had ever taken a lover—at least publicly. Yet here I was, a new Queen breaking all the rules.

It was up to me now to control the damage, to set a new standard for what Queens could and could not do. And that started with facing the Lords.

I crumpled the note in my hand, the fine, thick paper crackling inside my closed fist. I dropped the balled-up paper onto the floor and took a final sip of my tea. Then I rose from my seat before the wall of windows in my room.

I was the Queen and this time I would remember it. I would hold my head up and defend myself rather than shrink away. I was the Queen.

In the golden morning light streaming through those windows, Kaiht and Mara helped me dress. I chose a gown of gray, severe in color and just as uncompromising in cut. The long sleeves and bodice hugged me but fell in the standard billowing floor-length skirt. The neckline was cut in a wide V that was low enough to show the very top curves of my breasts. The back mirrored it, dropping in the same V to show a portion of my spine.

There was no adornment, no embroidery on this gown, but the material was well-made and heavy. It felt like armor on my skin—armor I would need in the Council Chamber this day.

Kaiht and Mara brushed through my curls, braided my hair, and pinned it up around my head. Finally, they nestled my crown onto my head.

I stared at myself in the mirror for a moment, taking in the full picture of a defiant Queen. For that was what I was—

a monarch yet also a woman with her own mind and heart. The months with Finn had been the best thing to happen to me since I arrived in the Alterealm, and I was not willing to give that up.

I did not know if I loved him, but it did not matter. That was not what this fight would be about. I needed Finn only to be exactly as he was—a friend, a lover, a confidant in this new world where everything else was harsh and unfriendly. And I would go to battle to defend my ability to choose that for myself.

"Your Majesty," Kaiht called, pulling my attention from my thoughts. "It's time."

I nodded at her, squeezing her arm as I walked past her towards the door.

"It will be alright, if you don't mind me saying," Mara added quietly. It was so rare that she spoke that I stopped and stared at her. Then I gave her the widest smile I could manage.

"I think so, too. Thank you, Mara."

She curtsied as I continued on. My chamber doors were opened for me, and the Vikela fell in line as I made my way down the staircases and hallways that separated my rooms from the Council Chambers.

Since I had remained in my rooms yesterday, sending my apologies to whomever I had planned to meet with, this moment was the first time I was braving the court since news of Finn got out. It appeared that the entire court had heard about my unconventional relationship, and more nobles and servants filled the halls than ever before—well, except for my arrival to the Alterealm all of those months ago.

My gray gown swished behind me, pooling in a slight train as I walked. I focused on the sound of the material against the stone and wood floors to block out the whispers I heard around me, the buzz of too many bodies pressing in on me.

And then we were before the Council Chamber doors. And the doors were opening. And the eyes of every advisor turned towards me as silence descended down the long Council table.

I stood in the doorway for a moment, taking a breath to steel myself. I pulled my shoulders back and lifted my chin an inch. Then I made that long walk down to my throne at the far end of the room.

From where they stood, each Lord dropped into a bow as I continued onwards. I noticed all twenty of them were present, as well as Roland and Eliza. It had been a long series of days, what with the attack on Ukuwela and the trip to survey the damage. I could see the tiredness carved into the weary faces before me.

I did not want to be here. They did not want to be here. Yet, word of my indiscretion gave them no choice but to deal with this here and now, no matter what else was happening in the kingdom. Attack or not, news of the Queen sleeping with a soldier was pressing.

A part of me expected to see Finn, but of course he would not be asked to attend. He would not be given a chance to defend himself or the relationship we had started. No, he would be judged by us lofty nobles and accept whatever punishment we meted out.

I gritted my teeth at the thought as I mounted the dais and slowly took my seat, the folds of my skirt fanned out around me like the plumage of a great bird.

"My Lords," I addressed the chamber and each man rose from their bow. "Please be seated."

"Thank you, Queen Sahle," Grimly responded from the head of the table. "And thank you for accepting our invitation to this impromptu Council session."

"Lord Grimly, I believe it was less an invitation and more of a summons," I corrected, eyes trained on the Chief Advisor. Peripherally, I saw Eliza and Roland look at each other, and I wondered if they recognized the child they raised in this moment.

A heartbeat went by before Grimly responded. "Your Majesty, you are Queen. You are never summoned."

My lips twitched to throw out a sarcastic remark, but I reigned in the impulse. The only sign of my disbelief was the single eyebrow I arched as I looked down the table of Lords.

My gaze tracked past the kindly Lord Marcus, the cantankerous Lord Lionel. It snagged on Lord Anson. I expected him to look smug. Just days ago he had suspected there was more going on between Finn and me. Of that I was certain. But something in his face was not right. He looked uncharacteristically worried. That stupid, cocky smirk—the one he seemed to wear no matter how grave the situation—was gone. In its place, he stared at me with an earnestness I had never seen.

"At your leave, shall we begin?" Grimly asked.

I tore my eyes from Anson's. "Please do."

"Your Majesty, we called this special meeting to discuss a delicate topic that came to our attention yesterday. Lord Roland and I discovered that the Queen and her trainer, Commander Finn, have engaged in an inappropriate relationship."

I closed my eyes at the phrase but opened them a split second later. I would not hide. I would not falter. If there was any moment to be strong, it was this one.

"And what exactly do you mean by an inappropriate relationship?" Eliza called from her place beside Roland. I caught her eye as she looked back at me and she gave me one of her reassuring smiles, just as she had always done.

"A relationship of a sexual nature," Grimly stated, and the room began to buzz. The Lords spoke among themselves and threw furtive glances my way, but I stayed still. I stayed silent.

"And?" Eliza continued. "The Queen is not married. She is an adult. She may engage in whatever relationships she likes, assuming they are not detrimental to the kingdom."

"Surely you are not arguing that it is acceptable for a Queen to share herself freely, especially when the man in question is a commoner?" one Lord called from the far end of the table.

Eliza held up her head even higher as she responded. "That is exactly what I am saying."

The buzz of outraged voices rose in volume, and I smiled again at Eliza in thanks.

"With all do respect, Lady Eliza," another Lord said as he

stood from several seats down. "Her Majesty is young and impressionable, not to mention new to court—"

"As well as the entire Alterealm!" another Lord interjected in a near-shout.

"Quite right," the first Lord continued. "She is our ruler, but she is also suggestible. This relationship would put Finn in a position of great influence over our Queen and, accordingly, Izwe."

Another Lord stood, "It is unacceptable for a mere trainer to have such influence. He is a soldier for God and gods' sake! And now he means to run a kingdom through the Queen?"

Outraged scoffs echoed through the Council Chamber, and several Lords tried to talk at once. They drowned out each other's words.

I should have said something, but my mind was stuck, incapable of processing what the Lords were implying. In the conversations with Roland and Eliza, I had been led to believe the shock of my relationship with Finn would center around the fact that I was sleeping with someone, anyone, when not married. I was quickly realizing that was only a minor part.

The real problem was that Finn posed a threat to the Lords' power.

I took a deep breath to calm my mind. I tried to focus through the cacophony of voices, the simmering resentment I felt from the Lords. My anger had grown, and it would grow still if the Lords continued down this path.

I was sitting here before these men, being questioned about the nature of the relationship with Finn and all of this humiliation was due to their own need for control. Before I could judge the wisdom of speaking that thought aloud, I had opened my mouth.

"So, what you are truly concerned with is that Finn's influence may grow more important than your own?" I questioned everyone and no one. I spoke to the air, to the once-trees that now formed the great ebony table before me.

"Queen Sahle," Grimly started. "We—"

"No, Lord Grimly, I am speaking now." I felt the anger like pressure behind my eyes as I focused on the Lord. He inclined his head in my direction and sat. "With everything that has just occurred—an attack on Izwe, people dead, livelihoods lost—this is an outrageous proceeding. You summon me here to argue over which man at this table is losing the most sway by my sleeping with Finn. Is that truly the root of your concern?"

There was silence in the chamber, stunned silence, as if each Lord was wondering when I had grown a voice.

And it was a fair question, for I had only recently discovered that voice myself. I had spent too many months being quiet and observing in this realm. I knew I could be a smart aleck and throw temper tantrums and quips to those closest to me. Yet, in formal capacities, I had taken the role of a silent observer.

Now, something I cared about was under threat, something intimate and necessary to what little happiness I had found in this place. I had no choice but to use my authority to stand up for myself.

Out of all the men seated before me, Lord Grimly recovered first. "Queen Sahle, if I may…?"

I waved a hand, signaling him to speak.

"Your Majesty is still new to our ways and this kingdom. If your advisors seek to guide you, it is only so that you receive the best training on how to govern. What we fear is that Finn is not the best influence."

"Why would he not be?" I countered. "You've trusted me to him for physical and magical training, so you must hold him in reasonably high regard."

"We certainly trust him to lead soldiers and train men. But he is not a politician, nor is he a ruler or a landowner. His knowledge of what it takes to think strategically for a kingdom is what is in question."

They may have had a point, but just as the pressure behind my eyes was beginning to lessen, Lord Wiley stood and spoke.

"With all due respect, a commoner should also not be allowed to touch a Queen of the Alterealm. It is an abomination, and it threatens any future marriage prospects for the Queen."

The silence in the chamber shouted, so still and quiet it rung like a thousand voices yelling in a hall.

"Excuse me?" I said quietly, my gaze trained on Lord Wiley.

Grimly stood, however. "What Lord Wiley is attempting to say is that your future marriage will help secure Izwe internally and with our allies abroad. Any prior relationship, especially one with a commoner, will limit your options and threaten the kingdom's security. It is a delicate topic, Your Majesty, but we do need to ascertain some information from you…"

Vaguely, I noted that Eliza was rising from her chair. She made her way to my side, exactly as she had the first day. I felt her hand on my shoulder, and she squeezed it once. I wondered whether she was there to offer her support or hold me down for what I suspected was about to be asked.

I focused back on Grimly.

"…the exact nature of your relationship, what physical steps Finn has taken with you, and whether you have had sexual intercourse?"

My eyes widened and my mouth hung open. I was expected to sit before this room of gawking men and detail what Finn and I had shared over the last weeks?

"Queen Sahle?" Grimly asked when I did not respond.

I blinked twice in an attempt to shake myself from my own shocked outrage.

"Your Majesty, this information is critical for the Council to know. We must know what has already occurred so that we can accurately represent you as we begin to consider marriages for you."

"Queen Sahle," Eliza said quietly from my side. I turned, expecting her to be standing and therefore towering above me. But she was squatted down, at eye level with me where I sat on my throne. "Just tell them and be done with it."

And while I did not trust any of the men in the room—except for Roland, who had had his eyes fixed on the table since Grimly began speaking—I did trust Eliza. If she told me to tell these men what they wanted to hear, then I would do it for her. I never doubted that she had my best interest at heart.

I refused to look at any one man and rather focused, like Roland, on the table before me. I traced the wood grain with my eyes as I swallowed dryly. I finally spoke. "Yes. Finn and I have had sex."

This time the scoffs and murmurs were as shocked as they were disgusted, and I resented that. I may not love Finn, but he was my friend. He was worthy. He was the only good thing that was mine in this realm, and I did not countenance a lack of kindness to the one source of happiness I had.

I felt blood stain my cheeks in a heated, angry blush. Just as I opened my mouth to tell the Lords they could keep their opinions to themselves, a voice rang out.

And oh how I wished it had not. The last person I wanted to hear from was Anson, but here he was. He would finally have his say and, once again, I had given him plenty of fodder with which to humiliate me.

"My Lords," Anson's voice bit out. I quickly turned my head at the tone.

He, too, had the pinkened cheeks of a blush and his eyes shone with emotion. But where I was mortified, he was livid. I could see it in the set of his mouth and the line of his eyebrows, drawn down as they were towards his narrowed green eyes. "It is a wonder the Queen does not order your immediate execution for the trial you are putting her through. What happens between the Queen and whomever she chooses to share herself with is none of our concern."

"Lord Anson," Grimly said. "The safety of Izwe is at risk every time she spends the night with this man. It cannot happen again."

"What cannot happen again?" I asked, though it was a dumb question. I knew what he meant.

Grimly looked hesitant to respond, so it was not long before Wiley took up the baton. "You may have already given yourself to Finn, and while we cannot do anything about that now, we can protect you from further ruin by forbidding it from continuing."

"You cannot forbid me. I am your Queen!" I nearly shouted at Wiley, as the whole table of men turned to me in shock and outrage.

But Wiley was not done. "A Queen whose insatiable appetite for—"

"Wiley," Anson said simply. And although it was quiet, everyone heard. Everyone stopped and looked at Anson—such was the timbre of that single word. "If you finish that sentence, I will personally run through you with one of the ceremonial spears on this Council Chamber wall."

To his credit, it took Wiley two seconds to blink and then he snapped his mouth shut. He apparently did not want to see whether Anson was bluffing or not.

Anson waited a moment more before continuing. "Queen Sahle is correct. Regardless of what past rulers have done, what precedence they have set, she is the ruler now. We, as advisors, can counsel her as to the best course of action but ultimately the decision is and will always be hers. Is that not right, Your Majesty?"

Anson looked at me then, and I could feel his gaze roving over my startled face.

What was this? Why, after everything, was he defending me? He had to have known about Finn and me. I had given him a perfect weapon to continue his campaign of embarrassing me and destroying my credibility. Yet here he was, championing me.

Surprised or not, I nodded. "Exactly right."

"Grimly?" Anson continued.

"Lord Anson, this relationship cannot be allowed to continue. God and the gods forbid she becomes pregnant!" Grimly added, a mark of horror in his eyes. I half expected him to cross himself against evil.

But Anson just shook his head dismissively. "If that were to occur, I'm sure the Council would be able to deal with it. But perhaps that is the compromise that the Council and Queen Sahle could strike. There are preventative measures and if she consents to taking them, she can continue a discreet relationship as she sees fit."

"What if I wanted his child?" I asked, more to see the Lords' reactions than anything. I did not want a child. I never had, and I certainly did not care to have one now, in a strange land with a man I had known less than a year. "What if I wanted to marry Finn?"

"Sahle," Eliza whispered urgently, squeezing my shoulder.

But her whisper was drowned out in the cacophony of yelling and shouting that broke out. I did not care. I knew I was saying this only to spite them, and apparently so did Anson.

He caught my eye once more and looked knowingly at me. I considered smiling back but could not bring myself to feel any sort of camaraderie with the man who regularly found sport in humiliating me, even if he was being surprisingly kind in this moment.

"My Lords," I said, raising my voice above the noise. All twenty Lords looked back at me. "I have no plans to have a child, and I have no plans to marry Finn. Is that enough?"

But Wiley had been watching Anson, it seemed, for he jumped in before anyone could respond to my question. "Anson, why do you smile like that? One would think you out of all people would be opposed to the Queen taking a soldier to her bed?"

Anson turned a steely gaze on Wiley, his green eyes flashing menacingly. "I'm sure I don't know what you mean."

"Oh, I'm sure you do—"

"That's enough," Lord Grimly finally said from his seat near me. "What do we have to say to the Queen's proposition?"

"I accept it," a younger Lord said to me with a slight bow.

Roland stood and turned to me as he added, "It is a reasonable deal—she may continue a discreet relationship with Finn given that it does not result in marriage or children."

I nodded at Roland as he took his seat again.

One by one, each Lord voiced their opinion, and I was surprised to hear that all—even Wiley, begrudgingly—consented to it.

Finally, Grimly turned back to me. "A healer will be sent to you today. She will provide you with a preventative medicine and will administer it to you daily so that we can be certain you are taking it. Is that acceptable?"

I did not necessarily like the idea of these men scrutinizing my contraceptives, but it was better than any other alternative. "Yes, that's fine."

"Good, Your Majesty. Unless you have anything else you would like to speak to us about, we will now turn to rudimentary palace business…"

I knew my cue, and that was it. I stood quickly, eager to be out of the chamber and away from the gazes of these Lords. I could feel them running their eyes over my skin where it was bared above the neckline of my gown, and I wondered how many of them had spent the last minutes picturing me in bed.

The thought made my skin crawl.

I descended off my dais and past the Lords who had risen from their seats to bow once more. When I reached the door, I glanced once over my shoulder. As the Lords returned to their seats, they turned their attention to Grimly who continued on with his agenda. Or rather, all but one had turned their attention to Grimly.

Anson was watching me. He met my gaze and bowed his head towards me.

I did not return the gesture. No, I quickly turned and left, the heavy wooden doors closing behind the train of my gray skirt.

And as I walked away from the Council Chamber, thoughts swirled in my head.

I needed to find Finn. I needed to explain what had happened, and what the conditions of our relationship would be.

And I could not stop thinking about Anson's role in all this.

He had defended me, he had empowered me to make my own decision, to stand up to the Lords. For the life of me, I could not imagine why. Why had Anson been nice? And what had Wiley meant about Anson caring more than the other Lords that I was with Finn?

I knew there were no easy answers to these questions. But what I could do now was find Finn. I had to find Finn.

I KNEW EXACTLY WHERE FINN WOULD BE, AND I COULD not get there quick enough. My hands itched to bundle up the yards of fabric swirling around my legs and run the rest of the way down the palace halls and out to the soldiers' training grounds. But I forced myself to walk purposefully and calmly down the long checkered hallways, even if my pace was a touch too fast.

Just like on the way to the Council Chamber, courtiers and servants alike stared at me and it felt like that first day in the Alterealm all over again. I kept my head high this time, my eyes meeting the gazes of those who lined the hallways. I was the Queen, and I had just won my first battle—even if they did not know that yet.

I made it to the palace doors that led out the side yard and around to the stables and soldiers' quarters. I forced myself to breathe calmly. There was a warring emotion in my chest. I was riding a wave of adrenaline from my time with the Lords but as that tide calmed within me, a feeling of elation was taking its place.

For so many weeks, Finn and I had met in secret. We had shared guarded looks and whispered instructions of where to meet. But now…now the secret was out.

I envisioned Finn and myself walking the palace grounds hand in hand, lying lazily under the swaying jacarandas that lined the estate, sharing little kisses at the banquet table over our glasses of konstans.

It was a nice fantasy, but it was also a figment of my imagination.

The Lords may have compromised with me, but I knew they still expected my discretion. My relationship with Finn may be the worst kept secret in the palace, but it would stay just that— a secret. I could do the Lords that favor, at least. I could continue to see Finn behind closed doors, so as not to flaunt the controversial relationship in the faces of all those who opposed the match.

The sound of swords clacking and men grunting pulled me from my thoughts. I descended a final set of stone steps and turned a corner, and then I was standing before the training ground.

A dozen men were in the training circle. Each held a sword, shield, or some other kind of weapon, and each was dressed only in pants. The high arches of pectoral muscles and shoulders glinted in the sun—sweat on taut skin—and I knew they had been out here for some time already.

I was not a stranger to these training grounds, of course. Finn and I met here to train nearly every morning. There were hardly any soldiers about then, and the ones that were dropped a quick bow and "Your Majesty" before hurrying on their way.

But this moment was different. This moment I was standing on the edge of the training ground in a court gown rather than my usual training outfit of pants and a shirt. I was wearing a crown that shone with gold and jewels in the bright midday sun. Most importantly, I was no longer just the Queen—I was also Finn's mistress.

Well, technically, Finn was my "mistress" but I was not sure what the correct term for a male mistress would be.

In a split second, every man in the training ground broke from their paired fighting and dropped to a knee. I spied Finn on the far edge of the grounds, his head bent and eyes trained to the red earth as the other soldiers.

I froze.

I was not sure what to do. Did I ask them to rise as I usually would? Did I approach Finn and single him out? In all of my time considering being a Queen, nothing had told me what to do when seeking out your frowned-upon partner in the midst of your soldiers.

I wanted to run up to him, throw my arms around him, and kiss him with wild abandon—such was my elation and relief at having the Council's reluctant approval of our relationship. But a voice in my head told me that would not do. It was not the correct way for the Queen to conduct herself in public. The Lords would not approve, nor would Finn, nor—if I were being honest with myself—would I.

I took a breath, willed my twitchy limbs to still, and then projected my voice so that even the men as far away as Finn could hear. "Rise."

As one the men rose, but they did not take up their fighting again. They stood and watched me, and I noticed a few of their glances swivel back and forth between Finn and me.

They knew why I was here and, as I caught a few cheeky smirks, I realized that they had heard all about Finn being caught in my bed.

I resisted the urge to grimace as I stepped into the training ring with my head held high, my dress sweeping across the red dust and gravel and forever ruining the hem.

I met Finn's blue gaze as I made my way to him, walking past the near-frozen soldiers. Finn's face was serious and I could see, even from twenty paces away, that he was uncomfortable. He would not want me here, with all of the court gossip swirling around me. He respected my crown more than I did, and it was one of the reasons I admired him so.

And then I was in front of Finn and, in the slight breeze of midmorning, I could smell the sweat shining on his bare chest and arms. I knew that scent, its heady musk recalling images and sounds of our moments together. It made me smile.

"Your Majesty," Finn said between pinched lips. He glanced to the side, to the men staring at us. "Can I be of service?"

"I need to speak with you," I replied. "Do you have time now?"

"Of course." He nodded and handed his sword to the soldier next to him. "After you."

I turned on my heel and returned the way I had come, this time with Finn at my side.

I half expected a few of the soldiers to snicker, to make disgusted noises, or throw insults as some of the Lords had done earlier. But none of them did. Most had no reaction, trained as they were. The few who did were all smiles.

Finn and I did not speak until we broke out of the training ring's boundary. Then I asked him, "Why are they smiling?"

He glanced over his shoulder at his men, who were just now beginning to return to their exercises. "They like that you consider one of them an equal."

"Oh," I said, more breath than word. I glanced over my shoulder, too.

"Why does that shock you?"

"I have heard little pleasure about our relationship from anyone else," I replied simply.

We turned the corner to the stone steps I descended earlier, the soldiers now out of sight. Finn reached out and grasped my arm, stopping my ascent and turning me to him.

"Are you alright? Tell me what happened," he said, staring down at me.

I glanced around us once more to make sure we were alone. Then I stepped into him, threading my arms around his neck and nestling my head in the crook of his shoulder. Distantly, I wondered whether my crown was poking him in the jaw. "I'm fine. I was invited to a special Council meeting this morning. Needless to say, no one was happy about the situation."

Finn did not say anything. His hand ran in soothing strokes down my back, and I nestled a little closer to him.

"I'll tell you everything but not here," I said after a few moments enjoying his embrace. I pulled away just enough to see his face. "Come. Let's go up to my rooms where we can talk more freely."

Finn looked at me questioningly, his eyebrows rising in surprise. "Do you think that's wise? Especially after last night?"

But I smiled at him. "Yes. Yes, I do."

We took the back route to my chambers, ducking into a few servants' stairwells so as to avoid the main chambers of the palace where the Lords and Ladies would be congregating. I might have been given the go-ahead to see Finn privately, but I did not want to further inflame the court by parading him through their halls.

Not just yet.

We made it to my rooms having only passed a handful of servants who looked shocked to see us in their space. I made a mental note to send my apologies to them with Kaiht and Mara.

The two in question were dusting curtains when Finn and I entered through the servants' door. They dropped into immediate curtsies and nodded at Finn, too used to his presence around me to give any indication of shock.

"Can I assist you with your crown, Your Majesty?" Mara asked quietly as she put down the ostrich feather duster.

"Yes, thank you."

As Mara began pulling out the pins that held my crown securely into my curls, I noticed Kaiht approach Finn.

He was standing near the door, his stance wide and dominant. The alert rigidity reminded me of a policeman from the Humanrealm.

"Commander," Kaiht said in greeting. "Can I offer you a drink?"

"No…thank you," Finn responded, glancing my way.

Mara unhooked the final pin and pulled the crown free. She placed it in its leather storage box before turning back to me. "Up or down, my Lady?"

"Up is fine, Mara," I said, and Mara repinned the sections of my hair she had let loose to remove the crown.

When she was finished, she joined Kaiht near the windows. Finn was still standing ramrod straight beside the door. All three watched me, waiting for dismissals or indications of how to act. The last time Finn had all been here, everything had fallen apart.

"That will be all, Kaiht and Mara."

They bobbed in curtsies before departing. I turned to Finn. "Do you want to sit?"

"Will I need to once you've finally told me your news?"

"No, you won't," I smiled as I walked towards him. He tracked each step I took. "Still, you look awfully serious and uncomfortable standing there…"

In front of him now, I took his hand and laid a kiss on the back of it. Then I looked up into his eyes and said, "The long and the short of it is that the Lords agreed."

"What?" Finn asked, eyes widening in disbelief.

I laughed, the sound light and airy even to my own ears. "They were upset, of course, but in the end, they agreed to allow us to continue a discreet relationship."

"Why?"

"There will be time for questions later," I murmured, dragging my kisses from his hand, up his forearm. "But right now, no one can say you can't be here in my chambers. No one can say you can't hold me or kiss me. And I want you to. I want you to do more than kiss me."

He looked at me in disbelief for a moment longer. And then his lips were on mine.

He crushed me to his chest, his arms forming a vice around my waist and hips. I smiled against his mouth and he asked me what I was smiling about.

"I should have told Mara to leave my hair down."

Finn pulled away enough to shake his head at me. "The things you think about…especially right now."

"What should I be thinking about?" I whispered as he reached up and pulled the pins loose again. He undid the braids and ran his fingers through the freed cascade of curls.

He was quiet for a few moments, focused on my hair. "How beautiful you are," he finally murmured against the skin of my neck. He ran his hands along the arch where neck and throat met, the line of my collar bone on display above the neckline of the gown.

"I should be thinking of that?" I laughed.

"Yes, and how much I want you." He turned me in his arms so that he could access the laces holding me in my gown.

I arched so that my hips pressed back against his, even as he adeptly loosened the ties. A low, needy sound escaped his lips, and I felt his hips push forward against mine. Then my dress slipped down my arms and chest and I was bare from head to toe, Finn's hands the only things that touched my skin now.

"You are so beautiful," he murmured again as he turned me to face him. He ran his eyes down my body and then bent to take the peak of my breast in his mouth. His lips closed over the nipple and I moaned. My core tightened low in my belly and I wanted him—all of him—on me, in me, around me. I wanted to be consumed by him, and for the first time not have to worry about who might find out.

The mix of lust and freedom was a heady one. It urged me on.

Distantly, I was also aware that the high I was riding had as much to do with this newfound freedom of Finn as it did with the feeling of my own victory. I had defended us. I had held my ground and pushed back against the Lords' demands.

For the first time here in the Alterealm, I felt powerful and capable. I felt like a Queen—one being worshiped this very moment.

When Finn switched his attention to my other breast, my

knees buckled and suddenly he was sweeping me up in his arms. He carried me to my big four-poster bed and nestled me into the blankets.

He stepped back to unfasten his pants, but I stopped him.

"Allow me," I said, pulling myself to my knees before him.

I took my time loosening the buttons on his training pants. And when the last button was unhooked, he sprang free, thick and heavy and straining for more.

I took him in my hand, and met Finn's gaze as I slowly brought him to my lips. I ran my tongue over the head and around its tip, before taking him into my mouth as far as I could.

He tasted of salt and his own unique musk, and I moaned around him as I pumped my mouth up and down.

Finn watched me with focused eyes, eyes that were both adoring and hungry. And then, just as I was about to pump down one more time, Finn's hands were on my shoulders. He hauled me up from my knees and brought his mouth back to mine. His hands ran over my naked back, my hips, and my backside. And then he was pressing both of us back into the bed.

Finn hovered over me as I opened my legs to him, cradling his hips with mine. And then Finn positioned himself at my opening and pushed into me, thrusting to the hilt in one go.

I gasped. I could feel my nails biting into Finn's back where my hands held him to me, but I could not summon the nerve to care that I could be leaving little crescent moon bruises. It felt too good. Finn felt too good.

Finn continued his onslaught mercilessly, and I moved with him in a rhythm that was quickly becoming natural to us.

Each deep thrust was exquisite, a feeling that walked the line between pleasure and pain, and I could feel my core tightening and tightening.

Just as I thought I could take no more, that the tightening could not continue, Finn pulled me up so that we were sitting facing each other. I straddled his hips, still impaled on him, and we moved together, wrapped as we were in each other's arms.

He took my mouth in his and, as he thrust up and into me, the tightening broke. I tumbled into my own shattering release, and he swallowed my cries in his kiss. When he broke a moment after, I swallowed his.

Both spent, Finn lowered us to the sheets once more. And even though sweat coated our skin, I pulled myself closer to him.

I had fought for him and he was mine. And for the first time since we had started this, we did not have to hide.

Minutes or hours later, once our breathing had returned to normal and the beating of our hearts had slowed, I turned onto my side to look at Finn.

He was laying on his back with one arm thrown over his head. His eyes were shut and his pink lips were gently parted.

I reached out and ran a finger across those lips, trailing them down to trace the square angle of his jawline. He was a beautiful man, I realized. Finn had never been my type. He was not the sort of man I would ever have gone for in the Humanrealm, but there was an objective handsomeness to his rugged features. I knew more than one woman in the palace thought he was the most gorgeous man in Izwe.

With a shock, Anson's face popped into my head. And I was startled and annoyed with myself to remember that I had once considered Anson the most beautiful man I had ever seen. Those days were long past, and any beauty in his fine features had turned to ash with his personality.

Still, a begrudging part of me did admit that there was something to his dark looks, his too-long hair. He had a certain brooding mystery that caught my eye like no other had.

Thinking of Anson made me think of the Council, and the deal I had struck. I knew I had only given Finn one part of the story before I had pulled him into my bed once more. He deserved to know everything.

As if called by my thoughts, Finn opened his eyes and turned his head slightly to meet my gaze.

"My Queen," he whispered, lifting his own hand to sweep a wayward curl out of my face.

I let out a little tsk. "How many times do I have to ask you to call me Sahle?"

But Finn smiled. "A dozen more times, at least."

I smiled back at him, but then grew serious. "Why?"

He looked at me thoughtfully, almost as if he was reading fine print written on the planes of my face. "Because you're the Queen. It's that simple. I can never forget that, no matter how long I share your bed."

"Yes, but we're awfully familiar for you to be so formal with me."

He ran his hand absentmindedly from my neck, down my arm and across my thigh as he thought. Then with a smile, he said, "Hmm, that's true. How about I make you a compromise? Would 'Queen Sahle' be suitable for now?"

But my thoughts had snagged on the word "compromise."

I sat up, hugging my knees to my chest and staring out at the wide windows that lined my chambers. Light slanted through the glass, casting a luminescent glow on the cream walls and creating shadow creatures out of fern fronds.

Finn sat up alongside me. "What's the matter?"

I turned my head back to him. "There's more I have to tell you about the Lords."

"Ah," he said. "I assumed there was more to the story than them just being fine with this." He motioned vaguely at us and the white sheets tangled around our legs.

"Yes, well, they are fine with it…" I started. At Finn's raised eyebrows, I continued. "They just have conditions."

"What conditions?"

Suddenly, I felt restless and unsure. I had felt so confident when the Lords had agreed to the continuation of this relationship that I had not stopped to think about the conditions that had been set.

Would Finn be angry? Did he want to marry me? Did he think of us having a child one day?

We had never discussed such important topics, and perhaps that was because of my personal understanding of our relationship.

I did not love him. I knew that as factually as I knew I needed to breathe air to live. I had been in love before and that overwhelming, walking-on-clouds feeling was not what this was.

Finn was…my friend. He was the one person who understood me here. But we also had a kind of raw, animalistic passion that I had never known, and indulging in that passion felt good in a place where so much did not.

To me, our relationship was that simple. I cared for him, and he made me happy. I did not need more, but I had not stopped to think that he might.

I was up and moving to my dressing room before I could think any further.

"Queen Sahle?" Finn called, a slight note of alarm crowding into the edge of his voice. From inside the little dressing chamber, I heard the bed creak as he rose.

I pulled on a long, white shift. Then I slipped my dressing gown over it before I went back out into the room.

Finn was standing naked in front of the windows, and he turned as he heard my approach. "Please tell me the rest of it."

"OK," I nodded, swallowing. It was going to be fine, I told myself. I just did not want to hurt him.

"Do you want a robe?" I asked, starkly aware of his nakedness in comparison to my two layers.

"No, it's fine," Finn said, crossing his arms. He waited, eyes trained on me. He knew I was finding excuses to put off this conversation.

I spotted the line of decanters on the liquor cart next to the fireplace and hurried there on itching feet. "Drink?" I called as I removed a crystal stopper and poured myself a finger of whiskey.

"Queen Sahle," Finn said again, and I could hear the anxiousness in his voice. "Just spit it out. You're stalling."

I picked up my glass, turned around and leaned against the bar cart as I took a sip. "Fine…"

He looked at me expectantly.

With one more deep breath, I explained everything. I told him how I received the summons this morning, how I had dressed and met the Lords who were generally outraged that we had been carrying on with a relationship.

I told him about Wiley and the insults he had nearly thrown my way—to which I saw a muscle in Finn's jaw tense—and how Anson of all people had stepped in to defend me—to which I saw Finn's eyebrows quirk up in surprise.

I eventually sat down on one of the wingback chairs before the fireplace and Finn sat in the accompanying chair, still naked but entirely unconcerned.

Finally, I explained the rules that had been set: we could continue our relationship given that we did not have children, and that we did not marry.

I stared into my nearly finished glass as I said that part. I was a coward, too afraid to see Finn's immediate reaction as I gave him the guardrails that this affair would have to follow.

Then I heard him chuckle, and my head snapped up.

The corners of his lips were raised in a smile. "Is that all?"

"Yes…" I replied, unsure how to respond to this surprisingly good-natured reaction. "Are you not upset?"

"God and gods no," Finn said. He leaned back a little more comfortably in his chair. "Your Majesty, perhaps you do not understand. For what we have done, they could have taken much harsher action. They could have dismissed me from my command immediately. They could have declared you unfit to rule, and installed a regent for a set period of years to lead in your place. They could have ordered your marriage to one of the Lords or one of Izwe's allies."

Finn reached out a hand to me and instead of giving him

my own, I stood. I walked to him and sat in his lap. His breath tickled my cheek as he said, "While I do not like anyone guiding my relationship, or telling me what I can and cannot do in it, I am relieved that this is all they have said."

I let out a breath I had been holding. "Good."

"Why were you concerned?"

"I thought you might want those things…"

I felt Finn's hand on my chin and he gently urged my face up until our gazes met. "You are the Queen. I have never fooled myself into thinking there could be more than this. If you were a normal girl, then perhaps I would wish to marry you. Perhaps I would wish for you to bear my children. But that can never be. I am a soldier in the army you lead. You will one day have to marry another to secure our kingdom. Those are the sad facts of our situation, but right now…right now, we have each other and that is enough for me."

I listened to every word he said, and then I smiled up at him. I could not tell if he loved me. And I was unsure whether he would ever admit it if he did feel it. But it did not matter. We were on the same page.

We sat together, gazes locked for some time. Eventually Kaiht and Mara returned—I quickly removed my over-robe and handed it to Finn for him to wrap around his waist—with platters of food.

Sometime later, when the sky had eventually darkened, when the food had disappeared, when a few more drinks had been drunk, we climbed back into my bed. And for the first time we had no worries about the hour, or who might come knocking at the door. We made love again and we slept. And when I turned over in the night, moonlight streaming through the windows onto Finn's face, I smiled. He was here and he did not have to leave, and that was enough—for both of us.

THE NEXT MORNING STREAMED BY US AS DREAMILY AS the night. I opened my eyes to see Finn's bright blue ones staring back at me and I smiled at him as I stroked his cheek with the back of my hand.

He kissed it, before scooting close enough to kiss my lips. They still tasted of wine and me. "Good morning."

"Good morning."

He lingered there for a few moments, running his tongue gently along my pillowy lower lip, before pulling back with a faint groan. "As much as I'd love to stay here in your bed, I have to get back to the training grounds."

"Are we training this morning?" I asked, confused as to why he would say he, singular, needed to go.

"No," he shook his head as he scooted out of bed. His clothes were folded neatly on the chest at the foot of my bed—courtesy of the silent Mara, no doubt—and he shrugged them on. "It's too soon."

"What is?"

"You coming to the training grounds to train. You caused quite the stir yesterday when you came there to fetch me. If you don't want an audience while training, it's probably best that we suspend that for the next few days."

I was conflicted about that. While I often complained through my training, especially the attempts at magic, I had grown to enjoy my time down at the training grounds. For the hours I was there, I could almost forget who and what I was here. I could run and jump and swing a sword and get out all of the frustration and confusion I felt in my day-to-day life in Izwe.

Still, the thought of being able to lazily sleep in was a welcome one, and I reclined further back into my pillows just at the thought.

"I can see that little evil smirk," Finn said, as he buckled his belt. "I'm sure having a few days off is quite the hardship."

"It's awful," I replied, trying to pull the corners of my lips down into an approximation of sadness.

"Sure it is," Finn laughed at my attempt, valiant though it was.

But then another thought occurred to me. "When will I see you, if not at the training ring?"

Finn laced up his boots and then came to perch on the side of the bed. He took my hand in his, lacing the fingers together as if they were made to fit so easily. "Well, the good news about this no longer being a secret is that you can send word with a messenger anytime you want to see me."

"And what about you?" I asked, gazing up at him and how the sunshine lit up the edges of his sleep-mussed hair. "When do you get to call me?"

He smiled, his eyes roaming over my face, and I forced myself not to fidget even though I itched to smooth down the rat's nest that surely was my hair this morning. "I would not dare summon Her Majesty."

"Finn!" I hit him on the arm, and he laughed in response. He was being playful, but I needed him to understand this. I sat up, the better to look him in the eye. Absently, I realized the sheet had fallen away in the movement, and my breasts were bare to the morning air.

"I am serious," I told him. "I want you to be able to call for me when you want to see me. I know I'm the Queen, but we're also in whatever relationship this is.

"I don't wish to order you to me like you're one of my servants, or one of the courtiers. I want to see you when you want to see me. And if you don't want to see me when I call, then I want you to tell me no."

In the Humanrealm, this would not be a conversation. I would never have the sort of power I wielded now, the ability to command every man, woman, and child under the palace roof and across the kingdom. But here, my word was—supposedly—law.

That was all fine and dandy, but I did not want a man who came to my bed by force. I wanted a man who came to my bed because he wanted me in return, simply and naturally as a man wants a woman.

I knew Finn understood that, no matter how he was raised. He had heard me whine about Izwe and the Alterealm through many of our training sessions and even more of our rendezvous.

"Alright," he finally said, his blue eyes serious in comparison with the lightness of a few moments before. "I promise to send for you when I want you, and to refuse you when I do not. Is that acceptable, Your Majesty?"

"It's Sahle," I tsked. "And yes, that is most acceptable."

Finn leaned forward to press a final kiss to my lips and then was up and across the room before I could say anything else.

"Have a good day, Your Majesty."

"Have a good day, Commander."

Finn's chuckle echoed down the hall as he closed my chamber door behind him. And I smiled to myself.

Unfortunately, the rest of my day was not as lovely as the morning. After Mara and Kaiht brought me breakfast, drew me a bath and helped me dress, I had an appointment with the healer to discuss my contraceptive options.

The physician came to my chambers, clad in somber robes that were somewhere between a dark burgundy and rich brown in color. I had never seen robes this color in the Alterealm, and so could not distinguish whether she was a courtier or a servant. I made a note to ask Lisideria about them; perhaps this was the dress of all Izweian healers.

The woman either did not know any small talk or did not seem interested in speaking to me, for she was quick about her visit. She bowed formally and immediately explained that she was tasked by the Council to supply me with contraceptives, if Her Majesty allows.

I explained efficiently that Finn took a contraceptive of his own—something he and I had discussed at length months before—and that I would be fine with supplementing that if it would put the Councilors' minds at ease.

The healer did not seem to pick up on my sarcasm, or maybe she simply ignored it. Either way, I swallowed a pill of some sort with a glass of water. I was instructed to take one pill each morning to prevent pregnancy and venereal disease, and I had to admit I was impressed. Whatever contraceptive medicine or magic they had here warded off disease and pregnancy in one go.

Before she left, the healer told me she would come by each morning to give me my pill, and I had to restrain myself from rolling my eyes. But still, this was better than removing me from the throne and having Finn executed.

I smiled and nodded at the healer and then she was gone.

And so was I. The day was getting away from me and I was already ten minutes late for lunch with Lisideria. By some miracle, it seemed Lisideria had not heard the news about my relationship—or else she was good at pretending it did not exist. I did not bring it up, and I was happy to allow her to control the flow and topic of conversation.

I ate and listened as I always did. I asked my question about the healer, to which she confirmed that that peculiar color was meant to symbolize the blood and feces of the body, and that all healers in Izwe wore it.

I forcibly kept myself from vomiting into my soup when she said that, and I swallowed the remainder of the pea and carrot puree before I could think on it further.

Finally, having said goodbye to Lisideria, I was able to excuse myself and return to the library. So much had happened in the last two days, between attacks and affairs, that all I wanted to do was hide in my quiet corner and fall into the void that was my books. I hurried there, not caring which courtiers were staring. And they were—oh, they were.

I was so deep in thought, I did not feel another's presence until I finished a chapter and reached for my glass of water. A rustling from the far wall caught my attention and I looked up to find Anson.

He was leaning against a stack, arms folded, face half in shadow. And he was staring at me.

"Lord Anson. What are you doing here?"

"Can a Lord not wander the library?" he replied with a sarcastic tilt of his head as he ran his hand down the spine of a book.

"Of course they can. I have just never seen you here."

Anson nodded. "That's fair. I tend to purchase my books rather than borrow them. I collect them, you see. My ancestral seat has a large library which I enjoy contributing to."

I stared at him. While I could certainly appreciate a beautiful private library, I was confused why he was here and why he was telling me this of all things.

Shaking my head, I stood and returned one of my books to the reshelving carts. I could feel Anson's gaze on me, and I reluctantly met his eye from the opposite side of the table.

I folded my arms and raised one eyebrow. "Well?"

"Well what, Your Majesty?" Anson said with a smirk.

"Why are you here? Surely you have more important things to do than watch me read."

"Hmm, that's true," Anson replied thoughtfully. "Would you believe me if I said I was here to check on you? To see if you were alright after yesterday's Council meeting?"

I stared at him. Surely I had not heard him correctly.

The Anson I knew hated me. He thought I was incompetent and young and naive—exactly the worst ruler for Izwe.

Yet between yesterday and today, you could almost think he cared.

"Why do you seem so shocked, Your Majesty?"

I scoffed. "Have you met you?"

Anson chuckled, that smirk of his breaking into a surprisingly deep and warm rumble of laughter. "Come now. I'm not all that bad."

"You hate me, and you have no qualms showing it," I replied with brutal honesty.

But that halted him. The smirk vanished and all traces of laughter with it. "I do not hate you, Queen Sahle."

"You have a bad habit of acting like it."

I watched as Anson squeezed his fists into tight balls. "I do not hate you," he repeated.

I stared at him a moment longer, holding his gaze from across the room. He did not look away and I could feel that green stare as if it were boring into my very soul.

I broke away first.

"Why would you defend me?" I asked.

Anson shrugged. "Why not?"

I shook my head. "That's not an answer. You came here to check on me apparently, so this is what I want to know. Why did you defend me?"

To my own ears, my voice sounded petulant, and I wanted to lean away from the whiny edge it took on. But Anson smiled.

"I defended you, my Queen, because none of those men had a right to question you."

I raised my eyebrows in surprise.

Anson moved fully into the light as he stepped away from the bookshelf and up to the table that separated us. He placed his palms on the polished wood, leaning forward as he held my gaze. "You are the Queen of Izwe. You answer to no one but yourself."

"Grimly and the other Lords would not agree with you."

"Grimly and the other Lords are inflated by notions of their own importance. They forget themselves, forget that you have returned and they no longer rule in your stead."

I nodded thoughtfully at his assessment. I had never seen it that way before but it made sense now. They had been without a Queen for nearly twenty years, during which the fate of the kingdom had rested on their shoulders. Now that I was back, it was an adjustment to give up that control.

But there was something else I wanted to know.

"So you support my relationship with Finn?"

Anson's gaze had wandered from me, but it snapped back at that question. "I wouldn't go that far."

My eyes narrowed. "No? I could have sworn you knew about Finn earlier—that wink you gave me in Ukuwela certainly made it seem like it. Yet you didn't say anything to me or the Council."

"I suspected," Anson replied, a lock of his dark hair tumbling over his forehead. "And while I do not particularly enjoy the idea of you and Finn, you are your own person. You make your own choices about who you invite to your bed."

I watched him a moment longer before nodding. "Thank you."

"For?"

"For not being an ass, for once."

Whatever Anson was expecting me to say, it was not that. He tipped his head back and laughed. The sound was too big for this space, for the quiet confines of a library, but it was so warm and inviting that I did not have the heart to shush him.

Whoever thought such a good-natured laugh could come out of Anson?

"And to answer your question, I'm fine," I said, circling back to the point of this entire conversation.

Anson pushed off of the table and took a step away. "Good. There will be more important things to battle the Lords on, especially after the attack at the border. I would hate for such a piddling topic as Finn to be the most you could handle, Your Majesty."

And there was the Anson I knew. "Just when I thought you actually had a decent bone in your body…"

Anson smirked as he dropped into an overly exaggerated bow. "Good day, Queen Sahle."

"Good day, Lord Anson," I replied. I watched him walk away, still wondering why he would bother to come in the first place.

reality

Eliza and Roland left the palace soon after that embarrassing moment in my chambers. Although it had led to a happy resolution, an acceptance of Finn and myself as a couple, I could not shake the feeling that they were a little disappointed in me.

Eliza and Roland had come to see me privately the night before their departure. Roland had apologized for overreacting to seeing Finn in my bed, and I was fairly certain this was only being said on Eliza's encouragement. She had stood a breath away during his awkward and stilted apology, a knowing little smile on her fair face.

There was nothing to forgive, however. I understood it, even if it had been uncomfortable and painful in the moment. Roland was acting as the father he had always been to me. He had stepped in when he felt I was in danger, and I could never fault him for that.

I told him as much, hugging him around the middle until he lost the stiffness in his stance and draped his arms around my shoulders to return the embrace.

"I love you both," I whispered.

"We love you, too," Roland had replied, smoothing a hand along my wild hair.

But despite Eliza's little smile, despite Roland's apology, Roland's looks lingered on my face, and I caught Eliza sighing frequently. As well as they knew me, I knew them. I could sense that they disliked what was happening between Finn and myself, but I refused to be ashamed.

Having Finn was something I was doing for myself. Every touch, every kiss, every moment in my bed was just for me. And after months in Izwe, after leading a life that I thought I understood only to find it had all been a lie, I felt I deserved one thing true and happy and mine.

I refused to be ashamed.

It was with a touch of relief, therefore, that I bid Eliza and Roland farewell. I joined them in the yard this time, waving with the courtiers who came to bid them farewell. Wrapped up in my own thoughts of Finn, the attack, the trip to Ukuwela, I did not mind the amused glances cast my way.

Several more days passed in which I kept a low profile. I did not go to the training ring, and Finn and I kept our distance, but I did meet Lisideria for lunch as usual. Our conversations had been a bit clipped and tense at first, and I could instantly tell that Ms. Etiquette entirely disapproved of the relationship she was now clued into.

We did not discuss Finn, though. Lisideria's pinched mouth said enough of what she thought—that it was inappropriate, that it was unseemly, that I was sinking below my status as Queen. It was only when Sybil surprised us one day that the topic came up.

"So, Your Majesty," she whispered, leaning conspiratorially over her pasta salad as her eyes met mine. "Would you tell us about your new love interest? If you don't mind me asking…"

I did not mind, and I said as much. With a knowing smile, I stage-whispered back, "Well, I wouldn't call it new, if that's any indication of quality."

I thought Lisideria would have a stroke, and her face made all of the rest of the questions I had to deflect completely worth it. Sybil wanted to know how it had started, what had happened, and where it was going.

I was not comfortable telling her the details, lest she then recount it to other courtiers, so I shrugged off her questions except to again imply that I was very satisfied with Finn at the moment.

"I take it he is a good trainer, then?" she asked with a sly smile.

"An excellent one," I answered sweetly before plucking a dressed noodle off of the fork's tines with my teeth.

Sybil was not the only one who was curious. Finn's and my relationship had overshadowed the attack on Ukuwela in many ways. I knew the courtiers were obsessing about it, happy to talk and wonder about that gossip rather than worry about what an attack on Izweian soil actually meant for them.

But I had not lost focus. My trip to Ukuwela had been eye-opening in many ways. The idea of death and war and enemies was no longer an abstract conflict, some far-flung possibility that I might one day face. No, it was real. And the fate of this nation depended on me.

I let that realization propel me. And with that need for me to learn and understand and be the best Queen I could be, my determination set a new pace.

I attended more Council meetings, sending messages to the Lords inquiring about which days they were meeting and asking that they issue me invitations for any Senior Council meetings, as well. It was how I learned more about how the Council functioned. Lisideria could spend all the lunches in the world explaining the inner workings of the court and the Council, but nothing made up for being in the room with the Lords and watching their procedures and interactions.

It was also how I kept up with the latest intelligence from Trina Cheile, how rebuilding efforts were going in Ukuwela, and how our soldiers fared at their various posts around the kingdom.

We had lost seven soldiers in the attack at Ukuwela, and they were not factored into the count of the dead that Aurora gave me. Each time I thought of those nameless men in brown, fighting at the gates of Ukuwela and in the market square, I saw Finn's face. I feared for him, and for all of the soldiers—but mostly for him. I knew his duty required him to serve and fight, but I selfishly did not want something to happen to him.

I told him as much during our first morning back at training. We had just finished our run and set out for a quick hand-to-hand sparring session.

"You worry too much," Finn replied, between inhales. His fist glanced off of my shoulder as I jerked away from his hit.

Inhale, I told myself. Exhale. "No, I don't!"

"You do."

"No. You are a soldier. What if something happens to you like it happened to those in Ukuwela?"

Finn advanced on me in one, two, three steps. And then he pinned me against his chest with a quickly placed arm behind my back. "Then I die."

My breathing came in hard and fast. I had to keep my spike of fear in check as I leveled my gaze at him, his face just inches from me. "Be serious."

"I am," he replied, and I could see the soberness in his eyes. He was not making light of his words. "You just can't understand because you've never been a soldier. This is a fact of our lives. We live. We fight. Sometimes we come home at night and sometimes we're not so lucky. But we accept either outcome. It makes us who we are."

I breathed heavily and my eyes met his. "But I don't want to lose you."

He broke my gaze to glance around us. Seeing we were alone, he kissed me quickly, a glancing meeting of lips that left me leaning forward in wanting.

"I know. And one day, that might happen. But not today. Today, I'm all yours."

His next blow was straight to my gut, and I jumped back to avoid having the air knocked from me. Then I tried my best to return the favor, my own determination to land a hit pushing the worry from my mind.

From that day on, I trained in earnest each morning with Finn. Sometimes we snuck back to his hut afterwards, and sometimes I left quickly for a Council meeting. Sometimes lunch with Lisideria snuck up on me or I retreated to a session of independent study in the library.

As I dedicated myself more and more to my role, I tried to be true to my own identity as much as I was to the notion of being a Queen. I began to greet certain Lords and Ladies in the halls as I passed them, now that I knew them better. Many still stared and watched me with uncertain eyes, but at least I knew I was doing my best to be a Queen.

I took tea with Sybil, Lisideria, Genevieve, and Mary at Eliza's continued insistence. When Eliza was at the palace, she joined us. Her returns were always short-lived; she would come from her country estate every two weeks or so. Sometimes Roland joined her, and sometimes he did not. He was not an official member of the Council, so he had no requirement to attend regular Council meetings. He attended when I asked him to and was happy to remain in the country if I did not.

I found it odd that he had drawn away from me so completely. I was the only daughter he had ever known, and I could not lie and say it did not hurt. A part of me believed him and Eliza when they said it was for my own protection, but a less rational, more childlike part of my brain simply focused on the fact that he was not here. He was not looking after me.

Eliza always tried to convince me that I was being silly. She explained over and over that the distance was to stop any impression that I was being influenced by them. Yet, she was there. She arrived on her tall zebra every few weeks, curtsying and bowing in public and plying me with hugs and kisses when we were alone.

I valued that time, and even though I felt hurt by the distance between the three of us now, I relished the hours I had with her. And they were hours—Eliza would arrive in the morning and by mid-afternoon, be mounted on her zebra to return to her estate. She rarely stayed the night.

But no matter how my day unfolded, I could count on Finn to steal into my bedroom once night had fallen, the glinting stars peeking through my chamber windows. He would peel off my body whatever ornate court dress I had worn to dinner in the Great Hall. We would kiss and make love, our low moans devoured by the wispy ferns and that filled my chambers with life. Sometimes we would ask Kaiht or Mara to draw us a bath, and sometimes all four of us would sit before the fire and drink konstans. I made it a point to ask Kaiht and Mara to join us.

It was uncouth. It was not what a Queen did—drinking wine and fraternizing with a room full of servants and soldiers—but recently ravished by one, cared for by two others, and considering them all friends, I could not see a reason why I should not do what I wanted in my own chambers.

Mara needed more convincing than Kaiht to join us each time, but after a full glass of the sweet, golden liquid that Izwe specialized in, she relaxed. We all laughed and swapped stories of the court, and I felt like I was among friends for once, not Eliza's ladies, or the Lords, or the servants who were told to fetch and be silent and to mind me because I was the Queen. I had spent so many quiet moments missing Mer, Cecily, and Jenna, wondering if my friends were out there somewhere mourning me. I had felt so alone. But now, I was with people I cared for, and who genuinely cared for me in return.

And after we had polished off one bottle and then a second— me leaning progressively more and more heavily on Finn—I would collapse in bed. Kaiht and Mara would tuck me in and then they would depart for their own beds. Sometimes Finn stayed the night. Sometimes he did not. And we would begin again the next day.

I was conscious of every second that there was not another attack, every second that there was not a whispering of new intelligence or secrets that Trina Cheile was coming for us. I was thankful for each moment of peace that we had, and I trained and studied and listened closely.

I could become better at swordsmanship, better at bows and arrows, more adept at political maneuvering and trade negotiations in the Council. But try as I might, I could never become better at magic.

I refused to try again, for I did not have magic. It was that simple. I would be the laughingstock of the entire Alterealm, the fabled Sahle who was nothing more than a normal Humanrealm child.

I did not have magic, and so I did not try—until one impulsive day.

I was sitting in the bathtub one evening, hours after Mara and Kaiht had filled the tub, rubbed oils onto my hair, and left me to soak.

The sky had long since darkened, and I knew I should climb out of the murky bathwater soon. My stomach had taken on that hollowness that precipitated the full, grumbling bellow of hunger. Yet I was not ready to stand on my own feet yet. There was still time before the music that heralded dinner began, and I wanted to float in the water a bit more, safe and cocooned from the realities of the world around me.

I contemplated calling Kaiht and Mara to refill the tub with new hot water, but I hated to disturb them especially when I knew they were probably preparing whatever court gown I would wear this evening.

I tipped my head back in indecision, letting the solidity of the water cushion my head like a hand cupping my skull. I drew in a deep breath and released it past my barely opened lips.

And then I made a harebrained decision.

I sat up slowly, pulling my knees to my chest and looking at the dark water around me. My hands broke the surface, resting just underneath that barrier of air and liquid, and then I closed my eyes once more.

I put my concentration in my skin, and where my skin met the water around me. I tried to feel the water, as Finn had once told me. And, most importantly, I tried to will the water warm.

For as long as I had known about magic, I had vehemently told everyone that I had none. I did not have magic. I was sure of it.

But something in everyone's insistence made me want to try, on my own, in the lukewarm cocoon of my bathtub as the evening drew on.

What if I did have magic?

It was a preposterous thought, one that I had not let myself even consider before. But if my mother and my father had both come from magical lines, surely I should have some propensity for it.

I had taken high school biology and seen enough Punnett squares to understand basic chance when it came to genetics. Unless I had inherited some seriously recessive genes, then the courtiers and Finn and all of the others insisting I had magic should be right.

I refocused on the water and just like the times before, I could feel my own body but I could not feel the water. I tried non-elemental magic, focusing on my desire for warmth.

I gritted my teeth, my focus sharpening on that wish. But try as I might, the water grew cooler with every passing second.

Finally, I opened my eyes and stood abruptly from the bathtub.

This was a stupid thing to try, I chastised myself. I did not have magic, and I knew that, so why did I bother? It was silliness and wishful thinking.

I snatched my towel from the stool next to the tub and wrapped it around myself hastily in irritation. Then I stepped out of the water, grabbed my comb, and left the bathroom in order to sit before the tall mirror in my chambers and comb through my curls.

In that sixth sense they had, Kaiht and Mara appeared moments after I settled into combing my hair. I waved off their help and they made themselves busy straightening up the bathroom while I worked.

If my hearing had been better, I might have heard them clearly from where they spoke in the bathroom. I might have made out the words that I only registered as muffled background noise, absorbed as I was in my frustration and my detangling.

Kaiht and Mara cleared away the oils, the soaps, and the rough sponge I liked to wash with. Then they turned to the bathwater. As they drained the water from the tub, droplets splashing on their hands as they worked, Mara remarked to Kaiht in surprise, "Hmm, I thought she was in here for longer. The water is still hot."

30
celebration

I KNEW THE DAYS WERE PASSING QUICKLY BUT, TRY AS I might, I could not fathom how a year had passed. I did not feel a day older and Izwe felt as foreign as ever—as if I had not lived each moment here since the clock struck midnight on my twentieth birthday.

And to make matters worse, Eliza and Roland were throwing me a party. Not a kiddie bowling alley party, or a princess-themed picnic as my twelfth birthday had been; they were throwing me a banquet complete with a stuffed ostrich and other fare I was sure I had never seen back in the Humanrealm.

What is this place? I asked myself for the millionth time.

Home. That was what it was. And as much as I still struggled to understand it, a part of me understood that I knew. I could feel, in my bones, that this place was me. My blood ran through the soil and stone. My breath was the wind that whipped over the palace.

I was made of and for this place, even if I still struggled to understand the intricate society of the Alterealm.

A snag to my hair pulled me back to reality.

"Apologies, Your Majesty," Mara said as she gently eased the offending comb out of my curls. She proceeded to reapply it from a different angle.

"That's OK. I know my hair is unruly," I replied, spying the mass that sprung out of my head. Sometimes I wondered if my hair was immune to gravity.

"I wouldn't say it's unruly," Mara said quickly with an apologetic smile. "You have thick hair, and a lot of it. Your mother had the same, so they say."

I looked again at my reflection in the mirror and wondered about her, Bekha. My eyes wandered the curls, the bridge of my nose, the color of my eyes, and I tried to lay the portrait of my mother that was hung in the palace hall atop my own features.

In an abstract way, I could see it. I knew our coloring was the same, our hair texture the same. But it was hard to look at one's own face and see someone you had never met.

Still, a strange pang echoed through me.

Had my mother sat right here before this mirror and talked with her attendees as they dressed her? Given that no one had used these chambers in the years since her death, I was sure that the layout I found—and had never thought to change—was exactly what my mother had designed.

The thought made me wonder who she was. I did not care about who the court knew, but instead who she was at the deepest, most private parts of her soul. I did not mourn her, for I had never met her. But I did mourn never knowing the secrets within her, never being able to see if the quiet hum of our natures aligned.

Mara finished her combing and began twisting my hair into a low horizontal roll at the back of my head. As she fastened the last hairpin, Kaiht appeared with a wooden box.

She cracked open the lid and inside was a delicate tiara sitting atop a bed of white velvet. The tiara itself was crafted of gleaming gold and it was adorned with diamonds and rubies in an alternating pattern.

"It's beautiful," I said to no one in particular as I ran a finger across the highest point of the tiara.

Kaiht nodded, pulling the tiara away from my fingers to place it atop my head. "Lady Eliza thought you might like it. It's less bulky than your more traditional headpieces."

That was the truth if I had ever heard it.

Mara secured the headpiece with a few more hairpins and then stepped back to let me assess. I turned my head from side to side, watching my reflection in the mirror, and I could barely feel the kiss of the tiara. I much preferred that to the weight of my crowns.

It was perfect.

Distantly, I made out the sound of musical instruments—the magicians warming up for this evening's festivities. We must be getting close to the start of the banquet, and I was still not dressed.

I stood, my white dressing gown cozy where the soft material touched my skin. Reluctantly, I let Kaiht and Mara strip it off my shoulders and fold it away for my return. I had long since grown used to the two women seeing me naked, so I did not think twice about it. They spritzed my bare chest and neck with something that smelled of rose water. And then they brought over my dress.

The gown was light gold and, even draped as it was over Kaiht's arm, I could see the intriguing combination between a well-structured bodice and a supple, billowing skirt.

Kaiht and Mara helped me balance as I stepped into the long gown, then they laced me up from the back. They secured the ties, helped buckle the straps on the matching shoes, and then led me over to the full-length mirror to see the complete ensemble.

For a moment, I just stared at my reflection. I had never been a beautiful woman. I was not ugly, but no one would describe me as stunning. Yet now, in this dress, with my hair pulled back from my face and the soft gold of the gown playing off the caramel tone of my skin, I felt beautiful. I felt like the most gorgeous woman in the world.

The dress' material was thick, the bodice structured with visible seams that arched complimentarily down my waist. The skirt billowed out, pooling behind me in the slightest of trains so as to not impede my movement. Sleeves in the same material sheathed arms that felt more defined, stronger than a year ago.

If I could have designed a dress, it would be this one. It was perfect, as if it were made for me.

"Is this one of my mother's gowns?" I asked Kaiht and Mara from over my shoulder.

They both smiled at me in the mirror. "No, Your Majesty. Eliza and Roland had this gown made specifically for you."

Tears pooled in my eyes as I looked at myself again, with this new knowledge. I had never asked for gowns. Despite Lisideria's early instruction that I should have an assortment of dresses made, I had preferred to unearth my mother's endless wardrobe and have them fitted to me or altered slightly to current styles. It seemed a shame to waste so many gorgeous pieces given that my mother and I were nearly identical in size.

But there was something about having my own dress, my first dress made just for me, that touched me. It was only a dress, but it felt profound. It felt like, for the first time, I was not trying to fill the shadow of my mother. I was leaving my own mark, creating what suited me out of this realm. I was forging my own path.

It was a scary thought, but an exhilarating one.

I took a breath past lips that were painted a soft red to match the rubies in my tiara, and then I stepped towards the door.

The vibration of music playing many floors below gently skittered across my skin. The musicians had begun in earnest. My birthday party was waiting.

Like invisible hands beckoning me forward, I followed the music that floated on the evening air to the ballroom. The large fireplace at the far side was lit, and it lent the vast room a coziness it usually lacked. The smell of sugared bambara nuts and roasting meat filled the space. Musicians lined the walls, their various instruments nimble and malleable under their fingers.

The entire court was here, so it looked. Their colorful chitenge-cloth outfits were even more ornate and patterned this evening, and I spied more than one headdress that reminded me of portraits I had seen of Marie Antoinette in long-ago Humanrealm history classes. I smiled to myself, amused and intrigued by the prospect of a courtier adding tiny ships to their hair, right next to the miniature lions and protea flowers I spied on one elaborate headpiece.

"Queen Sahle," Eliza called from behind me.

I turned and nearly threw myself at her, such was the speed in which I hugged Eliza to me.

She half gasped, half laughed as her slightly shorter frame was swallowed by mine. "Happy Birthday, sweetheart," she whispered.

I closed my eyes, my face close to her coiffed blonde hair. Even under the lavender perfume she wore, I could catch the sun and grass smell of her. For as long as I lived, I would never forget that. It spoke to me on an innate level of protection and warmth, of comfort when I skinned my knees as a toddler. To me, it was the smell of motherhood, even if not biological.

I pulled back after a moment, conscious of the fact that the court was watching. I smoothed my skirts where they had crushed against Eliza's. I smiled a real, toothy grin.

"Thank you, Eliza. And thank you for this gorgeous gown."

As if only noticing the garment now, Eliza dropped her gaze to it, tracking her eyes across every inch of the skirt and bodice before her. "It suits you very nicely. It was our pleasure to gift it to you."

Our was indeed the correct word, for I noticed Roland had appeared on Eliza's right as we spoke. He bowed before taking my hand and giving it a strong squeeze.

"Happy Birthday," he said, and I could have sworn his eyes glistened more than normal. But Roland was Roland—stoic, reserved and opposed to making a scene. He did not hug me like Eliza, and I did not try to drag an emotional moment out of him here in front of the court.

Still, when I looked into his eyes, I could see the love there. He may have been more distant than usual since my arrival in Izwe but he was, at heart, the father I had always known.

"Your court is waiting," Roland said, pulling me towards him and looping the hand he still held through the crook of his elbow.

Courtiers stepped aside and bowed, forming a natural aisle from me to the banquet table near the fireplace at the far side of the hall. Roland escorted me up to my seat, Eliza floating one step behind us all the while.

Once I was seated, the courtiers rose and turned back to whatever they had been doing before I appeared—speaking to a group of friends, sipping at a drink, listening to the musicians whose upbeat playing toed the line between chipper and boisterous.

A crystal glass of sparkling konstans was placed before me. A bowing servant laid down a long tray of cheese and fruit. I sipped at the wine and watched the people before me.

My gaze cast down the long hall, I could make out most of the Lords and their Ladies. I noted several servants I had come to recognize this year. Besides each door and window, there were also two Vikela placed as guards.

Finn was a commander. He would not play sentry. Still, I scanned over the guards, looking for him. Each wore their dress tunics, the more formal version of their soldier tunic that was slightly darker in color, slightly closer in fit, and with double-breasted buttons that ran down the chest. The horned helmets were noticeably absent.

To my surprise, there Finn was—posted near the main door across the room from us. His blonde hair glinted in the golden light of the chandeliers that hung from the ceiling. I had never seen him in his dress tunic, and I took a moment to drink in the sight, squinting slightly to see better across the long hall.

He was speaking to the other guard posted beside him, saying something and gesturing over his shoulder with one hand while the other rested unconsciously on the hilt of the sword attached to his belt.

The dress tunic fit him nicely, I thought as I sipped again at my wine. It was cut in a way that left little to the imagination, a veritable show of honed muscle under the formal lines of the fabric. I smiled into my glass, wondering what God or gods had been so thoughtful as to put Finn on guard duty tonight and place him directly in my line of vision.

As if he heard the thought, Finn's head turned in my direction. Even from this distance, I could see the slight quirk of his mouth as he tried not to smile obviously at me.

I could feel my own lips begin to curve in response and I bit the inside of my cheek to stop myself. I took another sip, nodding at Finn slightly.

He bowed in response, and I looked away before I could get myself in trouble. Luckily, servants bearing platters of food began streaming into the hall. Trays of roast pork and stewed chicken, heaps of steaming yams and tossed kale were put down on the head banquet table where I sat, as well as those that ran perpendicular down the hall.

The dreaded stuffed ostrich came out last, its wings spread wide and reaching. It was a wonder that the servants could carry such a large animal on a tray, and I watched in disbelief as they placed the creature on its own table in the center of the room. I forced my eyebrows not to lift as I caught the glint of the diamonds that had replaced its eyes. From the chair on my right, I heard Eliza snicker. She knew me too well.

Servants put various dishes on my plate, and I ate whatever was before me. It was a blur of spices and aromas, a veritable feast for my senses, and I enjoyed each bite. The only thing I refused was a slice of the ostrich.

Before I had finished my plate, dancers emerged. Clad in form-fitting outfits that reminded me of ballet leotards, they hopped and spun to the music, providing a backdrop of entertainment over our meal. I glanced down the long tables to see how many courtiers were actually paying attention to the dancers, and was unsurprised to see few were.

A young teen clapped her hands excitedly as the dancers finished a particularly challenging stunt, but she seemed the only one who had become transfixed by the show. The rest ate and spoke, quite used to dancers and singers being mere background to their greater concerns of courtly life.

When the meal was over, more golden wine was poured and a singer took the stage while the servants cleared plates. The woman was tall and stately, and her voice was heavenly. I recognized an aria from Carmen, and I turned to Roland, one brow quirked.

"Did you teach her this?" I asked, genuinely curious how a singer from the Alterealm would know of a Humanrealm opera.

"I may have introduced her to a few arias," Roland said, shrugging dismissively. But I saw the playfulness in his eyes, and I smiled at it.

"Thank you," I told him. "You know it's my favorite."

"Only because it was mine first," he replied under his breath, and I laughed. It was true, but an appreciation of opera was something we had always shared. I wondered whether he had smuggled in a recording somehow for the singer, or how he had managed to teach her.

In my peripheral vision, movement caught my attention and I looked to see Finn and a soldier take a glass of water from a passing server. Try as I might, I could not catch his eye again. He was focused on surveilling the crowd and I was grateful for that.

But in my own fantasy world where we were just two ordinary people, Finn would be seated beside me, enjoying the music as I was and sipping at his own flute of wine. It was a pipe dream, a fantasy conjured up from my own romantic mind. There would never be that moment publicly for us; I had resigned myself to that. That was the price of keeping him and I was prepared to pay it because he was mine: my friend, my confidant...

I almost thought the words *my love* but I stopped myself.

I knew I did not love him.

I respected him and enjoyed his company, but I did not fool myself into thinking it went any deeper. I had realized it some time ago and I tried not to dwell on it. It made me wonder how this would end between us, because if it was not love, the sense of destiny that I felt—the certainty that there was someone out there for each of us—meant that one day a woman would come along more enthralling than I.

One day, a man would come along more enthralling than Finn.

That line of thought was equally as absurd as the idea of Finn and I sitting together at this high table. I took another sip of my wine, putting down the flute a moment later to clap heartily as the singer took a final bow and moved gracefully back into the shadows from which she had come.

The doors to the far chamber opened and I watched as a man entered the Great Hall.

Not just any man. Anson.

He was dressed in his usual dark pants and shirt, but this time a formal double-breasted jacket sat atop his attire. He made his way down the long hall and directly to my seat, nodding in greeting to the people he passed.

He stopped several paces before me, dropping into a low bow.

He froze there, and I realized he was waiting for me to tell him to stand.

"Rise," I called, over the buzz and chatter of the banquet.

"Your Majesty," Anson said by way of greeting as he stood straight.

"Is it possible for you to ever be on time?" I asked, thinking back to my very first Council meeting where he was also late.

Anson quirked a brow and smiled that stupid grin of his. I could almost see him decide to take the bait. "I apologize for my tardiness. I had pressing matters to attend to but, ultimately, nothing could keep me away from as joyous an occasion as the young Queen's twenty-first birthday."

"Hmph," I muttered, taking another sip of wine—a small sip. I could feel the beginnings of a pleasant humming in my blood, and I wondered how many glasses I had had. The servants were remarkably good at filling up the flute before I ever saw the bottom.

"May I propose a toast?" Seeing no refusals from me or anyone else at the high table, Anson had to merely glance to his left and a server bearing a tray of wine appeared. He took a flute and raised it into the air.

The Great Hall grew quiet, conversations stopping mid-sentence as courtiers turned to watch the scene in front of them.

Anson did not seem to care. No, he basked in the glory of being the center of attention. With his cheeky grin, he raised the glass an inch higher. "Your Majesty, we wish you a pleasant birthday, a fulfilling year, and many more to come. Long live the Queen."

He took a long drink, nearly emptying the flute in one go, and the courtiers followed suit. Their own versions of "Long live the Queen" echoed around the hall.

I nodded at Anson, still too weary of him to believe this show was for my benefit. He nodded back and then spun on his heel. I expected him to take a seat at the head table beside Grimly and the other Lords of the Senior Council, but he did not. A small gaggle of Lords scooted closer together to make a space for their compatriot at a table to my right.

Birds of a feather, I mused.

Unfortunately, Anson seemed to have started a trend. A dozen courtiers approached and made toasts, all following some variation of wishing me well now and always. And then presents began.

Eliza had explained to me earlier in the day that it was tradition for each House in Izwe to bring forth a present for the monarch, so I was not surprised when the procession started. One by one, a representative of each House stopped before me. The first time, I was about to stand and reach for the gift myself when a servant stepped forward to take the wrapped parcel.

Roland leaned forward to whisper, "It's customary for you to stay seated. Your gifts will be brought to your room, and you can go through them there."

I nodded in understanding, although I did wonder what the secrecy was about. "Thank you," I said to the middle-aged woman who had been the first gift-giver.

I said the same after each gift was given. Again and again, I said thank you until I wondered how many Houses there were at court. It was a rhetorical musing; I knew there were exactly twenty—one for each Lord on the Council.

The humming in my veins had not lessened, despite the fact that I no longer sipped at my drink. In fact, the humming had grown more intense. While it was a nice, buzzy feeling, I felt like I needed air.

After one more gift had been presented and before the next person in line could step forward, I stood.

Conversation stopped momentarily, and I wondered how easily shocked these people were that the simple act of me standing up could cause them to pause what they were doing.

"Are you alright?" Eliza questioned from my shoulder.

"Yes. I'd just like some air," I said, turning my head to spy the closest door. One of the adjoining balconies would be fine, as would the garden. I needed a break if I had to sit through another moment of gift giving.

Eliza nodded but before she could say anything else, I was off.

The music resumed and the discussions started again. I made my way to the closest balcony door, eager for the cool air and maybe even a glass of water if I could find a servant who had anything other than wine.

Before I could get there, though, Anson was standing in my way.

"Yes?" I asked him, not bothering to be polite. He never was with me.

"I could not help but overhear."

I looked at him, unsure of what he was getting at. "Yes…?"

He stared back at me, as if I was the one not making any sense. After a moment, he continued. "Might I suggest a walk in the garden? I passed through there just as I was arriving here late"—he paused to give me a pointed look—"And I couldn't help but admire the look of the jasmine in the moonlight."

"I would never take you for a sentimental type," I replied, even though it did sound beautiful. I could imagine what the clustered blossoms would smell like, their sharp citrusy scent heightened as it floated in the cool night air.

"You'd be surprised, Your Majesty," Anson replied so quietly I almost did not hear him.

I was about to ask what he meant when he held up a hand and snapped his fingers. "Finn," he called in a clear voice that somehow traveled the distance to the door Finn was at without sounding like a yell.

My eyes narrowed. "What do you think you're doing?" My voice was something between a sneer and a whisper, pitched and incredulous as it was.

Anson merely leaned conspiratorially towards me. "Assisting you, of course."

And then Finn was there, and I was willing my cheeks not to flame in an embarrassed blush.

He stopped in front of us, bowing to me formally before facing Anson. "Can I be of service, my Lord?"

Anson let his gaze linger on my reddening cheeks before turning to Finn with an innocent look. "Certainly. Queen Sahle was just saying she desired a walk in the garden. Given the recent attack, it would be most prudent for a commander to accompany her rather than one of your men. Do you not agree?"

Finn did not respond for a moment, holding Anson's gaze in a serious, unblinking way. Then he bowed again and faced me.

"Your Majesty," Finn gestured down the long hall that would lead us through the door and down the correct staircase to the garden.

I did not take Finn's arm as I had Roland's when I originally entered the ballroom. No, that was not appropriate. Although everyone here—save the children, maybe—knew Finn and I were seeing each other, it would be scandalous for him to touch me in any way publicly. He was a soldier, and I was the Queen.

I started walking, focusing on putting one foot ahead of the other under my long gown. Finn followed a step behind.

But to get to that door, I had to get around Anson. Just as I passed, he whispered quietly enough that not even Finn could hear. "Happy Birthday, Your Majesty."

I halted my step momentarily and glanced at him, his eyes catching on mine and boring into my soul. But whatever depth there was in those green eyes was gone in an instant. Before I could form a quippy response, Anson was walking away, called by a pretty young woman in a silver dress who I had seen flirt with him mercilessly on several occasions.

I shook my head and continued on, unsure of whether Anson was joking or not.

It took twice as long to reach the door as it had to travel from the door to my table when I arrived. I knew it was just my perception—the fact that Finn was behind me stirring up hushed discussions, and making the time move slower.

I itched to reach back and pull him in line with me. But of course I did not. I held my head up, my palms gently clasped together in front of me, and I walked directly down the center of the hall, through the door, and down the staircase that led to the ground floor.

Servants streamed past, carrying more wine and, I noted with slight longing, trays of sweets. Two even balanced a large iced cake between them. As much as I enjoyed a good piece of cake, fresh air was more pressing.

Only when we had made it to the grounds, to the edge of the gardens, did Finn draw up beside me. He matched his stride with my slow meandering one and gently took my hand in his.

I craned my neck to look up at him as we walked. "Hello," I said simply.

"Hello, My Queen," he replied with a smile on his fair face. "Happy Birthday."

"Oh, not you too!"

"What?" he exclaimed, dodging a playful swipe I half-heartedly directed at his forearm. "Isn't that what you say to the birthday girl?"

"It is," I replied cautiously. "But how you said it reminded me of Anson."

"Anson who entirely planned this for us?" Finn said.

"Anson who is always a little shit," I corrected.

Finn shrugged, then glanced behind him to make sure we were alone before he looped his arm around my shoulder and pulled me into his side. "Anson did not have to do that. He was trying to be nice."

I rolled my eyes. "I don't know why you're defending him. I'm sure he's up there in the banquet hall just rolling with laughter at what people are saying about us. He did that on purpose—to make a scene, to amuse himself."

Finn shook his head. "No, it was a favor. I've known Anson for many years. Not well, granted, but I've known the man. And while he acts like an ass most times, he is actually a very decent person at heart. You just have to crack through that shell of his."

"Pssh." My shock did not lend itself to full words. "You do realize he hates me, right?"

That made Finn laugh—the sort of shocked laugh that catches even the one laughing off guard. "Hate you? Whyever would you think that? The man is possibly the most devoted Lord in all of Izwe."

"Kaiht told me something during our visit to Ukuwela. Apparently, Anson had argued to leave me in the Humanrealm while I was gone…I knew he was not my biggest fan, but I had no idea his animosity ran that deep."

"I'm sure it's not the whole story. Anson's motives are often complex, but they are never malicious, especially where the crown is concerned," Finn replied simply.

I glanced at Finn, shocked. I did not know how I expected Finn to respond to Kaiht's words, but it certainly was not like that. "Why are you so complimentary towards him tonight?"

"I just think you should give him a chance," Finn said with another shrug. "He's a powerful man who has this kingdom's best interests at heart—much like you. Make him an ally. It's only a suggestion."

"I'll take it under consideration," I muttered, although the part I did not say out loud was that I would only do so when hell froze over.

Sensing I was done with the conversation, Finn turned me towards him so that we were facing each other. I glanced over my shoulder, but we had reached the briar of jasmine. Not even the tops of our heads would be seen from the palace, the stairs, or the garden path.

We were alone. And that was my favorite way to be with Finn.

"Happy Birthday," Finn said once more as he placed a flittering, warm kiss on my lips.

Leaving one arm wrapped around my waist, he fished into his pocket with his free hand. Finding whatever he was searching for, he pulled it free, and he held it out to me. In the dim light, I could not make out what was in his palm. Perhaps a slim little box or a thickly folded piece of paper.

"Wha—" I started to ask, but then the world shredded apart.

31
crash

MY EYES INSTINCTIVELY SNAPPED SHUT AT THE BRIGHT light that tore through the garden, illuminating every blade of manicured grass, every shadow behind a jasmine petal. But the sound was just as bad, overwhelming each of my senses. I clapped my hands over my ears as I prayed for whatever this was to stop.

My heart was hammering, my ears were ringing but I forced myself to open my eyes and see what was going on around me.

Fire, I realized. Fire and smoke and two more explosions popped, all but soundless behind my covered ears.

But my ears did not stay covered for long. Finn was pulling at my wrists, his muted shouting not getting through my compressed ear canals.

"Sahle," I heard as he pulled my arms down to my sides. "Come on!"

Finn grabbed my hands, and although I wanted to look back at the palace, I was being pulled further into the garden and away from the smoke and flames that lit up the sky in sickly shades of red and yellow.

We were running, but I did not know where Finn was leading me. I was too concerned with the screaming that had started behind me, far up where my banquet was taking place.

What was going on?

I forced myself to focus, to think. I did not know what was happening in the palace but if it was an attack rather than an accident, the surest way to get killed was to stand frozen in the garden, staring up at the attackers. Those who froze in panic were the first to die; those who jumped into action were the ones who survived.

Finn and I kept running until we were on the edge of the soldiers' grounds. He slowed to a jog, and then pulled me into the shadow of one of the rondavels.

I could hear rustling and yelling, the clink of swords and armor in the soldiers' buildings. I hoped they were preparing to go into the castle.

We crept around the corner of one outbuilding to get a better look, Finn motioning with a finger at his lips for me to be silent.

Soldiers were streaming out of their huts, some in armor and some in training tunics. All held weapons and, at the command of one senior soldier, all started at a clipped marching run towards the palace.

I wondered why Finn did not call out to them. Surely we were safe with the soldiers. "Why don't we signal them?"

Finn glanced at me and whispered his reply. "I'm not sure who to trust right now, and I'd rather you stay hidden until we know what is going on."

"You think it's an attack?" My blood ran icy at the thought.

Even in the shadowy night, I could see his reluctant nod. "Yes."

"What do we do?" I asked, hoping he had a plan. Because I certainly did not. I had seen the rubble in Ukuwela. I had heard the story of my parents' deaths. But until this moment, I had never faced the reality of me being next in line to die—that I could be drinking wine at a banquet in one moment, and then blown to bits in the next.

This was real. Living it was entirely different than being told, and the shock was like a slap to my face.

But Finn was a man of action. He did not panic. He did not muse on what to do. He just did. And now he was telling me to follow him and be prepared to grab whatever weapons were still in the armory.

He took my hand, and we set off at a cautious run. We slowed to glance around each corner and down each pathway before setting off again.

I willed my breathing to be silent, even as my chest heaved against the tight laces of my bodice. I could hear my heartbeat pounding in my ears. The sound was loud in the silent night, the only accompaniment to the far-off screams and clashing metal coming from the palace.

We reached the training ring and beelined for the weapons room. The door to the room was still open, such was the soldiers' haste in getting whatever they needed and hurrying to the palace.

All of the bows and arrows were gone, as were the spears and shields. Most of the swords were gone but Finn handed me one that was still on the rack. He strapped two daggers onto his sword belt and handed me another. I shoved it down the edge of my bodice, the cool metal biting into the skin of my ribcage.

I eyed a rack of weapon belts and began to reach for one when a clicking noise caught my attention.

Finn and I looked at each other and then towards the door, left slightly ajar in our haste. Finn motioned again to be silent and then crept to the open door and peered out.

I could not see what was out there, but the clicking I thought I had heard was growing louder. And I realized it was not clicking, but the clomping of hooves or hardened boots on the soil.

I could see in Finn's face that he was unsure of his next action, and I guessed at the choices: to stay here and wait to be found, or to make a run for it.

I did not have time to throw my own opinion in before Finn's hand was once more on mine, and he was pulling me through the door at a sprinting pace.

Whatever was out there was growing closer. That much I knew. I could hear its approach even over my ragged breath and the pounding of my heart.

We made it out of the weapons room.

We made it halfway across the training grounds.

We made it to the edge of the ring.

Then, out of the shadows of the rondavels, a figure appeared. I could not make out who or what it was, but I could hear the slide of sharp metal against metal as a sword was unholstered.

The figure did not come any closer, though. Rather, it began chanting. I had never heard anything like it. It was not a language I recognized from the Humanrealm, or from my studies of the Alterealm this past year.

Finn pulled me closer, sensing something was coming. I tightened my grip on my sword a second before I was falling.

32
alter

I REALIZED WHAT WAS HAPPENING THE INSTANT I FELT my stomach drop out from under me. We were traveling, Finn and I; traveling as I had traveled exactly a year before from the Humanrealm to here.

This time there was no spooling light, no glow of the stars. It was different. It was just the sensation.

Before I could blink a second time, the sensation stopped. I blinked again, whipping my head around.

We were still in the training ground—the buildings surrounding us all still the same, the trees in the surrounding forest sticking up over the low roofs of the rondavels. But this place, as much as it was the same, was also very different.

The light was no longer the black of night. It was a deep glowing purple. Although the palace was still visible, smoke did not emanate from it. Screams did not pierce the air. It was silent, all except for my breathing and Finn's.

We were here but not here. Sickly, I realized that if I did not even know where or when we were, no one else but this figure would either.

Finn's hand stayed firmly locked around mine, his strong body angled just slightly between me and the figure.

And then out of the purple glow, the beat of hooves began again.

THE SOUND GREW AND GREW, SPIRALING EVER LOUDER until it seemed the noise was no longer in the air around us. It was inside my head.

Suddenly, figures were all around us, surrounding us, boxing us in. Finn and I spun, back to back, as the creatures drew ever closer.

They materialized out of the very darkness. Their bodies took shape as they rounded the corners of the soldiers' huts and, even in the purple glooming I could see that their forms were not right.

Their limbs were too long. Their heads were too large. They were humanoid but only in the most rudimentary way. Even their movements—too twitchy, too fast—marked them as something else.

They streamed into the training ring. They surrounded us. But for some reason they were still. Clubs and swords dangled from twisted fingers but they held steady. They did not attack.

I realized with sickening clarity that they were waiting for something—an order, a command. And I wondered at the words that would ultimately end my life.

The original chanting figure stepped out from the others and its mouth broke in two. The top half of his head fell backwards until what was once a forehead rested on its upper back. The lower half dropped down until the chin was resting on the chest.

And from deep within the body cavity, a whisper as cold and cutting as ice slithered out.

"Sahle," it preened. I could almost see the cruel smile that must have accompanied that pleased and disturbed voice. "Our dear Sahle. Oh, how you've grown."

"Don't listen to it, Sahle!" Finn called. He reached behind him to grab at my palm.

The creature did not seem to mind Finn's warning. It ignored it altogether. "Sahle. Little Sahle. Queen Sahle. How your parents fought for you. How they died for you, screaming and bloodied. What was it all for?

"For you to die here, amongst these creatures—once men but no longer? It has taken us twenty years to find you, little Sahle. Twenty long years to finally see the end of your treacherous dynasty. With your death, we'll have peace. And it couldn't come soon enough."

The words made no sense. What did he—it—mean by peace?

I had been training and studying and fighting for peace. I had been told every day since I arrived that my destiny was to rule Izwe and the entire Alterealm into peace and prosperity after generations of war and upset.

But perhaps the prophecy was wrong. I suddenly wished I could remember the exact wording. Did it say my actions would usher in peace? Or just me? Could it be that my death was all that was needed—that I was born and kept safe for this very moment, for this very death?

Before I could contemplate anymore, the creature cackled. But it was not the creature. No, it was whomever spoke through the creature. Like a sick music box, the creature sang the last notes of its laugh and then snapped its head shut in a crunching of bone and wet flesh.

"SAHLE!" Finn yelled at the exact moment the creatures leapt forward, having seen with his soldier's eyes the shifting of weight that precipitated battle.

I moved into Finn in one uncertain back step, and then was lunging forward towards the nearest creature. My sword swung wide on the first strike, but it landed in a spray of watery pink blood on the second.

I did not stop to see if I had killed the creature before I turned my attention to the next that attacked.

This one swung a club low, forcing me to jump into the air to avoid breaking my lower legs into pieces. My skirt snapping at my ankles, I landed and spun with surer feet than I would have expected. And then I paid the creature back in turn, slicing my sword across its legs and severing foot from calf at the ankles.

Another and another attacked, and somewhere over my shoulder I could hear the clanking of swords and shrieking of creatures as they fell by Finn's hand.

I hazarded a glance and saw him skewer one creature through the shoulder, another directly through the head.

But he was tiring. I was tiring.

With each creature I took down, I could feel my actions growing slightly slower, my swings slightly less measured. I had trained for this moment yet with each creature I brought down, each minute I continued to push the limits of my skill with a sword, I knew I was expending precious energy.

Soon, I would be flailing.

The creatures outnumbered us. For each one of us there were at least a dozen of them. They were all waiting their turn to take a piece of us.

"Sahle!" Finn called as he kicked away a creature. "Use your power!"

Slashing my sword across the stomach of another, I called back to him, "I can't! I don't know how."

"You do know how! You have to use it. We're running out of time!"

I knew he was right. We had minutes maybe before the creatures grew tired of playing with us and swarmed, or worse, before one of us grew too tired to fight them off and fell.

Help needed to arrive. Help had to arrive.

I was never a praying sort, but I prayed then. I prayed that the Lords realized we were absent, that Anson had survived whatever blast had rocked the palace and could tell the others where Finn and I had gone. I prayed that help was on the way.

Because I was not the person who could save us. I was just Sahle. Just a girl who was snatched out of the Humanrealm. I had no powers, no matter what Finn or the Lords or anyone else in Izwe thought.

I was not the hero here.

Another creature lunged at me, aiming for my shoulder. I side-stepped to avoid the blade but could not move fast enough to avoid taking a glancing blow to my forearm.

I screamed at the stinging slice of pain that arched over and through my arm. I looked down just long enough to make sure my limb was still attached.

"Are you alright?" Finn yelled from a few paces away as I turned on the creature, angry and increasingly more desperate.

"I'm...fine!" I shouted. My words barely made it over the cacophony of the fight.

"Use your power, Sahle!" Finn called again.

I was shaking my head as I sliced another creature. "I don't know how," I nearly cried.

"Just like we practiced," Finn yelled as his sword crashed with a creature's.

I could feel the desperation growing, crawling like ants over my skin. We were going to die here. There were too many of them and not enough of us.

I knew I would not be able to use my power, but I had to try.

I could try.

That much I could do.

I took down one more creature before I nodded to myself in

resolution. "Cover me, Finn," I called.

In a second, he was at my side, fending off the creatures who dared to draw too near.

I closed my eyes, focusing on my gasping breath and trying to drown out the din and clatter of swords. I tried to visualize my skin, my bones, the sinewy tissue that held my joints in place. I tried to envision all of that magic they claimed I had leaching from those inner parts of me and gathering in my palms, spooling outwards from my very pores.

But try as I might, nothing came.

"Sahle!" Finn yelled, and I snapped my eyes open. I spun just in time to avoid a blow to the leg.

"It's not working!" I yelled back, dodging another blow and then another.

Finn moved towards me, reached out to me as if to pull me towards him.

But then he stopped.

His arm froze mid-raise.

His eyes opened wide, and he glanced down.

And I realized with a horrifying clarity that the tunic he was wearing was quickly blooming a thick burgundy. At the center of the tunic, the end of a sword protruded out of his belly, straight through from the other side.

"NO!" I screamed.

Horror and fear and desperation took over my mind as Finn sunk to his knees, his hands grasping futilely at the knife-end of the sword.

And suddenly the world was white, blindingly white, the white of starlight and there was no sound or air.

The only thing I was aware of was my horror and my fear for Finn. That, and my hatred of the creatures who had hurt him.

There was no thinking this time, no visualizing my body and my magic. And I realized, in some distant part of my brain, that magic was will. That was all it was.

And right now, I willed for those creatures to burn.

One by one within the white glaring world of my magic, they lit up in blue flame. Their mouths—those too gaping halves of their heads—opened wide as if in screams, but no sound came out. I willed for them to not make a sound and they did not.

As they burned, they dropped to the red ground like lifeless, still sacks of flour. I stared at their forms, watching the flame turn their clothes and mottled skin to flakey black char. I wanted them to rise, to heal, so that I could alight them once more— such was my anger, my sadness. It was overwhelming. I was overwhelming, consumed entirely by my emotions.

But then a wet cough, so quiet it was like a gurgling fountain, broke through the haze of my anger. I spun around, my eyes searching in the blinding white for Finn.

He was laying ten paces away, no longer on his knees but slumped forward in a boneless pile. Somehow he had managed to push the sword backward and it lay behind him, marked by his blood.

The white fog cleared as my anger abruptly lifted. And then I was running the distance to Finn, sinking to my own knees and pulling him into me so that his head was cradled in my lap.

"Finn!" I yelled at him, shaking him gently. "Finn!"

His eyes were closed but I knew he was still alive. His ruby-stained chest rose in an uneven, labored rhythm.

He opened his eyes at the commotion I was causing.

He smiled but the look was etched in agony, deep grooves cutting into the edges of his mouth in more of a grimace.

I pressed my hand into his stomach over the wound. "You're going to be alright, Finn," I told him even as dark blood seeped past my fingers.

Arterial blood, someone had once told me. That was what this was. I had limited medical knowledge but even I knew it was not good. There was too much of it, and it flowed too darkly, too thickly out of the through-and-through abdominal wound.

"Help is coming," I said to him, pushing down tighter as if I could single-handedly hold his life force within him.

"Sahle," he rasped through his barely open lips. He coughed to clear his throat and I saw a splatter of blood land on the right corner of his mouth. "I love you."

"Stop it, Finn," I shook my head. I knew this was not a declaration of love but a confession—a last confession. And I did not want it. "You're not going to die. Stop it."

"My little darling" he whispered haltingly. "I love you and I'm sorry I never said it sooner. I was a fool before. Remember when I told you, if you were a regular girl, maybe I'd want to marry you, maybe I'd want you to bear my children?"

"I remember," I whispered, my voice unable to rise past the overwhelming desperation clouding my mind.

Finn closed his eyes slowly and opened them again, a grimace on his face. "That maybe was a lie. All of those things…Having you in your entirety…it was the one thing in my life I ever truly wished for. I knew it was not possible, but in the moments when I let myself dream, there was only you as my love, with all that entails. I'm sorry I never said it sooner. I didn't know how.

"But loving you, in whatever way I was able…it had to be enough. Sharing your confidence, your friendship, your bed… was the greatest honor I have ever known."

He closed his eyes again and I was distraught. I shook him slightly, trying to jostle him. "Finn, stay awake!" I shouted at him.

I noticed little drops of water on Finn's face. I stared at them confused until another droplet fell in a splatter on the arch of his cheekbone, and I realized that the water was coming from me. I was crying.

Silent tears slid down my face and landed on his. "Finn, you can't die. I…need you."

I wanted to say that I loved him. I knew that was the customary thing to do when someone confessed their love for you. But I did not love him.

I wanted to—oh, how I wanted to.

He was kind and good and strong and handsome. He was everything a girl could ever ask for, and yet my heart told me that he was not the one. There was something missing.

But as much as I assured Finn he was not dying, I knew he was. I could feel it in my gut. The deep burgundy blood that had so freely flowed from his stomach was slowing. In a detached, clinical way, I noted that it was on the ground surrounding us like a night-darkened pool. The skirts of my light gown were soaked crimson, and I wondered how many pints of blood a body could hold.

Finn was dying. I did not love him, but I cared for him. And if he was going to die now, then I wanted him to go with as much peace as possible.

And so I did the one thing I thought I would never do.

"Please," I whispered. I dropped my head to his and kissed his lips. They were cold, and I felt the blood he had coughed up on my own lips when I pulled back. "Don't leave me here. I… love you, Finn."

The words felt hollow coming out of me. They were not at all how I had once pictured confessing my love to someone. I had always imagined the words would pour out in a flood of warmth and effervescent giddiness.

But these words were not for me. Even though they felt brittle and forced on my tongue, they were for Finn. And I would do anything for this man who had saved me in the Alterealm, who had given me a taste of joy in all of these months of confusion and fear.

Finn cracked his eyes open and a single tear slipped down his face. In my peripheral vision, his hand stirred. He tried to lift it towards me, but it fell back down.

I leaned forward and picked up the hand and pressed it to my cheek. "Finn, I love you. Stay with me."

Finn smiled, and something in his eyes told me he knew the truth. He knew I did not truly love him, but he was glad all the same to pretend, just for a while.

"See. I was right," he spluttered wetly, pushing the words past the blood in his throat.

"What?" I asked, confused.

"You do have power," Finn said, his eyes turning determined even as I felt the hand in mine going slack. "Use it…Sahle."

I was shaking my head, not because I did not believe in my power. I had just seen it firsthand. I was shaking my head because I did not want these parting words.

"I will. I will. Just stay with me," I pleaded. I leaned down again and pressed my lips to his.

But the lips were too still. I froze and waited for a breath to brush past my face.

No breath came, no movement.

I pulled back, staring down at Finn's face. "Finn?"

His eyes were shut and for a moment I could almost believe that he had merely closed them to rest as he had before. Yet there was a stillness to him that was undeniable. His chest no longer rose and the seep of blood had halted.

I knew what that meant.

Finn was gone.

"FINN!" I screamed. "FINN!"

I do not know how many times I screamed his name. I shook his shoulders. I planted my hands on his face and willed him to open his eyes and look up at me. I was a void of desperate pleas, and my actions were entirely outside of my control.

Then hands were on me, pulling at me and I was screaming and trying to fight them off.

"Queen Sahle!" someone yelled.

Hands were at my face, pulling my gaze from Finn and to something else.

Someone else.

Anson.

His green eyes bored into mine, and then his gaze dropped. It tracked across the blood staining my gown and hands, the cuts on my sleeves.

"Are you hurt?" I thought he said. His lips certainly moved in what looked like that formation, but I was not sure I could hear anything truly. There was a ringing in my ears that muted everything else out. My body was numb and the little I could feel felt shivery, as if my skin were dancing.

"Sahle!" Anson yelled for I was staring at him, but I was not really seeing him. Distantly, I thought it was impertinent of him to call me by my first name.

Not that it mattered now.

Not that anything mattered now.

I looked back at Finn—or at least tried to. My head turned in his direction and I got a glimpse of too-still feet before I was being pulled up and pressed into a warm chest.

"I've got you," Anson said from near my ear, and I realized he was holding me. He was carrying me, and we were moving further from Finn.

I struggled in his arms. "Finn," I called weakly. "Finn!"

"Shhh," Anson murmured. "It'll be OK now. You're safe."

But I did not care about me. I did not want to be safe. I wanted Finn to be.

"Finn," I called once more. And then, without knowing where consciousness ended and unconsciousness began, there was nothingness—blackness, nothingness, and utter peace.

AWARENESS IS A FUNNY THING. I WAS AWARE OF MY BODY, but not my mind. I was aware of the cold pressing in on my face as I leaned it against the wall of windows in my room, but not that my naked skin was wet from the bathwater I had climbed out of.

A hollowness consumed me in my waking hours and the only respite I could find was in sleep, sweet sleep. It was why I stayed in bed as long as I could. The healers told me my wounds were superficial, that I would be fine, that I could leave my chambers as soon as I felt well-rested.

But I did not feel fine. I did not feel well-rested.

I felt tired with a sort of exhaustion that ran bone deep. I felt exhausted and numb as if I would never again have the energy to walk more than ten paces. And beneath it all, I felt an overwhelming sense of guilt.

Finn was dead. It was an undeniable fact and, though I woke most mornings reaching straining fingers towards what had become his side of the bed, I realized anew each day that he was gone. That moment hit with the physical force of a blow.

Yet I was here.

The injustice ate at me, almost as much as my guilt over having lied to him. I ran that moment over in my head time and time again, when I woke from restless sleep in the still night, when I sat before the fireplace and tried to feel the flames.

I told him I loved him as a comfort, but it was not the truth. It had never been the truth, and I knew Finn had seen right through me. I only prayed that he understood in that moment what I had tried to do.

I might not have loved him, but I cared about him. He had been my one true friend here and now he was gone. And the loss of him felt like a bolt to the chest each and every moment.

Days came and went and the only marker that I registered was that of Kaiht and Mara forcing me from bed each morning to bathe. The first days after the palace attack, they tried to speak to me, to ask me how I felt, to inquire after the cuts and bruises dotting my skin. But I had no words for them. I simply stared emptily at the murky bathwater and sank further into its warm, weightless embrace.

Eliza and Roland arrived at some point, soon after my return. Eliza had held me to her and cried. Roland had watched on, alternately pacing my room and stroking my hair when he came within arm's reach. But I had nothing to say to them either. They had already heard what happened. By now, I was sure everyone knew. There was nothing for me to add that had not already been shared.

The days passed. The wheel turned. And I moved through it in a haze.

And then, a quiet tap sounded on my door one evening. Kaiht and Mara had gone…well, I did not know where, nor did I particularly care. All I knew was that they were not here to open the door.

I dragged myself out of bed, grabbed a discarded shawl from the back of a chair, and tiptoed towards the door. From outside, I could hear a soft murmur of voices but no yelling, no screaming. It must be someone the soldiers knew, then.

I cracked the door open hesitantly, leaving just enough space to peer out, and then made to shut it again just as quickly.

But his voice froze me.

"Queen Sahle," Anson said and the gentleness there sent me straight back to that night—straight back to the physical feeling of being pulled away from Finn who laid too still, Finn whose eyes were closed.

I closed my own eyes, willing the physical press of those memories to stay away. They had to stay away.

Then, from closer, his voice called again. "Queen Sahle, may I come in?"

I could feel his breath on my face, and I opened my eyes to find him mere inches from me. He looked at whatever part of me was visible through the cracked door with a kindness that went against his very nature.

I did not have the mental capacity to wonder about that. I did not have the space to think about his usual cruelty. I merely stepped away from the door, content to let someone, anyone, tell me what I should be doing now.

I made my way to one of the chairs before the fire and sat heavily, staring at the flames. I did not offer Anson a seat. In fact, I was not even sure he had followed me until I heard the click of the door closing and the sound of his boots moving across the polished floor.

The other wingback chair was in my line of vision so I know he did not sit there. I think he stood, somewhere to my left. I was beyond caring, too tired to wonder why he was here or how a good hostess should act.

He said nothing for a time, and a little voice in my head wondered whether he was watching me or the fire, or merely taking in the features of the Queen's private chambers.

"Thank you, Your Majesty," he said at last. "I would ask how you are, but I think it goes without saying."

I watched an ember pop in the fire and closed my eyes against the vivid swell of sparks. He was right to assume I had nothing to say.

I heard his footsteps again. I felt his presence near me. I could even smell the cold on his clothes—stone and damp wood and night.

And then he was pressing something into my palm.

A corner of it stuck uncomfortably into the pad at the base of my thumb, and I looked down. It was a small box—the box that Finn had given me moments before the explosions began.

I stared at it uncomprehendingly. I had forgotten about its existence in everything that followed.

"I found it in the garden when we went looking for you that night," Anson explained. "It has your name written on the side, and I've seen enough of Finn's reports to recognize his handwriting."

I nodded, a pressure building behind my eyes. I wanted to thank Anson for finding it. I wanted to ask him why he was being kind. I wanted to tear open the package.

Most of all, I wanted to be alone with this last piece of Finn.

As if he knew that, I heard the scuff of Anson's boots on the floor as he turned. "Majesty," he said simply in farewell, and then he was gone.

I could not tear my eyes away from the package. It looked much the same as it had on my birthday. It was the same size, the same weight. Only the edges where the thin wrapping paper had torn showed any sort of indication of the horror that had fallen around it.

I turned it in my hand until I saw my name written on one edge. And then I carefully slid my finger under a fold to open the package.

Under the wrapping sat a thin box made of polished ebony wood. I noticed it had a hinge on one side and so I cracked it open on the other.

Inside the box sat a single silver bracelet. It was a solid piece of metal, thin and delicate with a small opening at the back to help fit it on or off of a wrist. At the front of the bracelet, the metal twisted in three small turns—I could almost see the smith turning the red metal around itself as he formed the decoration—before continuing smoothly around to the other side of the back opening.

It was simple and thin. It was beautiful. I managed to put the bracelet on my left wrist through a haze of unshed tears. And then I let the box and wrapping fall to the floor as I buried myself in bed once again.

At some point, Council missives began to arrive. Kaiht and Mara handed them to me as the messengers dropped them off. Sometimes Eliza intersected them and read them aloud. Sometimes Roland, who had taken to sitting companionably at my side some afternoons after Council, simply told me the gist of the conversations.

The haze that had descended over me still hung heavily but, one day, Roland's hesitant report snapped me out of it.

"...and it was decided formally that, as Finn was not an acknowledged suitor or consort, you will not be permitted to be in public mourning."

I swallowed a sip of my rooibos wrong and coughed violently. "Excuse me?"

Roland cut his eyes to me, then away. He had never been one for strong emotions and he could sense the storm brewing in me. "Sahl, you cannot wear black."

I stared at him, flabbergasted. "Finn is dead, there was an attack inside the palace, and my choice of clothing is what the Council is bickering about?"

"I know it seems absurd—"

"It's disgusting!" I nearly yelled, my anger leaping up the sides of my throat. But that anger surprised me, too. I had felt so little since...everything. At least I felt something now.

Roland reached out and took my hand. "I know, Sahl. But you have to try and understand. For a monarch to wear black signifies the death of a family member or another monarch. The relationship you had with Finn was unacknowledged. You might feel his loss and mourn him the way anyone would mourn someone they love—"

I stood abruptly at the word love, but Roland did not seem to notice.

"—but this is a custom of Izwe that is very important. Please, Sahle, there is little they ask but this. They have not pressured you to sit in Council; they've accepted me in your stead. They have given you time and space to mourn. Yet to be seen in public mourning—when you do decide to leave your chambers— would cause an uproar internally and signal weakness to our enemies externally."

I stared at a group of sugarbirds swooping across the treeline outside, and then took a deep breath. "No black?"

"Anything else, but not black."

I nodded at the birds. Perhaps they could help me understand the preposterousness of this discussion.

As if the conversation with Roland had prodded something inside of me, my motivation to get out of bed returned. I expected it to happen slowly and progressively until one day I felt like myself. But my anger at the Lords seemed to shake me enough that I was energized—recharged if not back to my old self than some whole, post-everything self.

I was suddenly itching to do something, anything. I called Kaiht and Mara to me and told them my plan.

I wanted three gowns made.

They made the necessary inquiries. A court dresser was summoned to my chambers immediately to hear my requirements and then in two days the gowns were being hung on display in my chambers for me to assess.

I looked at them all, running my hands over the matching fabric. The cut and purpose of each was different—one formal, one semi-formal, and one simple—but the color was exactly the same. They were not black, as promised, but they were also not the colorful fabric so commonly worn by the Houses in Izwe. These gowns were serious and somber, their fabric of an unpatterned color that was a single shade lighter than charcoal. It would not be mistaken for black but it was close enough.

It was close enough.

And that thought made me smile for the first time in days.

I WOKE UP EARLY IN THE MORNING, JUST BEFORE THE SUN crept over the horizon and bathed this strange world in gold. I sat for some time, silent and contemplative, and I watched the dawn build across the sky, the early birds flitting about like little shooting stars, the way the maps on my walls changed shape in the growing light.

Even from where I sat on my bed, staring through the wide windows, I could tell it would be a cold day. And that was fitting. That felt right for a funeral.

Sometime after dawn broke, Kaiht and Mara arrived with a steaming mug of rooibos tea and a platter of rusks, but I had no appetite. I watched the steam climb into the air and disappear. I would eat later, I told myself, though even that was a far stretch.

I bathed in silence, Kaiht and Mara having guessed my mood without having to communicate anything to them. And then the two women were pulling out all three of my gray dresses and laying them on my bed for me to choose.

I did not need them to lay out options. I knew which dress I would wear. I had it created exactly for this day.

Although it was cut out of fine thick cloth, the gown was the plainest of the three: fitted long sleeves attached to a structured bodice with a neckline that ended mid-bust, and a skirt that gently fell to the floor in a graceful swoop. There was no ornamentation, no lace, no stones. This was a serious dress for a serious occasion.

I rubbed the stiff material of the skirt between my fingers. "This one."

Kaiht and Mara dressed me and brought out gray shoes to match. And then I asked them for the headdress I had commissioned.

I had asked Mara and Kaiht what was acceptable funeral attire in Izwe and they had told me with no reluctance or questions about what I was planning. It was not a surprise, therefore, when I subsequently sent them to the court dresser with my request.

Now, they brought the wooden box to me and opened it. A small charcoal headpiece sat inside, matte and dark.

As Queen, I was expected to wear something atop my head—training had become the exception—but I had no desire to wear one of the state crowns today. I lifted the little headdress and fitted it to my head.

It sat low and blended into my curling hair that I left free and unbound. The tips of the crown's charcoal points echoed the arc of my hair, like a black sun's rays peaking past the cloud of my curls.

"Your Majesty, it's time," Mara said quietly from near the door, her hand already on the handle.

I nodded to her reflection in the mirror I was looking into. "Indeed it is."

The funeral was being held at the military cemetery on the far edge of the palace grounds. I made my way there, flanked by two of my guards. They did not try to address me, aside from their usual bow of greeting when I had appeared outside of my bedroom door, ready to depart.

No, they too were grieving. Finn had been their commander, their friend, and their brother in arms. I noticed that they each wore a black armband on their right bicep today.

As we crested the small hill that led to the cemetery, I was surprised to see a crowd had gathered. Dressed in shades of black and charcoal—or the formal tunics of the soldiers—the people milled about.

A pang of anxiety and fear shot through me at the sight. I did not know what I had expected. I knew Finn was loved, but now the reality of approaching this crowd of family and friends was overwhelming.

Would they boo and hiss at me, tell me I was not welcome here? In my heart, I knew they should even if they would not say it. I was the reason Finn was dead. If he had not been so close to me, he would not have been out in the garden that fateful night. He would not be one more body stacked up around me.

I hesitantly approached the crowd and conversation died as every person turned to stare. There were many people I did not recognize in the sea of faces, and a fair few I did: members of the Vikela, palace servants, city residents. But the faces my eyes locked on were those closest to the casket I now saw sitting beside the open grave.

The older man was clearly Finn's father or uncle. The planes of his face were the same, as was his build and the fall of his hair although it was darker and tinged with gray.

I guessed that the woman was Finn's mother. Her hair was his exact shade of gold and, as her eyes fixed on me, I realized they were the same startling blue.

It was too much. Far too much. I quickly averted my gaze from the woman's sad but curious face. I did not have the heart to face her.

For a moment that felt like a millennium, the crowd stared at me as if frozen. Eyes trained to the ground, I waited for their scorn. I waited for them to turn me away. And I would not hate them for it.

No, I would understand. I was the cause of this pain.

But then they bowed, heads sinking low willingly. It was a welcome, if a quiet one.

I lifted my eyes and nodded once in acknowledgement. I wondered if I should say something, but then a Master was speaking from the center of the crowd near the casket.

The crowd turned their attention to him, and the moment passed. The funeral began.

Much of it was a blur and, even to this day, I wished I had had more presence of mind to listen carefully. I had often seen this Master at the Yesonto and during high holiday festivities, and I knew him to be insightful. I am sure whatever he said was profound and moving and comforting, but I could not focus my mind on his words.

I was too busy staring at the closed casket and willing my eyes to not betray me. I might be here in my gray, my near-black. That might be overlooked, but it would not do to have the Queen of Izwe crying visibly at the funeral of a soldier.

I had to be strong, and I thought about Finn's words to me, his ardent belief in the Queen I could be. He would not want me to cry. He would want me to stand tall, with my shoulders back and my chin up. He would want me to bear this as a ruler did—stoically and quietly.

And so I did just that. It was the best way I could think to honor him. I pulled my shoulders back and cleared my throat. I watched. I paid witness to Finn's sacrifice for that was what this was—a sacrifice to the crown, to service, and to me.

The Master began to close the service, and I hung on the edge of the crowd as six soldiers made their way to the casket. They lifted it and, using a series of ropes, began to lower it into the grave.

I could hear several people sniffling. I could see many more dabbing their eyes with handkerchiefs, but I willed myself to focus, to not dissolve.

And then it was over. The Master was closing his prayer book, and the grave diggers were pushing red dirt onto the casket in earnest, and the crowd was breaking apart, streaming around me like I was an immovable rock and they were the river water flowing past.

My eyes fixed on one figure in the crowd.

Finn's mother met my gaze again from her place beside the grave and then she was walking towards me. I forced myself to hold my head high as she approached. I willed myself to take whatever consternation she would throw at me with grace. I braced myself for her to yell, for her to spit at my feet and curse me. I was ready to take it all; I deserved it, after all.

But then the blonde woman was in front of me and she curtsied heavily, sinking entirely to the ground in a heap.

"Oh," I uttered in shock, reaching for her arm reflexively. "Please."

I grasped her under the elbow and helped her rise.

When she was righted, she looked at me squarely and I steeled myself to not flinch. "You're Queen Sahle," she said. It was not phrased as a question, but I knew she was seeking confirmation.

"Yes."

Her eyes were trained carefully on my face as if she could read me like an open book. I do not know what she saw, but she nodded suddenly and then said, "I'm Finn's mother."

I had guessed as much, seeing her hair and eyes and the man she stood beside earlier. Still, the confirmation made something in my chest squeeze.

I did not know what to say to that, and so I said the first thing that came to my mind. "I'm Finn's...friend."

The word felt hollow, lacking. And it was.

Friend.

It was not the correct word to explain what Finn and I had been, but there was no correct descriptor for that. There never could be, in this world. He was a soldier and I was a Queen, and we had shared something we never should have. And he had been my friend, my confidante, my everything in this realm.

But just as there was no word for a male mistress, there was no word for what we had been to each other.

My eyes filled with tears unbidden, my vision blurring as I struggled to see past them.

Finn's mother saw all of this, the futility of the word, the buried meaning behind it, the tears that lined my eyes. She reached out and took my hand in hers, giving it a little squeeze.

"I know," she said quietly. "I heard."

I made a noise at that, somewhere between a single sardonic chuckle and a throat clearing. "Heard?"

"Heard that you were close," Finn's mother added. "Word travels, even outside of the palace walls."

"Oh," I said. It was the only thing to say to that, to the reality that Finn's mother was laying bare. She knew exactly what Finn was to me. And I glanced over my shoulder, wondering if every other person here knew, too.

Then she looked down at the hand she was holding, the wrist that was attached to the hand, and the thin silver bracelet that was just visible under the edge of my sleeve.

She nodded at the ornament and then met my eye again. There was kindness and acceptance in them, underneath the obvious pain. "I gave him that, you know."

My brow crinkled in confusion, and I looked down at the bracelet.

"He came to me a week or so before. He asked for a piece of jewelry that he could give to someone special. I gladly offered him whatever he wanted."

"Why?" I asked before I could stop myself.

"Not because of who you are, if that's what you're asking," she said matter-of-factly. "I gave him this because he had never asked before. There had been other women, of course, but none that lit him up like you did. You made him happy."

I shook my head, still gripping Finn's mother's hands. "I'm so sorry."

"Me, too. But this was the death he would have wanted, in service to the crown. To your crown." The woman paused, and then gave the slightest smile, a mere lifting of the corners of her lips. "Thank you for making him happy."

I stared at her, and she stared back at me. And it was as if the entire world was laid bare between us. For a split second, I could imagine what it would have been like to sit at her table in the city with Finn, if we had lived in another world, another time.

"I tried," I finally said. It was the truth, the only one I could give.

"I know," Finn's mother replied. She patted my hand once more and then let go, the breeze suddenly cool where the warmth of her palm had just been.

Finn's father approached and I turned my gaze to him. He bowed before clasping his wife's arm. "Your Majesty. Thank you for being here."

I hated his thanks, but I nodded all the same, swallowing down my shame. "I'm sorry for your loss," I said mechanically, but Finn's father was already steering his wife away.

I stood there for a moment, staring at the empty space in front of me where Finn's parents had just been. I clasped a hand over the bracelet on my wrist and I sent up my own thoughts for Finn. It took only a moment to say what I wanted to say to him, to tell him the goodbye I never got to tell him, and to thank him for all he did for me.

Then I turned away from the grave, flanked by my two guards, and began the walk back to the palace.

The crowd was still there, I realized. They had just moved from the grave to give the diggers room to complete their work.

And as I passed through the crowd, hands reached out to me.

"Queen Sahle," they called.

"Your Majesty."

"My Lady."

Their calls sounded like prayers, and I grasped the hands one at a time. People bowed and kissed my fingers, and I nodded my head in acknowledgement of each one.

"Thank you for being here," one man said as he bowed before me. He was in a soldier's formal uniform, and I reached out and squeezed his arm, just above the black sash tied there.

"Of course," I murmured.

But he had changed the crowd with his words. Instead of calling my name, I began to hear more words of gratitude. My neck prickled at the sentiment. I did not deserve thanks, and my ears burned with shame to hear it.

Still, I nodded at the crowd as I passed through it. Just before I reached the stairs that would lead me back to the palace properly, I noticed the line of soldiers standing by. I had seen most of them daily, when I was still training with Finn, and I recognized them as Finn's Vikela unit.

I walked up to them, and they bowed deeply to me. But instead of telling them to rise, I dropped into a curtsy myself.

There was a shocked moment of silence, and then I rose. The soldiers followed suit, casting glances between me and the other members of their company.

"I'm sorry for your loss," I said to them, for they had lost a brother just as Finn's family had lost a son.

"Thank you, Your Majesty," several responded. Others just stared.

I nodded once more and then turned from them. I was tired and I wanted nothing more than to get back into my bed.

And so, without looking back, I walked slowly and quietly back up the stairs of the palace and into the main halls.

Numbly, I was aware of the courtiers flitting around me along the checkered floors, dropping into bows and whispering as I passed. I paid no mind to them or what they might be saying about my mourning-but-not-mourning gown. I did not see them, focused as I was on getting back to my rooms.

I pushed the heavy wooden door of my chambers closed with a resounding thud. Then I leaned my back against it, staring at the empty room with the wide windows, the veiled bed, and the wingback chairs before the fireplace.

All the tears that I had held back, all the emotions I had tried to lock down came rushing forward. Silent tears ran down my cheeks and I did not bother to stop them, not now that they had started.

I had not cried, not once since Finn's death. Now, it was like the force of all of those days came rushing in. My knees folded and I distantly realized I was sitting in a heap against the door to my chambers.

It did not matter, not as the first sobs ratcheted up my throat and finally passed my lips. I let myself dissolve, my head bowed over my bent knees. My tears stained the gray of Finn's funeral gown.

Sometime later, a glinting caught my attention through the haze of the tears: Finn's bracelet.

I turned my hand over to better see the simple metal twists, and I ran a finger over them once more.

As if Finn were there with me, I knew what he would say in this moment of grief. He would tell me that this was the end and the beginning.

I knew he was right. I could feel it in the air, a whistling charge of possibility that opened before me.

There were threats to Izwe, to the entire Alterealm. There were powers that I had only glimpsed but still had to master. There was a kingdom that needed me.

And because I knew Finn would want me to pull myself off of the floor, I made my way to all fours and then to my feet. I walked to the big windows where a certain slant of light danced across the clouds.

I would do this. I could be the Queen we needed, for I had no other choice.

Today I would grieve but tomorrow…tomorrow was a new day.

Tomorrow was the beginning and the end of everything, and I would be ready for it.

acknowledgements

They say it takes a village to raise a child. In my experience, the same can be said about publishing a novel. I would like to thank my own village—everyone who was instrumental in the birth and rearing of this story:

To my husband, Hannes, thank you for being my forever first reader. You've seen the worst of my writing and the best. You are my harshest critic and my biggest fan. And I wouldn't have it any other way.

To Whitney, thank you for your thoughtful questions and notes on the sloppy, nascent manuscript I asked you to read, completely out of the blue. When I realized I needed feedback from someone I wasn't married to, there was no one else I trusted more.

To Emily, thank you for your insightful editing, sage direction, and genuine enthusiasm. You were the first to fall in love with one of my characters, and the experience of seeing your "buy in" was a true pleasure.

To Allison, thank you for listening to my vision and lending your art to a beautiful cover design.

To the rest of the Fractured Mirror team, thank you for your tireless efforts in editing, designing, printing, and promoting this book.

To the countless friends and family members around the globe, thank you for your joy. Your excitement made the complex process of publishing a little easier.

To Matt, thank you for telling me that publishing a story could be more than a dream.

To you, the reader, thank you for spending some time in my imaginings. I hope you found a bit of yourself within these pages.

about the author

C.P. DU TOIT was raised in Northern California but spent six years as an expatriate in Scotland, South Africa, and Australia. She currently lives in Philadelphia with her husband and their two black cats. A born storyteller, she has been writing poetry and short stories since she was a child. *A Certain Slant of Light* is her debut novel.